HARMED AND DANGEROUS

JASPER BARK

Published by Crystal Lake Publishing
Where Stories Come Alive!

www.crystallakepub.com

Copyright 2026 Jasper Bark
Join the Crystal Lake community today
on our newsletter and Patreon!
https://linktr.ee/CrystalLakePublishing

Download our latest catalog here:
https://geni.us/CLPCatalog

All Rights Reserved

ISBN: 978-1-968532-42-0

Cover art:
Joanna Halerz—jo.widomska@gmail.com

Comic Art – Mick Trimble
Comic Lettering – Mindy Lopkin

This is a work of fiction. Names, characters, businesses, places, events and incidents are either the products of the author's imagination or used in a fictitious manner. Any resemblance to actual persons, living or dead, or actual events is purely coincidental.

No part of this publication may be reproduced, stored in a retrieval system, or transmitted in any form or by any means, without the prior permission in writing of the publisher, nor be otherwise circulated in any form of binding or cover than that in which it is published and without a similar condition including this condition being imposed on the subsequent purchaser.

Follow us on Amazon:

WELCOME
TO ANOTHER

CRYSTAL LAKE PUBLISHING
CREATION

Join today at www.crystallakepub.com & www.patreon.com/CLP

"For Freya Alycia
and Ishara Mairead

For teaching me to be a father and for making me a better person.
You're now both old enough to read my work without giving your mother a heart
attack!"

GREETINGS, GENTLE READER, WELCOME TO THIS LATEST FORAY INTO THE FORBIDDEN TERRAIN OF BARK BITES HORROR!
TO SEE THE WORLD THROUGH SOMEONE ELSE'S EYES IS USUALLY A CALL FOR COMPASSION. BUT FOR KYRA HUGHES IT'S THE BEGINNING OF HER WORST NIGHTMARE.
A NIGHTMARE THAT OCCURS IN A DARK CORNER OF CAJUN COUNTRY KNOWN TO IT'S RESIDENTS AS 'YEUXVILLE'. WHERE THE 'OLD WAYS' ARE KEPT AND THE HARMED ARE STILL VERY DANGEROUS.
PROSTHETIC EYES

CHAPTER 1:

When Kyra looked back on that long, strange fall, she came to realize everything went wrong when she woke on the bus to New Orleans.

It might have gone wrong sooner. When she decided to flee Chicago or steal ten thousand dollars. But for some reason it didn't.

The pivotal moment was when Kyra got out of her seat, with sleep-stiffened limbs, and shuffled down the aisle. That's when the whole trajectory of her life changed.

Sleep had been fitful since Memphis. In New Orleans she woke and glanced about, eyes sticky with slumber. The bus wasn't moving. The passengers had gone. How long had it been in the terminal? Had she missed her next connection? She checked the time on her phone. She had a couple of hours till it left.

Head bleary with snooze haze, Kyra stumbled to the exit. Lost in that liminal space all long journeys create, where she was neither home nor at her destination, but caught in a carousel of connections, each one a short hop to the next.

It was the tiny object that snapped her out of it. The minute she put her foot on it she was wide awake. If she'd climbed off the bus and continued with her journey, her life might have taken a different turn. She might not have invited the presence into her life.

The presence had been waiting a very long time.

It would enter her life as gently as a spring breeze. In time, it would become a hurricane, tearing down everything in its path. The moment Kyra lifted her sneaker to see what she'd stepped on, the wind changed and the presence blew into her life.

She shook her head, she wasn't seeing what she thought. She couldn't be. There was a human eyeball staring up at her. An eyeball she'd trodden on.

Kyra crouched to get a closer look. She reached out a finger and gave the eye a tentative poke. It wasn't soft and gelatinous, it felt like plastic.

She let out her breath. The eye wasn't real, it was prosthetic. The world made sense again.

Kyra picked up the prosthetic and dropped it into her palm. The eye was shaped like a soft-poached egg. Kyra thought it would be rounder, but this one was flat. The craftsmanship was so detailed, down to the tiny red veins around the edge. The iris was blue, positioned to the left of center, and flecked with green and yellow. So lifelike she felt it was watching her.

It was still warm with a crust of matter around one edge. Moments ago it had been in someone's eye socket. An intimate part of their body that only they had ever touched. They'd be lost without it.

Kyra had to return it, but she didn't know how. Some of the passengers might be in the terminal. If she hurried she could catch them, the rest would be gone. Was there a lost and found depot? Should Kyra hand it in at the nearest precinct? A precinct meant cops, and Kyra was trying to steer clear of cops.

Kyra regarded the eye in her palm. No longer a strange object of beauty, but a moral dilemma. She wanted to do the right thing, but she risked exposing herself. She let out a sigh and glanced around, hoping for a sign, something that would point the way.

A low drone issued from the back of the bus. Was that the engine? It couldn't be, the driver was long gone.

There it was again, shaking the windows. It was definitely coming from the back of the bus. Kyra headed up the aisle toward the back. There, on the backseat, she found the source.

A short, round woman in her early fifties was snoring loudly, a thin trickle of drool ran from the corner of her mouth. Her light brown hair was flecked with gray. She was dressed in high tops, light cotton slacks and a blue t-shirt with wolves on it.

Her left eye socket was empty. The eyelid flapped like a loose sail in a breeze. Kyra was filled with compassion by this tiny, delicate sight. The wry smile fell from her lips. The woman was alone and asleep on an abandoned bus, unaware of her lost prosthetic.

Kyra touched her gently on the shoulder. "Excuse me, ma'am, I think you dropped something."

The woman stirred. "What?"

"I think you dropped something," Kyra held out the eye for her to see.

"I did?" The woman peered at Kyra's palm as her good eye came into focus. "Oh my word, where did you find that?"

"Over by the door."

The woman put her arms out to steady herself and blinked as she got her bearings. Then she prodded her empty socket. Kyra glimpsed the white, porous implant. "It must have fallen out. What was it doing by the door?"

"I don't know, it could've rolled, or maybe someone kicked it."

"Well, that's not very hygienic." The woman felt around for her purse and produced spray and a red cloth. She took the eye from Kyra, spritzed and polished it with the cloth. "Where are we? Where are the passengers?"

"We're in New Orleans, ma'am. We have to change."

"New Orleans, already, how long was I asleep? Oh, never mind. Excuse me but I have to pop this back in." She finished polishing the eye, tilted her head back and lifted her eyelid with her fingers.

Kyra turned away, scratched the back of her neck and stared uncomfortably at the ground until the woman was done.

"Thank you for returning my eye, those things aren't cheap. Can't think what I'd have done if you hadn't." The woman got to her feet with a tired huff and offered Kyra her hand. "I'm Constance, and you are?"

"Kyra."

"Kyra, what a pretty name, and what a pretty girl. Now, tell me Kyra, are you going to a funeral?"

"What? Uh, no, I'm just going to see a friend."

"Then why are you wearing so much black?"

Kyra dropped her head and pulled her bangs in front of her face, drawing circles with the toe of her sneaker. The jeans and hoodie she wore were perfect for Chicago, but too warm here.

Constance squeezed her shoulder. "I'm just messing with you, hon. I'm indebted to you for finding my eye. I was only going to doze for a minute. Didn't get a wink of sleep last night, too busy worrying."

"That doesn't sound good."

"Oh, it's fine. I have an exam today, and I couldn't stop thinking about it. Anyway, listen to me going on when we should be collecting our bags. They might not even be there."

"You think our bags won't be there?" Most of the ten thousand was in her backpack. She was lost without it. Why had she left it in her backpack? How could she be so stupid?

"Relax, I'm messing with you. You got anybody waiting on you?"

"No, I'm traveling alone."

"In that case I'll buy you a cup of coffee."

"Oh, that's not necessary."

"You got some place you need to be?"

"No, my next bus isn't for a few hours."

"Then I'd say it's necessary. It'll help take my mind off this exam."

Constance lumbered down the aisle, stretching and yawning to shake off the sleep. Kyra was dragged along in her wake, like a minor planetary body, uncertain how to break out of Constance's orbit.

Stepping from the bus was like crossing a threshold. The cool, sterile air of the bus was replaced by the dirty, humid fug of New Orleans. The heat was so intense Kyra could taste it at the back of her throat, like cayenne pepper in a gumbo. Her pores yawned open and sweat soaked into her parched clothes.

The scent of baked asphalt and exhaust fumes wafted over as cars tore along the overpass. There were only two bags in the collection area, Constance's pull-along suitcase and Kyra's backpack. Her anxiety ebbed the minute she saw it and she said a silent prayer of thanks to the gods of luggage, promising she'd transfer the rest of the cash to her fanny pack at the first opportunity.

Constance lifted the handle of her suitcase. "You home from college?"

"No, I'm still in high school. I have another year till college."

"And you're travelling by yourself?"

Kyra didn't reply and hid behind her bangs again. She'd done that since eighth grade. Her hair was a stage curtain that let her exit, in her mind, when the conversation took a turn she didn't like.

The terminal loomed up ahead, *Greyhound* written in large blue letters over the entrance. Constance was asking too many questions, clinging to Kyra like a barnacle to a cruise liner. She'd have to keep deflecting the conversation.

"So, this exam, is it a community college thing?"

"Heavens, no, I'm going to qualify as a spiritual counsellor." Constance made a broad sweep of her arm, as if she was on a stage. "I have the gift, like my mother before me."

"Spiritual counsellor, how do you qualify for that?"

"Signed up for a diploma at a college here in New Orleans." Constance pronounced it 'N'yarlins'. "Takes a year to complete, online mostly, but I come in twice a month for workshops and lectures. I get letters after my name when I'm done, and I can advertise as an accredited practitioner."

"Is that what you want to do?"

"It's what I've always done, but it's time I was officially recognized."

"Is it a written exam?"

"Not this one, I've done the written part. Today is the practical, where I get to specialize."

"Specialize?"

"Yeah, in the main it's a general accreditation for healers of all kinds. You learn how to run a professional practice and not come across like a con artist. Some folks are skeptical, others think it's from Satan."

"Really?"

"You're in the south now, hon. Lotta devout folks down here."

The midday sun was relentless, Kyra would've killed for sunscreen. As wizened as the last hot dog at the concession, she waded through hot air, every step an effort and the terminal never getting closer.

She turned to Constance. "What do you specialize in?"

"I throw the bones."

"Throw the bones? Is that like dice or something?"

"No, it's an ancient method of divination."

"Really?"

"Oh yeah, maybe I'll show you, if you're lucky."

And that was it, right there in that moment her fate was sealed. One innocent question opened a door and an unexplained presence walked right through. It was about to make everything worse.

CHAPTER 2:

The cool air of the terminal was a relief. Kyra blew into the main hall like a leaf on the breeze. Constance stopped huffing and straightened her back, Kyra was relieved to see Constance struggle with the heat. It was good to know even Louisianans found it hard. How would Kyra cope?

Kyra drifted into the center of the Union Passenger Terminal and let her head fall back. She gazed up at the mural running along the walls. The first thing that struck her were the colors, some so vibrant they leaped from the walls, others were murky enough to sink into the shameful pasts they depicted.

Slain soldiers, vestal virgins, nuclear scientists and horsemen of an impending apocalypse moved along the murals. A frenzied display of yearning, greed and wrath. Their dramatic poses reached across the crazy angles at which each historic scene intersected with another, as if time here had an entirely new geometry in which every second of the past rubbed shoulders with the present. Kyra had seen photos online, but they didn't do it justice.

Constance ambled over to join Kyra's vigil. "Quite something ain't they?"

"What?" Kyra half hoped Constance would forget about her, but she seemed determined to have that coffee.

"The paintings. Four centuries of Crescent City history on display. Been up there more'n sixty years. Nearly lost 'em in Katrina, but they cleaned 'em up pretty good a few years back."

"Yeah, they're great."

"C'mon, there's a Subway right here." Constance put a hand on Kyra's shoulder and steered her through the crowds. Her hand was warm and intrusive,

Kyra wasn't a child and didn't like to be led. But she had no idea where they were going, and the terminal was full of passengers who were intent on being somewhere else. They stared down at the ground, or up at boarding times as they dragged their luggage behind them. They jostled and vied for position, gawped at phone screens and scowled at commuters who were in their way. All of them filled with a sense of purpose, a drive to reach their destination that Kyra just didn't have.

She was pulled along in Constance's wake instead, like an errant piece of luggage, or a helium balloon losing its buoyancy. She entered a strange dream like state where nothing seemed real, but everything seemed to have happened before. If she'd known in that moment that the presence was coming, perhaps Kyra would have sensed it.

They came to the Subway, drifted inside and Constance bought them coffee and cookies. They blew on their drinks and grabbed a booth in back, with lime green upholstery and wood-patterned laminate tables.

Coffee was a novel experience. Kyra wasn't allowed it at home and had only drunk it once or twice with friends. She'd never had it in adult company and wasn't sure how much she actually liked it. She added four sachets of sugar to be on the safe side and waited for it to cool to a drinkable temperature.

Constance seemed to enjoy her cup. She took a big slurp, smacked her lips and gave Kyra a look of appraisal. "I guess you're not hitting the casinos later?"

Kyra smiled with embarrassment and pulled at her bangs. "I wasn't planning on it."

"So, where you headed?"

Kyra dug her nails into her palm. She didn't want to lie, but she couldn't afford to give anything away. Better to be evasive with the truth.

"I'm going to Yeuxville. I still have another bus to catch, it's a few counties over."

"Call them parishes in these parts, hon."

"Oh, yeah, sorry."

Constance wrinkled her nose. "Why are you going to Yeuxville?"

"You've heard of it?"

Constance laughed and made a dismissive gesture with her hand. "In my line of work, everyone's heard of Yeuxville."

"Really, why's that?"

"Don't you know?"

"Uh, no."

"You don't have family there?"

"I might. I was born in Yeuxville but I had to leave. My mother died when I was young and I was put up for adoption. Why do you ask?"

"It's a remote place is all. Not many folks have reason to visit unless they got family there. Most people avoid it."

"Why, because of the murders?"

"What? Aw hell no! We got murders all over. Let's just say they keep the old ways in Yeuxville."

"The old ways?"

Constance leaned in. "Certain traditions are still practiced there, older than Louisiana, older than the whole damn country. It's gone underground since that business in the bayou."

"You mean the massacre? I read about that."

"It wasn't a massacre, damn tragedy was what it was. Didn't put an end to the old ways. They're more powerful than any Hoodoo you'll find in this town, so you'd best steer clear young lady."

Constance leaned forward, her brows knitted, eyes burning. Kyra could smell the coffee on her breath. Was Constance trying to warn her or make her feel like a child? She glanced at the time on her phone. How quickly she could dip?

"Are you saying I shouldn't go?"

"Would it make a difference?"

"I've kinda bought my ticket. What else am I going to do?"

"You could go back home. Unless you're in some kinda trouble?"

There she was, prying again. Kyra had given too much away. "I'm not in any kind of trouble. I'm going back to see if I remember the place."

"Just be careful, you hear. Communities round those parts are pretty closed."

"I'll be fine, honestly."

"Let's hope so."

Constance narrowed her eyes, weighing up something. Kyra stared at her coffee and willed it to cool. Constance raised her index finger as if she'd come to a conclusion. "You know what, I think it's time you learned how to throw the bones."

"What?"

"I'ma give you a reading."

Was Kyra being watched? She could feel eyes on her. She glanced about but no one was looking. She was being observed though, she knew it. The sweat on her neck became ice cold. She shook her head. "I'm good. I mean, thanks and all, but it doesn't sound like my kinda thing."

"I'm not letting you go till we've thrown the bones. You're in need of guidance, young lady. Don't know what kinda fix you're in, but I can tell you got no idea where to turn."

"I'm not... How could you possibly know that? You've only just met me. I could be anyone. You don't know what's going on with my life."

"Honey, I don't need no gift to see you're in some kinda trouble. Like I said, I don't wanna pry, but you need directing."

"If you don't want to pry, why give me a reading? Won't you learn stuff?"

"Honey, a reading is for your benefit. I'll explain what the bones say. You decide what it means to you."

"How about your test? Aren't you sick of this?"

"I go where I'm called, that's the deal with the spirits."

"The spirits?"

Constance glanced to heaven. "Spirits, saints, whatever you want to call them, the beings who guide me and the bones. Don't worry about my test. This'll be a good warm up. It'll take my mind off my nerves."

Constance took a wooden chest from her case and opened it. Inside were a square of black velvet and a wooden bowl which she placed in the middle of the table, with great solemnity. There was something else in the chest. Constance held it up for Kyra to see.

"Are they real...?"

"Bones? Yes."

"Are they animal?"

"Human."

Kyra peered at the fragments on the chest's silk-lining. There must have been thirty, some gray, others sepia, a few bone white.

"You have to choose the bones you want. Seven is a good number, but you can have up to ten. Don't think too much, go with your gut. Pick the fragments that call you."

Kyra reached out a hand then pulled it back. Her gut told her this would change everything. Did that have to do with being watched? The observer she couldn't see. The presence. She should get up and leave. But her hand had other ideas. It reached into the chest.

In a morbid way, Kyra found the fragments beautiful. She recalled the skeleton from middle school biology. It sat on a stand at the back of class and because it was real no one was allowed to touch. Kyra had always wondered what real human bones felt like. Now she'd find out.

Her fingers were drawn to a flat fragment, shaped like a diamond. One side was smooth, the other porous.

Constance saw. "That's a section of skull. From the top of the brain pan. Place it on the velvet or pop it back."

Kyra turned it over and decided to keep it. She pulled out a long thin bone with ridges on the ends, it looked like a bone a cartoon dog would bury.

"That's a metacarpal," Constance told her.

"A what?"

"A finger bone."

"Okay."

Kyra's fingers chose a thin, light brown bone, curved with a gnarled lump in the middle. Kyra stroked the lump before placing it on the velvet beside the others.

"That's part of a rib. The little lump's from rickets."

"Rickets?"

"A disease from the last century, caused by Vitamin D deficiency. It's pretty much disappeared. Might be my oldest bone."

Kyra was curious. "How do you know so much about them? I mean, they're only fragments."

"Google, mostly. I spend a lot of time online, reading up on bones."

"Where do you get them from?"

"Graveyards and cemeteries."

"For real?"

"Where d'you think they come from?"

"I don't know. You don't rob graves, do you?"

"Oh, hell no. I find'em just lying on the ground."

"Really?"

"The earth moves more 'n people realize, things get pushed to the surface. Then there's the flooding. Some graveyards are washed clean away, 'specially the old ones. When the waters come, they scatter coffins and corpses for miles. You can pick whole bones right out of the fields. Feller who taught me how to throw the bones, he found a whole skeleton once, carried it into the church and left it by the altar with a note saying to rebury it."

"Did they rebury it?"

"I have no idea. But I bet their next service was something, turning up to find that on the altar."

"So, you just pick the bones off of the ground?"

"Only the ones that call to me. I have to leave the others where I find 'em. Found that out the hard way. If I take a bone that don't want to come with me, no matter how much I like the look of it, I can get sick. All my readings are thrown till I put it back right where I found it."

"Is that why *I* have to choose the bones for the reading?"

"Exactly."

Kyra picked out five more bones and laid them beside the three she'd already chosen.

"You done?"

"Think so. What happens now?"

Constance pointed to the wooden bowl. "You put all the pieces in there."

Kyra collected the bones and dropped them in the bowl. Constance showed Kyra how to take the bowl in her hands with her right pressed over the top. "Now you gotta shake the bowl with the bones in it, gently mind, and ask the bones a question. Don't say it out loud. When you think the bones are ready, empty 'em onto the velvet."

Kyra rattled the bones in the bowl. Her eyes darted round Subway to make sure none of the staff came over. What would she say if they did? *Don't mind me, I'm just throwing human remains over your dining table.*

Kyra tried to focus on a question. There were so many things she wanted to know. She was nothing but questions at the moment. Questions, fear and rage. Kyra closed her eyes and tried to empty her mind.

It went blank, which was close enough, and a relief. She'd been overthinking since she left Chicago. Before she could enjoy it, a question raised its hand. Kyra knew it was the question to ask, but it surprised her.

Will my dad find me?

Which dad did she mean? Her adopted dad or her birth dad? Were the bones ready to give an answer? She shook them a few more times then turned the bowl out onto the velvet.

And...

...nothing happened.

The bones didn't fall out. Kyra shook the bowl, but they stayed put. She looked inside the bowl. The bones had jammed themselves together, so they were all stuck in the bowl. Kyra showed Constance.

"Never had this happen before. Try again."

Kyra put her hand over the bowl and shook it. The bones came free and rattled around. She asked the same question. Somehow it seemed more urgent. She held the bowl over the velvet.

And...

...the same thing happened.

Kyra checked the bowl, and sure enough the bones had gotten jammed together again.

Constance pursed her lips. "It's like the bones don't wanna talk to you, like they're refusing."Constance took the fragments from the bowl and put them in Kyra's hands. She put her hands around Kyra's and shook them, the bones rattled between Kyra's palms."We're gonna try something different. Something's going on, and I wanna get to the bottom of it. Ask your question again."

Kyra wasn't sure she wanted an answer. Maybe there was a reason the bones wouldn't talk, were they going to tell her something bad? Constance's wrists locked and her hold on Kyra tightened, crushing the bones between Kyra's fingers.

Kyra winced. "That hurts, please, let go."

"I can't."

"What do you mean?"

"I mean, I can't, I'm not doing this."

Before Kyra could ask who *was* doing it, she felt watched again. By something much closer but still out of sight.

Constance's grip got tighter. Kyra's hands tingled, an electric charge ran through them. It started in her palms, spread to her wrists and forearms, then receded altogether.

Kyra saw the hairs on Constance's arms stand up, Constance frowned and ground her teeth.

"Wait, you feel that too?"

"Uh huh."

The strange tingling returned, more intense this time. It traveled up to her shoulders, before retreating. Whatever it was, it seemed to be moving between Kyra and Constance like a circuit, building up energy.

"What's happening? Can you please let go. I don't like it. Can you stop?"

"I would if I could, but I told you I'm not doing this. I'm not in control."

"Then who is?"

"I don't know."

The bones began to move. So imperceptibly Kyra thought she imagined it. But she hadn't. They were twitching, like dying insects cradled in her palm.

Had she woken the spirits of their owners? Were the bones angry at being used this way? Kyra didn't want to know, she just wanted to get them away from her, but she couldn't let go.

The energy moved out of Constance and into Kyra again, like a mild electric shock. It raced up her arms, along her shoulders, and engulfed her head. Kyra's face and scalp prickled, then she heard a dull click, and everything went black. All her senses turned off. Then everything came rushing back, but she wasn't in the booth any longer. She was in a memory from her recent past:

Kyra is in her room, surfing the net, when the text comes through.

And as quickly as the flashback came, it was gone again. Like an instant regret or a shudder of revulsion. The bright lights of the Subway flooded her sight, and Kyra was back in the present. Her fingers ached from Constance's grip. The bones twitched between her fingers as the energy raced down her arms towards Constance.

Constance seemed to sense it was coming. She gritted her teeth and looked up in genuine fear. The energy entered her, Constance threw back her head and her right eye rolled up into its socket.

Kyra knew that as the energy moved into Constance it carried her memory, surfing the crest of that charge. Kyra was livid. Constance had promised she wouldn't learn anything, yet she was lifting a memory clean out of her head.

Constance gasped as the energy flowed out of her, she bared her teeth and her whole body shook. It charged back into Kyra, with a greater urgency. Her arm and neck muscles knotted as it tore through them and engulfed her head once again. The blackness followed and just when she thought she might fall through it forever, another moment from her recent past came into sharp focus:

Kyra is opening an envelope, standing in the kitchen while her mom and dad look on.

Then it was her turn to gasp and shudder as the energy retreated and went racing towards Constance. Kyra felt a wild burst of loathing for Constance. She was snatching such intimate moments from Kyra's memory. Kyra made one last futile effort to tear her hands away, but Constance's grip was inhuman, almost mechanical. The bone fragments jostled against her palms in a new flurry of activity and the energy circled back, moving into Kyra with a painful jolt:

Kyra is in the counsellor's office at school.

Then she wasn't.

She blinked away tears.

The energy moved back and forth between Kyra and Constance three more times. Each time it got fiercer and more painful, and each time they shared a memory from Kyra's recent past.

Kyra is in her bedroom, arguing with her Dad.
Kyra is on the doorstep while her dad embarrasses her friends.
Kyra is opening a book on her dad's nightstand.

The last jolt was too much for Kyra and Constance. Their hands flew apart, the bones dropped onto the velvet cloth, and they collapsed into their seats. The bones lay together in a clump, making no discernible pattern.

"What was that?" Kyra breathed heavily, hardly able to move, sweating in spite of the air-con. Constance was panting, staring at the floor. She muttered something Kyra couldn't hear.

Kyra lifted her head. "What?"

"I said, I *don't* know, and I don't *want* to know." Constance stared straight at Kyra. Sweat ran in thick gobbets down her face. Her lips were twisted into a snarl. Her prosthetic eye was askew, making her look in two directions at once.

"Was that... does that normally happen?"

"That ain't never happened before. I don't know what kinda trouble you're in, but I don't want any part of it." Constance got to her feet, stuffed the chest into her case, and stumbled out of the booth, leaving the bones and velvet cloth on the table.

Kyra sat up. "Wait, where are you going?"

"Home, then I'ma get drunk for a week."

"What about your exam?"

"What about it? I'm in no state to do it now."

"But your bones, you can't just leave them there."

"Watch me."

Constance shuffled out of the booth.

This wasn't right. Kyra forced herself to her feet. Her head swam and her limbs shook. She grabbed Constance by the arm, partly to steady herself.

"Wait, you can't just leave. I've never experienced anything like that. You've got to explain it. You owe me. You demanded I do this. You promised you wouldn't learn anything, then you stole memories right out of my head. You have to tell me what's going on."

Constance rounded on her. "Get your hands off me. I don't have to do nothing. This is on you, not me. You ruined those bones for me. They're as good as cursed. I don't know how you did it, but you brought some sort of dark energy to bear on 'em, I can't ever use 'em again. I should've stayed away the minute you said you were from Yeuxville, nothing good ever came out of that place."

"I was born there, I'm not from there, and don't put this on me. This was your idea. You said you go where you're called, that's the deal with your spirits."

"And I don't stay where I'm not wanted. You want to know something? Okay, here's all I know. You did something bad in your past, young lady. I don't know what it was, but it's coming back to haunt you. You got a presence coming for you, can't say what it is, but I felt it. It's coming for you. It's coming cos of what you did, and I don't want any part of it, or you."

She mentioned the presence. Said it out loud. It wasn't just in Kyra's mind. There really *was* something lurking outside of her line of sight, something watching her. Someone else knew about it and that someone had turned their back and lumbered towards the exit.

Kyra contemplated going after Constance. Taking hold of her and shaking her until she gave a better answer. But she was exhausted. She collapsed back into the booth with the cooling coffee cups, the cookie crumbs and the fragments of bone on black velvet.

A woman in her late twenties came to bus the plates and cups. Her eyes poisonous with suspicion. She'd heard the scene Constance made.

Kyra had wanted to ditch Constance since they'd left the bus. Now she was gone, Kyra felt abandoned. Constance was the only person Kyra had spoken to since she'd left Chicago.

She took a sip of her coffee. It was cold and overly sweet. Kyra was alone, thousands of miles from home with an intangible presence watching her. Because of something bad she'd done in her past. A past that was waiting in Yeuxville, whether she liked it or not.

EXCERPTED FROM
viewfromthekiller'seyes.blogspot.com

An unpublished blog by Kyra Hughes (with Delilah's comments)

WHAT'S A NICE GIRL LIKE ME, DOING ON A BLOG LIKE THIS?

Good question. See, the thing is I'm obsessed with serial killers. Always have been. Growing up, most girls have K-pop stars, or Dora the Explorer on their walls. Me, I had John Wayne Gacy and H. H. Holmes. (No really). Everyone has a favorite group or a favorite sports team (so I'm told), but not everyone has a favorite serial killer. I do. I guess that makes me kinda weird, but I can live with that.

My favorite serial killer is Billy-Ray Johnson from Yeuxville. Never heard of him? Don't sweat. Not many people have. He's kinda obscure. I guess that's why I like him. I only found out about him a year and a half ago, thanks to a local thrift store.

By the way, in case you're wondering, Yeuxville is pronounced Yer-vill. It comes from the French word for 'Eyes'. Thanks to Delilah for that bit of info. As a long time Scooby Doo fan, I was pronouncing the Yeux as 'Yoiks', until she put me straight.

D: LOL! Great intro, I'm hooked!

HOW I FOUND OUT ABOUT BILLY-RAY

So, I'm flicking through a clothes rack, in this thrift store, looking for something black and retro. Black's the only color I wear (and yes it is a color, and it goes with everything, especially black), but nothing is doing it for me. My eyes drift to the bookcase, and in amongst the James Patterson and Stephanie Meyers books is a black spine, with white letters, that calls out to me. The title was *Eyes for the*

Killer by Becky Eve Hirst. The minute I took it off the shelf, I knew it was one of my favorite books.

That happens to me sometimes. I just pick up a book, or an album (vinyl preferably, but cassette will do—did I mention I'm totally retro?), and I'll just know it's one of my favorites. I don't even have to read the cover blurb or check the track listing, I just know.

Like this one time, I'm in the school library with my friend Marie Vasicek and I pick up a copy of *In Cold Blood* by Truman Capote. Marie goes, "Ugh, we did that at summer book-camp, it's lame!" Her parents are always sending her off on educational trips, poor thing.

"Really?" I say. "It's one of my favorite books."

"How can you say that? Name me one good thing about that book, just one?"

And you know what? I couldn't, I didn't even know the book existed until I picked it out, like two seconds before. So, even though I was sure I would love the book, I simply blushed and shrugged and put it back. It took me two months to go back and check it out. And you know what? I was right, it *was* one of my favorite books!

The same went for *Eyes for the Killer*. I was so excited I went straight to the counter and paid. I started reading it right away and nearly missed my stop on the subway home. I kept reading as I walked up my driveway and through the front door. Three hours later I finished the book. Then I began it all over again.

I read it three times in all, then I hit Google to find out more about Billy-Ray Johnson. Turns out, there wasn't much to find out — not online. That's one of the reasons I started this blog. Most of my information comes from *Eyes for the Killer*, as well as *The Truth About Billy-Ray Johnson and His Satanic Cult* by Mandy Sandiford. Good luck finding a copy of that. It's this self-published book that was only available in Louisiana, and there were only about 500 copies ever printed. It's not well written and it's kinda hard to get through, but it does have some fascinating stuff you won't find elsewhere. Sandiford's born again, from New Iberia, a lot of scripture, but stick with it for stuff that Hirst doesn't mention. It was written before Hirst's book and Hirst quotes it as a source.

Major thanks to my best bud Delilah for tracking down a copy and helping with this blog. Couldn't have done it without you, really, I couldn't.

D: Aww, shucks, now you've got me blushing!!!

CHAPTER 3:

Three hours later Kyra had exhausted her data. She should have paid for more when she bought this burner.

Where the hell was that damn bus? Two hours late was where it was. No explanation, no apology, just sit your ass down and wait till we're good and ready.

When it finally rolled into sight, Kyra saw it was run by a local company. The bus was an old model, its paintwork older still. The driver smoked two cigarettes before he let anyone on the bus.

There was no luggage compartment. Kyra propped her backpack next to her on the front seat. The seat covers were worn, the windshield grimy, and the air-con barely took the edge off the heat. The engine coughed worse than the driver and pulled slowly out of the terminal.

Despite all this, Kyra felt safer to be on the move. Travel provided security. Streets, cities, and all the dangers that lurked there, simply rolled past the window and faded in the rear view. The motion of the bus was like a hand rocking a cradle, comforting and reassuring.

It was only when she stopped and got off that Kyra was vulnerable and the bad things could find her. Like the strange presence that watched her in the terminal. Was it still watching? No, surely she'd left it in the terminal, skulking in the shadows, searching for some other victim.

But hadn't Constance said it was coming for *her* because it knew what she did? What did she do? What could anyone possibly do to trigger an experience like that? Kyra probably didn't want to know.

Maybe, given enough distance, Kyra could turn the story into a charming anecdote. Proof she was a seasoned traveler now she'd handled human bones and dabbled in local customs. Something to show Delilah how worldly she'd become.

For the time being, she'd rather put it from her mind. She slid down in her seat and stared out at the submerged soil of the wetlands. The wire-like stems of the golden marsh grass plunged its roots, like fingers, into that soil, and held its sodden, brown crumbs together. Off in the distance, there were oak trees, raising their gnarled branches to the sky in defiance. Their branches trailing wisps of Spanish moss, their leaves not yet brown.

There were three other passengers on the bus. A skinny guy with a sandy beard and long hair dozed fitfully on the back seat. An elderly woman in a faded, floral-print dress scratched at her arms and neck, two seats in front.

A large black woman sat in the front seat, opposite Kyra, fanning herself with the *Times Picayune*. Every couple minutes she made "mmm-hmm" noises to herself, as if she was following a sermon no one else could hear.

Kyra gazed out at the road through the windshield. A two lane blacktop with white painted markings that had faded to a ghostly gray.

A tiny chipmunk scampered onto the road ahead. It sat up on its hind legs and held its tiny nose in the air, catching some scent. But it didn't catch the scent of the bus or recognize it as danger. It didn't even turn its head to see the large vehicle tearing toward it.

The driver didn't see the chipmunk either. He carried on his same old trajectory, going as fast as the engine and the faded road would let him.

The chipmunk was going to get crushed. It was directly in line with the bus's front left wheel.

Its fragile bones wouldn't withstand the impact. Nor would its furry hide and soft innards.

If it moved, the chipmunk could still save itself. If the driver swerved he could avoid it. Traffic was light and there was nothing in the other lane. But chipmunk and driver continued this game of chicken, neither aware they were playing.

Kyra was on a caffeine jag from the coffee she drank back in the terminal. She wasn't used to the feeling, her nerves raw from little sleep. She wanted to tell the driver not to hit the chipmunk, but she didn't want to come across as crazy. She was trying to avoid attention.

Why wouldn't the chipmunk just move? Why wouldn't the driver see it? Why couldn't she will them to do something by staring at them?

The bus bore down on the chipmunk. It had seconds to live. Kyra raised a hand to cover her eyes. A blue and brown blur passed in front of the bus, swooped down from above and immediately climbed to the skies. Kyra dropped her hand, blinking at this flurry of feather and claw.

The chipmunk was gone. The bus rolled on without hitting it. Kyra's eye darted upward and saw it in the talons of a hawk. It hadn't seen the bus. Hadn't known how close it was to a sudden violent death.

The chipmunk could see the hawk and how close it was to death. Kyra watched it thrash and jerk with terror in the predator's grip. Ironic that it fought now for a life that was already over.

The bus carried on down the road. The hawk and the chipmunk faded into the sky. There wasn't a thing Kyra could have done to help the critter.

Was she like that chipmunk? Was a terrible danger heading toward her, one she hadn't seen coming? Was that what she faced when she got to Yeuxville? Or was something even worse going to drop from the sky and sink its claws into her?

No, of course it wasn't. She was just on edge, she needed sleep, no need to make a big drama about it. Nothing was going to drop from the sky and she wasn't in any danger.

Then Kyra remembered the presence that had watched her. And she knew with deadly certainty that it had followed her from New Orleans.

CHAPTER 4:

A road sign loomed up by the side of the road. It said there were fifteen miles to Yeuxville.

The burner was almost out of battery. Delilah's number was one of the few Kyra had put into it. She was arriving late. She ought to give Delilah an update.

Kyra:
ETA in 20, maybe 30 the way this bus crawls

She got a reply straight away:

Delilah:
OK, look out for the Piggly Wiggly, that's where the bus stops, I'll be waiting in the lot

Kyra:
Great, can't wait to get off, so hot on this bus

Delilah:
Welcome to the South, noob

Kyra:
Thanks for the warning

Delilah:
Would you have come if I'd warned you?

Kyra:
Hell no! I'd have run to Alaska

Delilah:
I mean that much, huh?

Kyra:
You're my best friend, can't believe I'm gonna meet you for real

Delilah:
Yeah, about that... I won't have a chance to do my face before I come, or change

Kyra:
So what? I've been stuck on a bus for days, how'd you think I look?

Delilah:
Well, I might not look like you expect

Kyra:
I don't even look human atm

Delilah:
Just keep an open mind, OK?

Kyra:
Of course, don't I always?

Delilah:

See you soon, then

Kyra:

See you soon

That was weird. Why was Delilah worried what she looked like? She was stunning in every photo Kyra had seen. Elegant and in her early twenties.

Or was she hinting at something else? Her tone had been cool since Kyra left Chicago. She scrolled back through earlier exchanges.

When Kyra had told her she was on her way Delilah replied:

Delilah:

Are you sure? It's a long way, maybe rethink this

Kyra had been distracted so she let it go, now she was worried. They'd spoken about her coming to visit for months. Sure, Kyra had decided to come on the spur of the moment, but she expected a better response. When she texted to say she'd changed buses:

Delilah:

There's still time to change your ticket, you could turn around and get a bus home, no-one would be any wiser

Kyra had thought Delilah was just looking out for her. But it was obvious she didn't like Kyra turning up with a just a day's notice.

She was an idiot. She thought Delilah would be as excited as she was, but of course she had her own life to get on with. She'd only just forgiven Kyra for the lies she told. She didn't want someone five years younger turning up and forcing themselves on her. Kyra would apologize when she got there and go find a motel or something. Arrange to hang with Delilah when it was more convenient.

It was a big ask, turning up like this and expecting someone to put you up with so little notice. Were Kyra's manners really that poor?

"Mmm-hmm," went the lady opposite as if she'd just read Kyra's thought. Kyra turned and caught her eye, the lady raised an eyebrow as if to say: *and your problem is?*

Kyra looked away, embarrassed.

It was too late to turn back now. She'd just have to deal with Delilah when they met. Kyra would soon be in Yeuxville, scene of Billy-Ray's crimes. The town where he'd brutally murdered Caitlin Robichaud and four others.

In four days it was the fifteenth anniversary of Caitlin's death. Kyra was going to be in Yeuxville for that anniversary. Maybe she'd finally get some answers.

"Mmm-hmm," agreed the lady opposite.

CHAPTER 5:

One Week Ago, T-minus 7 Days to Departure:

Kyra was in her room when the text came through.

Her parents were downstairs, having some 'quality time,' which meant Netflix but no chill.

It was Delilah. What if she was mad? She'd been chill about Kyra's big confession but what if she started to ghost Kyra.

She needn't have worried, it was short, but sweet:

Delilah:

Check your e-mail, I've left a little something

... and breathe! Kyra was just stressing. Everything was fine. Delilah was emailing about the blog. Kyra had been working on it for months. Delilah had been great, reading her entries and helping her with the technical side.

Kyra's blog was about the serial killer, Billy-Ray Johnson. That's how she met Delilah, in a social media group dedicated to his murders. Most members posted memes about Jeffrey Dahmer and Ted Bundy. But there were a few diehards, like Kyra and Delilah, who were fascinated by Billy-Ray's crimes and the mysteries surrounding them.

Delilah lived in Yeuxville. There was little she didn't know about Billy-Ray. She liked to post photos of his crime scenes and compare them with shots of the town today.

Kyra became obsessed with her posts. She stalked Delilah for a couple weeks, before plucking up the courage to comment. After some mammoth thread exchanges, they began following one another and chatting every day.

Delilah had a sick sense of humor, and she was scary smart. She should have gone to college, but she had to stay home and work. Her aunt and uncle had taken her in when she was young, and her uncle, a deputy, was shot while off duty, when Delilah was in high school. Delilah had to work as a courier to pay her share of the bills.

After going through the changes Delilah suggested, Kyra shot her a text:

Kyra:
Thanks for the notes

Delilah:
Hope I wasn't too harsh

Kyra:
I appreciate your honesty, you're always straight with me

Delilah:
I'll always tell you what I think

Kyra:
Thanks, it means the world, I think honesty is one of the things I value most, and yeah, I know that's ironic coming from me

Delilah:
Hey, c'mon, we don't have to bring this up

Kyra:
I know, but you've been so good with this blog, and everything I've been going through, I just want to say sorry again, I shouldn't have lied

Delilah:
Already forgotten

Kyra:
It still plays on my conscience, I think I need to explain why I did
it

Delilah:
I'm listening

Kyra:
You're so smart and funny, and you know so many things, not just
serial killers, all kinds of stuff, I thought you wouldn't want to know
me if you knew I was some lame high school kid

Delilah:
Don't be silly

Kyra:
You're a grown woman, you've got a job and you're saving for
college, you've got your life all sorted, I wanted to be part of that,
I wanted to relate to you as an adult, so I pretended I was one, I
told you all those lies about having a job and I feel lousy

Delilah:
Will you stop, my life's far from sorted, high school is officially the
eighth level of hell, everyone pretends they're someone else, it's
how you survive, we all fantasize about who we're going to be when
we finally escape, that's all you were doing, I see the real you, dark
and quirky, and that's why we get on so well

Kyra:

Stop you're gonna make me cry!!!

Delilah:

It's true, now dry those tears Miss World

There was a knock at her door. Kyra's Dad popped his head round.

"Time to put your phone down, honey, and your laptop. I don't mind you reading, but it's time to give screens a rest?"Kyra didn't say anything. She slammed her laptop shut and threw her phone on the nightstand, without looking at her dad.

"So, it's gonna be like this, is it?"

Kyra shrugged and glowered at the wall, avoiding eye contact.

"Okay."

Her Dad's voice was soft and full of dismay. Kyra nearly dropped her guard, nearly reached out to him. But her anger flared and put a stop to it. She narrowed her eyes and turned her back.

He said nothing more and quietly closed the door.

CHAPTER 6:

The bus turned into a side road. Kyra opened a sleepy eye. A road sign moved lazily past the bus – 'Yeuxville 5 miles.' This interminable journey was about to end.

There was something she wanted to do, a ritual she'd promised herself. She'd been dreaming about visiting Yeuxville for years. She was finally going to see it for real.

Kyra took her battered copy of *Eyes for the Killer* out of her backpack. She turned to the passage in Chapter Three that described the town. She wanted to visit Yeuxville one last time, in print, before she climbed off the bus and walked its streets:

Nestled in the heart of Cajun country, and surrounded by bayous, Yeuxville is a sleepy little burg that seems happy to remain remote and historical. It's a close knit, blue-collar, community that keeps to itself, located off the beaten path.

Not many tourists make the long trek, despite the old buildings and charming town square. If you ask folks in neighboring towns they'll tell you 'they keep the old ways in Yeuxville', though they'll never say what those old ways are, and change the subject if you ask.

This shabby collection of historic buildings and suburban streets, of trailer parks and industrial estates, wanted nothing more than to carry on napping in the hot Louisiana sun. It would have gotten its way, if a twenty-nine-year-old mechanic hadn't followed a high school girl out to a canal and given in to some terrible urges. Urges that would place Yeuxville in the eye of a statewide investigation.

Kyra looked up from the page as a water tower came into view. As the bus pulled past, Kyra caught sight of the town sign:

WELCOME TO YEUXVILLE

Bienvenue en Yeuxville

At The Heart of Acadia

Home of the World's Largest Boudin

Pop. 5,155

She grabbed her phone. The battery icon was red. Seven percent left.

"Aw, goddamn!"

The lady opposite shot her a disapproving look. Kyra hunkered down in her seat to text Delilah:

Kyra:
Just pulling into your one-horse town, pardner, time to hitch the wagon

The reply came straight back:

Delilah:
Be right there cowgirl

The bus headed down Main Street and turned onto Sunset Avenue. It pulled into the Piggly Wiggly lot with a hiss of air brakes.

"Yeuxville," the driver shouted. "All passengers for Yeuxville."

Kyra stumbled down the aisle to the door. She was the only one leaving at Yeuxville. She tumbled off the bus and put a hand over her eyes to shield them from the sun. The bus's engine coughed and it pulled away.

Her Charles Manson hoodie clung to her damp skin. Her socks were a nylon swamp.

A woman stepped out of the Piggly Wiggly and narrowed her eyes. Kyra was something to avoid. She looked away and saw a man in a pick-up shake his head.

In Chicago, no one gave her a second look, here in Yeuxville she set curtains twitching. She wanted to melt like gum on asphalt.

Where was Delilah? What was keeping her? Kyra squinted at the buildings surrounding the lot. There was a gas station across the way and rows of clapboard houses further up. A road led to a small business park, and on the corner of Sunset and Main, a sign pointed to the town center. Kyra checked her phone, it was on five percent.

A battered van pulled into the lot. The guy behind the wheel was in his early twenties. He had long hair pulled back in a ponytail and his clothes were gender neutral. He parked up and took a good look at Kyra. She turned her back and pulled her bangs over her face, wishing they'd provide better cover.

Instead of leaving, the guy stayed in the front seat of his van, his eyes boring into her.

She texted Delilah, quickly:

Kyra:
Where you at?

Delilah:
I'm here, right now

Kyra:
Where??? There's some creepy guy staring at me and I'm beginning to freak out

Delilah:
Does this guy have long brown hair in a ponytail?

Kyra glanced over her shoulder.

Kyra:
Yeah, how'd you know?

Delilah:
That'd be me

Kyra heard the van's door open. She turned and saw the young guy leaning out.

"Kyra, it's me, get in." His voice was also gender neutral, with a distinct drawl.

She took two steps towards the van without thinking and then stopped. Something was very wrong.

"Are you, like, Delilah's brother?"

"I'm Delilah."

"No, you're not."

"Kyra, it's me, really. I texted when you were an hour away. I asked you to keep an open mind, remember?"

"No."

"Look, I know this is kinda awkward and I hoped we wouldn't have to do this here. Please don't make a scene, it's a small town, people know me. If you just get in I'll explain everything."

"Like hell."

Kyra stepped back, her right leg shook. Her left palm throbbed, she was digging her nails into it. She'd been catfished. Totally catfished.

This guy had been grooming her for months. Sending her pictures and messages, making her think she had a friend, all so he could lure her down here. How could she be so stupid? How had she been taken in?

She couldn't move, frozen by indecision. Should she punch him in the face, or just turn and leave? Some voice at the back of her mind said *Run!* Kyra gripped the straps of her backpack and marched out of the parking lot, her heart dashed against her ribs.

"Kyra, wait, please!"

Kyra neither slowed down nor looked back. She kept on walking straight out of the lot and onto the road.

Where could she go? He was between her and the store, she couldn't go back. No one liked her in the store. Kyra didn't know her way around, and she needed to shake this guy, she didn't want to be dragged into his vehicle.

Acting on instinct, she bolted for the small road that led to the industrial park.

It would be easier to lose him there.

EXCERPTED FROM

viewfromthekiller'seyes.blogspot.com

An unpublished blog by Kyra Hughes (with comments by Delilah)

BILLY-RAY'S BIO

Billy-Ray Johnson was born at Our Lady of the Lake Regional Medical Center in Baton Rouge. His mother, Darlene Johnson, was only sixteen and didn't put the father's name on his birth certificate. Billy-Ray was named after his granddaddy, a veteran killed in Vietnam. Once she got out of hospital, Darlene went to live with her mother in Yeuxville.

Darlene left Billy-Ray in the care of his grandma, who raised him, in the bayous near Yeuxville. When Billy-Ray was in middle school, he moved into Darlene's trailer, for a few years, but he eventually went back to live with his grandma. He never graduated high school, dropping out at seventeen to work as a trainee mechanic. In his early twenties, Billy-Ray went to work at a repair shop owned by Frank Mancuso, situated on Third and Main in Yeuxville.

Billy-Ray was always looking for father figures. Frank took him under his wing and was the closest thing Billy-Ray ever had to a real dad. Billy-Ray worked his way up to head mechanic, the youngest the shop had ever had.

Most criminologists agree that serial killers are made and not born. For instance, many serial killers are abused or neglected as children. A great many suffer head injuries, or other physical trauma. A lot of killers exhibit sadistic tendencies at an early age, torturing and killing small animals. None of this is true of Billy-Ray, and that's one of the things that fascinates me. He's a bit of an enigma. He worked hard, paid his taxes, and was never in trouble with the law. Yet, one month before his twenty-ninth birthday, Billy-Ray snapped and went on a killing spree.

No one can say what triggered him, but three weeks before his first murder, Billy-Ray split from his long-term girlfriend, Lucy-Beth Martin. Some profilers, like Paris Chavez, believe his hatred and rage towards Lucy-Beth sent him over the edge, and he took it out on the women he killed. However, Lucy-Beth's friends report an amicable break-up, neither was mad with the other.

Before he split with Lucy-Beth, Billy-Ray confided to two work colleagues that he'd discovered a "terrible secret". According to one, he claimed: "something has been kept from me, and it's going to change everything about my life." Billy-Ray wouldn't say what the secret was, but his behavior changed afterward. He became secretive and unreliable, disappearing for stretches without explanation.

In *The Truth About Billy-Ray Johnson and His Satanic Cult*, Mandy Sandiford claims this secret was black magic. Sandiford says he joined a voodoo cult that abducted and killed children, and this was why he drew voodoo symbols, in blood, on the walls of his victims' homes.

She also goes on about the 'Bayou Massacre'. I don't know much about this, but it seems to be this big tragedy that happened 25 years ago. According to Sandiford, a "disastrous fire" broke out when a "coven of satanic Voodoo worshipers tried to summon the dark lord". She claims: "a local group of Christians" tried to "intervene and save them", but this led to the tragic death of four "Christian martyrs" and several "Satanists". She claims this proves "satanic voodoo" was the cause of the murders.

Hirst argues Billy-Ray suffered a psychotic-break, and this changed his personality. Although rare, a brief psychotic disorder could explain Billy-Ray's behavior. They're usually triggered by stress or a traumatic incident and tend to manifest when a person is in their late twenties/early thirties.

The most common symptoms are disorganized thinking, unusual behavior, and incoherent speech patterns. Billy-Ray did show some of these symptoms, but not for long periods. Hirst believes this is because the disorder takes place, by definition, over a brief period of time, and Billy-Ray suffered a series of short breaks that drove him to kill, again and again, until he was captured.

It's likely Billy-Ray had a psychotic break, but you can't ignore the Voodoo symbols at the last three crime scenes. Was he part of a Voodoo cult like Sandiford claims? Did that trigger his mental problems? I can't say for sure, it's just one of the many mysteries surrounding Billy-Ray and his crimes.

D: Billy-Ray was never diagnosed by a mental health professional, nor did his defense counsel enter a plea of insanity, so be careful about giving too much weight to Hirst's theories. She's a journalist, not a psychiatrist.

Be careful about your references to a Voodoo cult as well, it might seem as though you contradict yourself in later entries, especially when you side with Hirst and her views on Billy-Ray's psychology.

CHAPTER 7:

The business park sprawled over a large lot. There were a handful of warehouses and a few rows of industrial units. Here and there, weeds broke the gravel that covered the ground.

Kyra stopped running. She had a burn mark on the inside of her thigh, a recent wound that was now throbbing. She bent forward, rested her hands on her knees and panted from exertion. Her clothes clung to her body as if afraid for their safety. Her backpack slid to one side, the straps tugging at her shoulders, threatening to overbalance.

She needed somewhere to hide.

She was exposed and defenseless. The guy who'd met her at the Piggly Wiggly could have anything in his van. A pipe wrench, a knife or even some rope. He was into serial killers. Maybe he was building up to his first abduction. Kyra might just have escaped with her life. Should she call the cops?

She didn't know what to do. The person she wanted to consult, more than anything, was Delilah. But Delilah was chasing her.

He'd stolen Delilah from her. How could he do that? Lead her on for months, pump her for information, learn everything about her, all so he could trick her into trusting him.

It was worse than betrayal, it was a violation of trust. She'd lost her best friend, and even though she knew that friend never existed, Kyra was still in mourning.

She checked her cell. It was dead. Maybe someone in one of the units had a phone she could use.

The first unit was a repair shop. Four men sat outside, in the shade of the building. None of them wore shirts. All of them had grease stains on their hands and their pants. They looked over as they heard her footsteps. Two men exchanged a look and raised their eyebrows.

Kyra needed help. She needed protection and all these men looked as though they could handle themselves. Should she approach, tell them what had happened?

A man on the far left scratched his nuts. His mouth broke into a grin. Like a lion about to invite a gazelle into his den. Kyra felt the eyes of all the men on her. Taking in her hair, her clothes and the fact she was alone.

She kept walking, increasing her speed with every step. She'd rather take her chances with the creep in the van. She glanced about, listening for the engine, or the crunch of tires on gravel, expecting his vehicle any moment.

She came to a row of small workshops. The shutters were down on the first three units, only the last two were open. The first had a pit-bull snoozing in the doorway, it growled when Kyra approached. The second had air-conditioning and the cool air drew Kyra in.

She popped her head into the unit. "Is anyone in here?" There was no reply. She took a few steps inside. The entrance had a makeshift corridor, made up of aluminum shelves.

The shelves were piled with plastic display cases filled with prosthetic eyes. Each one held eyes of a different color and a different shape. Kyra found herself watched by row upon row of unmoving eyes.

She was reminded of Constance, and her chest full of human bones. Until today, Kyra had never even seen a glass eye. Now she'd trodden on one and here she was in a workshop full of them. Was the universe trying to tell her something?

The last two sets of shelves had no display cases. They were full of silicon dolls on their backs, some pink and others brown. They looked creepily real. But creepier still, were their empty eye sockets.

The final shelving unit had a single shelf in the middle. It was covered with gold fabric, like an altar. There were wooden statues of Saint Anthony, Mary

Magdalene, and Saint Peter, who was holding a set of keys. Behind the statues were five multi-colored candles in long glass tubes. At the back of the shelf was a picture of a beautiful African woman sitting by the shore, dressed in gold.

A headdress of peacock feathers was mounted over the picture, and sitting in front of it, on the shelf were three small plates containing honey, pieces of squash, and five copper coins. In front of the plates was a little collection of mirrors, each with a gold border. It was unlike any altar Kyra had seen.

Kyra's eye fell on something that looked out of place. At the front of the altar, off to one side. It was a curious object, six inches high, carved from dark wood. It looked like an African fetish doll. Its center contained a small jar filled with soil. It had toy telescopes for eyes, and cowry shells for a nose and mouth. Tufts of real hair sprouted from its head.

Kyra had the sense the doll was scrutinizing her as intently as she was examining it. She had the weirdest feeling it had been waiting, had called her all the way to Yeuxville and this workshop. Before she knew what she was doing, she reached out her hand. The doll had demanded she touch it.

Kyra had the sensation of being outside herself, watching her actions from a distance. Time shifted for her, as if everything she was doing had already happened, many years ago. And she was simply watching a replay. Unable to change anything that had happened before.

Her world collapsed to a point. There was only her and the doll. Some tiny part of her consciousness was aware of footsteps and a scolding voice, loud and urgent.

"Hey, don't touch that. No. Put that down."

Kyra was holding the doll. A hand reached out to take it from her. She turned her head slowly, moving as if she was under water. She still felt outside her body. A tall, Creole woman with vibrant green eyes and dark hair was standing in front of her.

"Give that to me. What are you doing in here?"

The woman's fingers closed around Kyra's as she tried to take the doll. Hot, vibrant energy passed from her into Kyra. It felt like someone had punched Kyra's hand, but the punch kept traveling, right up her arm and through to her shoulder. She was thrown back and the weight of her backpack caused her to topple to the floor.

Kyra felt her life pivot on this moment, like a fulcrum. This one instant of falling would take her from her life as it had been into her life as it would be from now on. The immensity of it was too much for her and she began to black out.

Unconsciousness flowed over Kyra, like dark stagnant water. There was something waiting for her in its depths. It was the presence, it finally had her where it wanted.

CHAPTER 8:

Kyra was surrounded by cool, still water. She was lying on her back on a bed of mud. She couldn't see and she couldn't hear. It was like being at the bottom of a bayou.

What was she doing in the bayou? Did someone throw her in? How was she able to breathe down here?

She had to get out, swim to the surface, but she couldn't. Her limbs wouldn't work. Her body was numb, it wasn't responding to her entreaties. She couldn't move.

She couldn't see, but she had other senses down here in the dark. Like the sense that tells you someone is watching, even when you can't see them. And someone was watching her.

Not someone – something.

It was the presence that had been stalking her since New Orleans. Hiding in the shadows waiting for its moment to strike. And now it had her, down here in the dark water.

Without knowing how, Kyra knew it had been waiting a very long time for this moment. It didn't want to harm her, physically. There was something it wanted to give her. Some knowledge it needed to impart. And somehow

... this was worse.

Because this knowledge would change everything.

She didn't want it to reach her. She had to get away, but she couldn't even cry for help. She needed a lifeline. She wanted someone to find her and bring her back.

The water around her was vibrating. And the vibrations brought her sense of hearing back. There was a voice, faint and distant, calling to her, showing her the way out.

"Aa oo awl riiii..."

The water around her began to move with the vibrations. Lifting Kyra out of the mud and drawing her slowly toward the surface. The words called her up from the marshy bed. Leaving the presence below her, in the dark.

"Can oo ear meee?"

Light broke through the dark waters. Just a tiny beam at first, but it grew, becoming fiercely bright, until it hurt her eyes. She blinked to protect them.

"I said are you all right? Can you hear me?"

Kyra no longer floated. She was lying on her backpack. The back of her head throbbed, and her butt was cold. She blinked in the fluorescent light overhead. The lady with the dark hair looked down at her, her eyes full of concern.

There was no bayou, that was something her unconscious mind had constructed. But not the presence, that had been real. And so was the threat of it.

"Hey, you gave me a fright. Are you okay?" The lady's eyes were such a deep shade of green they were almost grey.

Kyra blinked and swallowed. "I think so," her throat was dry. "My head hurts, but I'm okay. Was I electrocuted?"

"I don't think so. There's no power in this part of the unit, 'cept for the lights."

"It felt like I was electrocuted."

"You just flew backwards. I thought you'd had a fit or something. You're not epileptic are you?"

"I don't think so. I mean, I've never been diagnosed or anything. I think I probably fainted. I haven't eaten or slept much recently. Sorry about your, um, doll thing. I didn't mean any harm."

The lady smiled and Kyra saw how attractive she was. She helped Kyra shrug off her backpack, then get to her feet.

"No harm no foul. But what are you doing in my workspace?"

"Oh, yeah, sorry about that. See, there was this guy…"

"Isn't there always?"

"No, it's not like that. I met him online, but he catfished me. He pretended to be another girl. We spent months talking, all so he could lure me down here. I'm from Chicago. I took the bus. She said – *he* said I could stay at his aunt's house. I don't know if there *is* an aunt, or what he had planned."

"Sounds like you had a lucky escape."

"I know, right? He came to collect me from the bus and I just ran. I ran to the business park, to throw him off. I thought I should call the police. I mean, he's into serial killers and everything, that's what we spoke about online, mostly, so, y'know, maybe he had something real bad in mind."

"Why didn't you use your cell?"

"It's a piece of crap and it's out of charge. I thought someone in one of the units might have a phone. I called out when I came in, but there was no answer."

"I was out back."

"Oh."

The lady reached into her jeans pocket and pulled out a phone. "Would you like to use mine?"

Kyra knew she should call her folks and tell them she was okay, that she was sorry, and she would catch the very next bus home, but she just couldn't. She was too angry. There was an invisible barrier she couldn't cross, keeping her in Yeuxville for reasons she didn't understand.

She shook her head. "No, that's okay. Thanks, though. I should be going."

"Hey, listen, I can't let you go out there now, not with some creepy guy lurking about. Why don't I make you an herbal tea and then give you a ride somewhere?"

"I don't actually have anywhere to go. Is there a motel nearby?"

"There's one on the outskirts of town. I can drive you, if you like?"

"Thanks."

She offered her hand. "I'm Béatrice, by the way."

"I'm Kyra." She took Béatrice's hand, it was smooth and warm.

"Now, how about that tea? C'mon back."

Kyra followed Béatrice to the back of the unit. There was a large workbench, covered with paint brushes and other artist's materials. On the wall above it were hundreds of photos of eyes.

Kyra scanned the unit, while Béatrice made tea. She saw several large tubs marked 'Polyacrylonitrile' and 'Methyl-Acrylate'. On a desk next to the bench, a series of molds were stacked. Lying on the desk next to them were an array of clear plastic shapes that looked like tiny fried eggs. On closer inspection, Kyra saw they were unpainted versions of the eyes she'd spotted on the way in.

Béatrice put a chipped teapot and two slightly stained mugs on the workbench. She filled the mugs and handed one to Kyra. It was warm, aromatic and surprisingly sweet.

"Did you put honey in this?" Kyra said.

"No, that's licorice root, it's naturally sweet."

"It's delicious, I don't normally drink herbal tea, but this is really good."

"Thanks, it's an old family recipe."

Kyra took another sip and turned back to the shelves. "Do you mind if I ask what you're doing in here?"

"I'm an ocularist."

"A what?"

"An ocularist. I make ocular implants, otherwise known as glass eyes, except they're not made out of glass anymore and haven't been since the 40s."

"Yeah, I noticed that. What *are* they made out of?"

"Acrylic mostly."

"And what's with the shape? How come they're all flat and squashed, like a wad of gum? I thought glass eyes were round?"

"No, these days they put an implant in the socket, where the eye used to be, and connect it up to all the muscles. Stop me if I'm boring you."

"No, no, I think it's fascinating. Go on."

"Well, next they take an impression of the socket, using this foamy gel that hardens inside it, and they use that to make a wax model, which is cast in plastic. And that's where I come in."

"What do *you* do?"

"I take a photo of the person's eyeball, and I paint the prosthetic eye, so it looks exactly like their old eye."

"Wow!" Kyra looked around the workspace. "That's amazing. How'd you get into something like this?"

"I kinda fell into it, I guess. I didn't know what to do with myself when I left art school. I was in too much debt to stay in Baton Rouge, so I came home, and a family friend said she knew a company who were looking for someone to paint eyes. I thought she meant portraits, but it turned out it was a local practice specializing in ocular prosthetics."

"So, you spend, like, all day looking at other people's eyes?"

Béatrice shrugged. "Sounds weird, doesn't it? But being creative *is* weird and obsessive. And I'm giving something back, you know. I'm actually helping someone, it's really going to improve their quality of life."

"So, the weird looking babies, are they, like, an art project?"

"Oh, those?" Béatrice laughed and shook her head. "No, it turns out there aren't enough people with missing eyes to pay all my bills. So, I make eyes for life-size dolls."

"People buy those things?"

"It's a niche market, but lucrative. I also make them for adult dolls."

"Eww."

"I know, but I figure, they aren't hurting anyone."

"I guess."

Béatrice put her head to one side and regarded Kyra. She shifted her hips, and for some reason this made Kyra blush. Too self-conscious to meet Béatrice's gaze, Kyra focused instead on Béatrice's long, elegant fingers as they cradled her mug of tea.

"So, you're a long way from home, huh?"

Kyra cleared her throat. "Well, sort of. I live in Chicago, but I have connections here."

"Connections?"

"I was born here. My birth mother died when I was very young."

"I'm sorry. I lost my mother when I was young too."

"I was a toddler, so I don't remember much. It's one of the reasons I came back. To try and reconnect."

"I thought you were meeting the creep?"

"Well, yeah. I told her I was coming and she, I mean *he*, agreed to pick me up. I still haven't come to terms with the fact that she doesn't exist. It's kinda hard to take. We shared everything, we were so close. I can't believe it was all a lie."

"You've had a rough time."

"Yeah, listen, I don't mean to be rude or anything, but I'm kinda tired. Could you give me a lift to that motel now?"

"Are you sure? That was a pretty bad fall you took. You're not seeing double or anything?"

"No, no, really, I'll be fine." Kyra felt the back of her head with her fingers. "There's a small bump, it's not that painful."

"Okay, I guess I've done enough work for the day. Will you do me a favor though?"

"Sure."

Béatrice opened a drawer beneath her work bench and pulled out a small bottle of pills and handed it to Kyra. "Take a couple of Tylenol before you leave."

Kyra shook out the pills and swallowed them with the last of her tea. Béatrice showed her to the back door.

"Gimme a second to lock up. I'm the blue Chevy Impala, parked in back."

CHAPTER 9:

Kyra stepped out the back entrance, swaying with the weight of her backpack. Maybe it was the late afternoon heat, or perhaps she was woozy from fainting.

She hadn't been in Yeuxville more than an hour and she'd been catfished and passed out in a stranger's workplace.

So much for being old enough to look after herself. She'd been on the run a couple days and already needed help. She couldn't even get to a motel without someone dropping her off.

Kyra's legs shook as she stumbled to the Impala. The burn on her inner thigh stung. It was all the running. Walking through the thick heat of the afternoon was like wading through molasses.

She put her backpack down and glanced round. A small canal ran along the edge of the lot. The water flowed in a steady and somnolent fashion. As though it too was weary from the sun.

Clouds of flies swarmed the water, rising and falling like pistons on an invisible engine. Drawn to the canal's hypnotic pace, in love with its cool depths.

Kyra sensed the darkness beneath the surface of her own mind. She recalled the presence that lurked in the bayou down there and wondered when it would break into her waking world.

Béatrice locked up and helped Kyra stow her backpack in the Impala's trunk.

"You sure you're okay?"

Kyra nodded, making her bump throb. "Honestly, I'm fine."

"No strange visions or anything?"

"Nope. Why, was there something trippy in that tea?"

"It's not the tea, it's that fetish."

"Fetish?"

"The doll, the little statue thing you picked up, just before you passed out."

"Oh, that."

Kyra didn't understand the question. She hadn't seen any visions. Should she mention the bayou, or the presence she sensed down there? Béatrice would think she was crazy. They pulled out of the lot.

"I'm sorry for picking up the fetish thing. I didn't damage it, did I? It's not valuable or anything?"

"Oh no, it's not valuable, it's just something I made when I was younger, before I went off to LSU. I found it the other day in a trunk. I don't even know why I put it out."

"Were you trying to reconnect with your past?"

"Hell no, there are things that need to stay in my past. That fetish being one of them."

"Not everything from the past is bad, is it? I mean, the eyes you create for people, that's a part of their past, a part they want to hang onto. You help them do that."

Béatrice stared at the road, gripping the wheel. "You're right, I do bring something back with the eyes, but it's not my past, so it's a one-way thing, I'm just taking pride in my work. I look at the eye and it's just an object. I can look past it and it doesn't look back at me, you follow me?" Her voice sounded tired.

"I think so."

"There are things from the past that have a way of looking back at you, looking through you, and you don't always like what they see."

Kyra didn't know what to say, and Béatrice said nothing else for the rest of the short journey. Kyra stole sidelong glances at her. She didn't know about her past, but Kyra liked what she saw now and she hoped to learn a little more about her mysterious rescuer.

CHAPTER 10:

Béatrice drove to the north side of town, where the houses were bigger, the driveways longer, and the lawns better kept. On the outskirts a sign said, 'EXPRESS INN MOTEL'.

Béatrice pulled up in front of the office, a pink stucco building with a glass door. The clerk at the counter, a stout woman in her late forties, sat behind a small desk with an electric fan. Her roots showed through her dyed red hair.

On a shelf, on the wall behind the clerk, was a wooden statue of Saint Peter, holding a set of keys. It looked similar to the one she'd seen in Béatrice's workshop. There was a little glass of brown liquid in front of the statue, along with a plate of candies and a cigar. It struck Kyra as a weird choice of decor.

"Hey Barbara," Béatrice said.

"Hey Béatrice."

"Do you have a room for my good friend?"

"Always have a room for a friend of yours."

"This is Kyra."

"Hi, Kyra, are you here with your folks?"

"Um, no. I'm by myself."

Barbara glanced uncertainly at Béatrice, who shook her head with an expression that said: 'it's fine, don't sweat it'.

"Well, it's seventy-five dollars a night, how long you planning on staying?'

Kyra had no idea. This wasn't what she'd planned. She'd never stayed in a motel or rented a room. This was a whole new experience.

"About a week, I think."

"For a week I can do you a special discount of four fifty, seeing as you're a friend of Béatrice."

"Is it okay to pay cash?"

"Honey, you can pay how you want, so long as you don't ask for credit."

Kyra took the notes from her fanny pack, being careful not to show how much money was in there. Barbara took the cash and handed her a form.

"Okay, you need to register. Then I'll get your key, and some towels, and show you the room."

Kyra filled out the form using a false name and address. She didn't feel good about doing this, but it was necessary.

"So, you gonna see my brother later?" Barbara asked Béatrice.

"If he turns up. He's usually pretty reliable."

"You have no idea how much that group has helped, honestly, it's been a godsend."

Kyra looked up and caught Béatrice's eye.

"I volunteer at a group for recovering meth addicts. It's where I'm headed next."

"What? Here in Yeuxville?"

Barbara wrinkled her nose. "Oh, it's an awful problem round these parts. Wasn't always. Time was, everybody had a job, not anymore. It's like a plague. C'mon, I'll show you the room."

They left the office and Béatrice climbed into her car. "Okay, I've gotta run, I'll see you guys later. If you have any problems, Kyra, just call."

Béatrice pulled out of the lot. How could she call Béatrice when she didn't have her number?

Barbara set off towards the rooms. "This way. You're in number six."

The motel was L-shaped. A single-story structure in back of the office. There were twelve rooms in total, all with a blue door, a single window, and the same pink stucco. Barbara let her in and handed her the key along with some towels.

"You need anything, I'll be here until twelve."

"Okay, thanks."

The room was clean and simple with no frills. There was a double bed, a TV, and a nightstand with a light and a Gideon Bible. The bathroom had a small shower, a toilet and a sink with some complimentary toiletries. Kyra inspected it with anxious curiosity, pretending it was all a big adventure, and she wasn't the least bit nervous about spending the night in a strange place so very far from home.

When she took off her backpack, Kyra realized how tired she was. She lay down on the bed, without unpacking, closed her eyes, for a few minutes, and fell into a deep sleep. Despite her tiredness, if she'd known what was coming next, she wouldn't have slept a wink.

EXCERPTED FROM

viewfromthekiller'seyes.blogspot.com

An unpublished blog by Kyra Hughes (with comments by Delilah)

BILLY-RAY'S MURDERS

Billy-Ray's first victim was seventeen-year-old Mary-Jo Bernard. Her death has all the hallmarks of a 'crime of opportunity'. Billy-Ray followed Mary-Jo out to a canal near Yeuxville, where the local kids hang-out. The murder weapon was never recovered, but Billy-Ray either killed her with a blow to the head or pushed her off the top of the levee. The levee was high enough for the fall to have killed her. There was blood on the rocks around the body, so she may have struck her head when she landed.

D: Okay, these are tiny points, but they separate the women from the girls when it comes to Billy-Rayology (yes that is a word, even if I just made it up). The spot isn't a hang-out for local kids, just lonely misfits and potential suicides. That's just something Hirst made up, but she's from New York so waddayagonnado? Secondly, it's not a levee, that's something that both Hirst and Sandiford get wrong. Canals don't have levees, rivers do. The big mound of grassy earth, which runs along one side of the canal, was left there by the oil firm that dug it. They just never bothered to move it.

Many killers have a murder signature, and Billy-Ray's was removing his victims' eyeballs. According to the coroner's report, Mary-Jo's eyeballs were removed more than 24 hours after she died. Mary-Jo's body was found three days after her parents reported her missing. Two witnesses said they'd seen Mary-Jo walking to the canal with a girl of the same age. This girl has never been identified, and after routine enquiries, the police stopped searching for her.

D: Always wondered why, wish I could ask my uncle.

Billy-Ray's second victim was Frances Donovan, another teenage girl. Frances was drugged and poisoned in the living room of her three-bedroom house, while waiting for her father to come home. Once she was dead, Billy-Ray removed Frances's eyeballs with a large hunting knife.

There's a lot of mystery surrounding this crime, such as how Billy-Ray broke into Frances's house and poisoned her. It's unlikely Frances let him in, her father was strict about answering the door to strangers, but there were no signs of forced entry. The doors were still locked when her father got back from his nightshift. He found Frances dead on the sofa, with no eyeballs and her homework half done.

The third victim, Alison Comeaux, was in her late twenties and came from one of Yeuxville's most prominent families. The Comeaux's were well connected and involved with the local church. Alison, however, was known as a 'party girl'. She drank at a few of the same bars as Billy-Ray, and they may have known each other.

Alison's condo showed no signs of forced entry either. All visitors had to report to the front desk, and only one visitor was recorded that night, a Girl Scout, who was tall for her age, selling cookies and lemonade.

Billy-Ray incapacitated Alison with the same poison he used on Frances. If he forced her to drink it there are no signs of a struggle. He removed Alison's eyeballs, then left without being seen. His violent urges seem to have escalated, because he returned to the apartment, eight hours later, and mutilated her corpse.

D: Also worth mentioning there were no traces of the drug on any cup or glass in her apartment. Even weirder, the toxicologists ran multiple screens on all the victims, and they were never able to identify the drug he used. It's not on any database. It's unknown to science!

Billy-Ray removed several of Alison's organs and drew crude Voodoo symbols on the walls in her blood. Mandy Sandiford, who was Alison's second cousin, points to the Voodoo symbols as evidence of Billy-Ray's part in a satanic cult.

It was almost two months before Billy-Ray killed again. His fourth victim, eighteen-year-old Elizabeth Boudreaux, was his most daring murder yet. Billy-Ray killed her during a party, that at least twenty other teens were attending.

It's heartbreaking to think Elizabeth might have been saved. Sheriff Hawkins called at the party in search of his daughter, less than half an hour before Elizabeth's death. Billy-Ray would probably have been watching the party at this point, he may even have been inside the house. Unfortunately, the Sheriff's daughter was no longer at the party and he left to look for her elsewhere, leaving Elizabeth and the other partygoers to their fate.

No-one saw Billy-Ray near the house, but he managed to drug everyone at the party. Then he took Elizabeth Boudreaux to the master bedroom, removed her eyeballs and internal organs and painted Voodoo symbols on the wall in her blood.

Elizabeth's corpse was found, a few hours later, when the police returned to check on noise levels. This was lucky for the partygoers, all of whom eventually regained consciousness. If the police hadn't called when they did, Billy-Ray might not have fled the scene, and who knows how many more he might have killed.

A crack team of forensic investigators descended on the house next morning, but even those hardened experts were appalled by what they saw in the bedroom. The evidence they gathered was invaluable in apprehending Billy-Ray.

D: This is great, but you could play up the weirdness a bit more. This happened on a suburban street. The house has a white picket fence, for goodness' sake. There were twenty kids at the party, not one of them saw Billy-Ray, but he managed to drug them all. He took Elizabeth's eyeballs out downstairs, while her friends lay unconscious around her.

Then he dragged her corpse upstairs and tore it apart. A lot of those kids still live in town, and most of them are in therapy a decade and a half later.

CHAPTER 11:

Kyra woke to the sound of the air-con losing its battle with the heat. The darkness and the warm air smothered her like a pile of blankets she couldn't crawl out from under. The clothes she'd worn the past two days were stuck to her body with sweat.

She switched on the bedside light, her stomach groaned with hunger. Her armpits stank. She needed a shower, but first she needed something to eat.

She found a vending machine on the porch. It served meat snacks, but nothing vegetarian. Kyra made do with chips, a candy bar, and a can of soda. She hadn't charged her phone, so she had no idea what time it was.

Kyra plugged her phone in before she got into the shower. When she stepped out it was a little after ten. She was still hungry. Could she get a pizza delivered? Barbara was still in the front office, would she know a good place?

Kyra changed into clean clothes and was toweling her hair. There was a knock at the door.

"Just a minute," Kyra went to answer the door.

A tall, glamorous woman with long, dark hair and immaculate make-up stood on the porch. She was dressed in a black mesh batwing dress, with an ankh pendant and black thigh length boots. She had a pizza box in one hand and a bottle of wine in the other.

Was that? No, it couldn't be.

It was.

Delilah was standing right in front of her.

But it couldn't be Delilah. Delilah didn't exist.

The woman had a honeyed drawl. "I brought a peace offering. Aren't you going to invite me in?"

There was something really familiar about her. It was her voice, not the feminine pitch or timbre, but the nuance and inflection. She'd heard a voice very like it earlier today. And the woman's eyes. Kyra had looked into those earlier today too, but they hadn't had such long, luscious eyelashes.

It was the creep from the Piggly Wiggly. Visions of being grabbed and forced into the back of a van flashed through Kyra's mind. She slammed the door.

Why had she done that?

There was a gentle knock. "Kyra, hon, please open the door. The pizza's getting cold. It's your favorite—olives and artichoke hearts. I got it 'specially."

There were only two people who would know what her favorite pizza was, her dad and Delilah. She was so confused.

"Kyra, I know this is a lot to process, but if you open the door, we can talk it all out."

Kyra froze, she couldn't speak or move.

"Do you remember the last thing you promised me? You texted and said you'd keep an open mind. This isn't keeping an open mind. Do you know what I risked coming here, dressed like this, in a small town like Yeuxville? I thought you were my friend."

She *was* Kyra's friend, one of the best she'd ever had. Kyra had looked forward to meeting her for so long. But when she showed up to their meeting, she'd taken Kyra by surprise. Kyra thought the guy in the van was an imposter.

Now she realized what Delilah's texts had meant. The guy in the van wasn't an imposter. *Kyra* was. She prided herself on being a trans ally. She'd even been suspended for standing up for Sam's right to be recognized for who he was.

But in a moment of weakness, in a strange town, in a strange part of the world, she'd turned her back on her best friend and ran. Could she feel more disappointed in herself? She thought she was more open minded. Thought she was better than this.

There was another polite knock. "Kyra?"

Oh God. What was she doing. She'd left Delilah out there all this time. Kyra opened the door, cringing. She wanted to die. She didn't have bangs long enough to hide behind.

Delilah sighed. "Finally."

"How did you find me?"

"It's a small town. Everyone knows everyone. There's only one motel. I called Barbara and asked her if you were here. Can I come in?"

"Sure."

Delilah sauntered into the room on six inch heels. She was holding the pizza box like a cocktail waitress would hold a tray of drinks. If Kyra tried to sashay in heels that big she would have ended up on her butt.

"Okay, so this is awkward."

"You said a mouthful."

Delilah put her hand to her mouth and giggled.

"What?"

"Did you really just say that?"

"Stop."

"What are you, eighty years old?"

"Don't, I already want to die."

Delilah held out the box. "Do you want some pie?"

Kyra felt the juices in her stomach churn. "Oh God, yes."

The pie was hot and greasy with a nicely charred crust, just the way Kyra liked it. They ate in silence, perched on opposite sides of the bed with the box between them. As the food hit her stomach, Kyra felt her whole body cry out in relief. She'd been hungrier than she realized.

Delilah dabbed at her lips with a napkin. How did she do that without smudging her lipstick? "Shall I open the wine?"

"I'm all right, thanks, I don't really drink wine." Kyra didn't really know anyone who drank wine, except for Delilah. Most of the parties she went to had kegs.

"What does it taste like?"

Delilah picked up the bottle. "This is a good one, it's not too dry. Would you like to taste it?"

"I'm not sure I'd like it."

"Only one way to find out."

"Will it get me drunk?"

"If you drink enough."

"Maybe later. What do you mean by 'dry'?"

"There's wines which are sweet and dry wines which aren't"

"Oh."

"You okay?"

Kyra sighed. "You're so sophisticated. You know about wine and stuff. You must think I'm really dumb. No, I am really dumb, I'm so sorry for how I acted back there at the Piggle Wiggly. That's not me. I was surprised and I panicked, sorry."

Delilah reached across the bed and took Kyra's hand. "I don't think you're dumb at all."

"I acted really dumb. I saw the van and the way you were dressed and I thought I'd been catfished and you were going to abduct me or something."

"You've been reading too many true crime books."

"Look who's talking."

"Touché. I get it though, I can see why you were surprised. I tried to warn you."

"I know, I thought you were just being self-conscious, I didn't realize you were trans."

Delilah flicked her hair back with her hand and frowned. "I don't think of myself as trans, I'm just a woman."

Kyra was confused. "But you don't always dress as a woman."

"I live in a small town. My aunt needs me, I can't leave her. So, I can't always present my full female self."

"Cos everyone's prejudiced here?"

"They're good people, Kyra. I know you come from the big city and think we're all rednecks."

Kyra pulled her knees up under her chin. Now she felt even worse. "I didn't mean that."

"I know you didn't, hon. But the folks round here are basically very decent. If you're in trouble they'll come running. If you're hungry they'll feed you, if your car's broke they'll fix it. They'll give you the shirt off their back and ask for nothing in return. They just have their ways, is all, and I respect that."

"Have their ways, you mean like 'keeping the old ways'?"

Delilah raised her eyebrows and put her hand to her chest in surprise. "Where did you hear that phrase?"

"It's a long story."

Delilah closed the pizza box and pushed it toward Kyra. "Here, the last two slices are for you."

Kyra rubbed her stomach. "Like I need those extra calories."

"Wait till you try my Aunt Mimi's cooking. And you have nothing to worry about, you're beautiful."

"No, you're beautiful."

"Can't argue with that. Is there anything else you want to ask me?"

Kyra thought for a moment. "Have you always known? That you're tran... a woman, I mean."

Delilah's eyes traveled to the ceiling, she looked thoughtful. "I've always known I was different. I never fit in anywhere, but I wasn't always sure why. I was into odd things."

"Like serial killers?"

"Exactly. I was drawn to the outsiders in school, but I never really found my tribe. I was in Debate Club and Model UN cos I was smart, but I was also into fashion and make up. I used to help the emo girls with their hair in recess. Had a bathroom that we used as a salon."

"For real?"

"Oh yeah. I suppose I did know, but I hid it from myself. It's a big thing to come out, especially in Yeuxville and I guess I was scared. Eventually it all got too much. My anxiety was out of control. I hated everything about myself. I hated my face, my body, I couldn't look at myself down there, I went to the bathroom in the dark so I didn't have to look at it. I was avoiding everyone, stopped going to school, or even leaving my room. I couldn't understand why I couldn't just be normal. Eventually my aunt got me a therapist and she was great. She got me to admit what was really troubling me. As soon as I said it out loud everything fell into place and I knew I had to be true to the person I really was."

"Wow."

"I know."

"Have you, you know, fully transitioned?"

"It's expensive, but I'm saving. I'm doing hormone therapy and vocal therapy."

"And while you're in Yeuxville?"

"I dress gender neutral. It just makes things easier. Speaking of which, I don't want to drive home like this, can I use your bathroom to change?"

"Sure."

Ten minutes later Delilah stepped out of the bathroom in a plain, blue t-shirt, jeans and sneakers. Her hair was tied back and she'd scrubbed her face. She was still beautiful, but in a homey way.

"Are you sure you want to spend the night here? I've made up the spare room for you."

"I've paid till the end of the week, and I'd feel a bit weird leaving."

"You certain about that?"

"Yeah, I'm certain."

"Well, the offer's there, if you change your mind."

"Thanks, are we good, then?"

"Yeah, we're all good. You wanna hang out later? We could do that murder tour we've always planned."

Kyra cupped her face in her hands. "This trip around Yeuxville you've always talked about? Visiting Billy-Ray's murder sites."

"You'll be the only tourist I ever take sightseeing."

"I'd really like that."

"I'll call you tomorrow."

There was an awkward pause. Delilah picked up the unopened wine and Kyra went to open the door. Delilah put her arms round Kyra and drew her into a hug. For a moment Kyra thought she was going to cry and she clung to her friend. This was how it was supposed to be.

Kyra whispered. "I really am sorry."

"It's already forgotten."

They broke the clinch and Delilah sashayed out to her van with the wine. Kyra waved to her as she pulled out of the lot then went and lay down on the bed.

She wriggled out of her clothes and lay in her underwear. Her left leg was throbbing at the top. The skin had come away from the burn on her thigh, exposing the wound. The flesh as raw and angry as it was when the cigarette was first held against it.

Kyra had no ointment or Band-Aids. She'd forgotten to pack any. She'd have to buy some tomorrow. In the meantime she'd be careful not to let anything touch the wound. She'd have to be careful how she slept.

Kyra needn't have worried. Sleep eluded her. Was it because she was alone in a strange place? No, it was because she *wasn't* alone. There was something in there with her.

It was the presence. It had been stalking her since New Orleans. Waiting to get her alone.

Kyra could imagine it slipping from the corner of the room, inching closer to the bed. She stared into the darkness, forcing it to take a form.

If she could spot it, she could hold it at bay, freeze it in its tracks and expose it, but it was too determined. Staying in her peripheral vision. Circling her. Wearing her down. Waiting until she was defenseless.

Kyra thought of the chipmunk on the interstate. Oblivious to the oncoming bus, seconds from death and scratching its hide.

Was she any different? Alone in a motel room, miles from home with no one to rely on? Was she just as oblivious to the fate that was bearing down on her? Or was something worse going to swoop down and burrow its talons into her? Snatch her up like prey?

Was the presence doing that?

Suddenly it was all around her. Her imagination painted talons onto the darkness. Reaching for her, ready to lift her from the bed and away into the night to be torn to shreds.

And she honestly began to wonder if she'd make it through this night.

CHAPTER 12:

Two Days Ago, T-minus 8 Hours to Departure:

It was a single sheet of paper, but explosive as a nuclear device.

It came in a brown envelope addressed to Kyra. Propped against a glass of orange juice, next to her cereal bowl. It was Saturday morning, but her mom wasn't making pancakes, and her dad wasn't dressed for his morning run.

They were standing by the table, like it was her birthday and they were waiting for her to open her presents. Kyra had said little to them for days. She was too mad.

She was angry all the time, at many things. But mostly she was angry at herself. Kyra didn't really know who she was.

Her identity was a fragile construct. A shelter thrown together from whatever she could scavenge. Superficial things like the TikTokers she followed, her playlists and the clothes she wore. Things that altered all the time. If it wasn't for her anger, Kyra felt like every part of her could fall down and blow away.

Things might be different if she knew where she came from. How she started out in life. Not just the place, but the people who raised her, the experiences she had. Kyra's Mom and Dad had adopted her when she was a toddler.

"We didn't have you, we chose you," as Kyra's Dad put it.

She couldn't remember her early life. Those memories were locked behind a huge door in her mind, like the door in the Bluebeard story, that his wife was forbidden to open. And like Bluebeard's wife, Kyra wanted to kick that door right down, no matter what was behind it.

The search for her birth parents started six months ago. Her Dad had been supportive, like he always was, but the support and encouragement couldn't make up for the frustration and disappointment.

It should have been simple, but every letter they sent, every enquiry they made was met with refusal. Everywhere they turned another road block was thrown up. It felt as though someone much higher up didn't want Kyra to find anything. And this only fed her anger.

The rage had corrupted every part of her life, especially her relationship with her parents. Communications had broken down and now they hardly spoke. Her Dad was stoic, as if their bond was strained and needed time to heal, like an inflamed tendon.

Her Mom was infuriated. She couldn't stand Kyra's shrugs and single word answers. Kyra knew this, but she couldn't stand her mom's attempts to connect. They left her awkward and enraged, she wanted to crawl somewhere deep inside where she wouldn't have to listen to her mom's entreaties. So she waged a campaign of minimal communication.

Today, she sensed a temporary truce, like animals approaching a watering hole.

Kyra sat at the table and reached for the letter. "What's this?"

Her mom cleared her throat. "It's from the attorney's office who handled your adoption. Your father got in touch."

Kyra's fingers were damp as she held the letter. "It's probably another dead end."

Her dad took her mom's hand. "We don't know that. These things are complex, this might be the lead we're looking for."

"You always say that Dad. You said that every time the adoption agency wrote to us, every time they said the records were sealed and they weren't allowed to tell us anything."

"Honey, that's not entirely true. They did tell us what state you're from."

"And a lot of good that did. You petitioned the court in Louisiana and they told you the same thing—the records were sealed!"

"We just have to find out why those records are sealed and then we can petition to have them opened. Louisiana does allow people access to this information, it's the law, it's on the books, but these things are complicated and take a while to unpick."

"But if it's the law then why did the courts turn us down?"

"Because it's part of the game."

"Game?"

"Yes, game. Law is a game, we pretend it's about inviolable rules, but half the time it depends on which clerk is sitting in the office when your petition comes through. Everything's open for interpretation. You just have to stick to your guns, be patient, and wait for a break. This could be it. The court turned down our initial request. It's a legitimate request, but they denied it. All we know is they denied it because of one or both of your parents. We just need to learn *who* one of your parents is, or *what* those circumstances are, and we come up with a new strategy."

Her Mom put a hand on his shoulder. "Your father knows what he's doing, dear. This is his job."

"It's not my specialty, but I know courts, and I know how to work the system."

Kyra huffed. "So, what does this letter have to do with that?"

"I approached the law firm that handled your adoption. I spent time talking to them, one colleague to another, explained my situation, and asked if they could look through their records. They said they'd drop you a letter if they came across anything."

Kyra put the letter back on the table. "What if they say 'no' again. I can't take more disappointment. Maybe the universe is telling me something."

"Honey, you take all the time you need. We'll take this at your pace, no pressure. You don't have to open the letter now. When you're ready we'll be right here."

Her mom threw her hands up. "Oh, for God's sake, Kyra, open it already! You're going to give me a heart attack."

Kyra sighed, she tore the envelope open. The letter was from the offices of Giardina, Hunt, and Magee, written by a lady who signed herself 'Ann'. Her tone was official but sympathetic, it was obvious her dad had worked his charm.

Dear Ms. Hughes,

Further to my conversation with your father, I'm writing with regards to your petition to the court of District 18, Louisiana. Your father has explained the circumstances of your petition and the obstacles you've encountered. It's his understanding that my office is in a position to help with your case, due to certain documents in our possession.

We are not unsympathetic to your situation, we accept the validity of your case and the emotional pressure it is placing on you and your family. To this end, after careful consultation with my senior colleagues, we've agreed to release the enclosed document, <u>to your family only</u>. We cannot divulge the full contents of the document because it contains sensitive information that pertains to another case, which is not within our remit to disclose.

In accepting this document, it's important that you understand Giardina, Hunt, and Magee accept no responsibility, nor liability, for any actions, legal or otherwise, that arise from your possession. Acceptance of said document constitutes, under civil law, full recognition and acceptance of these conditions.

    On a personal note, I would just like to wish
you luck with your search, and I hope the final
outcome is of benefit to all.

Sincerely,
Ann
(Junior Partner)

The document was a photocopied court file. Most of the file was redacted. Thick blocks of ink covered practically every line. It contained only three discernible pieces of information.

The date of her birth mother's death. The town she lived in—Yeuxville—and her name, Caitlin Robichaud.

Kyra felt she was looking at the document through the wrong end of a telescope. She had the same hyper-awareness that came with déja vu, but this was different. This moment had always existed in the timeline of her life, like a landmark or a signpost. Inevitable from the moment she was conceived, and it was going to change everything.

At first, her brain refused to process what she'd was reading. She saw the words, she knew what they meant, but she didn't want to put them together, because she wasn't sure she could accept what they conveyed.

"Damn!"

Her mom barked. "Kyra Hughes! What kind of language is that?"

Kyra ignored her. The meaning was unavoidable. She had to admit the truth about her birth mother, even if she couldn't accept it.

"Damn!"

"Kyra!"

"I know who my mother is."

Her dad's face brightened. "They've given you a name? That's fantastic news!"

Her mom shook her head. "No, I don't think it is."

Her Mom knew Kyra was about to throw an emotional hand-grenade into the room.

"It's Caitlin Robichaud. Do you know who that is?"

"You sound as though you know, honey."

"It's Billy-Ray Johnson's final victim."

"Who's Billy-Ray Johnson?"

Her dad scratched the back of his neck and his eyes darted to the floor. "He's a serial killer. Kyra has his picture in her room."

"One of those awful posters? Why would you want your birth mother's murderer on your wall?"

Kyra's voice rose. "Because I didn't know he murdered my birth mother until I opened this fricking letter!"

Kyra's Mom raised her voice. "I will not be spoken to like that! I don't care for your tone and I certainly don't care for your language!"

Her Dad extended his hands in a conciliatory gesture. Ever the family peacemaker. "Okay, why don't we all step back a minute. Kyra's facing some big news, she's not herself, and she's just had a big shock. So, we can give her a bit of latitude."

"Latitude?"

"Yes, latitude, but that doesn't mean we're going to let the language go. When you've had a chance to let this sink in, you're going to apologize to your mother."

"Dad, do you even know what this means?"

"The people I spoke to at the law firm said there was a connection between your case and a high-profile case in Yeuxville. They intimated it might be what's causing the hold up. But the important thing is now that we have a name there are all kinds of options open."

Kyra put the document back on the table and looked straight at her dad. "Wait, you knew my mother was connected to Billy-Ray Johnson? Why didn't you say anything?" Her mom turned to her dad with the same look as Kyra. "Yes, why didn't you say anything?"

"I didn't know your birth mother was connected to Billy-Ray Johnson. I just knew there was a connection between your petition and a high-profile case. I didn't know *which* one it was."

"Oh, come on, Dad. Yeuxville is a tiny town with a population of a few thousand. It's not like Cabot Cove. There's not a murder every week. How many high-profile cases do you think it's gonna have?"

"I don't know. You're the expert, not me. I'd never heard of Yeuxville till you became obsessed with it."

"Don't play dumb. You helped me order that poster. You knew exactly what happened in Yeuxville."

"Yes, I knew about the Billy-Ray Johnson case, but I didn't know for sure it was *the* case connected to your parents. That was just a supposition, I didn't have any evidence. How could I say anything without confirmation?"

"How could you not say anything? You knew my birth mother came from Yeuxville, you knew that town meant something to me. How could you not tell me?"

Her mom crossed her arms and frowned. "I'd like to know that too."

"It was precisely because I knew the town meant something to you, that I didn't say anything. This whole search has put you under tremendous emotional strain. I mean, look how you've been acting out."

"Acting out?"

"What else would you call your recent behavior? Suspended from school, sneaking out to parties, it's classic teen rebellion."

"Well, I'm glad you think I'm such a textbook case."

"I'm not saying that. I just thought, given your emotional state, that I didn't want to add to your stress. You were bound to worry. You might have imagined anything, and it could have been months before we got any information."

"Dad, I couldn't have imagined anything worse than this. You could have warned me, but you said nothing. How could you do that?"

"I've just told you why. I've always had your best interests at heart, Kyra, why can't you see that?"

"Why can't you see how big a thing this is to me, Dad? I've been reading about Billy-Ray Johnson for months and months and now I find out he killed my actual mother! I put his picture up on my wall. I know what he did to all his victims, and one of those victims was my birth mom. I would have been alive when he did it."

"I know that. Don't you think I know that? If I could have spared you this pain, don't you think I would? That's why I didn't say anything, because I didn't want you to feel like this until we knew anything for sure. Not with everything else you've been going through, and how you've been acting."

Kyra stood up and pounded the table with her fists. She'd lost the ability to actually talk to her dad. He was being so pigheaded. The only noise she could make was a half scream, half growl. Why did he keep deflecting this onto her? Her actions had nothing to do with this. This was entirely his fault. Why wouldn't he admit it?

Her dad raised his hands as if calling for calm. "I think we're missing one vital and important point here."

Her mom looked anything but calm. "Oh, really Dennis, and what would that be?"

"I know this changes everything, I know it's a huge shock, but it's also an important breakthrough. We have an actual name. I know it's probably one of the last names we would have wanted, but it changes everything in our investigation."

"You're right, Dad, it does change everything."

"I know there's a bad side to this, Kyra, and I know that's going to take a while to get over, but there's also a good side. Now we know who your mother is, we're more than half way to finding your birth father. We wouldn't have found any of this out if I hadn't worked my butt off. I've been doing this for you, working nights, giving up my lunch hour. I realize you're upset, but you've got to give me some credit."

Her mom indicated Kyra. "This isn't about you, Dennis. Can't you see what a state your daughter's in?"

"Of course I can, but why am I the bad guy, all of a sudden? I didn't kill anyone."

"For God's sake, Dennis, why would you say a thing like that?"

"Yeah, Dad!" Kyra literally threw her hands up in the air. She couldn't even, she just, how could he? She turned on her heel and left the kitchen, stormed into the hallway and stamped up the stairs.

"Now look at what you've done," she heard her mom say, as she went up the stairs.

"Why is this my fault?"

"Why can't you see how badly you've handled this?"

The last thing Kyra heard before she slammed her bedroom door was her dad saying: "We've been looking for her birth parents for six months now. I'm the only member of the family who's made any progress, and now everything's my fault. How is that fair?"

Kyra had flown up the stairs like a cinder carried by the inferno of her rage. Her door had shaken in its jam.

What was it with her dad? Why was he so impossible? So pigheaded and patronizing just because he was a lawyer. So he knew the law, that didn't mean he knew how this was affecting her.

All his stupid insinuations. What gave him the right to withhold information from her? When he knew what it meant to her to find her birth mother. To learn where she really came from, so maybe she could begin to understand why she felt the way she did and did the things she was doing.

It wasn't acting out. It wasn't some adolescent cry for help. She was fighting for survival. She was going under and this was the only lifeline she had. It was all she'd been grasping at for months. And she'd just found Billy-Ray Johnson at the end of that lifeline.

How had Billy Ray gotten mixed up in this? Was this why Kyra was so obsessed with him? Because he'd touched her life back before she could remember. Before she even knew what she had. Had Kyra known on some level? Was she drawn to Billy-Ray's story because she was a part of it?

She didn't want to be a part of it. She just wanted this pain and anger to let up, to leave her alone so she could breathe for a few minutes. But it didn't. It built and built inside her. A pressure with no valve and no release.

There was only one place she could turn. One thing she could do. One way to bleed off this poison.

Kyra pulled out the drawer of her nightstand. Taped to the back of the drawer were a pack of Winstons and a cigarette lighter. She took a cigarette from the pack and unpeeled the lighter. She replaced the drawer and slipped off her jeans, pulling on a pair of gym shorts.

She listened for the sound of footfall on the stairs, and when she was sure there wasn't any, she opened her casement window and stepped out onto the roof. The autumn air was cool on her bare legs, but she needed to be outside, so her parents didn't smell the smoke. Kyra crouched down and lit the cigarette, cupping the lighter flame to keep off the breeze.

She hated the taste of tobacco. Pulled a face as she blew the smoke out. She hated everything about cigarettes. Hated the sweet scent of the leaves in the paper tube. Hated the stupid Surgeon General's warning on the packets. Hated how the stench of the smoke clung to everything it touched. There was nothing she hated more than cigarettes and that's why they were perfect.

She'd tried other things in the past. Knives and scissors, razors, anything with a sharp enough edge, but she didn't hate them enough. They bit but they didn't sear, they wouldn't let her sink low enough to come back up.

Kyra blew on the end of the cigarette until it was a glowing ember, then she peeled back the leg of her shorts, exposing her thigh. Her soft, ripe thigh, so tender, so filled with nerve endings. Kyra's confidante, keeping her crime from parental eyes, nestled beneath nylon and denim.

Kyra had tried other parts of her body, but none of them gave her the same relief. She always came back to her inner thighs. They demanded she punish them, like a child playing up for mommy's attention.

So Kyra brought the glowing end of the cigarette onto the most sensitive part of her inner thigh. Her skin crackled where it bit. Hot scent of charred flesh.

Blinding, white flash behind her eyes. The pain so sudden and intense her brain went offline.

She was out and then she was back. White light fading as the pain collapsed to mere agony, clustered around the fresh burn mark on her thigh.

Then the high. The soaring spike of adrenaline that flooded her system. Turning up the volume on her senses. Making her hyperaware of herself and the world around her.

Her breath was short and shocked, coming in quick, shallow gasps. The burn an open wound, soothed by the night air, throbbed its morse code of pain. But the rest of Kyra was empty, the pain and the anger all spent.

She was hollowed out inside and so much lighter. Empty in a way that brought serenity, peace and calm to her mind.

And in that moment Kyra could think clearly for the first time. She knew what she had to do. She knew how dangerous it was.

And she knew it could not be avoided.

CHAPTER 13:

A truck door slammed. Kyra opened an eye. Sunlight filled the room. The blinds powerless against it.

Where was she? Had she slept? Vague dreams floated up from the murk of her subconscious. Endless bus journeys, human bones rattling together. Someone chasing her in a van. Guilt at letting her best friend down.

Kyra groaned. A rattle at the back of her throat. The last two days came back. Everything that brought her to this motel room.

A slow shudder as she recalled last night's darkness and the presence it harbored. She'd read until dawn. At some point, the book must have slipped from her fingers, as she slipped into slumber.

She wasn't ready to wake. There was too much noise outside. Boots on gravel and a voice like a foghorn. Barbara's voice joined it, discussing something with a delivery guy.

Kyra pulled a pillow over her head. She wanted to snooze some more and blot out the sounds. But sleep had gone.

"Shut up," she moaned, as the delivery guy dropped off half of Walmart, talking the whole while with nothing to say.

Kyra threw the pillow at the door and blinked open blurry eyes. Gunky from sleep, unable to focus. She rubbed them with her knuckles, but they wouldn't clear. She'd left so quickly, she'd forgotten her reading glasses. It was a while since she'd had her eyes checked. Maybe she needed a new prescription.

She padded to the bathroom and threw cold water on her eyes. It helped but she still had problems focusing. Maybe she should get her eyes tested while she bought ointment for her burn. There was an optician in town. She'd seen it yesterday from the bus.

She found the ten grand and took out a few hundred dollars.

Should she call her parents? She didn't feel up to it. Besides, the signal was bad here. She'd call them later, in town. Maybe.

Kyra went to the office for the free Wi-Fi and grabbed a couple of Twinkies for breakfast. There was complimentary coffee as well as Wi-Fi in the office. Kyra poured herself a cup. She still didn't know if she liked coffee or not. She added lots of sugar and creamer as a precaution.

She searched bus routes on her phone and found it was only a fifteen minute walk into town. The heat wasn't bad this time of morning.

The walk into town was quite pleasant. Kyra had read everything she could find about Yeuxville. Now she was here, up close and personal.

The town had changed since Billy-Ray's day. There were new streets and new buildings. Starter homes and apartment blocks thrown up to cash in on the sudden revival in the housing market.

Kyra would have paid more attention if her eyes weren't so blurred. When had they gotten this bad? Was it a stress reaction?

She reached Main Street and couldn't make out the map on her phone. Kyra had to stop outside a pink cupcake store, called Gateaux, and lean against a tree. One side of her vision was filled with colored lines. Forming a zigzag pattern like a broken stained-glass window.

The optician was three doors away. They could probably tell her what was wrong. Kyra took a few more steps and shivered, the temperature had been rising since she'd left the motel, but now it plummeted. Her skin broke out in gooseflesh like she'd plunged into ice water.

Her legs and arms were suddenly heavy, as if something was resisting her movements. It felt like she was moving underwater.

What was happening to her? Was she having some kind of seizure? Was it epilepsy? Is this what it felt like? The sensation of being underwater brought back memories of the bayou. The street seemed darker. A cool panic gripped her as she recalled the presence.

It was here again, only nearer now, closer than it had ever been. What did it want with her? Could it get to her in broad daylight? What would happen if it did?

The zigzagging lines formed one great mass that swallowed Kyra's vision. It reminded her of an old projector when the film sticks and the bulb melts it, disintegrating the picture. Leaving only a white screen.

The lines moved to the periphery of her vision and the whiteness swallowed everything. Wherever she turned all she saw was white. She was helpless. Kyra reached out a hand for anyone, or anything, that could help her. There was nobody.

She had no defense against the presence. The shapeless, formless presence she'd never seen. It drew closer by the second, she could sense it, sense its intention to take her, and there was nothing she could do to stop it.

It had been waiting for just this moment. Ever since she picked out those bone fragments, it had marked her out for its own. How do you avoid something you can't hear, or touch, how do you avoid it if you can't even describe it?

Kyra didn't even know where it was, just that it was close, too close. She turned about, thrashing her arms, until finally, it struck. It was swift, gentle, and undeniable in its advance. It enveloped Kyra and she realized it had been all around her since she'd lost her sight. Even as it crept into her head, Kyra had no idea what it was.

And then,

Kyra's sight returned.

Everything came back into focus. In fact, she could see better than before. Images were sharper and clearer. She couldn't feel the presence anymore. She was all right, there was nothing wrong with her. Kyra almost laughed with relief.

The mid-morning heat was back, and the chill she'd felt was gone, but strangely she must have moved further down the road. She could have sworn she hadn't moved, but her surroundings had changed.

Instead of the cupcake store, she was in front of a craft shop called Thimbles, but the building itself looked exactly the same. Four doors down, instead of the optician, there was a drug store. Again, the building looked almost identical to the one the optician had been in.

Kyra walked without knowing where she was going, as though someone else was compelling her to move. She had the sensation of having grown a foot or more. She was viewing everything higher up. She wasn't used to seeing things from this height.

She looked around the street, not knowing why, searching for someone. Kyra hadn't the faintest idea who it might be. The buildings on the street looked different, as though there were suddenly less of them. She didn't recognize where she was. She should check her phone.

Before she could get it out, her hair fell in her eyes. It had changed color, for some reason. It wasn't dyed black anymore, it was mousey brown. She reached up to brush it away, only to find her hand had also changed. It was calloused and covered in grease, the fingernails bitten down to nothing. The hand of a car mechanic.

Maybe there was something wrong with her after all. Kyra's breathing quickened and the panic crept back. The sounds she heard did not match what she saw, like she was watching one film, but listening to another soundtrack.

She passed a vacant storefront on the corner of Main and Seventh. It was dark inside. The sun turned its window into a mirror. Kyra caught her reflection as she passed.

What she saw made her stand dead still and stare at the window. She raised a hand. The reflection in the glass raised a hand. Only it wasn't her hand she saw in the glass, or her reflection.

The ground swayed. Her temperature fell. Nausea rose in her stomach and sweat broke out on her back. The face that stared back at her wasn't hers. It was a face she knew intimately, from books and blogposts and the poster on her bedroom wall.

It was the face of Billy-Ray Johnson.

CHAPTER 14:

No.

This was wrong. Wasn't it?

Kyra didn't have time to process. She was walking again. She wanted to stand still, to work out what was happening, but her eyes kept flicking back and forth across the street, searching for someone. Forced to walk at a brisk pace, faster than someone her size would walk.

She wasn't in control, and she wasn't seeing Main Street as it had been five minutes ago. But she knew this Main Street, it was in the photos Delilah posted of Yeuxville, before the development.

She was looking at Yeuxville fifteen years ago, and she was looking at it through Billy-Ray's eyes. How was that even possible? Was this a psychotic break? A hallucination? It was vivid.

Something struck Kyra's shoulder. She charged down the sidewalk.

"Why don't you look where you're going?" a voice shouted. Kyra would have turned and apologized, but she wasn't able to, she was not in control.

"You on drugs?" the voice called. Kyra didn't know. Had she been spiked? When? All she'd had was a coffee and stale Twinkies.

Her eyes were scanning the street again. She was nearing the end of Main Street. There were fewer shops, more houses. Kyra's gaze moved to a woman across the street. She stepped behind a shrub in a front yard.

The woman crossed at the intersection, pushing a stroller. The two year old in the second-hand stroller was dressed in hand-me-downs. The woman was wearing a leather jacket, red crop-top, and jean shorts. Her hair and make-up immaculate. She was very familiar, but Kyra couldn't place her.

The woman turned down Saloppé Avenue. Kyra stepped out from behind the shrub and followed her. She hung back at a safe distance.

The woman turned into another street. Kyra saw her at a better angle. She knew where she'd seen her before. It was a photo in *Eyes for the Killer*. She was Caitlin Robichaud, Billy-Ray's fifth victim.

Kyra was following her birth mother.

But wait.

If that was Caitlin, the child was…

It was her.

The ground spun. Or was it her head? Kyra couldn't tell.

That was her mom. Her first mom. The woman who gave birth to her.

She felt tears and a tightness in her chest. But her eyes were clear. Because Billy-Ray's eyes weren't misting up.

Kyra wanted to run, throw her arms round Caitlin. She wanted to warn her. Tell her to run. Cherish the time she had with a daughter who'd soon forget her altogether.

How had this happened? A door to the past had swung wide and Kyra was allowed a glimpse. Allowed to view those forbidden memories.

Billy-Ray Johnson was showing Kyra her past, stalking Caitlin and bringing Kyra along for the ride. She'd read everything she could about Billy-Ray Johnson. Now she was accompanying him as he committed his worst crime.

Caitlin crossed the street and turned into another avenue. Kyra hung back, then followed.

She heard a car horn. She couldn't see any cars. Brakes screeched. Shooting pain in her hip and ankle.

Her feet left the ground. She was rolling across warm metal. She stopped rolling when she hit something smooth. It felt like glass.

Her vision went white and then cleared. She no longer saw through Billy-Ray's eyes. He had crossed the road, fifteen years ago. Kyra hadn't. She was pressed up against a windshield.

The minute she realized, Kyra rolled back down the hood. She slipped off the end of the car and hit the road. The breath knocked out of her. Her hip and ankle ached.

Her face was inches from the front tire.

CHAPTER 15:

Kyra heard a car door open. Feet hit the asphalt.

She propped herself on her elbow. The pain in her hip and ankle made it difficult to move. The driver peered down at her. A short, round guy in his late fifties, wearing Bermuda shirt and shorts.

"You okay, young lady? Stepped out of nowhere. Gave me a start."

Kyra fought tears. "I didn't see you."

"You hurt bad?"

"I don't think so. I'm just a bit sore."

"Need a doctor?"

"No, no, I'm fine really." Kyra got to her feet, winced at the pain in her hip.

"You don't look fine. How come you didn't see? You walked right into the road."

"I had something in my eye."

Kyra looked around. She didn't recognize the street, or the houses, she was all turned around. She'd been seeing the world through Billy-Ray's eyes. It was disorienting.

Her arms and legs shook. She'd been hit by a car. She could have been killed. She hadn't even known it was there. She'd had no say in her actions.

"Are you on drugs?"

"Why does everybody ask me that?"

"You look like you're on drugs, way you're dressed and all."

"I don't do drugs. I don't like them."

"Are you sure you don't need a doctor?"

"I told you, I'm fine."

Kyra took a step. A searing pain shot up her left leg. She cried out, lost her balance, arms flailing. The driver stopped her from going over.

"Don't look fine to me. That leg could be broken. It's my Christian duty to get you a doctor."

The driver steered Kyra to the passenger door. She hobbled as best she could. The interior smelled strangely exotic. It wasn't pine air-freshener, it was more like church, incense and fragrant oil.

A strange root hung from the rearview mirror. An ivory statue of a saint sat on the dashboard, dressed like a Roman Centurion, holding a cross and a feather. The driver reached inside his shirt and squeezed a red flannel bag, hanging from twine around his neck. His other hand was over the statue. He muttered a quick prayer.

When he was done, the driver winked. "A quick prayer to Saint Expedite. Ain't nobody gets you there quicker."

"Never heard of that saint."

"You Catholic?"

"Umm, no."

"Don't make no difference. He's peculiar to these parts, and our customs."

The radio came on as he pulled out. A preacher hollered, in a southern drawl: "The eye is the lamp of the body, so then if your eye is clear, your whole body will be full of light. But if your eye is bad, your whole body will be full of darkness. If then the light that is in you is darkness, how great is the darkness!"

"Amen to that. Name's Thibodeaux by the way, friends call me Bob."

"I'm Kyra."

"What's that?" Bob turned down the radio.

"Kyra."

"Well now, ain't that a pretty name."

"Thank you."

"Ain't never run into you before, 'scuse the pun. You from out of town?"

"I'm visiting family friends."

"First time in Yeuxville?"

"Sort of, I was born here, but I moved away when I was young. This is my first time back."

"Happy homecoming, welcome to Cajun country. Won't get a warmer welcome anywhere."

Saint Expedite did his work. The roads were suddenly clear. Bob pulled onto a small clinic's forecourt. He helped Kyra out, she found it easier to walk.

The receptionist was a thin woman with a pinched face and large glasses. She sat behind a small window. Beneath her blouse, she wore a brown, flannel bag on a ribbon.

Bob helped Kyra to the window. "Morning, Marge."

Marge regarded them over the top of her glasses. "Morning, Bob."

"I'd be most beholden, if you could take care of this young lady for me."

"What's the problem?"

"Well, she ran out in front of my car, and I'm afraid I clipped her, so I brought her straight over. Couldn't live with myself if she was badly hurt."

"She ran out in front of you?"

"Yes, ma'am."

"She on drugs?"

Kyra bit the inside of her cheek. "No."

Bob put a hand on her shoulder. "Know how she looks Marge, but she assures me she doesn't do drugs and I believe her."

"Why did she run out in front of your car?"

Kyra glowered. "I had something in my eye."

"Oh," Marge turned to her monitor and tapped a few keys. Kyra glimpsed several hand carved statues next to her keyboard. They were saints, part of some local custom, she'd been seeing them everywhere.

"Dr. McFadden is fully booked."

"Could he squeeze one more patient in? Do me a solid?"

Marge pointed to the waiting room. "Take a seat. I'll try and fit you in. You might have a long wait, though."

Bob beamed. "Marge, you're an angel. Always have been, always will be. Make certain to send me the bill."

Kyra shook her head. "That's not necessary."

"That's Cajun hospitality. We look after our own. You take care now, Marge."

"Be seeing you, Bob." She handed Kyra a clipboard with a form on it. "I need you to fill this in while you're waiting."

They needed personal details. Things that could identify her. Kyra needed medical attention but not if it gave her away. What if she was arrested?

EXCERPTED FROM
viewfromthekiller'seyes.blogspot.com

An unpublished blog by Kyra Hughes

BILLY-RAY'S PROFILE

The FBI profiler, Paris Chavez, did a psych report on Billy-Ray. It played a big part in his capture. I thought now would be a good point to go into it. I haven't read the full report, just excerpts from *Eyes for the Killer*. So I'm going to paraphrase.

Chavez believed Billy-Ray had to nerve himself up to kill. That's why there was often a time lapse between the murder and the mutilation of the victims. Chavez believed Billy-Ray had mood swings, shifting between aggression and remorse, confidence and insecurity.

Billy-Ray took bold risks, because he thought he was invulnerable. He needed to show he was smarter than the police. This stemmed from a deep-seated inferiority complex.

This was why Billy-Ray mutilated the corpses. Removing the eyeballs was a way of hiding from his crimes and avoiding detection. If his victim couldn't see Billy-Ray, then neither would the police.

The Voodoo symbols painted in blood were part of a ritual against getting caught. That's why he kept returning to the bodies. Once he'd committed the act, the bravado would pass, the panic would set in. Billy-Ray would return to tamper with evidence and create—what he believed—was magical protection. Chavez contacted Voodoo practitioners to find out what the symbols meant. He found they were meaningless, drawn by someone who'd encountered Voodoo but had no working knowledge.

CHAPTER 16:

"Can't see anything wrong with your eyes."

Dr. McFadden clicked off his penlight. A tall man with grey hair and a kindly face, he smelled of expensive aftershave. "The symptoms you described sound like an ocular migraine."

Kyra blinked, "But I didn't get a headache."

"An ocular migraine isn't always accompanied by a regular migraine, though it can precede one, so I'd be careful the next few hours. Stay away from chocolate, cheese or smoked meats."

Kyra spent three hours in the waiting room to receive this advice. Dr. McFadden examined her hip and ankle. He found no major damage. He put a dressing on her elbow.

"I'll write you a prescription for painkillers and dressing. Arnica will help with the bruises. My grandmother swore by it. Don't put pressure on your ankle till the swelling goes down. My receptionist will call your parents."

"My parents aren't here, they're in... I mean they're out of town. I'm staying with friends."

"Who are you staying with?"

Who could she say she was staying with? She'd planned to stay with Delilah, but that had changed, she was at work. Who else was there? Maybe Béatrice would help. Kyra didn't know her second name.

"She'll be at work right now. She, uh, makes glass eyes."

"I know Béatrice, been treating her since she was a babe. Go take a seat. I'll get my receptionist to call."

Kyra fretted. What if Béatrice told the receptionist they only met yesterday? What if they called the police? She wouldn't know where to run, or where to hide.

When Béatrice finally walked in, Kyra didn't know if she'd be mad, but she just smiled sympathetically.

"Been in the wars, huh?" She looked stunning in a black dress and white scarf. Kyra loved her fashion sense. She wished they could meet in different circumstances. It was embarrassing to be picked up like a school girl.

Béatrice smiled at Marge. "It's okay, I got this." Marge nodded and got back to work.

She turned to Kyra. "Do you need a hand?"

"No, I'll be fine." The ankle was easier to walk on.

"What happened?" Béatrice asked as they pulled away.

"Didn't see the car that hit me. It's no big deal."

"Says the lady with a limp."

"I should be fine in a day or so. Can you take me to a drugstore to get my script filled?"

"Sure, but I do need to get back to work. There's a big order and my boss is a bitch."

"Thought you worked for yourself."

"That's why my boss is a bitch. Can't get away with anything."

She smiled at Kyra, who blushed and turned her head.

"Thanks for picking me up. Sorry for calling you away. They wouldn't let me out without a ride."

"'S'okay, it's not like you could call on your creepy stalker."

"Actually, we patched things up."

"Really?"

"Well, more or less. It was a big misunderstanding."

"So long as you're safe."

"I think so."

"You think?"

"She's not a threat. I overreacted."

"She?"

"It's a long story."

"Okay."

They drove in silence till they got to the drugstore. Kyra winced as she tried to climb out the car. Béatrice plucked the prescription from her fingers. "I'll get this, you rest up. I'll give you a lift back to your motel."

"But you've got work to do."

"It'll wait. Besides, it won't take but a minute."

"You gonna say a prayer to Saint Expedite?" Béatrice looked genuinely surprised. "Where'd you hear about Saint Expedite?"

"Guy who hit me. He said a prayer before he gave me a lift."

"Aren't you full of surprises."

"It might have worked. The traffic disappeared."

"How about that," Béatrice shot her a wry look. She closed the door and went into the drugstore. Five minutes later, she came out with a paper bag and handed it to Kyra.

"Do you want to tell me why you stepped in front of that car?"

"I didn't see him."

"C'mon Kyra, you're not the sort of person who steps out into traffic. What's going on? Was someone threatening you? Did you see something strange?"

How much could Kyra say? She wasn't sure if she was losing her mind, her eyesight, or both. Had she really seen what she thought she saw?

Would Béatrice think she was nuts? Dr. McFadden would have thought she was losing her mind. Would Béatrice be more open minded? Could Kyra trust her? She needed to trust someone.

"I was having trouble with my eyes when I woke up this morning."

"What kind of trouble?"

"They wouldn't focus properly, so I went to the optician to get new glasses, only I didn't make it."

"How come?"

"My vision went all strange, and..."

"Go on."

"This is going to sound really crazy, but I thought I was seeing the past."

Béatrice's knuckles whitened on the wheel. "What do you mean?"

"It was like my body was here in the present, but my eyes were seeing what happened fifteen years ago, as though I was looking out of someone else's eyes."

Béatrice changed gear and pulled over to the curb. They weren't anywhere near the motel. Béatrice stared out the windshield, gripping the wheel. She took a breath and turned to Kyra. The compassion left her face. Her expression that of a teacher scolding a student without a hall-pass.

"You didn't tell any of this to Dr. McFadden, did you? Tell me you didn't."

Kyra didn't know what to say. She couldn't understand the change in Béatrice. Had she said something wrong? Should she have kept this to herself?

Kyra found her words. "No, of course not. I wasn't even sure about telling you. It only happened for a second. I probably imagined it. I'd just got hit by a car, I wasn't thinking straight. Are you mad at me? Have I said something wrong?"

Béatrice dropped her gaze, breathed out and her features relaxed.

"I'm sorry, that was a bit intense, I didn't mean to raise my voice. I'm just trying to look out for you."

"Okay." She didn't want Béatrice to think she was crazy.

"Look Kyra, I know McFadden comes on with that small town doctor act, but you can't trust him. You can't trust anyone in this town."

"He said he'd been treating you most of your life."

"He has. He was the one who sent me to the nuthouse."

"What?"

"When I was about your age, he had me institutionalized. My mother died when I was young, I never got over it. I was going through a dark period, thought I was seeing things and I confided in him. Next thing I know, I'm locked away for two years."

"Oh my God."

"Exactly. I got better, in time, but not because of the institution. No one gets better in those places. I got better in *spite* of being there. I just don't want you making the same mistakes I did. You don't want to lose your best years to the mental health care system."

Béatrice bowed her head. Kyra was speechless. She reached out and placed her hand on Béatrice's arm. Her skin was warm and smooth beneath her blouse. Béatrice put her hand over Kyra's and squeezed it.

Kyra's mouth was dry as she spoke. "I had no idea."

"Of course you didn't, I've put all that behind me."

"Do you think I'm losing my mind? Is that why I'm seeing things?"

Béatrice squeezed her hand again. "You're not losing your mind. There's more to the world than most people realize. Let's get you back. I've got stuff to do. Those eyes won't paint themselves."

Kyra thought of her own eyes. Billy-Ray had painted a vision of the past on them. It was the strangest and most unsettling thing she'd ever experienced. She didn't ever want it to happen again.

But Kyra was suddenly certain it was going to.

CHAPTER 17:

Twenty One Days Ago, T-minus 3 Weeks to Departure:

Kyra hated the counsellor's office. It was smaller than a broom closet. This told her all she needed to know about her school's policy on mental health.

She didn't hate it because it was small. But because every time she went there it felt like a punishment. Kyra would have welcomed proper support for her mental health. Her parents had chosen this school because of its reputation for pastoral care.

But the reality was different. As long as the Principal showed the school board the proper statistics, that was all that counted. The students' experiences didn't matter.

Kyra had to see the counsellor when her teachers accused her of acting up. This might have been a blessing if Mr. Bradley hadn't been so ill-suited to his chosen profession.

He was a tall man, in his late thirties, with stooped shoulders, thinning hair and a sparse beard. His breath smelled of medicated mouthwash, it filled the air around his desk.

His fingers were steepled, he was breathing heavily through his nose, gazing at Kyra like a bug on a slide. Kyra hid behind her bangs.

Eventually he cleared his throat. "So, you know why you're here?"

"Actually, I don't. I thought we'd sorted this out with the Principal."

"You're referring to the locker search?"

Kyra huffed. "I don't know why the school does them, they're an invasion of privacy."

"The school has a mandate to search all students' lockers, to ensure the safety and welfare of everyone in the building."

"But you found a book," Kyra gripped the arms of her chair. "You didn't find a bomb or an AK47, you found a book. I'm here because of a book. Is it a crime to take a book to school now?"

"It was a book about a school shooting, I'm sure you can understand why that raised flags."

"No, I can't. It was a book about Columbine. So what? Like my Dad told the Principal, it's been read by a million people, and none of them went and shot up a school. There's educational resources for schools to download on the book."

"We all know how lucky you are to have a lawyer for a father, Kyra, and I'm sure he argued very eloquently, but that's not what we're here to discuss."

"If someone on the faculty had downloaded those resources, or read the book, there wouldn't be anything to discuss."

"I'm not talking about your reading matter, we can come back to that later, if you wish. I'm talking about your attitude and behavior. You're displaying a problem with authority."

"I think authority's displaying a problem with me."

Mr. Bradley rubbed the bridge of his nose. "You see, that's exactly what we're talking about. I'm not here to condemn you."

"Sure feels like it."

"I honestly want to help. That's what this meeting is about. You're not here as punishment, you're here because someone at the school needs to hear what you have to say. It's confidential. This is a safe space to share."

"You won't tell the Principal?"

"If it's not illegal, or likely to cause harm, it'll stay between us."

"Okay."

Mr. Bradley leaned forward, his elbows on his desk, his hands folded. "Your parents told the school you're looking for your birth parents, and it's affecting your moods, is that right?"

"I have a right to look."

"I'm not saying you don't, I'm just asking if it's been affecting the way you feel?"

"It would affect anyone's mood."

"How has it affected *your* mood?"

"I just get so angry all the time. I can't remember what it feels like to not be angry."

"Is anger all you feel?"

"No, I also feel disappointed and let down, but mainly angry."

"Are you angry at your parents?"

"What? No! Well, sometimes my mom winds me up, but that's moms for you. My parents are the few people I'm not angry at."

"Are you angry at your teachers?"

"Some of them."

"What makes you angry?"

"When I can't trust them."

Mr. Bradley made a note on his pad. Why did he do that? Just how confidential was this meeting?

"When you say you can't trust them, do you mean you don't feel safe, or you don't believe them?"

"I hate when someone can tell me what to do, how to dress, what to say, and not have my best interests at heart."

"You don't think your teachers have your best interests at heart?"

"Not all the time, no. It's like, when I ask a question in class, because I'm interested, and the teacher acts like I'm just trying to be difficult. Or they accuse me of changing the subject, when I try and broaden the argument.

"Or I see someone in the hallway, and I can see they're going to make trouble for me, so I try to avoid them. But then I get a detention from some stupid teacher, cos I walked up the wrong staircase at the wrong time, and they don't even want to hear my side of the story. They're not interested in why I did it, they're just enforcing some pointless rule."

"And that makes you angry?"

"Doesn't it make everyone angry?"

"We're not talking about everyone, we're talking about you. Do you think your teachers are causing your anger?"

"They're not causing it, they're just the focus of it."

"Would you say the search for your birth parents is causing it?"

"I don't know what's causing it. I think it might help me if I find out where I came from. There's this puzzle piece missing from my life and until I find it, the only thing that fills that space is anger."

"Anger at your teachers?"

"Anger at anyone who has authority, I just don't know if I can trust them."

"Do you ever feel the need to act on this anger? To take it out on your teachers, or the other students?"

"Do you mean violently? I'm not a violent person."

"But you read books about violent people. I understand your favorite book is about a serial killer?"

"What's wrong with that? Most of the students watch violent sports or play violent games on their consoles, no-one accuses them. I get good grades. Why am I persecuted for reading books? I thought you were supposed to encourage literacy."

Mr. Bradley put his fingers to his chin and dug his nails into his beard. They made a rasping sound as he scratched it. His eyes flicked to the window and his cheek bulged as he ran his tongue along his molars. "The school encourages students to read as widely as possible. Your last three book reports were on the same subject—serial killers. Do you think that's appropriate for academic study?"

"A lot of people study serial killers – psychologists, criminologists and the FBI, for instance. This gets me so angry, people think there's something wrong with you if you're female, and you read books about murder. It's fine for middle aged men to study serial killers, but not high school girls."

"Do you think your anger makes you interested in serial killers?"

"Why don't you tell me?"

"It might be one of the reasons, but there could be others."

"Such as?"

Mr. Bradley jotted something else in his notebook. Then he closed it, steepled his fingers. Kyra looked up and met his gaze. His eyebrows were furrowed, hair twitched in his nostrils. "In your reading about serial killers, have you come across the term hybristophilia?"

"No."

"It's sometimes referred to as 'Bonnie and Clyde syndrome'. It's a type of paraphilia."

"That doesn't sound good."

"It's not. It describes people who are sexually aroused by violent murder and the people who commit it."

"That's gross."

"Does it arouse you to read about serial killers?"

"Are you allowed to ask me that?"

Sweat formed on his cheeks. His breathing got heavier. "I think it's appropriate, given the context. I'm trying to help, Kyra."

"By asking if serial killers turn me on?"

"No, by getting you to understand your motives, by showing you the reasons behind your anger, and your interest in things like serial killers. You can't say it's a healthy interest."

There it was again. The same old prejudice. Nice girls didn't read about serial killers. Only sickos and perverts.

Bradley just wanted to belittle her with insinuation. To think she'd believed him when he said this was a safe space. Had considered really opening up, making herself vulnerable.

And what had he done? He'd accused her of being a deviant. Was it any wonder she hated coming to this office?

Mr. Bradley pulled at his beard. "Have you considered other reading matter? Something more suitable to your age?"

"Have you considered other professions? Something more suitable to being an asshole?"

Mr. Bradley's eyes widened and he drew breath. "I don't see what my career choices have to do with this matter and that's not appropriate language to be using on school grounds."

"But it *is* appropriate for you to ask me if I get turned on by serial killers?"

"I've already addressed that matter. You can't avoid your problems by deflecting them onto me."

"No, but I can avoid talking to you."

Kyra stood and knocked over her chair. It didn't hit the floor, just wedged itself against the far wall. Kyra grabbed her backpack and glowered at Mr. Bradley.

His eyebrows furrowed. "You have twenty minutes left. We're not done yet."

"We are *so* done."

The door crashed into the corner of Mr. Bradley's desk as Kyra flung it open. In that moment she didn't think her life could get any more messed up.

What happened later, when she reached Yeuxville, would prove how wrong she'd been.

CHAPTER 18:

The bus shuddered and came to a stop. The doors clanked open like it was too much effort. Kyra opened her eyes much the same.

The bus was empty. Where had the other passengers gone? Kyra looked out the window but didn't recognize the street. Where the hell were they?

She'd caught the bus from the stop near her motel. She'd taken painkillers for her ankle. Kyra hadn't slept much. She'd spent most of the night worrying if she'd lost her mind. Or worse, that she'd had a genuine supernatural encounter.

But what sort of supernatural encounter? She hadn't seen a ghost. It felt more like she *was* a ghost, or looking through the eyes of a ghost. Seeing the past, exactly fifteen years ago.

She'd lost control of her body, something else had been in charge. It wasn't like being possessed. More like she was the one doing the possessing, carried along for the ride inside of Billy-Ray.

Kyra got to her feet and swayed, woozy from the heat and the codeine rush. This wasn't Main Street, they weren't anywhere near the town center. She'd closed her eyes for five seconds and the bus must have lulled her to sleep.

Delilah had texted last night to see if Kyra wanted to do the murder tour today. She wasn't free till after work, so Kyra had decided to kill time in town.

She looked out the window. All she could see was trees and fields. She staggered down the aisle to the driver staring at his phone, cap pushed back on his head.

"Excuse me, sir, where are we?"

"Last stop, you have to get off."

"But I don't know where I am. I fell asleep and missed my stop. Does this bus go back into town?"

"This bus goes back to the depot, there's another in a couple hours."

"I can't wait two hours, not in this heat."

"Then you'll have to walk. Head south along Bourque Avenue, turn right onto North Broad Street, should be there in half an hour."

Half an hour! It would have been quicker to walk from her motel.

Kyra's shoulders drooped. She sighed and nodded. "Okay, thanks."

She climbed out of the empty bus. There was no sidewalk. Only a long, dusty blacktop with the occasional car or truck roaring down it.

Kyra was out in the middle of nowhere, miles from town with no lift and no bars on her phone. And things were about to get a whole lot worse.

CHAPTER 19:

Kyra thought about kicking the tires of the stupid bus. But it wasn't the bus's fault, or the driver.

It was her fault she was stuck out here. This whole trip, everything, it was Kyra's fault. She'd kick herself but that would only hurt her ankle.

She'd come here for Caitlin. She needed what? Closure? Answers? She wasn't certain. Was that why she hallucinated, thought she was seeing Caitlin yesterday? Was it a hallucination?

Whatever it was, real or imaginary, seeing Caitlin had woken something inside her, an unnamable ache. A desire for something she'd lost. Something denied her. Knowledge of her birth mother. Something that would fill the empty, screaming void at her center.

She needed to know who Caitlin Robichaud was. How she laughed. What she sung in the shower. The way her neck smelled when she held Kyra.

These memories had been kept from her, just like her birth records. Locked behind some secret door, like the one in the Bluebeard legend the bride was forbidden to open.

Kyra continued down the roadside, thankfully, the painkillers were working. She was fine to walk so long as she didn't put much pressure on her ankle. After ten minutes a sidewalk appeared. Another ten minutes and the first houses came into sight. They were single story structures on pilings. Their screens were rusted, paint peeled and porches sagged. Their yards ran wild with weeds and high grass. There were engine parts in one and an old truck on cinder blocks in another.

She passed a bull terrier chained to a post. It yapped and growled, spittle flew from its bared teeth, but its tail wagged as if it was grateful to Kyra for breaking the monotony.

A man yelled, "Shaddap Duke! I said shaddap. Don' make me come out there!" But Duke was having too much fun. Kyra hobbled by as quickly as her ankle would allow.

On her right she passed a turning. A wooden sign read *Trenchard Trailer and RV Park*. A light breeze carried odors to Kyra, rotten eggs, and mild sewage. Kyra pulled a face and moved on. The smell faded as she turned onto Montaigne Street. There were fewer trees and less shade. The sun was higher and Kyra had to squint to see. The sun caught every window and car windshield, its rays burned her retina. Red and green after images floated before her eyes. Kyra blinked them away, but there was one persistent image that wouldn't leave. It started as a small golden blob in the corner of her sight. It shimmered and grew. Wherever Kyra looked, there it was, swallowing up more of her sight until her whole field of vision was a shimmering mass of gold.

She stumbled along the sidewalk, unable to see, her hands out front to stop her colliding with anything. She was effectively blind. What if she stepped in front of another car, or something worse? What if someone grabbed her? She wouldn't even see them coming.

Kyra felt the skin on her arms and the back of her neck pucker, causing all the hairs to rise. The sun had been smarting on her cheeks and forearms, but the temperature around her dropped.

Like a cloud passing in front of the sun, Kyra felt something move in on her. It was something she couldn't avoid or outrun. It was the presence.

Except, it wasn't just a presence anymore, it had a name and a purpose, one that couldn't be denied. Kyra knew who the presence was, she'd probably always known.

The shimmering expanse that filled her vision hardened into jagged, complex patterns. She felt the presence all around her, seeping into her, melding itself with her body and mind, taking away any control Kyra had over herself.

She shrieked and stamped her foot. "No! No, no, no!"

She was two years old again. Tiny and vulnerable and unable to deny the power someone bigger and stronger had over her. This was worse than a teacher or a counsellor being able to control her.

Was this an actual memory, an emotional flashback? Was this the root of her *attitude problems*?

Kyra didn't know. She just knew she didn't want Billy-Ray to take over her again. To take away her ability to act independently. It wasn't right. It wasn't fair. It just wasn't!

The vibrant patterns that shimmered before her eyes shattered, like a windowpane hit by a brick, and Kyra's sight cleared.

She was on the same street, but different cars were parked by the curb, the paint on the houses was newer, and the front yards had toys or shrubs that hadn't been there a moment ago. Kyra walked back the way she came, only it wasn't her choice, and it wasn't her will that carried her along. The pace was too brisk for her ankle and the pain crept up her leg.

Up ahead, she saw a well-dressed woman pushing a shabby stroller. She followed the woman for a few minutes, keeping a safe distance. Why was she calling her 'the woman'? Kyra knew who she was.

She was Caitlin. And Kyra was watching her through the eyes of her 'favorite' serial killer.

Could she call him that anymore? Now she knew that in two days' time Caitlin would be dead. She would never get to see Kyra grow up. Kyra would never get to know her outside of these stolen moments, spying on her through the eyes of her murderer.

Kyra felt more emotions well in her chest. There was longing, a need to throw her arms around Caitlin and bury her face in her mother's chest. To be comforted and told that everything was going to be all right.

But there was also fear. A palpable fear that gripped and shook her as though she was a child in the hands of an adult, being punished for reasons she didn't understand. Why was she frightened by her birth mother? Or was she frightened of what Billy-Ray was going to do to her?

Did Billy-Ray know what he was doing to Kyra? Was this some sick game he was playing from beyond the grave? It wasn't enough to take Kyra's mother from her, he needed to force her to watch.

Caitlin turned off the street onto a footpath, and Kyra found, to her relief, that the pace was slowing. Rather than follow Caitlin up the path, Kyra snuck alongside the dense shrubbery that bordered it. When Caitlin stopped by a tree, Kyra squatted down to watch her through a gap in the shrubs. Caitlin lit a cigarette and stared into space, while the child in the stroller slept.

There was a wistful look on Caitlin's face, as if her mind were away in a more peaceful place, unaware of what would happen in just forty-eight hours. The wistfulness suited Caitlin, it chased the anger and frustration from her face, doing more for her looks than the make-up she'd applied. Caitlin wasn't classically beautiful, but there was something attractive about her. She had the sort of quirky good looks Kyra aspired to. The more she watched Caitlin, the more of herself Kyra saw.

As she watched, little things about Caitlin became familiar. The door to those lost memories opened a crack. Nothing specific crept out, no definite recollections, just a sense that Kyra had gazed up at this face, had loved this woman.

This was what Kyra had been longing for. Recovering this tiny scrap from her past was almost worth being forced to squat behind a shrub. If Kyra could only reach out and stroke Caitlin's face, throw her arms round her and tell her how much she missed her, then she'd endure this a hundred times over. But Kyra wasn't going to get that. She had to be content with these snatched moments of second-hand intimacy.

Caitlin finished her cigarette and the child stirred. Kyra still thought of her as *the child*. It was hard to think of the person she was stalking as Caitlin, her birth mother, but it was even harder to think *she* was the tiny girl curled up under the threadbare blanket. Caitlin carried on down the path. It led to a field.

Kyra followed her on the other side of the shrub, completely unseen. Caitlin pushed the stroller across the grass until she got to a gate, in the lower end of the field.

Caitlin pushed it open.

Kyra stepped out from behind the shrub and hurried to catch up. The uneven ground of the field and the sudden, quick pace brought a stab of pain to her ankle. The gate was a back entrance to the trailer park.

Kyra saw Billy-Ray's roughhewn hands reach out and open the gate and at the same time felt her hands mimic his actions perfectly. As the gate swung open Kyra had a sudden presentiment. She was crossing a threshold.

What she would learn on the other side would change everything she thought she knew about her life and herself.

She would never see either in the same way again.

CHAPTER 20:

Kyra followed Caitlin through the park, keeping at least one trailer between them the whole while.

Caitlin came to a trailer surrounded by a low picket fence. Broken toys and a plastic slide were scattered in the mud of the yard. Kyra knelt by the wooden steps of another trailer and watched as Caitlin knocked at the trailer door.

A man in a Slayer t-shirt answered, he had a sandy mullet and a thick moustache, he grinned at Caitlin as she put her hand on her hip and pushed her chest out, smiling coquettishly at him. The man shouted something into the trailer and a few seconds later a woman, with limp, blond hair and an AC/DC t-shirt joined him at the door.

In the stroller, Kyra saw her younger self reach up her arms for the woman. The woman beamed down at her and lifted the child out of the stroller. Young Kyra seemed happy to be held by the woman and snuggled into her shoulder. Caitlin chatted with the two of them for a while, laughing and playing with her hair, winking at the man when the woman was distracted. After about five minutes, Caitlin kissed the woman on the cheeks and left the child with her.

Twenty seconds later, the man slipped out of the trailer and followed Caitlin down the path. Caitlin turned and smiled mischievously as he caught up to her.

Kyra trailed them at a distance. As they came to the main gate, the man slapped Caitlin's butt and put an arm around her waist. He pulled her into a small grove of trees by the entrance.

Kyra crept up to the fence and spied them through the trees. The man had his tongue down Caitlin's throat and his hand on her breast, squeezing it playfully. Caitlin's hands were on his butt, her fingers kneading his buttocks.

This was all wrong. How could Caitlin do this? Her friend was back in the trailer looking after her kid. She shouldn't be stealing her man. She was betraying her friend, betraying Kyra.

Caitlin pushed the man gently away. She smiled regretfully and pointed at her watch. He tried to pull her back, but she wriggled free, pecked him on the cheek, and made her way toward the main gate. He made one last attempt to smack her butt, missed, and loped back to his trailer.

Kyra tailed Caitlin as she left the trailer park and headed to the road. Caitlin glanced at her wristwatch and stared at the traffic. After about five minutes, a black SUV pulled up. There was a guy with a goatee behind the wheel, somewhere in his forties. Two younger guys sat in the back seat, their eyes dead, their faces blank.

Caitlin climbed into the passenger seat, and one of the guys in the back offered her a glass pipe. Caitlin took the pipe and the guy dropped some tiny white rocks into it. He lit the rocks with a Zippo and Caitlin inhaled deeply.

The white guy put his hand on Caitlin's chest, fondling her breast as she inhaled. When she exhaled, he leaned in and kissed her. She put her hand on the back of his head and pulled him to her. The windows rolled back up and the SUV took off down the road.

Kyra stepped out from behind the tree and watched the SUV drive away. There was no ground at her feet. She was plummeting into a dark place and the only lifeline she had was her anger.

Moments ago she'd wanted to throw her arms around Caitlin, now she wanted to wring her neck. Was that where her fear came from? Fear of learning what kind of woman her birth mother had been.

Her memories had been insubstantial and incomplete. Kyra wasn't certain she wanted to see the wider picture. There was pain and anger standing in her way, like rabid guard dogs.

Don't go there, they snarled. *You don't want to recall this, turn around and leave it in the past.*

Kyra kept breathing deeper and deeper, but she never seemed to get enough air. Her head spun. Was she going to hyperventilate?

Did she just hear someone calling her name? She wasn't sure. Who would know her out here in this trailer park?

No, there it was again.

Billy-Ray was looking at the road, he still had control of her, so she couldn't turn to see who called. She wouldn't have seen them anyway.

A hand gripped her shoulder. Was that her name again?

She was being shaken, but she couldn't see who it was. Billy-Ray turned to go, and Kyra made to go with him, but the hand was still on her shoulder. She felt Billy-Ray leave and carry on his way, and for a second she was bereft. The world around her collapsed into a gray haze. She couldn't see a thing, her name was being called and she couldn't see a thing.

Then the haze cleared, and her sight returned. She looked at the road, but the vehicles were different. Her body moved back and forth as someone shook her. She heard her name again:

"Kyra, what's the matter with you, girl?!"

She turned and saw Delilah was shaking her. Delilah had no make-up and was dressed gender neutral, t-shirt and jeans. Her brow was furrowed with concern.

"Stop with the shaking."

Delilah's voice was deeper. "You're standing in the road, you could've got hit."

Kyra looked down and saw she was standing on asphalt, not the grass she'd seen a moment ago. "Wait, did they move the road?"

"A long time ago, maybe. Are you all right? You looked out of it."

"I, uh, it's kinda complicated. What are you doing here?"

"I'm delivering a package. This is my day job. What are you doing out here? I thought you hurt your ankle?"

Kyra remembered she'd told Delilah in their text exchange last night. "I did. I took the bus into town, only I fell asleep cos of my meds, and I woke up on the other side of town. There wasn't another bus for two hours, so I kinda wound up here."

"I'd have given you a lift into town if you'd asked."

"You weren't free till later, and I got bored. The only thing I had planned was your tour."

"Yeah, 'bout that, do you mind if we take a rain check until the day after tomorrow? I've got to run to New Iberia on an errand. It's pretty urgent."

"Oh," Kyra couldn't hide her disappointment.

"I'm sorry, I can't get around it. I need to do this now. Listen, I can take a break if you'd like to go get a coffee?"

"Can you *get* a decent cup of coffee in this town?"

"I might know a place, and the beignets are to die for."

Kyra's ankle throbbed. Her limbs felt heavier and her stomach had that faint nausea she always got when her meds were wearing off. She couldn't walk back to town now.

Kyra shrugged. "Sure, let's go."

She'd been looking forward to the tour. If only because it would have saved her another night alone in her motel room with her intrusive thoughts. Thoughts that would only get darker after what she'd just seen.

Kyra couldn't escape the fact that she was either losing her mind or a long dead serial killer was taking her over and forcing her to watch as he stalked his last victim. That this victim was Kyra's birth mother was bad enough, but what she'd just learned about Caitlin could shatter everything she thought she knew about herself.

A cold, sick feeling spread over Kyra as she followed Delilah back to her van. It wasn't her meds wearing off this time. It was the certain knowledge that what she'd learned so far was nothing compared to what she was about to discover.

CHAPTER 21:

Delilah parked off Main Street in Church Square. Most buildings dated to before the Civil War. Including the old church that dominated the north side of the square. There was a green in the center, surrounded by a cast iron fence with a memorial to the fallen Confederate soldiers.

The Naked Bean sat on the west side of the square. It was a tasteful mix of contemporary decor and period detail. There were prints of old Yeuxville on the walls, and a large sack of coffee beans with merchant's scales at the back.

The coffee was okay, Kyra still wasn't sure if she liked drinking it, but the beignets *were* to die for. Kyra realized she hadn't eaten since yesterday. Her diet was awful at the moment, but she was glad they'd ordered a big plate.

Delilah raised her eyebrows. "Kyra Hughes, have you been starved and locked in an attic the past week?"

"Sorry, I missed breakfast. Wait, did I eat all of this plate?"

"I had half a beignet."

"You must've had more."

"I'd have lost a finger if I tried."

"Sorry. You're right, they're to die for."

"So they get Chicago's seal of approval?"

"For sure."

Kyra grinned. Delilah handed her a paper napkin.

"What?"

"You have some powdered sugar on your chin."

"Do I?" Kyra wiped her face. "How long's that been there?"

"A while."

"Well, thanks for telling me. How come you didn't say something?"

"I thought you were rocking a new look."

"Remind me never to hire you as my stylist."

"Couldn't do a worse job than your current one."

"Ouch! Way to boost my self-esteem."

"Oh my, have I hit a sore spot?"

"Maybe, I mean I don't exactly blend in with the locals, everyone thinks I'm on drugs."

"Can you blame them?"

"What's that supposed to mean?"

"Nothing, baby girl, you're just not something they see round these parts. We don't get many visitors from up north. It's why I like you so much."

"Because I scare the natives?"

"No, because you don't fit in, and neither do I. Because you dress differently and think differently. You're the only person I know who's as obsessed with Billy-Ray as I am."

"Do you ever wonder why that is?"

"What do you mean?"

"I mean, do you ever wonder why we spend so much time thinking about Billy-Ray? Like how he spiked the drinks of a party of teens without anyone seeing him? Or how he got into so many of his victims' houses without leaving a trace?"

"Or what his big secret was? The one he mentioned to his work colleagues, that sent him over the edge."

"Yeah, but why do we obsess about this so much? Do you ever think about that?"

"You're in an introspective mood."

"I suppose I am."

Delilah placed a hand on her chest and let her eyes drift upward. "Well, I love a mystery, and it all happened locally, but part of my fascination is my uncle worked the case before he was killed. I've never thought about it much, but I guess studying the case brings me closer to him. In fact, I may be about to turn up some new info, thanks to my uncle."

"Really?"

"I can't say too much yet, and it's probably nothing, but it's part of the reason I have to run this errand. So, how about you? I've read your blog, I know some reasons you're fascinated with our friendly neighborhood serial killer, but you don't have a personal connection."

"Actually I do. It's why I'm here. You know I'm adopted right?"

"Yeah."

"Well, just before I left, I learned that Caitlin Robichaud was my birth mother."

"No way!"

"It's true."

"Oh Kyra, I'm so sorry. I had no idea."

"That's okay. I didn't want to say anything by text, because I was still processing. I still am, I guess. And then when I got here..."

"We didn't get the chance for a heart-to-heart."

"No, sorry."

"Is this why you've been acting so out of it?"

"What do you mean?"

"Stepping out in front of cars."

"Okay."

"When I saw you at the trailer park you were zoned. You didn't hear me when I called."

"No, it's not that, I've had a couple of episodes."

"What kind of episodes?"

"Nothing important. I just zone out a bit. I'm sorry, I'm on some heavy painkillers, and I might have taken one too many."

"How's your ankle?"

"It's fine. It's a bit sore, but it's a lot better than yesterday."

Delilah pointed to the bandage on her arm. "How about this?"

Kyra peeled back the dressing to reveal the damage beneath. "Wanna see?"

"Whoa, nice scab."

"Nice scab? Where are we, kindergarten?"

"I'm just saying, gonna have a sexy scar when it's healed."

"So, that's what you look for in a lover—scar tissue."

"Maybe. Sorry to burst your balloon, honey, but you're not my type."

"You're gonna let a little thing like being gay stand between us."

Delilah shot her a bemused look. "Honey, I'm straight."

"Wait, of course you are, because you're... I mean you're into men and ..."

Kyra's cheeks reddened. Why did she say that? She'd messed up again.

Delilah reached over and touched her arm affectionately. "It's okay. If you do need to talk about this thing with your birth mother you know I'm here, right?"

"Thanks, but actually I'd rather do something to take my mind off it."

The waitress came to take their plates. Her top lip curled when she spoke to Delilah. "Can I get you anything else, *sir*?"

Delilah's voice went up a register. "I'll have another latte. How about you, Kyra?"

Kyra swilled the last of her americano in the bottom of her cup. "No, I'm good."

The waitress turned her nose up and sashayed back to the counter.

Kyra nodded toward her. "What was that about?"

Delilah waved the matter away. "Some people have fixed ideas. Anyway, weren't we going to take your mind off something?"

"Why don't you tell me about this church," Kyra pointed out the window, at the steeple, which was visible from their table. "I've seen photos, but I had no idea it was so big."

"You mean Notre Dame."

"Wait, isn't that in Paris?"

"That's a different one."

"So, this one doesn't have a hunchback?"

"Not at the moment. Its full name is, 'Les Yeux de la Notre Dame'. It was built in the 1760s by French speaking Arcadians who came here from Nova

Scotia. The British kicked them out, and the Spanish, who controlled Louisiana, let them settle here."

"Lousy British."

"Tell me about it. The party of settlers was led by a priest called Henri Louis Boudreaux, who founded the church. The whole town grew up around it. It was originally called 'Yeux de la Notre Dame Ville', but that got shortened to Yeuxville over time."

"*Yeux* means eyes in French, right?"

"That's right. Legend has it Henri's daughter, Madeleine, had this vision. Are you sure you want to hear all this?"

"Hell, yeah!"

"Okay, well, allegedly, the eyes of the Virgin Mary appeared to Madeleine in an oak tree, and suddenly there were angels in all its branches. She told her father and he said it was the miracle they were looking for. So they built the church on the very spot where the oak tree stood. Apparently, a lot of the wood in the rafters comes from that original tree."

"So, they cut down the sacred angel tree with the Virgin Mary eyes?"

"Yep."

"And they made a church out of the wood to celebrate?"

"No-one said they were smart."

"How come you know so much about this?"

"I read a lot. Plus I did a project on it for history, in middle school."

"I can't get over how beautiful this square is. It's nothing like the rest of the town."

"There's been a lot of development the past decade. Katrina hit us pretty bad and so did Ike."

"I thought that was mainly New Orleans."

A bitter tone had crept into Delilah's voice. "That's what everyone thinks. We weren't big enough to make the five o' clock news. A lot of places round here were hit worse than the Big Easy, only no one ever hears about them. More than half the town's been rebuilt in the last ten years."

"How come you don't have more tourists visiting the square?"

"We get a few, around May and June, on day trips to the church. But we're off the beaten track and there's not much else for them to do."

Delilah checked the time on her phone. "Listen, I've got to get back. I can drop you at your motel if you like?"

"No, that's okay. I can get the bus. I'd like to look around for a while."

"Just don't fall asleep again. I don't want to have to come get you if you wake up in St Martinville."

"I won't, I promise."

"About that murder tour, with everything you learned about Caitlin, do you still want to do it?"

"Yeah, no, I'd love to."

"How about we try for tomorrow then? We can start around noon if you like? I've got a half day."

"Sounds great."

"Okay, I'll just get the check, then I've got to run."

"That's okay, I can get this."

"No, I insist. I'm the one standing you up, so it's my treat."

Kyra didn't want Delilah to leave. When she'd gone, the dim lighting stopped being atmospheric and took on a sinister edge. Now she was alone, Kyra could almost feel the presence circling her.

She was still calling it the presence when she knew who it really was. She knew he was waiting and she knew he had worse things to show her.

CHAPTER 22:

Kyra wandered round the square, browsing in the shops and admiring the architecture. She spent a long time in the church. A plaque by the door said the current church was rebuilt in 1890, replacing the wood-frame building that had stood on the site for 150 years prior.

It pleased Kyra to learn the current building was constructed in a Gothic revival style with Romanesque motifs. The exterior of the church had one central spire surrounded by four miniature spires, with four further medium spires at the corners. Was there a fire sale on spires in the 1890s? Or should that be 'spire sale'?

The interior was a white marble dream of swooning spires and descending columns. Hanging lanterns illuminated rows of oak pews that demanded you kneel and genuflect. Three stained glass windows blazed above the altar, the main window showed the Virgin Mary gazing heavenward, in front of a tall oak tree, surrounded by angels singing her praises.

Roped off, on the left of the main altar, was a side chapel. Kyra peered in and saw it contained a small altar. She couldn't resist removing the rope and stepping inside. The altar contained three wooden statues.

The central statue was a black Madonna, someone had carved the words *Erzuli Dantor* into the base of the statue. In front of the statue the parishioners had left tiny bottles of perfume and chocolate liqueur as well as costume jewelry and gold rings. To the Madonna's right was a carving of an African St. Peter and to her left was an African St. James. In front of St. Peter were bottles of rum, cigars and coins. Before St. James were peppercorns, kola nuts and snail shells.

Kyra's sneakers squeaked on the flagstones, she looked guiltily about, afraid of being caught. Over in the corner was a sign on a wooden stand, that might normally have been at the entrance. It read 'THIS AREA CLOSED TO PUBLIC'. This wasn't something tourists were supposed to see.

The church door banged and Kyra heard footsteps. She stole out of the alcove and replaced the rope. Then she hurried down the side aisle and left the church.

Outside the sun hung low in the sky, pain crept across Kyra's ankle and up the side of her leg. Her pain meds were back at the motel, but there was a drugstore on the corner of the square, she could pick up some Tylenol. She checked her phone and saw she had twenty minutes before the next bus.

The interior was an intriguing blend of new furnishings and old-world fixtures. The pharmacy counter was at the end of the store, Kyra browsed the shelves on her way. She lingered for a minute at the cosmetics-counter but didn't see anything of interest.

Behind a beaded curtain a glass cabinet caught Kyra's eye. She stepped through the curtain to examine the cabinet. It was old and dusty and must have dated to the last century. It ran the length of the back wall, and its glass shelves contained jars and phials of powders, and liquids.

All the containers had handwritten labels, with names like: Dragon's Blood, Sacred Sand, Black Cat Oil, Boss-Fix Powder and Get Together Drops. Some of the bigger jars had little type-written notices next to them. Kyra bent closer to examine one:

```
BRIMSTONE

Burned to keep away evil spirits and enemies, and
to break spells that have been cast on someone. Can
be used to fumigate infected apartments, clothing,
etc. Do not remain in room while burning.
Disclaimer: We make no claims for this product,
which is sold for novelty purposes only. Everyone
is entitled to their own beliefs and many people
```

```
gain satisfaction from practices that others would
consider unorthodox.
```

Each of the notices had a similar disclaimer. Kyra turned to leave and saw a counter assistant standing on the other side of the curtain.

She was tall, African American, and in her late twenties, her hair was in braids and she wore a long white lab coat.

"Can I help you?" The assistant's tone was sharp and showed little interest in helping.

"Sorry, I was just browsing."

"Those items are mainly for local people, a select clientele."

"People actually buy these? I thought it was just a display."

"I doubt there's anything that would interest you, unless you're a servant?"

"A servant?"

"Of the Loa."

"I don't know what that is."

The assistant smiled a tight, knowing smile. "Maybe there's something else I can help you with?"

"Um, yeah, I came in for Tylenol."

The assistant led her to the pharmacy counter. Kyra paid for her goods and left the store as quickly as she could.

There were other things than the presence lurking in Yeuxville. Every nook and dark corner hid another secret. Kyra had the sense that if she stumbled on the wrong one, it would be the death of her.

EXCERPTED FROM

viewfromthekiller'seyes.blogspot.com

An unpublished blog by Kyra Hughes

BILLY-RAY'S FINAL MURDER

By now, Yeuxville was crawling with cops. A multi-agency task force was put together to catch Billy-Ray. This is probably why he waited before killing again. According to Chavez, his final choice of victim shows his confidence bordered on arrogance.

Caitlin Robichaud, a single mom from the poor side of town, definitely knew Billy-Ray. There were rumors they'd had an affair, a year before. Several witnesses testified Billy-Ray was stalking Caitlin. He was seen following her around town and watching her while she was in her apartment. Chavez thought Billy-Ray harbored a murderous rage for Caitlin, because of their affair. All his previous murders were rehearsals for killing her.

Billy-Ray kicked down Caitlin's door to get into her apartment, showing none of his previous ninja-like skill. He left forensic evidence behind, and this would eventually lead to his capture.

Billy-Ray lost it once he was inside. He didn't drug Caitlin, he grabbed a kitchen knife and removed her eyeballs while she was still alive, damaging her brain and killing her. The ferocity of his actions, and the lack of caution, seem to support Chavez's theory.

According to the coroner, the murder took place around six pm. Billy-Ray was seen running from the crime scene carrying what was described as 'a small bundle'. An anonymous caller tipped off the police and Sheriff Hawkins arrived shortly thereafter. He secured the area and made sure no-one entered. Somehow, between the Sheriff securing the crime scene, and leaving to inform the FBI, Billy-Ray's mojo returned, and he re-entered the property to mutilate the body, without anyone seeing him.

Police canvassed the surrounding area, and eyewitnesses identified Billy-Ray as the culprit, leading to his arrest. Six different traces of Billy-Ray's DNA were found at the crime scene and, the knife that removed the victims' eyeballs was recovered from his house. Billy-Ray was charged with the murder of all five women.

Billy-Ray maintained his innocence throughout the trial, in spite of the evidence against him. It took the jury fifteen minutes to return a guilty verdict. He continued to plead his innocence, for five more years, as the Supreme Court turned down every one of his appeals. On August 24th, on the eve of his execution, a representative of the victims' families requested Billy-Ray make a full confession of his crimes. Billy-Ray refused and died by lethal injection the following day.

CHAPTER 23:

Kyra bought a bottle of water at a grocery store and limped to the bus stop. She washed down a handful of Tylenol and waited for the bus to arrive. Naturally, it was late.

There were two other people at the stop. An older lady in a sun dress and sneakers and a black guy in his early twenties. He wore shades and was nodding his head to whatever was on his AirPods.

The sun had been roasting Main Street all day, and though it was low in the sky, the temperature was high. Kyra gazed down the two lane road, crawling with traffic. Trying to summon the bus with will power.

The asphalt was sticky from the sun's rays and the heat shimmered in waves. The hard lines of the approaching traffic were soft and malleable in the haze. License plates and head lamps softened and swayed, road signs and streetlights vibrated. The sleek solid forms of cars became fluid and inconstant, the haze robbing them of shape and substance.

It was disorienting. Kyra couldn't see the bus, so she looked away from the road. Unfortunately the shimmer didn't leave her vision. Wherever she looked she could still see it. The lines of the haze got sharper and more defined. They began to form patterns.

Kyra saw nothing but these patterns, no matter where she looked. She heard the bus pull up but couldn't see it. Her temperature plummeted and so did her mood as she recognized what was happening once again.

No! He *wouldn't* do this again. He wouldn't.

She didn't want this. It was against her will. Twice in one day was too much. It was *all* too much. She just wanted to get back to her motel and rest up.

Kyra stamped her one good foot and shrieked in defiance and frustration. As the doors of the bus clanked open she heard the older lady say, "They're all on drugs these days."

The noise of the engine reminded Kyra of the chipmunk, frozen in the path of the bus. That's how she felt. Unable to get out of the way of the fate that was charging down the blacktop toward her.

Kyra sensed the familiar presence descending as if from a great height, swooping down, like a bird of prey.

And then his talons were in her. She couldn't fight him, she couldn't struggle. He took control of her body. Her vision cleared.

There was Main Street, just as it had been fifteen years ago.

She turned away from the stop as the bus pulled away. Kyra's view of Main Street was from a different time. She took off in the rapid, loping pace with which Billy-Ray always seemed to move, hoping the Tylenol would kick in soon, so the pain in her ankle would subside.

She slowed as she got to the corner of Main and Saloppé Avenue and slipped into the same place in the shrubbery as yesterday. Billy-Ray, it seemed, was a man of habits. Kyra stood behind the shrub, while Billy-Ray smoked two cigarettes and scanned the street. Her hand moved in time with his, she took deep, sharp breaths as he inhaled the smoke and watched it leave his mouth as she exhaled.

The sun sank lower in the sky, Kyra's calves were stiff from standing so long. Caitlin finally sauntered into view, pushing the stroller. She was scowling. Her make up did not look fresh, and she walked with a sullen air.

Resentment emanated from Caitlin in waves. Kyra could only surmise that she'd been called back from her session to pick up her kid. She only had visual clues to work from.

Kyra's younger self was just as unhappy. Tears streaked her reddened face as she bawled and fought her straps. Caitlin's knuckles were white on the stroller handles. She crossed the road and stopped. She shook the stroller, tilted it back so she could scream in her child's face. This only made the toddler cry more.

Caitlin crouched down, so her face was level with young Kyra's. She raised her hand as a threat, but the child cried harder. So she brought her palm down on her daughter's cheek with such force the child's head snapped to one side.

Young Kyra's eyes bulged in surprise. Caitlin brought the back of her hand, even harder, across the other cheek. The child in the stroller breathed heavily, obviously in shock, her face completely pale.

Caitlin stood, smoothed her skirt, and fixed her hair. Young Kyra shook, looking up at her mom, tears filling her eyes. Before she could do anything, Caitlin raised her hand again and young Kyra curled into a defensive ball.

Caitlin remained still for a moment, watching her daughter, a hard, vicious look on her face. Then she nodded with satisfaction, as if she'd done her job, took hold of the stroller and continued down Saloppé Avenue.

Kyra felt her hands turn into fists. She looked down and she saw Billy-Ray's big oil-stained mitts were clamped around a branch in the shrubbery, their knuckles also white, the branch torn and splintered. Was Billy-Ray mad? Had Caitlin's behavior affected him too?

Before Kyra could consider this further, she'd snuck from the shrubbery to tail Caitlin. Caitlin took the same route as before, as much a creature of habit as Billy-Ray.

When they got to the road where she'd been hit by the car, Kyra's stomach clenched. It looked clear, but she wasn't seeing the present. What if another car was coming? She wouldn't see it and she couldn't stop crossing.

Billy-Ray moved her to the exact same spot where she'd crossed last time. Kyra strained her ears for traffic but couldn't hear any.

The curb was like a cliff edge. Stepping from it was a leap into the abyss. When her foot touched the road and she kept on going, she tensed her muscles against the car she was sure was coming.

Kyra wanted to scream, to turn back and run. To curl up into a ball and lie there in the road, but Billy-Ray wouldn't let her. He plowed on in pursuit of Caitlin.

At the end of the avenue, the two-story houses gave way to apartment buildings. Keeping a good distance, Kyra followed Caitlin to the last building, where she let herself in.

As soon as Caitlin was inside, Kyra walked up to the building and followed the chain-link fence to the rear of the property, where a clump of bushes grew at the back. Kyra stepped into them and crouched down to look through the fence, hidden from view.

The ground floor apartment had two large windows, and a glass door, that allowed Kyra to peer into the living room and kitchen. A light went on in the living room, and Kyra could see a threadbare couch, a stained carpet and peeling wallpaper. There were a couple of comforters in the room, and a widescreen TV. The floor was strewn with beer cans and pizza boxes.

Caitlin led young Kyra to a comforter and made her sit, then wagged her finger to warn the child to sit still and be quiet. Caitlin threw herself onto the couch, grabbed the remote, and started flicking through channels on the TV. Within ten minutes, she was asleep.

Kyra watched the room from the bushes. The longer she stared, the more she recalled. The furniture was familiar, so was the TV. Smells and emotions rushed back to her. Cigarette smoke and the dust of the comforters. The scent of her mother's perfume, how frightened she was when she smelled it.

The door to her memories inched open a little further. She'd regret seeing this, but she couldn't stop herself. Anger and pain, those twin guard dogs, bared their teeth and snarled.

Kyra's younger self sat incredibly still. It wasn't normal for a child that age to be so immobile. Kyra must have been terrified. Eventually, her restlessness won out. She sidled off the comforter and went to check Caitlin.

When young Kyra had established her mom wasn't going to wake, she padded over and picked up a toy from the floor. It was a stuffed patchwork duck. Seeing the toy set off a depth charge in Kyra's memory. Her first real and palpable memory returned, not a vague recollection or a series of impressions. This was real and visceral.

Kyra recalled how the duck's fabric had felt against the skin of her cheek, how it had smelled of feather stuffing, and her own bodily odors. The memory hit her right in the chest, and Kyra would have given anything to gather her younger self in her arms and comfort her. Tell her things would get better, in a few months she'd have new parents and they'd look after her properly.

Caitlin had left her cell on a table by the couch. It lit up and vibrated, but she slept on. The cell caught young Kyra's attention. Forgetting her fear, her curiosity got the better of her. She ambled to the phone, took it from the table and touched the screen. Then she held it to her ear, smiled and spoke. Caitlin stirred, opened a groggy eye and saw young Kyra on her phone.

It took Caitlin a few seconds to register what her child was doing. When her functioning brain cells registered, she leapt from the couch and shouted at the child, snatching the phone away. Caitlin spoke into the phone, her expression changing from tired and puzzled, to worried and apologetic.

When she was done, Caitlin rang off and glared at young Kyra. The child knew she was in trouble and shifted from foot to foot. Caitlin had been abject on the phone. Smiling, wheedling and placating whoever called.

The shift in her emotions was seismic. The conversation had not gone well and Caitlin knew who was to blame. Veins throbbed in her temples, tendons stood out in her neck, she turned her ire on the hapless toddler. Caitlin grabbed her child by the neck to stop her fleeing and spanked the backs of her legs.

This made the child howl. You could see the pain and fear on her little face. This only enraged her mother further. She dragged her daughter across the room by her wrist and opened the small broom closet door.

Young Kyra understood what was happening and she didn't like it. She kicked and flailed, tried to pull free, pleaded with her mother. Caitlin didn't listen. She dragged the child into the closet and slammed the door. Her face had the same pitiless expression.

Caitlin went back to the couch and changed the channel on the TV. The closet door shook and rattled, kicked or pushed from inside. The rattling got frantic, Kyra's younger self was hysterical.

Outside, in the bushes, Kyra watched with horror. Another memory kicked at the door in her mind, not a welcome one. She remembered what it was like in that closet, the lack of light and the choking smell of damp and shoeshine. She'd been in the closet many times. Kyra's chest tightened as the details came back. She fought for breath.

Kyra had hated that closet more than anything. Hated the confinement, and the darkness. Hated the shame of being punished and how powerless it made her feel. How unfair it had seemed. It *was* unfair. It was abuse plain and simple. No adult should ever terrorize a child like that. No wonder Kyra had shut off those memories.

The door continued to shake. Caitlin found a pack of cigarettes and shook one out. They were Winstons – why did that not surprise her? Caitlin lit the cigarette and pointed the remote, turning up the sound. Kyra watched as a malign detachment crept into Caitlin's expression. She was building to something.

She lit a fresh cigarette, walked purposely to the closet, and threw open the door. Inside the closet, young Kyra shrank back, shocked and terrified. Her defiance crumbled and she tried to withdraw into the dark corners of the closet.

Caitlin grabbed a handful of her child's hair and yanked her into the living room. Young Kyra's tiny hands closed around Caitlin's wrist. Caitlin picked her up and tossed her onto the couch. Young Kyra stopped struggling when she hit the couch, winded by the impact.

Caitlin took a deep drag on her cigarette, looking down at her prone daughter. The end glowed fiercely, illuminating the scorn on her face. Young Kyra waved her arms and kicked her legs to keep her mother off.

It did no good.

Caitlin grabbed her daughter's ankles and tore her diaper off. It was full. The child needed cleaning.

Surely she was just going to clean her up. That's all that was happening, right?

The tiny scars and blisters on the child's buttocks told a different story. Hidden from prying eyes by the diaper they kept her mother's dark secret.

No. This wasn't right.

Kyra did *not* want to see this.

Caitlin crouched closer to her child's behind. Young Kyra screamed and cried, unable to get away, probably begging her mother to stop. Caitlin was impassive. She blew on the end of her cigarette, raising an angry, red ember.

Stop!

Kyra couldn't watch. This was her absolute limit. This was one truth she didn't want to tear from her past.

She hated Billy-Ray for making her see this. Forcing her to live through it again. But she hated Caitlin more.

God help her, if Billy-Ray had jumped up and murdered Caitlin right there, she would have cheered him on.

But Billy-Ray didn't jump. He just sat there, in the bushes, watching impassively.

Kyra couldn't move her head, couldn't close her eyes, but she had to look away. Her teeth clenched until her temples throbbed. Her neck muscles were taut wire. Her eyes headlamps on a runaway vehicle, swerving into oncoming traffic.

She fought for the wheel. A sob broke in her chest. She wrenched his head sideways. Made him look aside. His gaze moved from the window to the bushes around her.

She'd done it. She'd shifted his gaze, in spite of the effort. It was like moving two heads with one set of muscles. She felt her head start to turn back to the window, and she stopped it, dragging her gaze away a second time.

She was doing this!

She was moving her head. Kyra was still seeing the world through Billy-Ray's eyes, but she was looking where *she* wanted. She tilted her head back and looked up at the evening sky as it grew darker. How was she doing this? How was she able to take control?

"...won't ask you again," said a voice behind her. Damn, someone was there in her time. "Miss, I will use this on you if I have to!" It was a male voice and it was angry.

"Wait, she's just a girl," said a woman's voice. "She's not dangerous, let me handle this."

Kyra felt a hand on her shoulder, but she was still viewing the world as it had been fifteen years ago. She couldn't see who was talking to her.

"Miss," said the female voice. "Can you hear me? I need you to step away from the fence and come with me."

Billy-Ray turned back to the fence, and his view of the ground floor apartment. Kyra didn't. His presence separated. His vision detached itself from hers. The world around her swam. Colors and shapes flowed together, fuzzy and indistinct, then they became clearer, and Kyra saw who was talking to her.

Two police officers were standing over Kyra. One of them was pointing a taser.

CHAPTER 24:

"Name?"

Deputy Patterson didn't look up from the arrest form. She was a short, well-built, African American woman.

"Kyra."

"Kyra what, what's your surname?"

"Robichaud."

Why had she lied? She was lying all the time now. Was she trying to protect herself? The more truths Kyra learned, the less she was able to tell anyone.

"Address?"

"I'm, um, I'm stopping with friends. I'm afraid I don't know their address."

"Why not?"

"What?"

"Why don't you know their address?"

"They drove me from the bus station. They never told me the address."

Patterson looked up from the form and held Kyra's gaze for the first time. "Really? You want me to put 'No Fixed Abode' on your form? Cos then I'ma need to charge you with vagrancy on top of everything else."

Kyra shrugged and stared at the floor. This attitude wasn't going to help her, she knew that. She kept flashing back to that tiny cupboard she'd seen and the memories it had dredged up. She was overwhelmed when the two Deputies found her. After what she'd seen they couldn't expect her to explain herself and they didn't give her the chance.

They just grabbed Kyra and stuck her in the back of their car. There she was, powerless in the face of what she'd just learned, trying to process how she was treated as a kid, and two more adults were grabbing her, abusing her, and locking her away in a tiny space just as Caitlin had done. She pretty much shut down at that point.

The worst Deputy had been Guillory, he was tall and broad shouldered but ran to fat around the middle. He was the one who'd nearly tased Kyra. He was on her case the whole trip to the station, telling her how much trouble she was in and how he'd seen her sort before. But Patterson was nearly as bad, shaking her head and tutting like Kyra was some errant child that needed to be locked up.

And that's exactly what they planned to do. Lock her in a holding cell, with as much room to move as a two year old in a broom closet. Only this cell wouldn't smell of damp, shoe polish and despair. It would smell worse.

Guillory walked with a mean, violent swagger that warned people not to mess with him. He loomed over Kyra, with a joyless smirk. "On your feet, Sheriff Hawkins wants a word. You're in trouble now."

Guillory led her down a short corridor to a small interrogation room. "Let's get something straight, I don't like you, and I don't like your attitude. I'ma see you get a record and do some time. Don't think I don't have enough on you."

Kyra balled her hands into fists and stared at the floor to stop herself flipping Guillory the bird. He snorted then left. The interrogation room had only one small desk and two chairs. Kyra slumped in a chair and found her breath coming quick and shallow. There was a fan in the corner stirring the somnolent air without affecting the temperature, cold sweat broke out on Kyra's skin as she considered how much trouble she might be in.

She jumped to her feet in a sudden panic and tried the door. It was locked. The walls of the room began to close in. Something was sucking all the air out, she was unable to take a deep breath. For a second she thought she might start kicking the door as if back in that broom closet.

It was okay. She'd done nothing wrong. She was the victim here. It's likely she was losing her mind. Should she tell the Sheriff about her weird incidents?

No, she didn't want to get committed like Béatrice. Better to play dumb. And Kyra was beginning to suspect she wasn't losing her mind at all. Where was that Sheriff?

The door opened and a tall man in a Stetson walked in. He had a handlebar mustache, flecked with grey, and his light tan shirt was open at the neck, showing grey chest hair. His sheriff's badge was pinned prominently to his shirt pocket.

He walked with a rolling gait that made Kyra think of gunfighters of the old west, all he was missing was a six shooter on his hip.

"Well, now, aren't we in a heap of trouble." His voice was genial, and his manner was easy going, but his eyes were cold, like a predator's, prying for signs of weakness, or hesitation.

"I haven't broken any laws."

"That's for me to decide, young lady. This is my town and I'm the law around here. Now, when I get a call from a cousin of mine, saying she's seen someone suspicious in the bushes, watching her apartment building, I'm likely to take that very personally.

"So, when I send a couple of my deputies to check it out and they tell me you're on drugs, you can understand why I wanted a word with you. So, I'd be very careful about what you say from this point on."

Kyra's Dad once told her when you deal, one on one, with people in a position of power, first they'll try to charm you, and then they'll remind you how dangerous they are. Sheriff Hawkins was emphasizing his danger far more than his charm.

"I'm not on drugs. You can test me if you like."

"I just might, at that."

"You can't charge me with anything."

"Well, I beg to differ. Seems to me we've already got you on loitering, public intoxication, attempted burglary and vagrancy. Anything else you want to cop to? If you tell me now, it might go better for you later. So, why don't you just cut the bullshit and tell me what you were doing in those bushes."

"I was looking at the ground floor apartment."

"Scoping the place out, you mean? So you could rob it?"

"No, I was just looking at it, I was in the area and I spotted the building. I wanted to get a good look at it."

"From the bushes?"

"I wanted to see it from in back. The bushes were in the way."

"Okay, so you're taking a walk, in a rough district, and you decide you want to look at the back of a building. Heaven knows why, but that's what you decide, and there just happen to be bushes in the way."

"Yes."

"You know where your whole story really falls apart?"

"No."

"The fact you stayed there for what must've been an hour, judging from the time my cousin called till the time my deputies picked you up."

"I was lost in thought."

"Lost in thought. You expect me to buy that?"

"Yes."

"And just what were you thinking about?"

"Memories."

"Of what?"

"I used to live in that apartment."

"When?" Hawkins leaned forward, his gaze hard and insistent, burning under thick black eyebrows. He was a predator bringing down his prey, ready to administer the killing blow. "I know just about everyone in this town, I make it my business to, but I don't know you, and that leads me to believe you're lying."

Kyra dropped her head, Hawkins thought he had her, thought he'd destroyed her story and caught her in a lie. His smugness, his attempts to intimidate her, enraged Kyra. She wanted to shout in his stupid face that he wasn't as clever as he thought, but for once the gravity of the situation stopped her. She had to be careful what she said, she was in real danger here, everything about Hawkins' manner, from the moment he had walked in the room, had told her as much.

"I lived there with my mother. I was only two years old, that's why you don't remember me, but you'll remember my mother."

"I will?"

"She was Caitlin Robichaud, and she was killed there. I was put up for adoption. This is my first time back."

Hawkins sat back in his seat and pushed the brim of his Stetson up. A certain tension slipped from his muscles. His jaw relaxed and his eyebrows moved up his forehead. "I worked that case."

"I know."

"Do you now?"

"I read about you in *Eyes for the Killer* and the other book by Mandy Sandiford."

Hawkins chuckled, but his eyes showed no mirth. "She sure has some crazy ideas, that Sandiford woman. But tell me, why would a nice young lady be reading books like those?"

There it was again, that old prejudice that pushed all of Kyra's buttons. The stupid assumption that nice girls would never read a book about serial killers. It wouldn't help to get angry, though. Hawkins had backed off, and she needed to play this carefully.

"Because I wanted to find out about my mother, and what happened to her," she said.

Hawkins broke his gaze, his eyes flicked up and to the right. His expression that of a man weighing the odds.

"These friends of yours, ones you say you're staying with, there any number I can call 'em on?"

Kyra's mind raced, this was where her whole story could unravel. She'd lied about staying with friends and if the Sheriff found out he might start doubting everything she'd said.

Should she give him Delilah's number? Delilah was a close friend, but she'd been raised by her uncle who was a deputy. She could be a bit of a Dudley Do-Good. She might not lie to the Sheriff, even to help Kyra.

That left one other person. She'd covered for Kyra before, but would she do it again?

"Do you know a lady called Béatrice? Has a workshop out in the industrial park?"

Hawkins raised both eyebrows. "Do I know her? Reckon I ought to, given she's my

daughter."

CHAPTER 25:

Hawkins' eyes were shards of ice crystal. His smile was the kind a lion shoots a gazelle.

"Surprised? Didn't she tell you about her old Dad?"

"I didn't know."

"It never came up? I'm her guilty secret, the only blot on her spotless Creole heritage. Makes me wonder how well you know my daughter. Just how did you two meet?"

"We, uh... we met when I got into town."

"And she's putting you up?"

"For a few days."

"Well, I guess I'll go ask her, see if we can't clear this up. 'Course, she's helping out at her soup kitchen in Lafayette, so she may not answer her phone. But you knew that, right?"

Kyra didn't say anything. Hawkins might be trying to catch her out. He narrowed his eyes and considered Kyra, as though he knew what his daughter was going to say, whether it was true or not.

Hawkins got slowly to his feet and left the room, closing the door behind him. Kyra heard the lock turn, like a period at the end of a sentence. She had no idea how long she'd have to wait, or what Béatrice would tell her father. She wouldn't do anything to hurt Kyra, would she?

Kyra had lied and now she was hoping Béatrice would lie to her father. Was she pushing things too far? She shouldn't have lied in the first place. A dumb thing to do. She was making one bad decision after another since she'd come to Yeuxville.

But what other choice did Kyra have? She couldn't tell the Sheriff and his deputies she'd been seeing the town as it was fifteen years ago through the eyes of a man who murdered her birth mother. If she told him she was staying in the local motel they might start asking more questions and find out she was technically a runaway.

Was Kyra wrong to put her trust in someone she'd only just met? Béatrice had gotten pretty heavy with her on their last drive. What did Kyra know about the woman?

She knew Béatrice volunteered a lot. She hadn't known about the soup kitchen, but she did know about the recovering addicts. She knew Béatrice spoke about, "giving something back". She obviously liked to help people, so maybe she'd help Kyra again.

Kyra also knew Béatrice had the deepest green eyes, and long, expressive fingers with a grace and a dexterity all their own. She had a smile that made Kyra's palms damp and her breath quicken. She was intelligent and artistic and...

And Kyra really shouldn't be thinking those things.

God, she was stupid. This was all her fault. Why did she get herself in these situations? She was so angry right now. Angry at the stupid Sheriff and his deputies, but mostly angry at herself.

Kyra pulled her knees up to her chin and curled into a defensive ball. She felt the walls of the room move closer and closer until she was in a tiny box from which she'd never escape.

When the door opened she didn't hear. She only heard the harsh voice. "Quit that and stand up."

It was Patterson, and she didn't look pleased. "Come with me." She refused to look at Kyra.

Kyra followed her down the short corridor and into the main office. The knot of tension between her shoulder blades began to unwind and her fists unclenched the minute she saw Béatrice, wearing a tan leather jacket. Guillory looked more pissed than Patterson. Hawkins was perched on the edge of his desk. His face was impassive, like a pro poker player. He could have a winning hand or a busted flush, and you'd never know.

Béatrice smiled, the first genuine smile Kyra had seen in hours. Patterson handed a plastic folder to Hawkins containing Kyra's cash and phone, but not her Tylenol.

Hawkins held out the folder then snatched it back when Kyra reached for it. "You might want to put my daughter's number in that phone, seeing as you're BFFs. Reckon she'll set up her own homeless shelter, soon enough."

Béatrice took the folder from the Sheriff's hands and gave it to Kyra. "That's enough, Daddy, we don't want to be rude to our guests."

"If you want to take in your little soup kitchen rejects, ain't nothing I can do."

"I'm glad you know that. Be hell to have a Daddy who did nothing but meddle."

"Be hell to have a Daddy who didn't clean up your mess."

"Just as well I don't leave no mess."

Hawkins turned to Patterson and Guillory and motioned to the back of the station with his chin. They got up and left. Hawkins got off his desk and stood with his shoulders back and his hands on his hip. "A man don't expect thanks for the things he does. It's his job to look out for family. He just knows when he's not there, they'll come to appreciate what he did."

"Long may the Lord keep that day away. Hate to be appreciating you when you're not here to gloat."

"Amen to that."

A huge wave of gratitude washed over Kyra as they left the station. Béatrice hadn't let her down. She could have left Kyra to rot in some holding cell, but she'd come and rescued her.

Béatrice hunched her shoulders and pulled her elbows in, a frown furrowed her brow. She wouldn't meet Kyra's eyes, just fished in her purse for her keys.

Kyra cleared her throat. "Listen, I..."

"Forget about it. It's fine." Béatrice's tone was curt and Kyra's words dried on her tongue. Was Béatrice mad? Of course she was.

They drove back to the motel in awkward silence. The gulf between them reminded Kyra of her dad. She wanted to reach out, but she couldn't think of a thing to say.

Kyra bowed her head and sighed as they pulled onto the motel's forecourt. "I'm sorry."

Béatrice looked genuinely bemused. "Why?"

"For being this dumb little kid you've always got to save. For making you lie to your dad. I don't blame you for being mad at me."

Béatrice reached over and cupped Kyra's chin in her hand. Béatrice's touch was so tender it made Kyra ache. Filled her with so much yearning she almost flinched.

"I'm not mad at you."

"You're not?"

"No, I'm sorry if I made you feel that way. It's just my daddy. He's the one I'm mad at. It doesn't matter how old I get, how much I achieve, how much I work on myself. He has this way of making me feel like a stupid little girl. Like I can't do anything without making a mess that he has to clean up. Does that make sense?"

"So, you're not mad at me?"

Béatrice shot her a sad but kind smile. "No, I'm not mad at you. Why were you arrested? My dad said something about attempted burglary."

Kyra lifted her chin and rolled her eyes. "I went to my old home. The apartment I lived in before I was adopted. I just wanted to see it after all these years. One of the neighbors must've seen me. I didn't even see the deputies until they arrested me. They didn't even ask what I was doing there."

Now it was Béatrice's turn to roll her eyes. "I'd keep out of trouble if I was you, you don't want to be on my daddy's radar."

Kyra felt a twinge of apprehension. "Okay."

Béatrice reached across her and opened the passenger door. Kyra caught the scent of her leather jacket and the sweet musk of her perfume. She had another pang of yearning as Béatrice's arm brushed her chest.

The passenger door swung open. Béatrice started up the engine and put her hands on the wheel. "You take care of yourself now. And stay out of trouble, hear?"

Kyra nodded and climbed out of the car. Béatrice waved as she pulled out of the lot. Kyra waved back but she didn't see.

Kyra walked reluctantly to her room, the pain in her ankle flared up again. Behind that door lay all her old demons and some brand new ones from today. There was no one she could call and nowhere else she could go.

All she could do was lock the door behind her and pray she survived until morning.

CHAPTER 26:

Two Weeks Ago, T-Minus 12 Days Until Departure:

Kyra ran her finger along the embroidery. The guy she'd found online had done a great job. She was glad she'd chosen him.

Kyra laid the handkerchief out on her bed to admire. It was a present for her dad's birthday. In one corner, it had an image of *The Little Prince*, from the drawing by the author, Antoine De Saint-Exupéry. The Little Prince's scarf caught the air and next to him sat the long-eared Fox. The rest of the handkerchief had the Fox's quote on it:

"One sees clearly only with the heart.
"What is essential is invisible to the eye."

Her dad was gonna love it.

She was folding it to put away when her phone buzzed with a text from Weezie:

Outside your house, Rob and Sam here too

Kyra finished up her eyelashes and texted back:

Be right down

She was at the top of the stairs when she heard the front door open. Her Dad called out, "Hey guys, don't hang around the driveway, come on in."

Kyra's heart sank. She thought he was out. She'd have to get them out quick, before things got awkward.

The trouble with Kyra's dad was that he still acted like all her friends thought he was cool. When she was younger, all her friends loved him. She sometimes worried they liked him more than her.

She'd told him this one night as she was getting ready for bed. She hadn't wanted to, but he'd spotted she was down and he had a way of getting her to open up.

He pulled a shocked face when she told him what was up. "No way! The only reason people like me is cos my daughter's so popular. The cool kids at work only sit at my lunch table because I know you." He could always make her laugh. Even her mom said he always knew the right thing to say, especially when he got into trouble.

Her tenth birthday was a classic example. This was back in the days before cliques formed, so if you invited the whole class to your party, pretty much everybody came. Most of her friends' parents hired a magician or some dopey clown. Not Kyra's Dad, he organized the entertainment himself.

Kyra's birthday was in summer, so her dad would always fill the pool in their back yard and host the party there. Everyone came in their swimming costumes, which was for the best because things often got messy. Her dad organized water balloon fights, a chip eating contest, and another competition to see who could put the most lifesavers and soda in their mouth. He'd topped that off with a soda explosion, where her friends dropped a whole roll of lifesavers into a bottle of cola, then saw how far they could run before the cola erupted from the bottle in a fountain of sticky, brown liquid.

When everyone had dried off, he dug out Kyra's special crash helmet and gave everyone a ride round the block on the back of his Harley. This was so popular, the kids begged him for another go.

He was just pulling up to the curb, with Tommy Edwards clinging to his back and shrieking with laughter, when Rachel Kauffman's mom pulled into their drive. Her dad lifted Tommy off the bike and all the other kids swarmed round him, desperate for a third go.

The clamor of voices was cut short when they heard the car door slam. The way Rachel's mom's heels clacked across the driveway told them something was wrong. She was wearing jeans and an expensive blouse. Her eyes were narrowed and her lips were pursed.

She marched straight up to Kyra's dad as Kyra and the others backed away.

"Mr. Hughes!"

"Call me Dennis." Kyra's dad took off his helmet and shook out his hair. He wore it long at the sides and back, like a surfer.

"Irresponsible is what I'd call you. Have you been taking these children on that motorcycle?"

"They were perfectly safe, Mrs. Kauffman. I'm a careful driver and I took every precaution."

"That's not the point. I didn't give permission for Rachel to go on that machine. I wouldn't have let her come if I'd known."

Everyone kept backing up the driveway. Suddenly they were in trouble and they didn't know why. Their parents would turn up any minute and no one wanted to get told off. They glanced nervously at each other, trying to work out what they'd done. Many shot Rachel dirty looks and her eyes filled up with tears.

"You're absolutely right."

Kyra's Dad straightened his back and looked her right in the eyes. His manner was earnest, contrite and charming. It was an approach, Kyra was later to learn, that he took with both judges and clients when they admonished him.

"I *should* have asked your permission, and you have every right to be mad at me. I take full responsibility for my actions. Please don't be mad at Rachel, she's not to blame."

Mrs. Kauffman's shoulders relaxed and she put a hand to her chest. "I'm not mad at Rachel. I'm sure she was perfectly safe, I would have liked to have known beforehand, is all."

"And I was wrong not to tell you. It was a spur of the moment thing, I hadn't planned it till it happened, but I should have checked with you."

"I mean, I'm sure the kids had fun, it's just, you know, the principle."

"No, no, you're right, principles are important."

"I get that it was spur of the moment, but it would have been nice to get a call."

"Absolutely, I should have thought of that, and I promise that's the first thing I'll do next time."

"I mean I don't want to spoil anyone's fun. It is a Harley, after all."

Kyra's dad flicked his hair back with a toss of the head and gave a crooked grin. "Hey, you know your bikes."

"I wouldn't say that. I had a couple boyfriends in college."

"Scare your parents?"

"Did they ever, why do you think I dated them?"

Kyra's Dad broke into a full smile, turning the charm up to max. "Get a load of the dark horse."

Mrs. Kauffman laughed. Her neck and chest flushed. She ran her fingers through her hair. "I have my moments."

Kyra's dad patted the seat of the Harley. "So, wanna go for a spin?"

Mrs. Kauffman's eyes widened. "What? No. I couldn't possibly."

"Why not?"

"Well, I mean, it's been so long."

"There are some things you never forget. I bet you're a natural."

"But I've got to take Rachel home."

"Party doesn't end for another fifteen minutes. We've got plenty of time. Hop on."

He patted the seat again and winked at Kyra. "Go get your mom's helmet."

Kyra raced into the garage.

When she got back Mrs. Kauffman was smiling with her hand on her chest and her eyebrows raised, looking down the street. "What will your neighbors think?"

"That I'm the luckiest guy on the block."

Mrs. Kauffman actually giggled. Kyra handed her the helmet. She put it on. Kyra's dad helped her adjust the strap.

"I can't believe I'm doing this." She turned to Rachel. "Don't you dare mention this to your father."

Rachel hopped from foot to foot and clapped her hands. "Can I have extra cake?"

"No you can't."

Kyra's dad threw a hand in the air and revved the engine. "Extra cake for everyone."

Mrs. Kauffman put her arms around his waist and he took off down the driveway.

Everyone looked at each other and laughed with relief. A moment ago, they were going to catch hell from their parents and now they were off the hook. Kyra's dad had won Rachel's mom over and no one was mad anymore. Rachel's mom even had a guilty secret that Rachel couldn't tell her dad.

Jenny Kowalski put her hand on Kyra's shoulder and watched as her dad tore down the street. Jenny had long blond hair and wore the most fashionable clothes. Everyone wanted to sit at her table at lunchtime, she was the most popular girl in Fourth Grade.

She grinned at Kyra. "You have the coolest dad in the world."

That night they read *The Little Prince* again. Only this time Kyra read it to her dad, without stumbling over any of the words. Snuggled into the crook of his arm, she turned the yellowed pages of the copy her dad first read as a child.

They loved *The Little Prince*. Her dad said it was one of those stories that grew as you grew, so you never got tired of it. As you changed and matured over the years, you saw new meanings in the story and what the characters said. In this way, he explained, it becomes a yardstick to measure yourself against.

This was before the anger and the intrusive thoughts. Before Kyra had learned to hate herself. She'd never been prouder of herself than on that night. And she'd never been prouder of her dad.

That was Fourth Grade. A lot had changed since then. Jenny had moved to Utah. Tommy Edwards was on Adderall. Rachel's mom disowned her when she came out, and Kyra's Dad was no longer cool. Not even a little bit.

But he wouldn't be told.

Kyra left her room feeling a mess. She'd rushed her make up to try and head her dad off. She was too late. She heard her friends traipse into the hallway.

As she raced downstairs she heard her dad say, "Anyone like a beer?"

Rob was staring at the floor with this hands in his pockets. Sam had his hood pulled down, his eyes on his phone, still uncomfortable about his masculinity, he liked to hide. Weezie curled a wisp of blue hair round her finger.

She smiled, embarrassed. "No thanks, Mr. Hughes."

"You're not straight edge are you?"

Weezie's smile faded, she had no idea what to say. She didn't understand what Kyra's dad said. Rob and Sam were pretending they weren't there.

Kyra felt her bones crawl back into her skin. She didn't have enough bangs to hide behind. She closed her eyes and willed her dad not to say anything else. *Please stop talking, please stop talking, please stop talking.*

"You guys don't know about straight edge? It was really big when I was your age. It's an underground movement that started in the punk scene, in Washington, in the early 80s, then got really popular and spread throughout the States. There was a song by the punk band, *Minor Threat*, called *Straight Edge*. That's what kicked it off. People who were straight edge didn't do drugs, drink alcohol, have sex or eat meat, crazy huh?"

He laughed, and the sound seemed to fall to the hall floor and shatter in the silence. Her dad was smart, everyone knew that, but he didn't have to turn every conversation into a lecture.

Kyra ran for her leather jacket, which was hanging by the door. She had to get her friends out as quickly as possible.

She grabbed the door latch and wrenched it open. Her friends saw their opportunity. It was time to get out from the awkward glare of adult attention.

"Okay, thanks, Dad. We gotta go now."

And that would have been that. The escape would have been quick if not painless. But Kyra's dad had one last salvo in him. One last shot at the cringe bullseye.

He pointed at Rob's shirt, which had a Pearl Jam logo on it. "Wicked shirt. You know, I worked back-stage at Lollapalooza when *they* first played, even got to share a beer with Eddie Vedder, really nice guy."

Rob just froze, mouth open, blinking rapidly at her dad. Kyra grabbed his arm and pulled him toward the door. "Uh, great story, Dad. Never knew that. I'll call you when I'm on my way home."

As a final coda, just to show he wasn't finished, he followed them through the door and onto the porch. He waved from the front step. "You guys have fun now."

Kyra shepherded her friends down the driveway. *Why were they going so slow? Why was her dad always like this?* These were the only friends she had and it was hard enough hanging on to them without her dad making it any harder.

Why didn't he realize there was a silent détente between kids her age and their parents? A thin line of toleration that neither were supposed to cross.

"Quit pulling me!" Rob yanked his arm away. Kyra had forgotten she was still pulling it.

Rob rubbed his forearm and glanced back at her house. "What was all that about?"

Kyra pointed to the logo on Rob's chest. "Your shirt, Pearl Jam are his favorite band."

Rob curled his lip and laughed derisively. "Pearl Jam's a clothing label, everyone knows that."

Kyra shook her head and headed out to the L station.

Looking back, Kyra came to realize this had been the point of no return in her relationship with her dad.

CHAPTER 27:

Kyra opened the door, flicked on the light, and stared at her motel room. The self-loathing and intrusive thoughts were like many-legged creatures only she could see, crawling up the walls and under the bed.

The space was alive with dark notions, and she didn't want to face them.

Kyra shut the door, went to the vending machine, and bought one of every candy bar. She took the bars back to her room and stood at the foot of the bed.

She tore open the wrapper on the first bar and ate it in three bites. She didn't even taste it, just ground it to bits between her teeth, working her jaws angrily until it was gone.

She pulled the second bar from the wrapper and crushed it in her fist. Letting the nougat and caramel ooze out between her fingers. She pushed the candy and her fingers into her mouth, forcing it down her throat until she gagged.

Then she crammed another bar in her mouth. And another. She kept at this until her jaw ached and her face and hands were covered in chocolate and tears. The floor littered with torn and discarded wrappers. Her muscles twitched and her eyelids spasmed, she wanted to puke from all the sugar.

For a second, Kyra wished she was back in the interrogation room being grilled by Hawkins. Even riding with Patterson and Guillory would be better than standing here, face to face with the truth of her childhood.

The crazy thing was, she still ached to be in Caitlin's arms. To curl up against her and be comforted. She needed it now as much as she'd needed it then. But she didn't have it fifteen years ago and she couldn't have it now.

How could Caitlin do those things to a two and a half year old? How could she do it to Kyra? As much as she wanted to be held, Kyra wanted to lash out at Caitlin. Smash her fists into her mother's cruel, painted face, wiping away the make-up and the self-regard. Reduce it to a beaten pulp.

She thought she was angry before. She wasn't. She was barely annoyed compared to the raw, biblical fury she felt now. Every molecule of Kyra's body vibrated with rage. She wasn't big enough to physically contain such wrath.

The root of all her anger had been revealed. The door to her lost memories had been kicked open. The guard dogs weren't keeping secrets from Kyra, just protecting her from the fear and anguish of an abused child, who didn't want to remember. If anything, the door had been there to protect her, but, like Bluebeard's wife, she couldn't leave it alone. She had to find out what was behind and now she'd damned herself.

Every time she closed her eyes, Kyra saw Caitlin blowing on the end of the cigarette. Her tired features twisted by spite and lit by the red glow. She saw that tiny pink behind, and the fierce, red scars, hidden by her diaper.

The agony and the humiliation Kyra had felt in the moment, welled up in her chest. Like an emotional loop, playing over and over. She was trapped in that lost memory.

Kyra collapsed onto the bed. The rage tore through her like a live current. She dug her fingers into the duvet, lifted it from the bed and threw it from her. She plunged her fists into the soft, yielding fabric of the pillows. She pictured Caitlin's face beneath her knuckles, then Hawkins', then Guillory's and finally her own. She could feel the pressure build inside her. Her hand went reflexively to the burn on her inner thigh. If only she had a pack of Winstons.

No.

Not after what she'd just seen.

Kyra pictured her two year old self. The raw, angry blisters on the inside of those little legs where the diaper would hide them. Caitlin wasn't here to do that anymore. She didn't need to be. Kyra was continuing her work, like a good little daughter, without ever realizing, as if she'd held her two year old self down while Caitlin burned her.

And now that had to stop. She had to break the cycle of abuse. Had to find another way to relieve the pressure.

She had to stop punishing herself in this way. Had to stop the work that Caitlin had started. She was not her mother and no longer two. She'd never deserved the way she was treated. She was substituting her own hands for her mother's and she mustn't do that anymore.

Kyra's throat was strangely sore and ragged. The wall by her headboard shook as someone pounded on it and told her to keep it down. And only then did she realize how long and loud she'd been screaming.

The scream stuck in her throat and shriveled to a wet sob. Then her stomach gave out. She crawled off the bed, stumbled to the bathroom and bent over the toilet bowl.

The candy came back first, followed by thick strings of bile. There was an endless flow of poison that rose from inestimable depths within and she needed to purge it. Finally, her arms gave out. She rested her chin on the edge of the bowl and her stomach quivered from all the retching.

Kyra limped back to the bed and lay on the tangled sheet. Her duvet discarded. Tears flowed in a constant stream down her cheeks. She sank into the welcome oblivion of sleep.

Later, in the cruelest hours of the morning, Kyra awoke. As soon as she opened her eyes she was aware she'd come to a terrible decision. One that would change her life forever.

A distant and dispassionate part of her brain wondered if she was considering suicide? But ending it all was only a fleeting consideration.

No, what she was considering was far worse than killing herself. And its consequences were even more profound.

CHAPTER 28:

Kyra was not going to get back to sleep. She was dressed and her t-shirt smelled faintly of vomit. She slid off the bed and went to look out the window.

The sky was lighter but hadn't yet given way to the dawn. Kyra watched a rat scurry across the lot. It stopped, sat up on its hind legs and scented the air as if deciding where to go next.

It reminded her of the chipmunk she'd seen on the bus. Kyra had come to identify more and more with that chipmunk, facing two horrible fates and powerless to avoid either.

She could no longer deny that she was seeing through the eyes of Billy-Ray Johnson.

She'd thought she might be losing her mind. It could be that you had to lose your mind in order to see the things she was seeing. But Kyra was experiencing a genuine paranormal phenomenon.

Constance said a presence was coming because of something she did in the past. Kyra had no idea what that was, but she knew the presence was Billy-Ray. They were connected in some way. And that connection went both ways.

Up until yesterday, Billy-Ray had all the control. He could take her over, make her walk where he'd walked and see the things he saw.

But he wasn't alone in that power. For a moment, Kyra had made him turn his head. She'd reached back into the past and controlled his actions.

If she'd done it once, Kyra could do it again. But she had to test it out, had to make sure she was right.

Because if she was, it changed everything not only for her life, but for Billy-Ray's and Caitlin's too.

EXCERPTED FROM
viewfromthekiller'seyes.blogspot.com

An unpublished blog by Kyra Hughes (with comments by Delilah)

MY PERSONAL CONNECTION WITH BILLY-RAY JOHNSON?

Why am I so obsessed with Billy-Ray Johnson? That's a hard one to answer. I guess there's a lot of reasons. The first is the mystery surrounding Billy-Ray's case. There are so many unexplained things. Like how he was able to break into places without leaving clues behind. I mean, he drugged an entire party of teenagers, and no-one even saw him in the house. That's gotta be some kinda record, right?

But then, after proving what a criminal mastermind he was, he loses it on his fifth murder, goes into a killing frenzy and leaves a ton of evidence behind. What's that about? How does someone, so skilled, suddenly snap and go into such a homicidal fury? What kind of hold did Caitlin have over him?

Then there's his refusal to admit his guilt. He didn't try for a plea bargain or plead insanity. He insisted he was innocent to the bitter end. According to Hirst, at one point in his interrogation, Billy-Ray claimed he'd seen Caitlin die, but it was important to him to protect the person who killed her. He wouldn't say why, and he never revealed the identity. I respect that. In spite of everything he did, I think Billy-Ray lived by a code and that's one thing you can say in his defense.

I also admire his defiance. He didn't back down or give in. He stuck to his guns, no matter what the courts threw at him. That takes conviction and it takes guts. I won't go into it here, but I know what it's like to have the weight of a whole institution pitted against you. To have everyone pointing fingers and accusing you of something you can't admit to, even if there's evidence that says different. I know how hard it is, I know what it does to your spirit, and I think Billy-Ray stood up to that with dignity, right up to his lethal injection.

There's also that lost, melancholy look Billy-Ray has, staring out from the custody photos. I actually had one of those photos blown up and made into a poster. It's up on my wall, looking down on me as I type this. Every time I see that look, I want to put my arms around Billy-Ray and comfort him.

Don't get me wrong, I'm not one of those girls who fall for serial killers, I'm not into dangerous guys. I'm not sure I'm even into guys at all. But I do feel a personal connection to Billy-Ray Johnson. It's like it's in my blood. It sounds weird, but I sometimes feel like he's an older brother or a distant cousin, or something. I'm probably not explaining this well, and I'll probably go back and delete a lot of this post but, even though he's been dead for over five years, I still feel like I want to look out for Billy-Ray. Does that make any sense?

D: It does make a strange kinda sense, but it also sounds unhinged. I think you need to edit this post or, better yet, shelve it and do a bit more work on it. Maybe you could expand the post into a more general entry on why people are interested in Billy-Ray, or why they ought to be, and take out a bit of the personal stuff, so people don't judge. Anyway, that's just my opinion, it's your blog and you can do what you want with it. I'm just here to help in any way I can.

CHAPTER 29:

Kyra stopped on the corner of Main and Saloppé, leaned up against the grocery store and took a long breath, mopping the sweat from her brow.

She lifted her right foot and eased her sneaker off. There was an angry, red blister on her heel. It took her mind off her aching ankle. She'd walked more in the past few days than the previous two months.

Kyra's heel stung from the burst blister. It gave her a weird rush, like touching her skin with a glowing cigarette end.

No!

She wasn't going to go there. She wasn't going to do that. Not ever again. Not after what she'd learned.

She'd been following the same circuit all morning, covering every site where the presence – She corrected herself, *where Billy-Ray* had taken her over. From Church Square, she walked down Main Street to Laveau and then up to the trailer park on the other side of town. A good four miles in all, an hour and a half on foot and this was her third time around.

Kyra was feeling the strain in her calves and thighs. Her diet was lousy and she'd hardly slept. No wonder she was exhausted.

But, for all her efforts, Billy-Ray was nowhere to be seen. Her eyesight was fine, no blurring, no spots, no whiting out, nothing. She stopped every few minutes and glanced about, but she couldn't sense any presence creeping up. It was as though Billy-Ray knew she was looking for him and was avoiding her.

Kyra grew tired of looking at her naked foot, wrinkled and pink as a boiled ham. She pulled her sneaker back on and tried not to enjoy the pain. The door of the store opened and a man stepped out. He was tall, with a thick black beard and a red baseball cap. He was wearing denim overalls, he folded his bare arms and glared at Kyra.

The message in his eyes was a simple one – *you're not from these parts, you're not one of us and you're not to be trusted.*

It wasn't the first time Kyra had seen that look. Yeuxville was a small town and strangers stuck out. When they toured the same spots over and over in the course of one day, they tended to draw attention. None of it good.

Kyra said nothing, but it was hard to ignore the man's gaze. She could feel him glowering as she limped down Main Street to the bus stop. The same stop where Billy-Ray had taken Kyra over for the second time yesterday. Would he be passing this way? Would she finally catch him?

Kyra had spotted a pattern in her strange experiences and had started to form a theory. She'd arrived in Yeuxville exactly four days before the fifteenth anniversary of Caitlin's death. The routes that Caitlin took as Billy-Ray followed her, would have been the exact routes she took fifteen years ago to the very minute.

For the episodes to occur, for Billy-Ray to take Kyra over, their paths had to cross. Kyra had to be in the very same place that Billy-Ray had been fifteen years ago. When that happened, some strange convergence took place and Kyra was able to see what Billy-Ray had on that day, fifteen years ago.

She lost control of her actions and was forced to act the same way Billy-Ray acted. However, unless yesterday was a fluke, this strange connection might not be entirely one way. She just had to test this theory and prove she wasn't losing her mind.

But that meant she had to put herself in the same place that Billy-Ray had been, at some point on this day, fifteen years ago. And so far she'd completely failed. Even though she'd visited every place she'd been when she was seeing the world through his eyes over the last couple days.

The thought of walking one more step, let alone another couple miles, made every muscle in her legs throb. Besides, Billy-Ray did not look like he was going to show. Unlike the bus to the trailer park, which pulled up at the stop with a hiss of airbrakes and clank of automatic doors.

Kyra decided to ride out to the trailer park and give her feet a rest. She'd do a few circuits of the trailer park and call it a day. Surely Billy-Ray couldn't avoid her all day?

The bus ride was hot, but Kyra was glad of the rest. She had at least caught her breath and gathered her thoughts.

She approached the park by the back gate, using the route Caitlin took. As she was about to open the gate a dog started barking. Kyra saw a pit-bull chained up at the back of a trailer on the far edge of the park. It was straining at the end of its chain, gnashing at the air as foam dripped from its sharp, bared teeth.

Two guys with their backs to the gate turned to look at Kyra. Both were bearded and heavily inked. From the hostility on their faces, whatever deal they were in the middle of wasn't strictly legit.

Kyra pulled her bangs over her face and backed quickly away from the gate. She breathed deeply to keep the panic at bay. Okay, that entrance was off-limits. She'd have to try the front.

Kyra retraced her steps and followed the road around to the main entrance. She found the tree where Billy-Ray had hidden, as he spied Caitlin climbing into the SUV. She tried to adopt the same position, without drawing attention to herself, to see if that would summon him, but it didn't.

Had she scared him away yesterday, by making him look away? Was he avoiding her? Kyra wasn't sure how she felt about this. She didn't like being taken over by a serial killer and forced to stalk her birth mother. She hadn't wanted to see the things he saw.

But now she did. She needed him to come and he was staying away.

Kyra decided to stay away from the back gate and the shady dealings going on down there. The trailer park had grown in the last fifteen years, with hundreds of new trailers. Kyra concentrated on the older homes that she'd seen through Billy-Ray's eyes.

She tried retracing the route Billy-Ray took and came on the trailer where Caitlin had left her. As she approached, Kyra felt certain things stir at the back of her mind. They weren't memories, more the ghosts of lost memories, glimpsed among the ruins of her missing childhood.

She recalled smells and emotions. Excitement at spending time away from mom and eating proper food. The way her clothes felt unwashed. How desperate she was to get out of her stroller.

Kyra wandered around back of the trailer to its tiny yard, surrounded by a two-foot fence that was missing many pickets. It was mostly baked, cracked dirt now, the white paint of the fence gray and peeling. Kyra remembered it having more grass. The little playhouse in the far corner of the yard came back to Kyra, as did the tiny slide and the paddling pool that had been there.

The longer Kyra stared, the more she could recall where each item had been. She could almost see them, waiting at the periphery of her vision and if she inclined her head just right, they'd come into focus.

She pictured herself playing in the yard, running between the slide, the pool and the playhouse. The sharp, polyvinyl smell of the pool's inflatable plastic came back, and the dank earthy smell inside the playhouse, where she'd served imaginary tea to her patchwork duck on a set of toy cups and saucers.

The longer she looked at the yard, the more Kyra imagined herself playing there, watching a ghost from her past. Kyra was drawn to a clump of bushes a few feet away. They were growing around the base of an oak tree, with Spanish moss in its branches like an old woman spinning yarn.

Kyra ran her hands along the furrowed bark of the tree. There were no marks or scratches on its surface. This was exactly what she needed. This was the place. It had to be the place.

Kyra slipped into the bushes and moved the branches so she could see the trailer's back yard. Some instinct, some vague connection to Billy-Ray told her she should shift a few steps to her right.

This was it.

This was the spot. Kyra had no idea how she knew, but if she was going to encounter Billy-Ray anywhere, it was going to be here.

She thought of the yard when she was a toddler. She imagined her younger self climbing the tiny slide, dropping toys in the pool and hiding in the playhouse.

The longer she looked, the clearer the picture became. It was like willing a ghost into being. Conjuring up an after image of her forgotten childhood from memories that had faded to white, like old Polaroids left in the sun.

At first Kyra just envisaged her younger self at play in the yard. Painting pictures on her mind's eye. But the longer she looked the more the memory came to life.

She was no longer picturing herself as a child. The image she conjured began to move of its own accord. The definition sharpened and the colors deepened. Kyra was no longer visualizing but watching.

Her vision blurred and was filled with a sudden white flash that washed everything else out. She was aware of Billy-Ray all around. He lowered himself into the very spot where she crouched, waiting for him.

She had called him to her and he finally came.

Not as a hawk burying his claws, but a wary guest.

The white flash faded and her eyesight came back. But the view had changed.

Kyra was looking at the yard as it had been fifteen years ago. And there was her younger self, in almost the exact place she'd imagined.

If her chest hadn't been rising and falling in time with Billy-Ray's, Kyra would have breathed a sigh of relief. She was afraid Billy-Ray would never come. But now he was here, she was afraid of what she had to do.

Because if it proved what Kyra thought it would, she was going to change not only her future, but her entire past as well.

CHAPTER 30:

The grass was back in the yard, and the fence had most of its paint. The inflatable pool, the slide and the playhouse were all there and so was Kyra's two-year-old self.

Kyra expected Caitlin to show up at any minute to collect Kyra. But she never showed. Kyra assumed Billy-Ray would get bored and go hunt Caitlin, but he didn't. He stayed put.

Billy-Ray was more comfortable crouching behind a bush than Kyra. Her ankle and her calves ached and her bladder needed release. But, because Billy-Ray had taken her over, she couldn't move unless he moved, so she was forced to hold her position.

The woman who looked after her came out several times. Once to bring young Kyra milk and cookies, which she devoured. The other two times to smoke a cigarette and play with the infant. The child toddled over, a single daisy between her thumb and forefinger. She presented the daisy to the woman who broke out into a broad smile.

The child pointed to her ear, where the woman should put the daisy. She tucked her hair behind her ear and popped the daisy in, causing the child to clap her hands and jump with glee.

It was strange seeing herself as a tiny child, back before there were any photos or video. Kyra had seen the horrors this infant had to face on a daily basis. Watching her play with joy and abandon, absorbed by the tiniest task, full of wonder at the simplest things, brought a hard lump of yearning to Kyra's chest.

She wanted to let the child know life wouldn't always be this way. She wouldn't always have to live in fear. There were better parents, and a new home, waiting for her in just a few months' time. But most of all she wanted to gather the child in her arms. To snatch her from Caitlin and keep her safe.

As she thought this Kyra sensed a deepening connection with Billy-Ray. Up until now, Kyra had shared only two things with Billy-Ray, what he was seeing and how he acted. But now she felt an emotional resonance, their feelings were harmonizing, like tuning a guitar to a piano.

This was worse than being forced to watch the last hours and minutes of her birth mother's life. Kyra now had to face the fact that not only was her birth mother stalked before her murder, but so was she. That her last days with Caitlin lay under the shadow of this monster.

Rage rose inside Kyra, strong enough to bring her to her feet. It came with such white-hot intensity it lifted both Kyra and Billy-Ray from their crouch. Kyra wasn't just turning Billy-Ray's head, she was controlling his whole body. Controlling it across time.

From their newfound emotional connection, Kyra knew that Billy-Ray was confused. He didn't like having control taken away. *Welcome to my world, asshole.* He wanted to go on watching Kyra as a tiny child, but Kyra was through with that, through with giving in to his sick demands. This was what she was here for.

She made him turn his head and his upper body toward the trunk of the tree. She couldn't move his legs though. They stayed rooted to the spot. His jaw was clenched and he ground his teeth, causing Kyra to do the same. They were fighting for control of the same body.

Billy-Ray was bigger and heavier. He had more muscle mass than Kyra was used to commanding. She had never tried to navigate a physique this big before. It was like she was moving his body from inside it, using her weaker muscles to direct his bulk as he fought her.

She felt him turn away from the tree and she realized she was losing him.

No.

That wasn't going to happen.

Billy-Ray was so busy fighting for control of his upper body he forgot about his legs. Kyra stamped her foot and his at the same time. Billy-Ray wasn't expecting this and stumbled against the trunk.

Kyra took this opportunity to seize back control. He was confused and disoriented. She was full of righteous indignation.

My turn. I'm in charge!

Kyra turned Billy-Ray around till he was looking at the smooth bark of the oak tree. According to *Eyes for the Killer*, he always kept a knife in his boot. A standard issue army blade, that had belonged to his grandfather. It was there when Billy-Ray was arrested, so it should be there now. Kyra forced him to bend and reach into his boot.

Though she could see what she was directing Billy-Ray to do, she couldn't feel it. The only sensation in her fingers was her own. She pushed his fingers into his boot, she saw the shoe leather bulge, but she couldn't sense his fingers closing around the hilt of the blade. She had to hope they made contact without the certainty of touching it.

She brought Billy-Ray's thumb and forefinger together and they seemed to have found something because she couldn't close them. There must be something between them. She withdrew Billy-Ray's hand from his boot.

The knife came out, but it dropped from his fingers and landed in the dirt at his feet.

Goddamn it!

In her frustration, Kyra felt her hold on Billy-Ray weaken. He slipped out of her clutches. Then he noticed his knife on the ground and bent to retrieve it. As soon as his fingers closed about the hilt, Kyra seized him again.

Kyra made Billy-Ray stand and place the tip of the knife in the bark of the tree. Guiding Billy-Ray's hands she gouged three lines in the bark, forming the letter 'K'. When she'd done this, she carved a circle around it. Kyra watched the knife slice into the bark, she felt her arms moving in unison with Billy-Ray's, but she had no sense of holding the knife in her own hands. She saw what the end of the blade did to the tree, but she didn't feel the bark resist and splinter as she carved the letter.

The knife blade slipped in her fingers and Kyra couldn't prompt Billy-Ray to hold it any longer. Billy-Ray sensed this and took control of his limbs.

Kyra was too tired to fight him. Energy slipped from her like the last grains in an hourglass. Sickening fatigue stole into her limbs, brought nausea to her stomach and dimmed her sight.

Billy-Ray turned himself around, but Kyra didn't go with him. She dropped to her knees instead. She found it impossible to remain upright and her body lurched sideways. She fell but she never felt the impact. Her sight was dimming. She was slipping out of consciousness.

The prolonged strain had been too much, but she'd made her mark on the tree. She had proof of what she'd done, inside Billy-Ray's body, fifteen years ago, feet from where she'd played as a tiny, neglected toddler.

What she'd done was supposedly impossible.

And now she'd have to live with the consequences.

CHAPTER 31:

How long was she out? Was it fifteen years or seconds?

Probably both.

Pain ran in a tight ridge from her eyebrows to her temples. Her eyes stung as she blinked them open. The sky was darker, the air cooler.

Kyra was lying with half her face in the dirt. Crumbs of soil on her cheek and lips. Something tickled her face. A large beetle crawled up to the bridge of her nose.

Kyra sat up, intensifying the pain in her temples. She brushed the bug away and pressed her fingers against the side of her head. The pain brought bright, flashing colors to her eyes, then died back to a throbbing ache and she got her breathing under control.

Brushing her face a few more times, to make sure the beetle had gone, Kyra put a hand on the oak and climbed unsteadily to her feet.

A wave of dizziness and disorientation overcame her. She had to cling to the tree to stop from toppling. Her eyes blurred. When they were back in focus she turned to inspect the bark of the tree. She saw a sign had been carved into the oak.

It had weathered in the last fifteen years, and the bark had grown back around it, but there, on the tree, Kyra saw a crude K surrounded by a circle. The letter she forced Billy-Ray to carve, seconds before she passed out, was now old and faded, but it was exactly where she'd made Billy-Ray carve it.

It hadn't been there when she'd walked around the trailer. The tree had been pristine, untouched, but now it was clearly marked. That badly carved K was proof of what Kyra had done.

She'd reached back in time, to alter the past, and she'd used Billy-Ray Johnson to do it.

This was immense.

This changed everything.

CHAPTER 32:

Kyra stared out of the windshield of Delilah's van. Water lapped at either side of the dirt track they rode. The track led to a bank of scrubland, where five clapboard houses lay perched on pilings above the bayou.

Delilah had picked Kyra up from the motel just after lunchtime. She was dressed in a t-shirt and jeans with her hair tied back in a ponytail. She managed to look glamorous and gender neutral all at the same time.

Yesterday evening, after riding the bus from the trailer park, Kyra spent a troubled night wrestling with a moral dilemma. Her thoughts chased themselves like dogs biting at their own tails. This did nothing for her headache.

Sleep had come in the early hours and lasted till late morning. Her headache had gone, but not her dilemma. This long-promised murder tour was a welcome diversion.

Delilah pulled off the dirt track and parked near the houses. Kyra glanced out the window.

"Are we even in Yeuxville anymore?"

"We're outside the town limits, but most people count it as Yeuxville. It's in the parish."

"A parish is what the rest of the country calls a county, right?"

"No, a county is what they mistakenly call a parish in Chicago."

"Glad we could clear that up."

They climbed out of the van and walked past the frame houses. Some had a single story, others two, but all were built at least partly over the somnolent waters of the bayou.

They came to the last house. There were no lights inside, many of the windows were cracked or missing. The roof lacked shingles and paint fell in large, brittle flakes from the wood cladding. Warped planks pushed at the rusted nails that held them captive, others had escaped into the bayou long ago.

Delilah put her foot on the first wooden step. "This is it."

Kyra squinted at the abandoned house. "Where Billy-Ray Johnson grew up?"

"Yep."

A screen door creaked, a lady with gray hair and a plaid shirt came out from the house next door. Her voice was hoarse. "Help you people?"

Delilah's voice dropped, becoming a southern gentleman. "Thank you, ma'am, we're just here to take a look at the old Johnson house."

She crossed her arms and narrowed her eyes. "Ain't nobody lives dere, pas pour longtemps, been empty since old lady Johnson died. What you want wid it?"

Kyra heard her own accent stray south of the Mason-Dixon line. "Billy-Ray killed my momma, ma'am. When I was a little girl. I don't really know what I want here. We're not causing trouble, I just want to see where he lived, is all."

The lady looked Kyra over and nodded as if she understood. "See you don't make any noise, my grandkids are napping." She opened the screen door and went back inside.

Delilah raised her eyebrows. "Well, Scarlet O'Hara, I do declare!"

Kyra blushed. "Shut up."

Several steps were broken, all of them creaked. Kyra went up as lightly as she could, thinking of the lady's grandchildren. Delilah set off a chorus of groaning boards. Kyra put a finger to her lips. Delilah held out her hands in apology.

The porch smelled of damp wood and mildew. Kyra peered through a grime laden window but couldn't see much. She shone her phone flashlight through the pane and saw peeling wallpaper and worn carpet. A rotted couch frame sat by the far wall.

Kyra tried to imagine Billy-Ray growing up here. Pictured him as a teen, slumped on the couch, avoiding homework, watching shows, like *The Fresh Prince of Bel Air* or *Friends*.

Strange to think Billy-Ray had lived in this building. Had leaned on its walls, walked through its rooms and opened its doors. It wasn't how she pictured his childhood home. It wasn't how she pictured the tour would be. What was she doing here anyway?

The man she'd obsessed over was a poorly educated murderer from a deprived background. Not a misunderstood individual, defiant in the face of public disgrace. He'd affected Kyra's life in a deep and significant way. He was as responsible for her rage and confusion as Caitlin.

So, how did she see him now? In light of everything she'd learned and everything she knew she had to do, Kyra realized he'd become her opponent.

And she knew what she was doing on this tour. She was on reconnaissance for the battle she was about to fight. Gathering intel on her combatant.

Delilah peered into the window next to her. "What you thinking about?"

Kyra shrugged. "Stuff."

"Secret stuff?"

"Yeah, like Billy-Ray's big secret."

Delilah pulled a scared face. "Ooh, the big secret!"

"Do you think it was real?"

"Sandiford and Hirst thought so. They both wrote about it."

"I guess. But, if something had been kept from you, like Billy-Ray said it had, and that something changed everything about your life..."

"Like Billy-Ray said it did."

"Would that be enough to make you snap? To send you on a killing spree?"

"Depends how big the secret was. Have you ever had a really big secret?"

Kyra peered into the abandoned room, weighing her thoughts. Should she say something to Delilah? Where could she begin, without sounding crazy?

"I might have. What about you?"

"Not sure it's enough to send me on a killing spree, but I've uncovered some stuff to do with my family. I can't say more until I've done more digging."

Kyra held her flashlight under her chin and pulled a face. "Ooh, mysterious."

"Says you. At least I told you what mine was about. You didn't give me anything."

"Noted."

"You know you can tell me, right? I know things have been weird since you came to Yeuxville, but I'm still your friend."

Kyra took Delilah's hand and squeezed it. "I know."

Delilah's gaze shifted, something caught her eye. Kyra turned to see a large bird, with a long, flat beak, a white neck, and dark pink underbelly fly over the house. Delilah pointed. "Spoonbill, don't see one of those every day."

"Do you think it's an omen?"

"Of terrible secrets uncovered?"

"Or terrible décor gone to seed."

They both laughed. Delilah squeezed Kyra's hand and let go of it. A sudden breeze blew off the bayou. It shook the frame-house, timbers shrieking in complaint. The building listed. Kyra and Delilah held onto the wall to keep from falling.

No other buildings were affected, not a branch of the surrounding trees rustled. The breeze flew up from nowhere and disappeared just as quickly.

In its wake came the marshy scents of the bayou and something else, heavier odors that lingered and swirled around the porch. Old Spice and Jack Daniels, worn leather and the thick musk of a male body. It wasn't just the odors that lingered. There was a presence there on the porch with them. A presence Kyra knew all too well. She thought for one awful moment Billy-Ray had come to take her over, that by a horrible twist of fate he'd been standing in the very same place on that porch exactly fifteen years ago.

But he hadn't.

Kyra wasn't the only one who sensed him. Delilah sniffed the air, catching the same odors. Her eyes darted back and forth, looking to see who was watching.

They looked at one another and the odors faded. The building stopped swaying and for one moment there was no sound at all. The bayou, usually a riot of noises, fell deadly silent.

Then, after a beat, the crickets started up, the frogs resumed their croaking and the high-pitched wail of a limpkin could be heard in the distance.

Delilah shuddered, in spite of the heat. "That was weird."

"Yeah."

"We should get to the next stop. A lot to see yet."

"Okay."

Delilah clomped back down the steps. Kyra took a moment to look around. Taking in the ambience of Billy-Ray's childhood home, one last time.

He knew Kyra was coming for him. He seemed to welcome it.

"Hope you're ready," she whispered.

And I hope to God I am, she thought as she staggered down the steps.

CHAPTER 33:

The water receded the further they got from the bayou and soon they were on a dry blacktop.

Billy-Ray's presence also receded and Kyra's resolve with it. She'd come to a crossroad in her life. The road ahead mirrored this, intersected by another. As they approached, something caught Kyra's eye.

She put a hand on Delilah's arm. "Could we pull over?"

Delilah looked puzzled. "Right here?"

"If you don't mind."

Delilah pulled onto the verge and they climbed out. Kyra crossed the road to investigate what looked like a small shrine.

Someone had carved a statue out of a wooden stake. It depicted St. Peter as an African American. He was holding a cane in one hand and a huge bunch of keys in the other. There was a corn cob pipe in his mouth and a wide brimmed hat on his head.

The neck of the statue was draped with bead necklaces, all of them red, white, or black. On the ground in front of the statue someone had left a bottle of rum. There were other offerings scattered around, cigars and cigar butts, lots of candy, all of it with red and white wrappers. Even some horseshoe magnets and pennies.

Kyra bent to pick up a penny.

"Don't!" Delilah's tone was full of warning.

"I wasn't going to take it, I was just looking."

"I know, but you don't want to be disrespectful."

"Of course not."

"Besides, you don't want to get on the wrong side of Elegua, it's back luck."

"Elegua?"

Delilah pointed at the statue. "This is his shrine."

"I thought it was Saint Peter."

"It is. That's one of the names we give him in these parts, also Papa Legba, sort of a local custom."

"Is there a church nearby?"

"No."

"Why is he all the way out here?"

"He's the spirit of the crossroads. This is his place."

"Yeuxville is weird."

"You only just noticed?"

"So what's with all the pennies and stuff?"

"I'd guess you'd say they're offerings."

"So, when people say, 'they keep the old ways in Yeuxville', this is what they mean?"

Delilah shrugged. "I guess."

"Do you think Billy-Ray ever came here?"

"Most people in Yeuxville have been here at one time or another."

"Including you?"

"Sometimes I need a bit of guidance. Elegua is an opener of the way, a guardian of the gates."

Kyra bit at her thumb. "The pearly gates you mean?"

"That's one way of putting it. He lets things out as well as welcomes people in."

"What sort of things?"

"Saints, Spirits, whatever you want to call them?"

"Spirits, like dead people?"

"Sometimes. But they're more like forces that show you the way when you don't know where to turn."

Kyra put her head to one side and regarded the statue. "That makes sense."

"Do you want to head on?"

"Can you give me a minute?"

"Sure."

Delilah headed back to the vehicle. Kyra rooted through her pockets. She found a dime and placed it carefully on the ground in front of the wooden statue.

Kyra cleared her throat. "I, um, I really don't know how to do this, and I don't know if you let Billy-Ray out, so he could come back. But I've got to make a choice and, um, I could really use your help. If that's okay?"

A crow cawed somewhere in the distance and a wisp of cloud moved across the sun, causing the shadows on Elegua's face to move. In that moment, Kyra was sure she was going to do the right thing.

CHAPTER 34:

Kyra bent over and tried to catch her breath. The walk to the mound had been long and arduous.

It was over twenty feet tall and the sides were sheer. Scrambling up had taken its toll, while Delilah didn't seem the least tired. Luckily, Kyra's ankle held up.

The canal on the other side didn't seem worth the effort. Its brackish water flowed sluggishly between crumbling, concrete banks. Here and there an outcrop of boulders marked the point where the mound met the water.

Kyra wiped her forehead. "Are you sure this isn't a levee?"

"Canals don't have levees, this is just the earth the oil company left when they dug the canal, they never moved it, and the grass grew. Only rivers have levees, and that's what's causing the grief."

"What do you mean?"Delilah pointed to a stretch of wetlands on the other side of the canal. "See that water out there? two years ago it was marshland, covered in trees."

"It's not part of the bayou?"

"Used to be wetlands as far as the eye could see."

"That's not possible."

"I'm afraid it is."

"Where did all the water come from?"

"Coastal erosion. We lose fifty acres a day, that's a landmass larger than Manhattan, every year, and the Federal Government does nothing about it."

"Why doesn't anyone know about this?"

"Cos we're too remote. Everyone wrings their hands about the Everglades but forgets Louisiana. If an invading army was taking this much land from our country every year, you can bet Congress would do something, but because it's water, and because it only affects a bunch of Cajuns and Rednecks, everyone looks the other way."

"Is it a climate change thing?"

"Climate change is a myth. It's the levees that are causing this."

Kyra blinked in astonishment. "What?! How can you say that?"

"Because it's true! Every year the Mississippi would burst its banks and flood, washing sediment and alluvial soil down through ten states, to deposit at the coast. That's what replenished the land. But now it's so hemmed in with levees, it doesn't flood, and we lose more coastland every year."

"So, you admit the problem is manmade? And the environment can be affected by human activity?"

Delilah wagged her finger. "Okay, I can see where you're going with this, and you're being very cute, but I don't want to fight."

Kyra held up her hands in surrender. "Sorry, I can see this is important to you. I've never heard about it."

"Hardly anyone has."

"Why don't we get back to the murder tour."

"Why don't we. Because this," Delilah pirouetted with her arms spread to indicated the top of the mound. "Is the scene of Billy-Ray's first murder."

"Where he hit Mary-Jo Bernard with a rock."

"Or he might have pushed her."

"The autopsy said the skull fracture came from a rock."

Delilah pointed to boulders at the base of the mound. "Which she could have struck after he pushed her."

"Good point. But you know what's been bothering me?"

"Not flatulence? I have to drive home with the windows closed."

Kyra laughed. "No, silly. How did he sneak up on her?"

"What do you mean?"

"Look around. We can see for miles. There are no trees or bushes. How could you follow someone out here without being seen, let alone sneak up on them?"

"You're right, that is strange. I never thought about it before. Maybe she had her back to him the whole time or she fell asleep and he crept up and woke her? Maybe Billy-Ray was a ninja."

"And what about the girl someone said they saw Mary-Jo with?"

"You don't think that was Billy-Ray in disguise?"

"It's another mystery."

"This whole case is full of mysteries."

"I guess that's why it fascinates us."

"Indeed," Delilah shielded her eyes with her hand and glanced back the way they'd come. "Want to head on to the next site?"

"Back to the Mystery Machine, Velma."

"I am so not Velma. I have far more style."

"What's wrong with Velma's style?"

"Orange? Don't get me started."

"But she's smart and funny and the cutest character in the show."

"See, that says more about your sexuality than I care to unpack."

CHAPTER 35:

The next two stops were even less impressive. They almost missed Frances Donovan's house.

Fifteen years ago, it had been a ranch home on a secluded road. But there'd been so much development the road was unrecognizable, and the current owners had renovated.

They drove past the house three times before they identified it. The current owner was watering the lawn, so they stayed in the van.

The complex where Alison Comeaux lived had been bought by developers. It was surrounded by scaffolding. There was a sign promising 'Real Estate Opportunities—Coming Soon!'.

Kyra and Delilah walked around to the side of the complex and Delilah pointed to a window on the third floor.

"That's Alison's condo."

"Which one?"

"Fourth and fifth windows in from the left, see it?"

Kyra squinted. "I think so."

"How do you think Billy-Ray got inside the building?"

"Didn't he just come through the main doors?"

"The front desk was manned the whole time. There was security footage with no sign of Billy-Ray."

"Is there a back entrance?"

"I don't think so."

"What about underground parking?"

Delilah pointed to the complex. "Do you see any underground lot?"

"No. Maybe the guy at the desk was asleep, or in the john? The only visitor he remembered was a girl scout selling cookies."

"You don't think that was Billy-Ray?"

"Billy-Ray is six-two."

"The guy did say she looked big for her age."

They both giggled. Delilah took Kyra's arm and led her back to the vehicle. "Time to visit the swankier part of town."

Delilah wasn't kidding. The scene of Billy-Ray' grisliest murder was on Yeuxville's most affluent street. An air of opulent self-satisfaction hung over every building, like the fine mist that rose from their sprinklers.

Every yard boasted the attention of landscapers. Every driveway resembled a car dealership. The Godin house, with its pitched roof, dormer windows and large covered porch, supported by Doric columns, was no exception. It hadn't changed a bit in the last fifteen years. It was just like the photo in *Eyes for the Killer*. This was the house where Billy-Ray drugged a party of drunken teenagers then took Elizabeth Boudreaux up to one of the bedrooms and dismembered her.

The residents were used to delivery vans, so they didn't get a second look parked by the curb.

Kyra wound down her window. "How come all the houses have raised foundations?"

"In case of flooding. It's a big hazard, even in this part of town."

"Are they big enough to hide under?"

"Think that's how Billy-Ray got into the party?"

"Could be, but how did he drug everybody? Unless he put something in the water. You don't think he got to the plumbing, do you?"

"I don't know. Sounds too elaborate. Most of the teens were drinking beer, don't think they drank from the faucet. But it might explain one mystery."

"Which is?"

"Conflicting reports about the timeline, especially when Billy-Ray mutilated Elizabeth's body."

"Wasn't it straight after he poisoned her?"

"That's the official line, but there's an earlier report, that must have been suppressed, which claims when Elizabeth's body was first found, only the eyes were missing. The mutilation might have happened afterwards, which means Billy-Ray returned to mutilate the body, *after* the police had arrived. Just as he did with Alison Commeaux. If that's the case, then maybe he was hiding under the house the whole time the police were there."

"Where did you learn that?"

"I might have found a new source. Can't say too much, but I can show you when I know more."

Kyra shrugged. "Sure, I guess."

"Would you like to take a look round back?"

"No, I'm good."

"Is everything okay?"

"Yeah, I'm fine."

"You don't sound fine. I just told you I might have uncovered a new source on Billy-Ray, and you just shrugged. Who are you, and what have you done with my friend?"

"It's just, all these locations make it real, you know. Billy-Ray actually killed the people that lived in these houses. Standing on his porch I could imagine him going about his life, doing day to day stuff, and he didn't seem so bad, but seeing all these people's homes makes me think about their lives, and how they can't go about them anymore, because of Billy-Ray."

"Brings it home, huh?"

"Yeah. Suddenly Billy-Ray's not just this guy I can project my angst onto. Plus tomorrow's the anniversary of Caitlin's death."

Delilah put her hand to her mouth. "Kyra, I totally forgot. I am so sorry. We'll quit the whole thing. I can't believe I'm so insensitive."

"No, no, really, I'm fine, we're good. You've been great all afternoon. The anniversary has been throwing up a lot of things."

"Want to talk about it?"

Kyra stared out of the window at the Godin house, collecting her thoughts. "Can I ask you a question?"

"Sure."

"Do you think anyone deserves to die?"

"Whoa, ask me something deep, why don't you?"

"Humor me"

"Okay, well, I don't think it's a black and white thing. I think it depends on the person, and how they're going to die. Billy-Ray's victims, for instance, they probably didn't deserve to die."

"None of them?"

"I can't say for sure. They were just in the wrong place at the wrong time. If you're asking whether an unborn child deserves to die, then I'd say hell no! If you're asking me whether I support the death penalty, the answer's hell yeah! There are some crimes you can only pay for with your life."

"Wow."

"What?"

"Didn't figure you for a conservative."

"Didn't figure you for judgmental."

"Ouch."

"Back atcha."

"Okay, so what about someone who abuses children, do they deserve to die?"

"Damn right, pedophiles go straight to hell, the sooner the better."

"Not a pedophile, just a mother who hurts her own child. Does she have a right to go on living?"

"Where's all this coming from?"

"I've been wrestling with a lot recently."

"Okay."

"If you could stop someone getting killed, even though you knew they were hurting someone you cared about, would you save them?"

"I honestly don't know. I mean it depends on how much they were hurting the people I cared about."

"But if you didn't stop this person being killed, and you could have stopped it, then you'd be just as guilty, right? Of murder, I mean."

"Okay, now you're scaring me. How hypothetical is this conversation? Are you in some kind of trouble? Is this happening back home or here?"

Kyra sighed. "Actually, it happened a long time ago."

"Fifteen years ago tomorrow?"

"Yes."

"Okay, I see what's going on. This tour's affected you more than I realized. You're not responsible for your birth mother's death, Kyra, you couldn't have prevented it. You were only a child."

"But what if I could do something now?"

"Kyra, I lost someone when I was young too, you get all kinds of notions. You know my uncle was shot by one of his best friends?"

"No, I didn't, I'm sorry."

"It's okay, it happened a long time ago. He also shot his friend in self-defense, it happened in our garage. Our families used to be real close. My Aunt Mimi won't even look at them on the street. After my uncle was shot, I would fantasize about all kinds of stuff."

"Like what?"

"Like having super powers. I used to picture myself swooping into the garage and letting the bullets bounce of my chest."

"You never mentioned this."

"I don't think about it much these days. It was a crazy notion, born of grief and impotence. It's part of the grieving process. That's what you're doing. You're grieving for the mom you never knew. It's okay to have thoughts, but you can't hold yourself responsible for what Billy-Ray did. I think we should skip the house on Conqueror Street."

"Actually, it's on Laveau Street, the last building on the row."

Delilah looked genuinely surprised. "I thought Caitlin Robichaud lived on Conqueror Street."

"No, we lived on Laveau Street. I took a trip there the other day, after we had coffee, and it all came back. I spent a while looking at the place. That's why the cops picked me up."

"You got arrested? You never told me!"

"It's no big deal, a cousin of the Sheriff's saw me. He sent two deputies, we had a chat, and I explained why I was there. They didn't charge me."

Delilah threw up her hands, then dropped her forehead onto the steering wheel. "You have no idea how much trouble you could be in. The cops round here, they're not like cops in Chicago."

"But they let me go. It's all dealt with, it's over."

"You don't know Hawkins. Once you're on his radar it's never over. He's a dangerous man."

"It's fine. I told him who my birth mom was and he laid off me. Then his daughter, Béatrice, came and got me."

"Why did his daughter come get you?"

"I sort of met her when I was trying to avoid you that first day." Kyra rubbed at a mole on the back of her neck, avoiding eye contact.

Delilah folded her hands in her lap and stared into the footwell. "Oh."

"Anyway, I thought you were all Thin-Blue-Line, now you're saying I should fear the police."

"I'm not saying fear them. They're good men and women, even Hawkins. I'm saying they do things differently round these parts."

"Everyone keeps saying that."

"Because it's true, you should have seen by now."

"I have."

"And it's no different with the Sheriff's Department. I should know, my uncle used to work there, he knew Hawkins real well. Just promise me you'll be careful?"

"Okay, I'll be careful. Can we change the subject?"

"I care about you."

"I thought we were changing the subject."

"We were."

After an uncomfortable pause, Kyra said. "Would you like to see our old apartment, the one where I lived with Caitlin?"

"I thought we were skipping the last stop."

"It's no big thing."

"If you're sure?"

"Sure."

Kyra directed them to the end of Laveau Street. The sun was sinking lower in the sky and the heat was coming off the day. They could breathe again.

As she guided Delilah through the streets, Kyra had a tight knot in her chest. A reconnection to a past that was lost before she even knew, an acceptance of everything she could have had, but never did.

Finally they pulled up at the apartment block. Delilah glanced at the graffiti on the walls and the broken glass on the ground. "Are we safe?"

"It's your town, you tell me."

"I've never been here before."

"For real?"

"Not even a delivery. Can we see the apartment from the street?"

"It's around back. Is it okay if we don't look? After what you said about the cops."

"I think that's wise. So this is where you grew up."

"The first couple years of my life."

"Remember much?"

"Bits and pieces come back."

"You've taught me something about Billy-Ray, thanks."

"Any time."

"Even if there's mysteries we still haven't answered."

Kyra had hoped this tour would bring her some answers. Would help her with the dilemma that was tearing her apart. But she already knew the answer. Had always known the answer.

What she needed was the strength to do something that would set her past, present and future on a wholly new course.

And she wasn't going to find it in Billy-Ray's old haunts.

CHAPTER 36:

Kyra set her jaw as they pulled up to the Express Inn Motel. "You can drop me here."

"Are you sure, I don't mind taking you to your door."

"That's okay. I think I'm going to take a walk and do some thinking."

"What about your ankle?"

"Took some painkillers, there's more in my room."

"You've done a lot of walking today, shouldn't you rest up?"

"What are you, my mom?"

Delilah frowned. "No, Kyra, I'm your friend and I'm concerned about you. And speaking of moms, have you called your parents yet?"

"I've been meaning to."

"Kyra Hughes, they'll be worried sick!"

"I know, I know, I'll call them. I've had a lot on my mind."

Delilah's tone softened. "You know I'm here, if you need anything, a shoulder to cry on, place to crash, help burying a body."

Kyra smiled. "How many bodies have you put in the ground?"

"Tell you that when they catch me."

Kyra unbuckled her seat belt. She reached for the door handle then paused and turned back to Delilah. "Thank you for being my friend. Sorry for being distant. I really enjoyed today."

"Me too."

Delilah leaned across and pulled Kyra into a hug. It was the first physical contact she'd had in days.

Delilah broke the clinch and Kyra let go with reluctance. She climbed out of the vehicle and closed the door. Delilah wound the window down.

"Take care of yourself, Kyra. Here if you need me, for anything."

"Okay, thanks."

She waved as Delilah pulled out of the lot. The van took off and Kyra's hand dropped like a stilled metronome. All that awaited her this evening was an empty motel room and an impossible decision.

As Kyra drew nearer to her room she was concerned to see a cop car outside. Her steps got quicker and so did her breath. Cool tendrils of apprehension tugged at her gut.

The car door opened.

It seemed to take an eternity. When the door had swung all the way out, a leg appeared, with a size fifteen cowboy boot.

A Stetson emerged next. Below it was Sheriff Hawkins' profile. His features lean and hard, chiseled from granite.

When he drew himself to his full height it seemed impossible that he'd ever fit in the front seat. Had Hawkins grown since Kyra last saw him or was it just the light in the parking lot? How was he towering over her?

He leaned on the hood of his car. "There she is. I'd almost given up on you."

"Is everything all right?"

"Why don't you tell me."

"I'm not sure what you mean." Delilah's warning came back to Kyra, *once you're on his radar it's never over.*

Hawkins gestured to her room with his chin. "My daughter behind on her rent?"

"I don't know."

"Cos you told me you were living with her, and here I find you staying at a motel. So I figure either she's been evicted, or you were lying. Which is it?"

Kyra froze. She had nothing to say.

Hawkins dropped his chin. His eyes bored into Kyra from under his brim. "I'd be careful what you say next. Lying to an officer is a federal offense. If I knock on that door, right now, will my daughter answer?"

"No."

"So, you lied about staying with her?"

"Yes."

"Something more to add to your rap sheet."

Kyra flashed back to grade school. When it was her turn for show and tell. She'd brought her grandmother's antique doll. It had pale porcelain skin and a hand-stitched black dress with white embroidery.

Her mom had encouraged Kyra to pick something else, but Kyra was adamant. She loved the doll. To Kyra it was the most beautiful and precious thing in her house, she couldn't wait to share it with her class.

As she was heading into class, Kyra passed some older girls in the corridor. One of them pointed to the doll she was carrying.

"What is that?"

The other girls shrieked and giggled in mock horror.

Another put her hand over her mouth. "That is the creepiest thing."

Kyra shrank into herself. She couldn't show the doll to the class now. What if they reacted like those older girls? She hid the doll in her locker and told the teacher she'd forgotten it.

Her teacher, Ms. Hanson wasn't pleased. She made Kyra stand in front of the class and explain how she'd let the class down, she'd let Ms. Hanson down and most of all she'd let herself down.

Kyra had cried the whole while. Tears of shame for lying about not bringing her doll.

That's how she felt now. Just as powerless, just as ashamed of being caught in a lie.

For one awful moment she thought she might cry. "What are you going to do?"

"Depends on you."

"What do you mean?"

Hawkins pushed the brim of hat back. "You been seen round town with the Landry boy."

Kyra was confused. "With who?"

Hawkins smirked. "Thought he was a friend of yours. Delbert, young feller who fancies he's a woman and thinks we don't know."

He was talking about Delilah. No wonder she hid her true self. "Is that a crime?"

"It's a free country. But see, today you were sniffing round old crime scenes, making a nuisance of yourselves. Now, I knew Delbert's uncle, and Dan was a good man, damn shame I had to lose him, so I'm inclined to let him slide, but not you."

"What have I done?"

"Report crossed my desk 'bout a missing person, one Kyra Hughes, missing five days. Figure your second name isn't Robichaud anymore, figure it hasn't been for a while."

Kyra felt sick from her shame and fear. "Are you going to take me in?"

"Like I said, that depends."

"On what? You keep saying that, but you haven't told me what."

Hawkins got to his feet and meandered over to Kyra. Maybe it was the light in the lot, but with each step he seemed to grow in stature. He towered over Kyra by the time he stood toe to toe with her. When it came to intimidation, Hawkins was the real thing.

"There's a bus leaves the parking lot of the Piggly Wiggly at 13:45. I want you on it. Takes you all the way to New Orleans. From there you can catch a bus back to Chicago. You'd save me a lot of paperwork, and the people of Yeuxville a lot of bother, if you'd just go back where you came from."

Another impossible decision. Kyra felt the panic rising in her chest. "Can I have one more day? I'll be gone the day after I promise. There's something I need to do tomorrow, and I have to be in Yeuxville to do it. It's real important, otherwise I wouldn't ask."

Hawkins put his fists on his hips and bent forward, craning his neck till his face was an inch from Kyra's. She could smell the peppermints and rye on his breath. "Do I sound like I'm giving you a choice? Do you think you come into my town and dictate your own terms? If you ain't on that bus tomorrow, I will come find you and I will put your ass into the system. You'll be taken into custody and held in a correction center and it will be a long time before your mommy and daddy will be able to come get you out. Do you understand what I'm telling you?"

The import of Hawkins' words hit Kyra like a body blow. It was a moment before she could catch her breath. "Yes, I understand, but…"

Hawkins tilted his head. "Don't you 'but' me missy. There's no 'ifs' nor 'buts' about this. Am I clear?"

"Yes."

"Yes what?"

"Yes, sir."

Hawkins took a step back. He touched the brim of his hat with his fingers. "You have a good night now. I'm glad we had this little talk. It's good when two people understand each other, don't you agree?"

He ambled back to his cruiser with the loose-limbed confidence of an apex predator. He didn't turn or acknowledge Kyra as he climbed into the car and pulled out of the lot.

It wasn't until he'd pulled away that Kyra remembered to breathe.

This was untenable. Kyra was wrestling with a choice that would change not only her future but also her past.

On the one hand she could lose everything. On the other, she could go to jail.

CHAPTER 37:

Kyra looked at the door to her room. Opening it was beyond her. Her feet just wouldn't move.

All it promised was a night of no sleep and intrusive thoughts circling like vultures. Kyra had never felt so many negative emotions as she had in that room. It was blighted. Maybe she'd ask Barbara if she could change in the morning.

She'd told Delilah she wanted to walk, that seemed like the best course of action. The sun was sinking, and darker skies were edging in. She needed to exhaust herself if she was going to sleep. She crossed the parking lot and entered the first field, going where her feet took her.

Hawkins wanted her out of town. He'd refused to listen when she asked for one more day. Tomorrow was the fifteenth anniversary of Caitlin's murder.

Kyra had no idea how Billy-Ray was able to take over her or why she started seeing the world through his eyes. But she did know she had to be in the same spot as Billy-Ray for it to occur.

She also knew she could change the past. She could take control of Billy-Ray, just as he took control of her. It cut both ways. There was a 'K' carved into a tree to prove that. A 'K' that hadn't been there when Kyra first came to Yeuxville. Except it had, because Billy-Ray had carved it fifteen years ago. Only Billy-Ray wouldn't have carved it if Kyra hadn't come to Yeuxville and made him do it. It was one giant paradox.

If Kyra stayed in Yeuxville, she could change the past one last time and save Caitlin's life.

Stop Billy-Ray stabbing Caitlin or warn her so she could get away. Perhaps she could just make Billy-Ray stab himself. Kyra wasn't sure how long she could control him, probably only a few minutes, but if she picked the right moment, she might ensure the murder never happened.

But what would happen if she did decide to save Caitlin? Would Billy-Ray go on to kill someone else? Caitlin's murder led to his capture. The DNA he left at the scene led to his arrest. If he didn't kill Caitlin, then he wouldn't be caught. What if he went on to kill more people before he was stopped?

Kyra might save one life, only to condemn more women to death. What if one of those women was supposed to give birth to a future president or the person who cured cancer? Kyra could alter the past and bring about a terrible future.

Kyra came to a wooden fence and climbed over it. She paid no attention to where she was going or where she'd been. After a few steps, the ground got marshy. Water pooled round her sneakers, soaking them.

It wasn't just Billy-Ray's victims she had to think about. If Caitlin lived it would affect Kyra's life. This was personal. Kyra would be raised by her birth mother, and she'd never get to meet her current mom and dad.

Her dad had always told her: "We didn't have you, Kyra. We chose you, and that makes you special."

If Caitlin lived, they'd choose some other lucky girl who'd grow up to have the coolest Dad in Fourth Grade. Kyra would never know the two people she loved most in all the world.

And who would she get in their place? Caitlin, a woman who couldn't raise a finger, let alone a child. The two and a half years Kyra spent with Caitlin had messed her up badly. Caused her anger, her self-harm and even her depression. How much worse would Kyra be after seventeen years?

She thought of the glowing cigarette end. The malice in Caitlin's eyes. The tears in her own. The tenderness of the flesh Caitlin charred and the depth of the scars she left. Scars that lingered in Kyra's soul, long after the burns had healed.

Why was she even considering saving that woman's life? She should storm into that apartment, and smash Caitlin's teeth down her throat. Take a cigarette to her behind, hell, she'd take a blow torch. She'd let Billy-Ray kill the bitch and happily watch.

No, she'd do more than watch, she'd take over, she'd do worse things to Caitlin than Billy-Ray ever did. She'd teach Billy-Ray a thing or two, and the child abuser who gave birth to Kyra would deserve every minute.

She ground her teeth till her jaw ached. Pain throbbed at her temples. If she murdered Caitlin, using Billy-Ray's hands, it would be the perfect crime. Caitlin had died fifteen years ago. The police had arrested, tried and executed her killer. No one would ever suspect it was really Kyra. She had the perfect alibi.

What would it be like to push a knife into Caitlin's abdomen, to use Billy-Ray's hands to do it? Would she feel it this time? Would the warmth of the blood touch her fingers as it spilled over Billy-Ray's?

Another image sprang to Kyra's mind. Caitlin's wistful face, leaning against a tree, smoking a cigarette, and with it came the memory of wanting to be held like a little girl. Was this really a woman Kyra could murder? Was there anyone she could actually kill, no matter how angry she got?

A numbness crept into her limbs. Her anger disappeared as quickly as a stove flame when you cut the gas. The world blurred with the tears that filled her eyes and spilled down her cheeks.

Kyra saw herself driving a knife into Caitlin's flesh, staring deep into her eyes. It went round and round on a mental spool, and every time it made her nauseous.

Kyra clutched her stomach and fell to her knees. Water soaked her jeans. She retched, bent forward and felt her lunch come rushing back up.

She didn't stop till the half-digested meal lay in a pool of bile. When she was done, she pulled a tissue from her pocket and wiped her eyes, and her mouth.

She looked up at the sky, it was dark and clear. Kyra rubbed her bare arms, cold and empty, purged of food and bad thoughts.

Glancing around, Kyra realized she had no idea where she was. She didn't recognize the scenery, couldn't see the lights from the highway or the motel.

Kyra had lost all sense of direction. She had no idea what she was doing. She was lost.

She'd never been more lost in her life.

CHAPTER 38:

Twelve Days Ago, T-Minus Ten Days Until Departure:

Kyra was in disgrace. Driven home from school with a seven day suspension.

The ride home was fraught. Her mom was furious. Kyra was so livid her mom's mood barely registered. Maybe this was why the screaming started the moment they came through their front door.

For once, Kyra gave as good as she got. The two of them retreated to their own corners of the house. Kyra to her bedroom, her mom to the kitchen. All they could do was wait for Kyra's dad to get home.

Kyra's dad was the peacemaker. He would step in when Kyra and her mom fought, making them both feel heard and placated. His secret was to listen without prejudice and get them to see each other's side. Her mom said it was what made him a good lawyer.

When Kyra needed advice or inspiration, she'd go to her mom. When she had a problem she'd go to her dad. She could depend on him to listen without judging and find a way to fix things, working with her until it was resolved. Right now, he couldn't get home soon enough.

Kyra heard the front door a little after six. Her Dad called out a greeting and was met with her mom's muffled tones. She was getting her side of the story in first.

Kyra only caught the gist. One comment her mom made was very clear.

"She's confused, Dennis. You don't give her enough boundaries. She doesn't know whether you're her father or her friend!"

She was taking her anger out on her dad. Kyra had seen this play out many times. Her mom would accuse her dad of being too lax, then she'd accuse herself of being a bad parent. Her dad would listen politely.

Later, her mom would apologize for most of the things she'd said, and her dad would apologize for anything he'd done to upset her. After that they'd come up with a plan for coping with the situation next time it happened. A plan they'd promptly forget *next time it happened*.

Kyra stayed in her room. She had to give them space to sort this out, then her father would come to her. The waiting was killing her.

She pulled out the drawer where she'd taped the cigarettes, then slid it back again. Her dad would smell the smoke, he could come in at any minute. There was nowhere to put her rage.

It was the prejudice and hypocrisy that annoyed Kyra. Her teachers were always telling her to speak out, be the change she wanted to see in the world, but when she did they punished her.

They find one little phial of testosterone in her locker and she's public enemy number one. It didn't even belong to her. And the school shouldn't be invading her privacy.

The new Principal was big on locker searches. Ever since they turned up her copy of *Columbine*, Kyra's locker was hit more than others. When they found her serial killer books the school insisted she see the Counselor.

The searches were supposed to be a surprise but most people knew they were coming. That's why Sam freaked out. Kyra didn't see the big deal, but then he showed her the phial.

She'd known Sam since middle school. He was Samantha when they first met, another quiet girl who didn't quite fit in. That's how they became friends. In high school he realized *why* he didn't fit in and began to transition.

Kyra shrugged. "Everyone knows you're seeing a gender therapist."

A pained expression crossed his face. "But she didn't give me this, I got it off the dark web. If my parents find out they'll cancel my treatment."

Kyra took the phial and the syringe he was holding. She placed them both on the top shelf of her locker. Sam looked nervous.

"Won't you get in trouble?"

"What if I do?"

She was so sick of adults and their handwringing. All their safeguards and false concerns were about controlling anyone younger. They were just jealous because the young had their whole lives ahead and they didn't.

Kyra was called to the Principal's office in third period. Her mom was waiting. They'd found the phial, of course.

The Principal wanted to know where she'd gotten it. He wanted her to understand it was a controlled substance and dangerous in the wrong hands. He told her she shouldn't be taking it without medical supervision, these changes weren't to be taken lightly, they could have far reaching effects that she wasn't old enough to understand.

Kyra wanted to scream in his ignorant face. Instead she crossed her arms, hid behind her bangs and stared at the floor.

Her mom hadn't even asked what Kyra's side was. She just repeated the same reactionary crap. It wasn't fair that she got to monopolize Kyra's dad.

When she heard her dad on the stairs she sighed, as much with frustration as relief. He came into her room and sat on the end of her bed, wearing that earnest expression that always pushed her buttons.

"Is what your mom says true?"

Kyra's tone was more flippant than she meant it to be. "No, dad, she made it up to freak you out."

Her Dad frowned. "Kyra, this isn't funny. You're facing serious charges. Your mom says the Principal's going to hand it to the police. You could get a criminal record, that'll affect your college applications, future employment, all kinds of things."

"Dad, it's just a hormone, it's not illegal."

"It *is* illegal if you got hold of this without a prescription. And, unless you've got a new doctor that I don't know about, I'm pretty sure you don't have a prescription. Do you have a new doctor?"

Kyra found his tone patronizing. "No."

"Are you thinking about transitioning?"

"Oh hell, no! I'm happy as a woman. Happy as I *can* be with my problems."A pained expression crossed her dad's face, then he composed himself. It was the look he always gave when she mentioned her mental health. It was a look of disappointment.

He wasn't disappointed in Kyra, but in himself. As though her mental health was his fault, if he'd only been a better parent he could solve all her problems. He had to make everything right.

"So how did you come by the testosterone?"

"It isn't mine."

He closed his eyes and breathed out, his face relaxing. "That's what I hoped. Who does it belong to?"

"Who do you think?"

"Sam?"

"Bingo."

Her dad moved around the end of her bed to get a little closer. "Great, so all we have to do is let the school know it was all a misunderstanding and they can give Sam back his testosterone."

Kyra drew her knees up to her chest. "It's not that simple."

"What do you mean?"

"I can't tell them it's Sam's testosterone."

"Why not?"

"Because Sam didn't get it off his gender therapist and if his parents find out he has it they'll stop his sessions."

"You don't know that."

"Yes I do, because he told me. You don't know how long it took to get them to come around and let him transition. He was nearly suicidal, you don't understand body dysmorphia."

"I know what body dysmorphia is, Kyra."

She threw up her hands. "You know what it is, but you don't understand it. No one in your generation does."

"Well, there's just as many trans people in my generation as yours and I'm pretty sure they understand it."

"Okay, now you're just lawyering me."

"I'm not certain that's an actual verb. But we're getting sidetracked. The important thing is to get this straightened out with the school, get your suspension lifted and get this off your record. I'll book another appointment with the Principal and we'll put your side of the story to him."

"Not gonna happen, dad."

Her dad looked perplexed. "Kyra, you need to work with me on this."

"I can't throw Sam under the bus. I'll just do the suspension and get on with the year."

"Do you think that's wise?"

"Yes, dad, I do."

Her dad put his hand on her knee. "Look, I admire your loyalty to your friend and your idealism. But this isn't about trans rights, Kyra. It's about your future. You're smart enough to get into a really good college, but not with this on your record."

"So I'll go to community college, it's not a big deal."

"It *is* a big deal. You're worth more than that. Sam has got many years yet to transition, you're going to college next year. If he's your friend he won't let you take the fall for his mistake. He'll come forward and admit what he's done."

"He hasn't done anything."

"Yes he has. If he'd come by that testosterone legally he wouldn't have pressured you to hide it."

"He didn't pressure me, okay. I took it off him and put it in my locker. We knew there was going to be a locker search and I wasn't going to let him get in trouble. I didn't hide it. It was out on show when they searched the locker."

Her dad took his hand off her knee and put it to his forehead. "You knew there was going to be a locker search and you put it in your locker for them to see?" Kyra put her chin on her knees and stared at her duvet. "Yes."

"Why would you do something that stupid?"

Kyra threw her head back. "Thanks, dad. Call me stupid, why don't you. That's really going to make me feel better."

Her Dad stood up, unable to hide his exasperation. "I didn't say you were stupid, I'm trying to understand why you'd *do* something so stupid."

"You're not in court now. Spare me your word games."

"I'm not trying to play word games. I'm trying to work out the best way forward. Your mom thinks we should ground you."

Kyra blinked in surprise. "Ground me? Do people still do that?"

"I'm trying to find other options, but you're not giving me much room to maneuver. We try and treat you like an adult, Kyra, but if you won't behave like one, if you don't take responsibility for your actions, what choice do you give us?"

Kyra ground her teeth. He shouldn't have called her stupid. She wasn't stupid. Even if what she did sounded stupid when she said it out loud. Oh God, it did sound stupid, didn't it? Why had she done that? Even still it was the principle her dad wasn't getting.

And what was all this talk about grounding? Since when had her dad become one of those adults who wanted to control her? Telling what she could and couldn't do, telling when she could and couldn't go out. The thought of it made her powerless. A toddler in the hands of someone she couldn't trust.

The words spilled out of her before she had a chance to think. "Well, perhaps you could start listening to me, and backing me up when the school keeps trying to victimize me. Perhaps you could try being a dad for once and stop trying to look all cool in front of my friends, talking about meeting lame ass rock stars no-one cares about. Perhaps you could stop embarrassing me with your pathetic lectures that just make you look sad, and awkward, and such a loser. How about that, Dad, is that enough of a choice for you?"

Oh my God! Had she really just said that? She should apologize right away. But the look on her dad's face told her there was no taking it back. He clenched his jaw, took a deep breath. He didn't raise his voice, but Kyra wished to God he had. He sounded colder than she'd ever heard him.

"All right, if that's the way you want to play this, then you are most definitely grounded for the rest of this term. You're only allowed out of the house to go to school, and you're to come straight back when it's over. If you're not back within half an hour of school finishing, your mother, or I, will come find you, and from then on, we'll make a point of picking you up and dropping you off at school. Am I making myself clear?"

"Dad."

"What?"

Kyra didn't know 'what'. Her last word was half plea, half complaint. She was scared and angry and upset. Kyra looked at her dad as if to say: *But this is me. Doesn't that mean anything? We don't treat each other this way.* Her Dad held her gaze and she saw the same look cross his face.

For a moment she thought the tension was going to break and they were going to drop this whole charade, that he would reach out and remake the connection they'd always had. They'd start to talk properly about what had happened and how they were going to fix everything, but neither one of them seemed to know how to do that. The moment passed.

A vivid memory from her childhood came back. Kyra was five, her parents had rented a cabin in the woods near Volo Bog. She was scared of the woods and wouldn't play outside in case a bear came. Her Dad had laughed her out of it, pretending to be a big, silly bear that kept falling over and bumping into things as it chased her.

He was chasing her round the porch, and she was running, and laughing, when she turned a corner and spied the wood pile. Kyra grabbed a small log and waited for her dad to come roaring round the corner. When he did, she dropped the log on his foot. Her dad stopped pretending to roar and cried out in pain.

His face went red and he raised his voice. "Kyra, what did you do that for?" He went from a pretend bear to an angry bear glowering and shouting. She hadn't meant to hurt him, she'd just gotten caught up in the moment, pretending it was a real bear chasing her and trying to defend herself. She'd thought it was funny and that her daddy would laugh, but instead he got red-faced and cross.

She shifted from foot to foot and then the tears came. She didn't like the daddy she had now, she wanted her old daddy back. She lifted up her arms to him for comfort and sobbed, "Daddy, Daddy".

In that moment, she saw him melt. The furious expression was replaced by the old gentleness and concern. He reached down and scooped her into his arms.

"I'm sorry Daddy, I'm sorry," she sobbed.

"That's all right, pumpkin. That's all right, let's go grab some hot chocolate." He carried her inside. The angry bear had disappeared and her strong, kind protector was back.

"Daddy, I was so scared."

"Don't be scared, Daddy's here."

And he *was* there. Kyra had reached out to bring him back and he'd come. He was no longer mad at her. He was her Daddy again.

Kyra wished more than anything she could reach out to him like that now, but she couldn't find the words. They were standing on opposite sides of a canyon and there was no semaphore, no smoke signals that would allow them to reach one another.

Kyra's Mom appeared in the doorway and spoke softly. "Dennis?"

"It's all right. We're done here, I'll tell you about it in a moment."

The door closed gently behind her dad. "You did the right thing," she heard her mom say.

How could she say that? How was locking her up in the house like a child *the right thing* to do? Kyra held a pillow over her face and screamed silently into it. For a moment she was sure she could smell damp closets and shoeshine.

Kyra felt utterly powerless, like a tiny toddler locked in a confined space. What did that mean? Where did these feelings come from?

Had she known, in that moment, where those questions would lead and what she'd discover about herself, she might never have left Chicago.

CHAPTER 39:

Kyra woke to a loud banging, like someone was trying to break down the walls.

No, it was coming from the door. She opened a sleep-blurred eye and closed it again, hoping it would stop. Maybe it was another door, not hers. Maybe the banging would stop soon and she could go back to sleep.

Kyra had only had a few hours' sleep. She'd walked for most of the night, tramping through field after field with no idea where she was. Finally, she'd chanced on a road and followed it until she got back to the motel. The sun was rising as she stumbled into her room.

The banging stopped. Kyra sighed and pulled the duvet over her head. But a shrill woman's voice called out. "I know you're in there, young lady, so you might as well come out."

Oh God, was she ever going to get any sleep? She was so tired, but this sounded serious. Kyra slid out of bed and grabbed her clothes from the floor. The bottoms of her jeans still crusted with mud. She hopped to the door as she pulled on her socks.

Barbara was standing outside her door. Kyra could feel the anger and disapproval coming off her.

"Did I treat you well?"

Kyra still had one eye closed from sleep. She blinked it open. "I'm sorry?"

"I kept your room clean, even when you scattered your clothes all over it. I treated you with respect and courtesy, didn't I?"

"What?"

"Didn't I?"

"Yeah, I guess."

"So why do you see fit to lie to me and abuse my hospitality?"

"I don't understand."

"You lied to me. You told me you was someone else and you registered under a false name. Sheriff Hawkins came calling first thing and let me in on a few things. You ain't tight with Béatrice, and you been causing trouble all over town. He don't want you around, and that means I don't want you in my motel. I can't offer you a room anymore. You have one hour to pack up and leave."

"That's not fair, I haven't done anything."

"You got yourself arrested."

"That was a misunderstanding. The charges were dropped."

"That ain't how the Sheriff put it. I run a respectable business, and I can't be harboring felons and troublemakers."

'Felons and troublemakers?' It was like a line from the last century. Why would she say that about Kyra?

"Like I said, one hour, missy."

"But I've paid till the end of the week."

Barbara reached into her pocket, pulled out a wad of crumpled notes and handed them to Kyra. "This should cover the balance. You can leave the key in the door. Don't make me come back here." With that, she turned and walked to the main building.

"Shit!" Kyra slammed the door and it rattled in its frame. Her stockinged foot shot out and collided with the bottom of the door, sending a stab of pain through her bad ankle. Kyra hopped away from the door, cursing herself and all of Yeuxville. How could Barbara say those things about her? Why couldn't Hawkins stop meddling in her affairs for just *one* day?

Kyra removed her clothes and tried to wake up by standing under the shower. She needed to plan what to do next. When she was done, she changed into new clothes and the last of her clean underwear, gathered her belongings and stuffed them in her backpack.

The room looked no different from the first time she saw it. There was nothing she could point to that spoke of her time here. Kyra had left no mark on the room, but the time that she'd spent here, the emotions that had gripped her and the thoughts that had crawled from its dark corners had left an indelible mark on her.

Kyra picked up her bag, closed the door and walked to the bus stop. She didn't see Barbara in her office, but she gave her, and the whole of the Express Inn, the finger anyway.

Kyra texted Delilah as she stood at the bus stop, the morning sun drying her hair.

Kyra:
I need a favor, can I crash with you, like we discussed? It'll only be a night, I don't
have anywhere to stay and I've got to do something before I go xxx

She waited fifteen minutes, but no bus came nor any text from Delilah. She tried again:

Kyra:
Did you get my last text???

Five minutes later the bus came, but there was still no text from Delilah. Kyra got off at the Piggly Wiggly, her backpack seemed heavier than normal and the straps chafed her shoulders. She walked to the industrial park to find Béatrice's unit.

The door was open, Kyra knocked, but there was no reply. She tried again, a little louder.

"C'mon back," Béatrice called.

Kyra lugged her backpack past the shelves, careful not to knock anything, especially the make shift altar. Béatrice was sitting at her desk, a tiny paintbrush in hand. She was wearing a pair of glasses, which made her look strangely more attractive. "What brings you here? Everything okay?"

"No, I've been kicked out of my motel."

"What happened?"

"Your daddy, that's what happened."

Béatrice sighed with annoyance. "What's he done now?"

"He found out I was staying at the motel, and not your house, and he came round last night. He told me to leave town on the next stagecoach."

"He said 'stagecoach'?"

"It was more like 'next bus', but he might as well have said it. This morning he told Barbara that I didn't know you and signed in under a false name, so she threw me out."

Béatrice put down her paintbrush, rolled her eyes and took off her glasses to massage the bridge of her nose. "Kyra, I'm really sorry about this. But I'm not surprised. Once my daddy gets something stuck in his craw he's not going to let up. As he sees it, Yeuxville is his little kingdom. He wants things done *his* way and most folks go along with that. What are you going to do now?"

"I have something I need to do today, after that I don't know."

"I'd let you stay at mine, but it's a one bed apartment and I just sold my couch. Guess that's why my daddy got suspicious."

"That's okay. What I really need is a place to store my stuff for a couple hours, I'll pick it up later today, tomorrow morning at the latest."

"Sure," Béatrice pointed to a pile of boxes. "Stick it in the corner over there and I'll make sure it's safe."

"Thanks, I appreciate it."

Kyra dropped her bag in the corner.

Béatrice got up from her stool, stretched her back and smiled, sympathetically. "So, aside from getting kicked out, how you holding up?"

"Okay, I guess," There wasn't much conviction in Kyra's voice. Béatrice picked up on that.

"No more visions?"

"What do you mean?"

"Like seeing the past through someone else's eyes? Remember, you told me about it on the way back from the doctors."

Could she trust Béatrice? The weight of everything she'd learned hung so heavily on her shoulders, she was afraid it would bury her. It would be wonderful to share the burden.

She liked Béatrice but what would she think if Kyra told her the truth? There was so many dark thoughts lurking in her mind she was afraid to share. It was safer to say nothing.

"That was just a crazy moment. I'd been hit by a car. I wasn't thinking straight."

"Okay, because if you had seen anything again, you know you could tell me, right?"

"Yeah, no, of course."

"I know I only met you a few days ago, but I care about you. If you need to talk to someone, I'm here."

"So, I'm not just some charity case, like your daddy thinks? I mean, you do volunteer a lot."

"Okay, I like to give something back, I admit that, and I volunteer a lot, but you and me, it's personal."

"I'm not just some dumb kid?"

Béatrice placed her hands on Kyra's shoulders and smiled. She could feel the warmth from Béatrice's palms through her t-shirt. The contact held a delicious charge. A cool anticipation that beat inside her chest like the wings of a freshly hatched chick. Kyra's breath was shallow, the back of her neck speckled with sweat.

"Kyra, you are a smart, charming, independent young woman. I don't care what my daddy, or anyone, thinks. I'm proud to know you."

Kyra wanted to stay and tell her everything, but there was something important she had to do, and a limited window in which to do it.

"Thanks for letting me stow my bag, I'll pick it up later, promise."

Béatrice squeezed her shoulders and let go of her. "Okay, you take care now."

Kyra left the way she came. She paused a moment at the strange altar. She noticed the weird fetish doll was gone. Béatrice had probably thrown it out.

Kyra wondered if its absence should bother her. She knew nothing about portents or omens. If she had, she would have been fearful as she left the unit.

CHAPTER 40:

The pain in Kyra's ankle was worse. The muscles hurt from all the walking last night.

She just needed it to hold up one more day. Kyra was about to make the most important decision of her life. A decision that would affect her future and her past. That would affect everyone she loved most. And Kyra had no way of knowing how it would turn out.

Her phone buzzed as she limped onto Main Street.

Delilah:
Sorry, only just got your message!! Of course you can crash, my aunt wants to meet
you, shall I pick you up at the motel?

Kyra:
I was kicked out, so unfair, tell you about it later, there's something
I need to do, I'll call
you when it's over

Delilah:
Okay, text me if you need anything

Her screen suddenly blurred. Kyra blinked and tears ran down her cheeks. Two tiny acts of kindness from two different women and she was overcome with emotion. Was this karma after Hawkins and Barbara had been so mean?

Kyra was grateful for their kindness but also embarrassed. She had a mental image of her mom on her birthday. Her dad made a big deal of birthdays.

He'd start with a breakfast of pastries and croissants from mom's favorite patisserie, along with fruit, cheese and sparkling wine. Then would come presents, always the exact things she wanted and she'd never have to drop hints. In the afternoon they'd take a trip somewhere special and in the evening they'd catch a movie. Her dad would organize the whole thing.

He did the same for Kyra on her birthday. When she was younger she used to love the attention. The older she got, the more she responded like her mom. When her dad lavished affection on her mom, she would blush and shoo him away, so moved she was afraid to show it.

"Enough already," she would say. Her dad would never listen, and she loved him all the more for it.

That's how Kyra felt now. Until a few days ago, she'd only met Delilah online and she didn't even know Béatrice. But they'd thrown her a lifeline when she needed it.

Their kindness was a comfort, but it was no substitute for the love that existed in her family. Like a phantom limb that throbs, Kyra needed the company and succor of the people she loved the most. And even as she admitted that to herself the old fury raised its head like a beast roused from its lair. She was still mad at her parents for everything they'd said and done before she left.

Then the doubt set in. Was it *them* she was mad at?

Yes.

But was it?

She was afraid to answer truthfully. She knew who she'd been most angry with all along.

She was mad at herself.

Mad for all the things she'd said and done. All the lies she'd told. For the cash that sat like a heavy burden in her fanny pack. Each a sin for which she'd have to repent.

That was why she had to make this decision.

She wished she could speak with her dad. Her poor, clueless Dad, who couldn't put a foot right these days. However much he embarrassed her, for all the times Kyra could have choked him, she still looked to him, in every decision she made, even when he wasn't there. He was her moral compass, she knew what he would do, no matter what, and that's how she knew the right thing to do now. Even though it meant she'd never see her parents again.

No, it was worse than that.

Worse than never seeing them again. She was going to make sure she never knew them at all. Kyra couldn't breathe when she realized this. She stopped and leaned against a storefront wall as she tried to catch her breath.

She needed to reach out to them. To hear their voices one last time.

Kyra punched her dad's number into the burner phone. It was one of two numbers she knew by heart. She stopped shy of the last two digits. Her dad would pick up. She knew this. If she spoke to him, she didn't think her resolve would hold. He'd talk her round, or he'd find out where she was, and she wouldn't be able to do what she had to.

She typed her mom's number in instead. Kyra knew her mom wouldn't pick up. She rarely knew where her phone was. It drove Kyra and her dad mad. They could never get hold of her. For some weird reason her mom hated cellphones, always had. They didn't have them when she was a kid.

She got a phone under protest. Kyra's Dad bought it, kept it charged, and talked her into turning it on in case of emergency.

Her Mom's phone went to voicemail, as expected.

Kyra froze when she heard the tone. Her mouth was open, her lips moved, but she couldn't find the words.

Eventually, she stammered: "Mom, dad, I'm sorry. I love you guys. Oh God, I love you. I miss you so much. I'm sorry about everything's that happened, about everything I did. I don't want to lose you, but I have to do something, because it's the right thing, because dad would do it too. He'd understand. You'd understand, dad, you would. You're great parents, I know that now, it's just that..."

A recording cut her off, telling Kyra her time was up. She could press one to re-record or just hang up. Kyra cut the connection and put the phone back in her pocket.

Kyra had been in a dark place last night. The thoughts she had about Caitlin had scared her, had made her look at what sort of person she was, made her think about all the bad choices she'd made. It was time to start making better choices, necessary ones.

She was going to save the life of a woman she hated. And to do that, she would have to destroy her own.

CHAPTER 41:

Kyra heard the phrase 'dead man walking' in a movie with Sean Penn and Susan Sarandon. It was what the warden called when escorting a prisoner to execution.

It was how she felt now as she turned off Main Street into Saloppé. She didn't know what her life was going to be like after this afternoon, but it probably wouldn't be good.

Kyra had decided to save Caitlin's life. She had proven that she could alter the past through Billy-Ray Johnson. That she could take over his body and control him for brief periods. That meant she could step in, as he was about to murder Caitlin and stop him from doing it.

Kyra wasn't certain how she would do that, but her window of opportunity was coming up. If she turned her back on the chance to save Caitlin and walked away, she'd be as bad as Billy-Ray and, much as she'd once admired him, that was the last thing she wanted.

Leaving a mark in a tree was one thing, it didn't affect the future very much, but saving the life of someone who'd already died could affect hundreds of lives, not least her own. Kyra had no idea what the present would be like afterward. Would she even remember her old life, or what she'd done to change the past? Kyra had no idea.

She turned off the avenue into Laveau Street, trying not to draw attention. Kyra sauntered down to her old apartment and walked around back. She peered at the ground floor as long as she could, without looking suspicious. Then walked back up the street.

She needed to trigger another episode, to let Billy-Ray take over so she could take control at the key moment. But she wasn't sure where Billy-Ray was fifteen years ago.

She checked the time on her phone, it was three fifty in the afternoon. Kyra didn't know exactly when Billy-Ray would come to the apartment. But she'd read everything she could find about that day. She knew that fifteen years ago today, a neighbor reported Caitlin's body, lying in her kitchen, in a pool of blood, at six thirty pm.

The coroner put time of death around five pm. This meant Billy-Ray was at or near the apartment from around four onward. If Kyra stayed near the building, she had the best chance of being in the same place at the same time. Once she was looking out of his eyes, she'd bide her time and pick her moment to save Caitlin.

"Hey there," a voice called. "Out of my way!"

Kyra jumped to one side as a huge, elderly lady, in t-shirt and sweatpants, trundled by on her mobility scooter. Her flesh seemed to have absorbed most of the seat and even some of the handlebars. She rolled off the sidewalk and onto the road, unfortunately one of her back wheels caught the curb and the scooter stalled.

The old lady turned to see what the hold-up was and listed to one side. Within seconds both she and the scooter had gone over. Kyra rushed to see if she could help. The old lady was sprawled on the tarmac like a piece of roadkill.

"Well, don't just stand there, help me up. This is all your fault!"

"How is this my fault?"

"You were hogging the whole sidewalk."

"No I wasn't."

"If you're gonna stand there and sass me, I'ma whoop your ass. Now get on over here."

Kyra stepped off the curb and went to help. She could smell stale sweat and urine as she drew close. Kyra took hold of the woman's elbow and wrist and tried to pull her up. The old lady shook her arm free.

"What are you playing at?"

"I'm trying to help you up."

"Not like that you're not, you gotta get under my arms to lift me."

Kyra sighed and reached under the old lady's armpits. Her t-shirt was dank and sodden.

"What in hell?! Git your hands offa my titties!"

"I'm not anywhere near your... I'm just trying to help."

The old lady balled her hand into a fist. Before Kyra could move, she smacked it into the side of her head. A sharp pain shot through Kyra's temples and colored sparks danced before her eyes. Kyra let go of the old lady and staggered back.

The sparks kept dancing. They started to split apart into even more sparks. Then those stars also fractured and before long Kyra could see nothing but sparks.

"Go on, backchat me again. See if you don't get worse. Now git me up."

Kyra's sight was engulfed by the sparks. She stepped away and turned slowly as she felt a familiar presence creep up and take hold of her. She didn't fear it, or struggle. This time, she welcomed it.

"Hey, what the hell," the old lady shouted. "Hey, come back here, I ain't up yet. Come back here. I'ma kick your ass for sure."

The old lady continued to holler as Kyra's sight cleared and Laveau Street, as it was fifteen years ago, appeared before her. Kyra's moment to change everything had arrived.

CHAPTER 42:

Kyra saw the sky as it was fifteen years ago – dark and overcast. A pall of gloom hung over Laveau Street. Kyra spotted Caitlin up ahead and, impelled by Billy-Ray, she stepped behind a wall. Kyra peered out from behind the wall and watched as Caitlin pushed the stroller up to the front door of the building.

As the front door closed, Kyra found herself walking round to the back of the building where she squatted down next to the fence. It was a better place to hide in Billy-Ray's time, she was more exposed in her own. She hoped the Sheriff's cousin didn't see her.

From the safety of the bushes Kyra and Billy-Ray watched the living room through its French doors. Caitlin came into the room with Kyra's younger self and dropped her into a collapsible playpen. Caitlin stabbed her finger at young Kyra, warning her not to leave.

Caitlin went into the kitchen, rummaged around in the drawers, and came back with tinfoil and a drinking straw. She hunted through her bag for a plastic baggie full of brown powder. Caitlin emptied the powder onto the tinfoil and held a lighter to it. The powder began to smoke, and Caitlin inhaled the vapors through the straw.

When she was done, Caitlin fell back onto the couch and clicked on the TV. The screen threw colors on Caitlin's face as a daytime soap played. Caitlin's head nodded, her chin fell against her chest, and she passed out. Young Kyra observed all this from inside her pen. She waited to make sure Caitlin didn't come round, then clambered out of her pen.

Summoning her courage, the child touched Caitlin's hand to see if she'd stir. When she didn't, young Kyra lifted the remote from her fingers and sat down in front of the couch, flicking through the channels until she came to *Elmo's World*.

For as long as she could remember, Kyra had hated Elmo. It wasn't the show itself or its characters. There was simply something about the dangerous redness of Elmo's fur and the high note of panic in his voice. It made her nervous, made her think something bad was just about to happen.

Kyra thought she'd always been this way. But now it seemed when she'd lived with Caitlin, it had been her favorite show. Her younger self was entranced, caught up in the careful homilies and life lessons the show imparted.

For ten minutes nothing happened, then Caitlin stirred. She came to with a stupefied look and blinked at the TV. It took her a second to realize it wasn't her soap, then she glanced at the playpen and saw young Kyra wasn't in it. Caitlin sat up and saw her daughter sitting on the floor.

Furious that Kyra had disobeyed her, she staggered to her feet, limbs heavy with the drug and raised her hand. Caitlin swung for the child but Kyra saw her and avoided the slap.

Young Kyra ran around back of the couch, gripping the remote. Caitlin stumbled after her. Young Kyra backed up against the wall, the remote behind her back. She shook her head and refused to hand it over.

Caitlin raised her hand in warning. Young Kyra flinched but shook her head and held her ground. Caitlin stamped her foot, her face red, the tendons standing out on her neck as she screamed at the child.

Young Kyra's legs were shaking, her mouth was set firm, and she stared right back at Caitlin. Then, out of nowhere it seemed, she shouted back at Caitlin. Even though Kyra could only see what was happening that day, she knew what she'd said. Her mouth formed the word, "NO!"

Good for me. Kyra was beginning to doubt her decision to save Caitlin.

Caitlin took a step back, her arms fell to her side, and her face registered genuine surprise. For the briefest moment, the whole balance of power in her relationship with her child seemed to shift. Then, like flames billowing through a burning house, Caitlin's temper came rushing back.

She grabbed young Kyra by the throat, lifted the child off the ground, and marched her into the kitchen. Young Kyra pulled at Caitlin's hands as her legs kicked the air. The kitchen window was smaller, so Kyra's view of what was happening was obscured. Caitlin appeared to slam her daughter onto the kitchen table. Kyra could see the child's legs still kicking. Caitlin held her by her throat, choking her.

The kitchen was small enough for Caitlin to open a drawer, while holding the child on the table. She searched the drawer and brought out a knife. Kyra's heart beat quicker. Was Caitlin about to do what she thought? Caitlin leaned over her daughter.

This couldn't be happening. Kyra needed to do something. She tried to seize control of Billy-Ray but he wouldn't respond. On the kitchen table, her younger self kicked more furiously. Kyra saw Billy-Ray's fingers grip the chain links of the fence. Caitlin brandished the knife at the child, her top lip curled in a sneer.

Not so sassy now, are you? Her expression seemed to say.

Caitlin leaned in to her child. Young Kyra was still kicking. Her tiny foot connected with the hilt of the knife. Caitlin's hand shot backward. It looked like she punched herself in the face. Her head jerked back, her expression one of genuine shock.

Before she realized what she was doing, Kyra had scaled the fence and jumped down the other side. Pain screamed up her leg as she hit the ground. She sobbed through gritted teeth. Billy-Ray was taking her to the ground floor apartment.

Kyra saw Billy-Ray raise his foot to kick in Caitlin's backdoor and felt her own carried with it. More pain shot up her leg as her foot connected with the backdoor. Caitlin's door rattled in its jamb, the plastic cracking around the lock.

Kyra had no idea if the door in her own time was giving way. She wasn't as strong as Billy-Ray and the door was newer. When Caitlin's door broke open, Kyra hoped the one in her time had too.

Luckily it had, because she charged into the kitchen to see Caitlin standing by the table while her younger self lay completely still, staring up at her. Caitlin was swaying, unsteady on her feet, a vacant expression on her face. She turned to face the door as if to greet Billy-Ray, and Kyra saw what was wrong with her. The knife was no longer in her hand. It was embedded in her right eye socket. It had lodged there when Young Kyra kicked her hand.

Blood streamed from the wounded eye, running down her cheek and soaking the front of her blouse. Her head lolled as her neck muscles gave out. Her left eye rolled up into its socket and she pitched forward, face first.

The hilt of the knife struck the floor, driving the blade further into Caitlin's skull. Though she couldn't hear it, Kyra could imagine the loud *Tok!* it must have made. The knife slid to one side as the weight of the body came down on it. Caitlin's head turned till she lay on her left cheek in a rapidly growing pool of blood. Her legs kicked randomly and her body shook with spasms.

Kyra looked over at her younger self, still lying on her back on the kitchen table, her face a mask of abject terror.

Nausea rose in Kyra's gut. Bile burned the back of her throat. She wanted to bend double and empty her stomach, but Billy-Ray was still in control and, for some reason that stopped her.

An older woman's voice, husky from whisky and cigarettes broke Kyra's attention. It was coming from Kyra's time and she couldn't see who was shouting. "Who the hell are you? What are you doing in my kitchen? Look what you've done to my door. Earl git your gun!"

"I got it," a male voice grunted.

"What are you waiting for? Shoot her! Look at her eyes, she's on drugs."

Kyra couldn't move or speak. Couldn't respond to the imminent danger in her own time because Billy-Ray had control of her body. She was too panicked, too confused to try and take over him.

And she was about to take a bullet.

CHAPTER 43:

Billy-Ray knew nothing of this. It was fifteen years in the future for him. A future he wouldn't be alive to see.

If he had known, would he have bent so softly to the child on the table? Would he have lifted her into his arms with such care?

Kyra didn't feel the weight of her younger self or catch her childlike smell. She simply felt her own arms moved into the same position as Billy-Ray's.

She heard a loud pop, similar to a firecracker. A noise like *pyyyong* parted the air to the left of her head. Was this it, was Kyra going to die? Would the last thing she ever saw, be a view of the past, through the eyes of the man that killed...?

No, wait. He *hadn't* killed Caitlin.

Kyra had just seen Caitlin die, and Billy-Ray wasn't responsible.

Kyra was.

Kyra had killed her own mother at age two and a half.

It was an accident. Caitlin herself was partly responsible. If she hadn't reached for the knife Kyra wouldn't have struck it with her foot. But Kyra administered the blow that took her mother's life.

She had no memory of this. Little wonder, the trauma, the guilt would have been too much for a two year old to process.

There was another *pyyyong*. The slipstream ruffled Kyra's hair. Then a loud crash that sounded like crockery breaking.

"Darn it, Earl that's my best china! Cain't you shoot straight?"

Kyra turned with her younger self in her arms and made for the door. As she went, her foot nearly went from under her. She was mirroring Billy-Ray's actions. She looked down and saw Billy-Ray had slipped in Caitlin's blood. It was pooling out all over the floor.

Dammit, Billy-Ray, you're leaving evidence, she thought, and wondered why she was concerned about a serial killer.

There was another loud crack and a splintering thud in the door lintel, just as she was rushing through it.

"Gimme that gun! You cain't shoot a blamed thing!"

Kyra was already out of the ground floor apartment and racing across the communal yard, at a speed she wouldn't normally make. She ducked through a side entrance she hadn't known was there. It led to a field of scrub grass which she raced across, with her younger self in her arms.

Why had Billy-Ray abducted her all those years ago? Had Kyra changed the past without realizing it, just by looking through Billy-Ray's eyes? Had she caused the timeline to go veering off in a terrible new direction? Instead of saving Caitlin, would she now have to stop Billy-Ray from killing her younger-self?

No, she couldn't have changed the past. She didn't make Billy-Ray do anything, so this must be exactly how it happened. Was Billy-Ray trying to get young Kyra out of the way so he could go back and cut up the body?

Was he looking to come back and get his kicks out of Caitlin's corpse? Maybe that would explain the time lapse between the murder and the mutilation? No-one knew Billy-Ray had to get Caitlin's daughter out of the way.

So why was he treating young Kyra this tenderly? Kyra couldn't read Billy-Ray's mind but she caught something of his mood from being forced to mimic his actions. Emotions were physical things and Kyra soaked up Billy-Ray's feelings by replicating his movements.

Billy-Ray was holding her younger self with such concern. How could a psychopath, a man who'd murdered and disfigured four women, be capable of such tenderness? Kyra was finding it difficult to process what she was experiencing.

In the split second that she'd stood in that kitchen, trying to understand what was happening, her mind had cast back for memories of that evening. But she'd drawn a blank.

Now the faintest of recollections was haunting her. Gossamer thin specters of recall.

They were triggered when she noticed her mouth was making words. It took her a while to register. She was finding it hard to catch her breath and every step was painful. Billy-Ray was running at a pace Kyra would have found it hard to keep up even if she didn't have a bruised ankle.

By the time they'd covered half a mile, over an unforgiving terrain of marsh grass, Kyra noticed she'd been mouthing the same words over and over. She couldn't hear the words, so it took her some time to work out what they were. Their rhythm was like a forgotten melody, that suddenly returned, transporting her back to the first time she heard it.

The wet, earthy scent of the marsh grass also triggered memories. It was what Kyra had smelled that night, fifteen years ago, along with Billy-Ray's aftershave, cigarette smoke, and the distinct aroma of his leather jacket.

The feeling was not unlike déjà vu. Previously, she'd seen this night over Billy-Ray's shoulder, now she was seeing it from his point of view. Her recall made everything more vivid and she recognized the words Billy-Ray kept saying, like a mantra:

It's all right, it's all right little darlin'

I ain't gonna let nothin' bad happen to you no more, not no more, not now.

It's all right

Daddy's here.

Daddy?!

Daddy?

Kyra's lungs were on fire. Her legs about to go from under her. But she recognized where they were. It was the field behind the trailer park. Billy-Ray must have known a short cut.

She ran through the back gate and thankfully slowed to a walk. Kyra would have collapsed with exhaustion if Billy-Ray hadn't been in charge of her body.

Kyra wove her way through the rows of trailers till she got to the small fenced-off yard she recognized, with the slide, the pool, and the playhouse. She bent over the short fence and put her younger self down on the grass.

Young Kyra reached out to her with imploring arms, her tiny fingers curling and uncurling as if they were tugging at the air to draw her back. Her eyes were full of tears and her little lips mouthed the same words over and over. Kyra remembered saying the words. The memory seemed to have lain dormant in the muscles of her body and now it surfaced like an angry sob.

She was there again, on that warm night, in the darkening twilight, crying and reaching for Billy-Ray saying the same words again and again:

No, no, Daddy. Don't go, Daddy.

Don't go, Daddy, no!

Why was she calling Billy-Ray daddy? Unless.

Unless.

Kyra glanced up just in time to see the trailer door open. Her cries had alerted the occupants. Billy-Ray didn't want to be seen. Kyra stepped into the shadows and slipped behind another trailer with no lights.

As she did, one final memory forced its way back from the black sea of forgetting that had swallowed her early years. She recalled Billy-Ray stepping back into those shadows, leaving her to Caitlin's friends.

Even then, at age two, Kyra had known it was the last time she'd ever see him. She remembered crying for hours. Nothing could console her.

Then the darkness closed in and there were no more memories. Kyra's body protested as Billy-Ray began to jog to the back gate. She couldn't catch her breath, her calves were knots of quivering muscle.

She knew Billy-Ray meant to go back to the apartment. Back to the kitchen where Caitlin lay in a congealing pool of blood.

Kyra didn't want to go with him. She didn't want to face the crime she committed when she was too young to remember. Too young to realize what she'd done or how it would affect her whole future.

The couple who lived there would have called the police. They would arrest Kyra and Sheriff Hawkins would find out she hadn't left.

If they hadn't called the police, they'd shoot at her again. And this time they might not miss.

There was no way to stop Billy-Ray or turn him around. Kyra was too weak, reeling from the shock of everything she'd learned.

Kyra couldn't take control of Billy-Ray. But if she didn't, she faced arrest or certain death.

CHAPTER 44:

Sharp, sudden pain exploded across Kyra's forehead.

Red light engulfed her vision. The red of sirens and stop signs. She was thrown backwards but Billy-Ray continued on to the apartment and their sight and bodies separated.

Kyra let out a cry of pain. It hurt to be severed from Billy-Ray. And her whole face throbbed as she landed on her back.

She lay on the grass in the trailer park. As her vision came into focus, she found herself looking at a metal pole, set in concrete. It hadn't been there fifteen years ago. She must've walked right into it.

Kyra tried to stand, fell to her knees. She waited for her head to stop spinning and tried standing again. Was this a concussion? Kyra touched her forehead to see if she was bleeding. There was a lump forming on her forehead, but the skin was unbroken.

She felt a hand on her shoulder. Heard a heavily Cajun voice. "Y'all right dere? Dat was a nasty blow ya took to de head."

The accent was thicker than gumbo. Kyra turned slowly, head pounding. A woman with long gray hair and a Lynyrd Skynyrd t-shirt was eyeing her with suspicion. Kyra was sure she knew her.

"I said are y'all right, êtes-vous bien, ça va?"

Kyra nodded and pain knifed through her left eye. "Yes, thank you, ma'am."

"Ya been over wid dem deadbeats smokin' rocks?"

Kyra didn't understand. "I'm sorry?"

"I know what goes on in dat trailer. Whole park's full of it, and I'm sick of it. Saw ya hangin' round de back of ma trailer."

Kyra stood and nearly fell. The ground spun then settled. Deep breaths settled her nausea. "Was that your trailer?"

"Sure was."

"I'm really sorry, ma'am. I didn't mean anything by it. It's just that I, I think I used..."

Kyra's voice trailed off as she recognized the woman. She'd seen her before, through Billy-Ray's eyes.

"Wait a minute, ma'am. Did you ever look after a two-year old? Caitlin Robichaud's girl, about fifteen years ago?"

The woman stared at Kyra, and then a light came on behind her eyes. "Kyra, is dat you, c'est vrais? Why, you're da spit of yer momma."

She stepped closer, brushed the hair from Kyra's forehead and gently stroked her bump. "You're gone have a nasty bruise in da morning."

"I didn't see the pole, ran right into it."

"Thought ya was one o' dem crackheads, hangin' round."

"What, oh no, I'm not into drugs. I was just visiting the area, and I thought I'd drop by, stir up some old memories."

"C'mon inside, I'll put some iodine on dat bruise." The woman helped Kyra to her feet and led her back toward the trailer.

"I'm really sorry, but it's been such a long time. I can't remember your name."

"I'm Gail. Ya used ta call me Gay-Gay."

The trailer smelled of cooking fat, cigarettes, and cheap air freshener. It was remarkably clean and tidy. Gail pulled out a chair and told Kyra to sit while she rummaged through her kitchen cupboards, emerging with an old brown bottle, some cotton swabs and a box of Band-Aids.

Gail applied the iodine to Kyra's bump. "Always wondered what happened to ya, we didn't hear nuddin after we handed ya over to da state. I'da kept ya if'n I could, but dey wouldn't allow it. Someone dropped ya off in our yard da night, well, ya know what happened."

"I didn't until a moment ago. You'll probably think me strange, but it all came back to me as I was watching your yard."

"Don't think ya strange. I knew ya quand tu étais un bébé. When ya was a babe. Wish I could've held on ta ya. Ma lagniappe, that's how I thought of ya, my li'l gift. Where ya been all this time?"

"I was adopted and taken to Chicago. No-one told me about my life here."

"Ya cried and cried dat night, tu étais si triste, weren't nuddin we could do ta shut ya up. Frank finally went off and slept in anudder trailer."

"Was Frank your husband?"

"Anudder in a line o' deadbeats I had kicked ta da curb."

"Can I ask you a question?"

"Sure."

"Did Caitlin ever mention who my Daddy was?"

"Well, I ain't one ta speak ill o' da dead, but yer momma knew a lot o' men."

Kyra swallowed and for some reason felt tears in her eyes. "I'm just finding that out."

Gail finished applying the iodine and gave Kyra a very sad smile. "She weren't always like dat. Time was she could light up a whole party wid her smile, give ya da shirt off her back if'n it would help ya. But she got into too many drugs and well, it didn't end well, as ya know."

"But did she know who my Daddy was?"

"Dere was a man she was tryin' ta get money off dat she told me 'bout. Said he'd been followin' her around since she mentioned ya to him. We didn't pay it much heed, she was on a lot o' drugs. Actin' paranoid da whole time. Den when she was killed, I put da whole mess out o' my mind. Sorry."

"That's okay. You've been really helpful. Listen, it's late and I've taken too much of your time. I should go."

"Ya sure? I could cook ya somethin' if ya like? I ain't got no chicken nuggets or fries, dat was yer favorite meal, but I could rustle somethin' up."

"You've been really kind, but I'm expected somewhere."

"Ya want I should call ya an Uber?"

"That's okay. I've got a friend who'll pick me up."

"In town long?"

"I don't know, think I'm leaving soon."

"Well don't be a stranger. Come see me 'fore ya go."

"Okay."

"Ya promise now?"

"I promise."

Kyra got up from the chair. Gail opened her arms and drew Kyra to her. The hug surprised Kyra and she tentatively returned it. Gail smelled of fresh laundry, cheap perfume and stale cigarettes. She was all skin and bone, but her arms held Kyra with an unexpected strength.

It was all Kyra could do not to cry. Gail hadn't seen her for fifteen years, not since she was a toddler. She was virtually a stranger and she'd taken Kyra into her home and cared for her. A wave of embarrassment overcame Kyra. She didn't deserve this attention.

She stepped out of the embrace. "Thank you again, I should really go."

"Remember what I said. Don't be a stranger!"

"I won't."

Kyra stepped out of the trailer and turned to wave. Gail returned the wave and stood in the door to make sure she got away safely.

Outside, in the warm evening air, Kyra almost regretted leaving. She'd missed the bus Hawkins wanted her to catch. She'd have to lay low and stay out of his way. Tomorrow she'd call her parents and arrange to go home.

Tonight she'd try to come to terms with what she'd learned. Though she suspected that would take the rest of her life.

Kyra was a murderer. She'd killed Caitlin at age two. Only one other person knew this and they were dead.

Kyra had idolized this person for years. Over the last few days, as she was forced to see the world through his eyes, she came to hate him.

Kyra had spent a year searching for her birth parents. Now she'd found them both. Billy-Ray was her biological father. This changed everything she thought she knew about him.

And everything she thought she knew about herself.

CHAPTER 45:

Kyra limped along the road to the main entrance. Her leg muscles sore from keeping up with Billy-Ray.

The lump on her forehead throbbed, pounding out a Morse code of pain.

Kyra found it easier to think about the pain in her body than concentrate on what she'd learned. It was as if someone had taken every part of her life and thrown it up in the air. Now she couldn't recognize the pieces when they landed. Everything she'd ever thought about her life was wrong.

She was a murderer.

No matter how much she tried to distract herself, her mind kept flashing back to the image of Caitlin with the knife sticking out of her eye.

As she approached the entrance, Kyra stopped, leaned against a tree and bowed her head. Billy-Ray was no longer in charge and Kyra couldn't control her gag-reflex. Everything in her stomach came up, including the bile and digestive juices. It lay in a steaming pool at her feet as she wiped her mouth. She felt empty to her core.

Last night, at what might have been the lowest point in her life, fueled by her hatred of Caitlin, Kyra had fantasized about killing her. This had shocked her. She hadn't thought she was capable of such thoughts. But she did have them and her guilt was overwhelming.

This guilt was partly why she'd risked everything to save Caitlin. She'd been ready to give up her parents and her family, to make up for wanting to kill Caitlin. For having that fantasy.

Then she learned it wasn't a fantasy. It was what actually happened.

When questioned about his innocence, Billy-Ray had said he knew who killed Caitlin, but he would never reveal their identity. No one was convinced by this answer. Some had postulated Billy-Ray had an accomplice, but no one had come up with a plausible candidate. There were lots of theories but no real evidence. In the end nobody believed there was anyone for Billy-Ray to protect.

But Kyra knew different. Billy-Ray was protecting *her*. Because *she* was his daughter.

Where had Billy-Ray gone after he left Kyra at the trailer? Did he head back to Caitlin's to cut her up, to make it look like she was killed by a serial killer? Those rough calloused hands had cradled Kyra as he spirited her to safety. The thought of them slicing and dismembering Caitlin was too much to consider.

But Caitlin's corpse had been viciously mutilated. If Billy-Ray hadn't done it, who had?

Caitlin's murder was the one for which Billy-Ray had been caught. There was forensic evidence tying him to the scene. Because this evidence was overwhelming, Billy-Ray had been charged with all the murders.

Kyra knew Billy-Ray wasn't guilty of Caitlin's murder, no matter what the evidence said. What did that mean for the rest of his crimes? Kyra was beginning to suspect there was only one conclusion, but it was too much to take in.

She needed to talk to someone, she needed a friend. Kyra pulled out her phone and texted Delilah:

Kyra:
Can you please come get me? Please, please come get me! I'm at the trailer park

Thankfully, she got a reply in less than a minute.

Delilah:
What in God's name are you doing there?

Kyra:

Please don't ask, just come get me

Five minutes later Delilah pulled up at the entrance and Kyra climbed into her van.

Delilah's eyes were wide with concern. "What happened to your face?"

"I ran into a pole."

"This another of your episodes?"

"Yeah."

"Listen, it might not be any of my business, but I'm worried about you."

"You and me both. There's things I found out today that change everything I thought I knew about my life"

Delilah started the engine and pulled onto the road, her mood seemed to darken. "I've had a similar day. I found something out, something about my family and something about Billy-Ray. You're the only person I know who'll understand how big this is."

"Billy-Ray Johnson didn't commit those murders."

Delilah took her eyes off the road and stared at Kyra, her mouth open in shock.

"How in hell did you know that?"

CHAPTER 46:

An uneasy silence settled. Delilah seemed to be wrestling with troubling news of her own.

Kyra cleared her throat. "Sorry, feel like I dropped the mic."

"No, I dropped the ball, it's on me. I'm stunned. I thought I was the only one who knew. How did you find out?"

"It's a long story and it's kinda complicated, I'm not sure you'll believe me. How did *you* find out?"

"That's also complicated. I'll have to show you when we get back."

Delilah lived on Montanet Avenue. She parked in the drive and led Kyra into a two-story clapboard house, with a wooden porch.

"Hi," a female voice called as they came through the door. Delilah took Kyra through to the back of the house. Everything was clean and tidy, but the furnishings were old, and the wallpaper faded.

They passed a little parlor, lit by a small table lamp. Against the far wall was an altar. Kyra stepped into the room and walked up to the altar. If she'd stopped to think, Kyra would have realized how rude she was being. But she was unable to stifle her curiosity.

In the very center of the altar was a statue of the Virgin Mary carrying a scepter and wearing a red cape and a gold crown. Two female, African carvings stood on either side of the statue, draped with gold material fashioned into skirts. One was topless, with an intricate gold headdress, her arms raised to embrace the sun. The other was seated by a riverside, she wore a tiara and chainmail top.

Behind the statues was a fan of peacock feathers, in front of them were several fans, an ornate mirror, a collection of toy boats, and a small stone vulture. Around the side of the altar were six large candles in long glass jars.

"So where is this girl?" said the female voice.

"She was right behind me a moment ago. Kyra, hey Kyra, come say hello."

Kyra blushed, she'd forgotten her manners. She left the altar and hurried into the kitchen.

Delilah introduced her with a flourish. "Aunt Mimi, this is Kyra, Kyra this is my Aunt Mimi."

A very striking lady, in her late fifties, was drying her hands on a tea towel. She wore jeans and a fashionable, red knitwear top. Her skin was dark brown, and her salt and pepper hair was fashionably styled. She enfolded Kyra's hand in both of hers and kissed her on both cheeks. She smelled of lavender and exotic spices.

Aunt Mimi grinned in amusement. "Oh, child, your face is a picture. You really aren't from these parts, are you? Yes, I'm black and yes, I really am Delilah's aunt. I married her mother's brother, God rest his soul."

Kyra felt a fierce, red heat in her cheeks. She wasn't aware she'd shown any surprise. "Oh, no, I wasn't, I mean I'm not, I just didn't... um, it's very nice to meet you."

Aunt Mimi laughed and cast a wry eye over Kyra. "What you do to your face, girl?"

"I ran into a post. I wasn't looking."

"I can see that. You're going to have an awful bruise if I don't see to that. Sit here." She pointed to a chair. Kyra sat and Mimi headed into the parlor and returned with a jar and a roll of Band-Aids.

The jar contained an unguent that Mimi rubbed on Kyra's forehead after she removed her current Band-Aid and washed off the iodine. The pressure of Mimi's fingers on the bruise made her wince, but after a couple of seconds it tingled. Mimi covered the bump with another Band-Aid.

"What's in the jar?" Kyra said.

"Don't ask, but in a couple of days there'll be no bruise and no pain."

"Really?"

"Never fails."

"You should take a look at her ankle too, Aunt Mimi," Delilah said.

"What's wrong with her ankle?"

"She got hit by a car."

"Girl, are you accident prone, or just plain dumb?"

Kyra hung her head. "These days, I'm not so sure."

Mimi took gentle hold of Kyra's chin and raised her head examining her like a medical professional. "You got a presence hanging around you, comes from something you did in your past."

Kyra's mouth fell open.

"Did I startle you?"

"No, it's just that someone else told me that in New Orleans, but I didn't realize what she meant."

Mimi raised her eyebrows. "Well, the woman knew what she was talking about. Even if she was from New Orleans."

Delilah gave a curt laugh. "Not my aunt's favorite place."

"Is it bad? The presence, I mean."

"It don't mean you no harm, but I think you already know that. It may even try to help you. It's connected to an old conjuring. I'ma think on this. Meantime, I've a pot of green herb gumbo on the stove."

"I'm vegetarian."

"I know. There's not a bit of meat or fish in it. I've been fully briefed. Delilah wanted to make sure everything was just so."

Kyra's stomach growled. Mimi and Delilah raised their eyebrows in unison. She'd forgotten how hungry she was.

The gumbo was thick, rich, and spicy. Her whole body cried with joy at the vegetables she'd been missing. "This is the best thing I've eaten in weeks."

"Would you like another bowl?"

"I wouldn't normally, but this is too good."

Aunt Mimi got up and ladled out another bowl for Kyra.

Delilah dabbed at her lips with a napkin. "Is there any of that Boudin left?"

"It's in the icebox."

"Stupid question, but what's a Boo-dan? Is that how you say it?"

Delilah pulled a Tupperware container from the icebox. "Not far off. It's a spicy sausage."

"Oh, I see, you can't have one meal without meat."

"You know me."

"This sausage is on your town sign isn't it?"

"Yeah, the world's biggest Boudin. That was the Mayor's idea. She wanted to do something to rival Abbeville with the world's biggest omelet. The town comes together in the Church Square every November. Aunt Mimi helps organize."

Mimi frowned. "Don't talk with your mouth full and come eat at the table." She smiled at Kyra. "It raises a lot of money for charity."

"Thank you for the meal and for letting me stay."

"You're welcome, child. It's nice to have company. It's only me and Delilah with my husband gone."

"I'm sorry for your loss."

"Not as sorry as I am. He served this community for eighteen years."

"He was a cop, wasn't he? I'm sorry, I mean a police officer?"

"He was Deputy Sheriff and look where it got him, gunned down like a dog by a junkie."

Delilah wiped her mouth with a napkin. "Aaron wasn't a junkie, Aunt Mimi, he was one of Uncle Dan's oldest friends. They were school friends, played football together."

"They found drugs in his system. His family is dead to me. I'm only glad your uncle killed him before he died."

"We all miss him, Aunt Mimi."

"No-one more than me. I light a candle to his name every day."

Kyra tried to change the subject. "Do you light it on the altar? I couldn't help noticing it when I came in. It's sort of unique."

"Not around these parts. We keep the old ways in Yeuxville, always have done. Sundays, I make my peace with the Lord, the other six I keep counsel with the spirits."

"Spirits?"

"Spirits, Saints, Orisha, Loa, I honor 'em all. If you look after them, they'll look after you."

"People talk about keeping the old ways in Yeuxville, but I have no idea what that means."

Delilah took their bowls to the sink. "A lot of early settlers were Haitian refugees, fleeing the revolution. They were supposedly Catholic, but they brought other religious beliefs with them, which go back to Africa. People refer to these practices as 'the old ways' or the 'old faiths.' It's been part of our lives for as long as we can remember. I guess most people would say it's Santería or Voodoo."

Mimi made a dismissive gesture. "Voodoo? That's a stupid name for the tourists in New Orleans. What we do in Yeuxville is authentic."

"They're all authentic, Aunt Mimi. What we do here in Yeuxville is no less syncretistic."

Kyra looked puzzled. "No less what?"

"Syncretistic, it's a religion made up of other religions. Like Voodoo is a mixture of Catholicism and African practices, so is Santeria. What we've got in Yeuxville is no different. It's a mixture of Christianity and Yoruba and Lucumí beliefs, even some stuff from Cuba."

"You'll have to excuse my niece. She likes to remind everyone how clever she is, cos she ain't gone to college yet."

"Aunt Mimi!"

Mimi rubbed her arm affectionately, "It's true, hon, and we don't love you any the less for it."

Kyra laughed, "My Dad's the same. Does everyone in Yeuxville follow the old ways?"

"It gets a little less every year. Public meetings have been on the down low for the last decade."

"Is that since the Bayou Massacre?"

A look of warning crossed Delilah's face. "Aunt Mimi's kinda sensitive about that."

Mimi looked solemn, "I lost my best friend that day. We don't mention it in this house."

Kyra put a hand to her mouth. "I'm so sorry, I didn't realize."

Mimi waved Kyra's apologies aside. "You weren't to know, child. Now, Delilah, why don't you show Kyra to her room."

Kyra got up from the table. "Do you need a hand with the dishes?"

"No, that's all right. You go on up."

Mimi made Kyra feel so welcome. A knot of tension unwound between her shoulder blades. For the first time since she'd come to Yeuxville, she didn't feel angry, panicked or depressed.

What Delilah was about to tell her would change all that.

CHAPTER 47:

Delilah showed Kyra to the back bedroom where she was staying. It was sparsely furnished with a bed, a dresser, and a single watercolor hanging on the wall.

"There's no storage, I'm afraid. The wardrobe's full, so you'll be living out of your bag. Hope that's okay? Where is your backpack, by the way?"

"I left it with a friend."

"Would that be the Sheriff's daughter, lady who paints glass eyes?"

"Béatrice, yeah. She's really nice, you'd like her."

"You must introduce us. Give me a few minutes to freshen up then come through to my room. It's the second door on your left."

Kyra lay down on the single bed and stared up at the cracks in the plaster ceiling. She touched the Band-Aid on her forehead. It felt like the bump had gone down and the throbbing had stopped. Maybe there was something to the 'old ways' after all. The whole of her forehead had gone numb.

It wasn't just her forehead. Kyra was emotionally numb from everything she'd seen and learned today. It was too much to take in and too much to process. Her mind and emotions had just shut down.

She didn't want to dwell too much on it. She figured Delilah would be done 'freshening up', so she went and knocked on her door.

"Just a minute," Delilah called. Kyra scratched the back of her neck, awkward about standing by herself on a landing in a house she didn't know.

"Come in."

Delilah was sitting at a vanity table, fixing her mascara, the stubble gone and her face fully made up. She'd ditched her jeans and hoodie in favor of a black, sequined top and a short, black skirt. She looked stunning as ever.

Kyra grinned. "This how you spend your evenings?"

Delilah shrugged, her voice had risen a register. "Sometimes I'm so wiped I just sleep. What do you think of my room?"

It was three times the size of the back bedroom. The decor was 19th Century bordello – plush carpeting, velvet curtains, chaise lounge, a double bed with voile canopy. There was a long rack of gowns on display, a tailor's dummy, and a small table with a sewing machine. Next to the sewing machine was a small desk with a laptop and a really old Apple Mac on it.

"It's stunning." She flicked through the gowns on the rack. "Did you make these yourself?"

"Some, the rest I bought. I even inherited, one or two."

"Really?"

"My momma was pretty much the same size."

"Lucky you, they're gorgeous."

"When I was younger I used to fantasize about having my own house, way out in the bayou away from prying eyes. I was going to fill it with dresses and mirrors and when I got home I would spend all night wearing the dresses and looking at myself and no one would ever know or judge me."

"Not everyone will judge."

"I know, I think I've always been my biggest judge. Anyway, that's not what I brought you in here to talk about."

"We're back to serial killers."

"One of your favorite topics, no?"

Kyra sighed, "I'm not so sure anymore. It's not going to be gruesome is it?"

"Says the girl who watched *Terrifier* for her twelfth birthday. It's not gruesome. It's more a mystery."

Delilah reached under her bed and pulled out a shoe box filled with floppy disks. There was a note in longhand on top of them.

Aaron, if anything happens to me, you know what to do with these.

Dan

Kyra gasped. "Wait, isn't Aaron...?"

"The guy who shot my Uncle Dan—allegedly."

"I don't understand."

"Neither did I. It's always been a mystery. Aaron was my uncle's oldest friend, and you know who his niece was?"

"No."

"Elizabeth Boudreaux."

"Billy-Ray's fourth victim, weird."

"I know, right?"

"Where'd you get these?"

"Aaron's widow, Sonya approached me in the Piggly Wiggly. I was surprised, our families aren't on good terms. She found them when she was cleaning out the garage. She said I could have them."

"They're ancient."

"I know, I nearly threw them away, but something stopped me. A couple weeks ago, I dug my uncle's old computer out of the attic to see what was on them."

"This old thing," Kyra pointed to the computer on Delilah's desk. "What's it powered by, coal?"

"My uncle wasn't a technical guy, he bought one computer his whole life and he never saw the need to upgrade."

"Does it even work?"

Delilah pressed a button on the computer and another on the monitor. "The mainframe does, but the monitor was dead. It took me a while to track down another one. You remember I had to cancel our first tour?"

"Yeah."

Delilah tapped the monitor. "This is why. Had to drive all the way to New Iberia."

"So, what's on the disks?"

"Here's where it gets interesting. I was expecting family photos, but it was police reports from a case my uncle was working."

"Which case?"

"Which case do you think?"

"Not Billy-Ray's murders?"

"One and the same."

"No way."

"Way."

Kyra breathed deeply. Today had thrown up so many questions. Had Delilah just found some answers?

"Did you learn anything?"

After what seemed like an age the computer booted up. Delilah stuck one of the disks in a slot in the front. "As well as the reports there were some other files."

"What was on them?"

"A journal."

"A journal?"

An icon appeared on the screen and Delilah clicked it. "In his last few weeks, my uncle had misgivings about the case, things he couldn't tell his colleagues, so he wrote them down."

"What sort of misgivings?"

"He thought they'd got the wrong guy. Most of the evidence was circumstantial, Billy-Ray even had an alibi for the night Frances Donovan was killed, but it was never mentioned in court. Not even the prosecution knew."

"How come?"

"It was suppressed, along with other evidence."

"Suppressed?"

Delilah paused and looked Kyra right in the eyes. "Yes, by the guy my uncle thought was the real killer. A guy who wanted revenge for his wife's death."

"Who?"

"My uncle's boss—Sheriff Hawkins."

CHAPTER 48:

"You're kidding."

"Nope."

"Your uncle thought Hawkins was the killer?"

"Crazy, right? I've been freaking out the past couple days. I didn't want to believe it. I was sure my uncle was mistaken. But I've been over the reports. I can't find a flaw in my uncle's thinking. I know it was eating him up. It's in his journals. It was killing him."

"What put him on to Hawkins?"

"Little things, at first, but they added up."

"Such as...?" "The reports that were filed. There were discrepancies. The first responders reported different things from the primary officers. These weren't small discrepancies, like you'd imagine, there were big differences."

Kyra pulled up a chair and sat down, staring at the flashing cursor on the ancient monitor screen. "Didn't anyone notice?"

"Yeah, my uncle. But he wasn't the only one. Hawkins was always changing the timeline of events and bullying his team to get on board, he even fired a guy who wouldn't play ball."

"Sounds like Hawkins."

Delilah shook her head. "My uncle thought he was a great boss. He'd go to bat for his whole team, that's why they were so loyal."

"Except the guy he fired."

"That's what rattled my uncle, it was out of character. But it got worse. He finds Hawkins tampering with evidence."

"For real?"

"Yeah."

Delilah scrolled down the screen. "You remember the girl scout who called at Alison Comeaux's condo?"

"The super tall one?"

"That's right. There were eyewitnesses but none made it into the final report."

"How come it was in Becky Eve Hirst's book?"

"She spoke to a local reporter, she'd been told to keep it out of the paper, guess who by?"

"Our friendly, neighborhood Sheriff?"

"Bingo. Did you know Billy-Ray had two more alibis?"

"Other than for Frances Donovan?"

Delilah nodded.

"Why didn't the Sheriff's department check them out?"

"Hawkins wouldn't let them. He lied to the investigators on the task force, and he lied to the courts."

Kyra shook her head in disbelief. "This doesn't sound good."

Delilah closed the file and ejected the disk. Then she slotted another one into the computer. The screen flickered and the machine gave a weird hum. "This is why my uncle started to document everything. You know what got him really suspicious?"

"No."

"Hawkins was first to every crime scene, but he wasn't on record as the first responder. It was often hours before he called it in. Why take so long? What was he doing all that time?"

"Tampering with evidence?"

"Or covering his tracks."

Delilah clicked out of one file and opened another. "This is a testimony Uncle Dan took from a rookie. He was troubled and needed advice. His conscience was playing up after he helped Hawkins take evidence from a crime scene and destroy it."

"What kind of evidence?"

"Two knives, covered in blood, and a bloodstained uniform shirt. The shirt was later burned."

"Oh my God."

"I know."

"What happened to the rookie?"

"Blew his brains out."

"Couldn't handle the guilt?"

"I don't know, but my uncle got paranoid, kept writing about something happening to him. Then he puts all these disks in a shoe box and gives them to his oldest friend. A few days later, that friend dies in a shoot-out with my uncle. It doesn't make sense."

"Unless," Kyra stopped mid-sentence. Delilah was hugging herself, rocking back and forth, staring at the flickering monitor.

Eventually she met Kyra's gaze. "Go on."

"Unless your uncle's friend didn't kill him, and the rookie didn't commit suicide."

Delilah threw her hands up. "You see why I've been freaking out?"

"It's a lot to take in."

"No, Kyra, you don't understand, my whole life I've been brought up to respect the police. To believe in the Thin-Blue-Line. It's the only thing that stands between us and total anarchy. Then I find out a man I've looked up to my whole life, could do something like this, could be..."

"A serial killer?"

"It doesn't bear thinking. Don't get me wrong, I know from dirty cops, but this is something else."

"Why would Hawkins do this? What's his motive? You said something about his wife. Was she murdered?"

"Not exactly, it goes back about twenty years, to the Bayou Massacre, one of our worst tragedies."

CHAPTER 49:

"Doesn't Mandy Sandiford mention that in her book? Some satanic mass where a bunch of people got killed."

Delilah rolled her eyes. "Mandy Sandiford doesn't know what she's talking about."

"So, what did happen?"

Delilah held up a finger to say, *wait* and reached for her laptop. "That's complicated, it happened twenty years ago, but we have to go back to the turn of the last century to understand it."

Kyra grabbed a pillow. "Uh oh, sounds like a long story."

Delilah threw her a box of tissues. "It's also a sob story, I'll try not to put you to sleep."

"I'm all ears."

"There have been ceremonial gatherings since Yeuxville became a town, but things really took off with the arrival of Letitia Papillon"

"Who?"

"Letitia was a disciple of Marie Laveau. She fled New Orleans to avoid jail."

"Marie Laveau, the queen of New Orleans Voodoo?"

"The very same, she trained Letitia. Letitia took over the ceremonies here in Yeuxville. It was secret at first, mainly local black folk, but after a while word got out and white folk began to come. Sometimes they'd watch, sometimes join in. In time, half the town was out there. It became a local tradition. Letitia set up a shop in the Church Square, right where we had coffee, most of the town would come see her."

Kyra inclined her head. "What for?"

"To cure an illness, win back a lover, beat a jury or fix a vote in the State Congress. Like Marie, Letitia had strange powers and she died a wealthy woman. She founded a dynasty that lasted to the present day, the title of Mambo was passed from mother to daughter."

"What's a Mambo?"

"It's like a head priestess."

"Okay, but what does this have to do with Hawkins' wife?"

"Céleste Hawkins was the great, great granddaughter of Letitia Papillon. She was killed leading a ceremony out in the Bayou. It was a local scandal, made all the papers."

"And this is the Bayou Massacre, right?"

"Right."

Delilah googled: *Bayou Massacre Yeuxville*. Kyra scooched round so she could see. The screen showed a bunch of results from *The Times Picayune*, *The Daily Advertiser*, and *Teche News*.

Delilah clicked on the results as she was talking. "Massacre is a misleading term. It was a tragic accident. Five people burned to death, including Céleste."

"Was it on purpose? Is that why Hawkins wanted revenge?"

"It's more complicated. There was a community intervention, led by a preacher from Lafayette."

"What's a community intervention?"

Delilah brought up a page from *The Daily Advertiser* showing a picture of Reverend Lee, a short man, with a red face, thick neck, and no hair.

"It's where the community comes together to stop something they don't like. Reagan had just left office, and a lot of people were worried about the nation's moral welfare, and not without reason."

"You sure do love that Reagan."

"Best President we ever had."

"What about Obama?"

"What is it with you northerners and Obama?"

"But with your aunt and everything, surely you'd..."

"Vote for Obama? In spite of my principles? One, I wasn't old enough to vote, and two, isn't that a bit racist?"

"Voting for Obama is racist?"

"No, but assuming I would because my aunt's African American is."

Kyra sighed and put her hands up to her temples. "I think we're getting off topic. You were telling me about this Reverend Lee guy."

Delilah took a deep breath. "So, Reverend Lee was looking to expand his ministry. He hears Yeuxville's holding what he thinks are satanic rites and he decides to get the whole town to put a stop to it."

"Did it work?"

"He came and spoke in the local church, addressed civic groups, held meetings, and his flock handed out leaflets on street corners. Folks were polite, they smiled and shook his hand and then went about their business. He was Evangelist, we were Catholic. He tried to rally the town for a demonstration, march into the swamp, confront the devil worshippers and put a stop to it. You know how many people he got?"

"How many?"

"Four. The Reverend marched out into the Bayou and got lost. They had to go find the Reverend's party so they didn't hurt themselves. The ceremony was in a big tent, like a revival show. No one knows what happened next, but there was an argument and a fire broke out. Five people were killed, Céleste and the four people the Reverend brought."

"That is tragic, but how does it link to the murders."

Delilah clicked on a page from the *Times Picayune*, it had a photo of Céleste next to the other four victims. Delilah pointed to each of them.

"Ethel Thompson was Mary Jo Bernard's grandmother, Loretta Donovan was Frances Donovan's mother, Nicole Patterson was Alison Comeaux's aunt, and Whitney Boudreaux was Elizabeth Boudreaux's cousin. Apart from Céleste, all four victims were related to the people Billy-Ray's supposed to have killed."

"And your uncle thought Hawkins killed them in retaliation?"

"My uncle thought he blamed their families. If those people hadn't been out there, it wouldn't have happened."

"Why did Céleste marry Hawkins in the first place?"

"He's from a prominent Catholic family. His brother's the town priest. They hate the Papillons. Case of opposites attract, real Romeo and Juliet stuff."

"But the murders took place a long time after the massacre, why wait?"

"He didn't have the power to cover it up back then. It had been eating at him for years and he probably just snapped. When the murders drew national attention he needed a patsy. Billy-Ray was the perfect candidate."

Kyra folded her arms. "Why choose Billy-Ray?"

Delilah sighed, as if Kyra wasn't keeping up. "Because Billy-Ray killed Caitlin Robichaud at just the right time to frame him for the other murders."

"Billy-Ray didn't kill Caitlin."

Delilah looked puzzled. "What do you mean, there was all that evidence against him."

"You said yourself that Hawkins suppressed evidence that should have cleared him."

"Of the other murders, not that one. There were forensics, there was DNA. He was definitely at the crime."

"He was at the crime, but he didn't commit the murder."

"Then who did?"

"I did."

"What!?"

"It was an accident. I was two years old, and I killed my own mother."

CHAPTER 50:

Delilah put her laptop down and put her hands on Kyra's, sadness sat in lines across her forehead.

"Kyra, you can't take this on yourself. You're not responsible for your mother's death. Billy-Ray is."

"No, I saw it, I saw everything."

"What are you saying?"

What *was* she saying? Kyra's throat tightened and she couldn't get her words out. Didn't want to get them out, because that would mean facing how immense her crimes were. But she couldn't carry this burden any longer, or it would kill her.

It had been killing her for fifteen years and she'd never known why she blamed herself for everything. Why she was angry all the time, angry at everyone but mostly herself. Why she took the naked end of a cigarette to the tender flesh of her thighs.

She was a murderer like the men and women she idolized. She'd killed before she was even in kindergarten. Driven by a mother who terrorized, dominated and physically abused her.

When her tiny foot had kicked the knife handle, she'd wanted Caitlin to die. And that was why she couldn't forgive herself.

How could she tell this to Delilah? What would she think?

Kyra opened her mouth to say something, anything, and a huge, wet sob broke from her lips. Tears clouded her eyes, the levee had broken and nothing would stop the deluge.

Delilah dropped the box of tissues back in her lap and put her arms around Kyra, stroking her hair. "It's okay, baby girl, it's okay. Get it all out."

She buried her face in Delilah's shoulder and let out sob after wracking sob. After a few minutes, Kyra was aware of the mess she was making of Delilah's top.

She took several deep breaths and took control of herself, blowing her nose with a tissue and dabbing at Delilah's shoulder with another.

Delilah took another tissue and wiped it herself. "So, what's really up?"

Kyra breathed in and let out a sigh. "You know these episodes I told you about?"

"Yes."

Delilah inclined her head, her face a picture of sympathy. How could Kyra explain this so she didn't sound delusional? She had to be selective with the details.

"I've been recovering memories from my childhood, my early childhood back when I lived here. Something about being in Yeuxville must have triggered them."

"What sort of memories?"

"Caitlin was a horrible person. She took drugs, she slept around, she cheated with other people's boyfriends, and she..."

Kyra saw Caitlin's face illuminated by the red glow of a cigarette end. She thought of the sting and the sizzle of a tiny thigh and she couldn't breathe.

Delilah took her hand. "Take your time."

"She abused me. She shouted, threatened and hit me. She used to take a lit cigarette to the inside of my thighs, where my diaper would hide it. Fifteen years ago today, she came at me with a kitchen knife. I was on my back, I was scared, and I was kicking. My foot caught the knife's handle and it went straight into Caitlin's eye. That's how she died."

"Why was Billy-Ray's DNA all over the apartment?"

"He was stalking Caitlin. She was trying to shake him down but, if I'm honest, I think he was concerned about me."

"Billy-Ray was concerned about you?"

"Yes, he was, when he saw what Caitlin was doing."

"Kyra, I'm sorry, but I'm not following any of this. Why was Caitlin shaking Billy-Ray down? Why was he concerned about what Caitlin was doing?"

"That's why I went to the trailer park. I spoke to a woman there who used to look after me. I had my suspicions, but she confirmed Billy-Ray Johnson was my biological father."

"She told you Billy-Ray was your father?"

"Not in as many words, I kind of inferred it. But the facts add up."

Delilah put her hands to her face, her eyes wide, her mouth open in shock. "Oh my days, Kyra I had no idea. Here's me obsessing over my issues, and you're wrestling with all this. Billy-Ray was your daddy? Are you sure?"

"As anyone can be."

Delilah put her arms around Kyra again and she hugged her back. They clung to one another. Two damaged souls whose worlds had been torn apart by lies and family secrets. Who'd just discovered their lives were built on a foundation of murder and mistruth. The blindfolds were off, the truth had been revealed, and everything they thought they knew about themselves had been overturned.

It was a lonely place, cut off from the pasts they had and the people they loved. Who could they tell? Who would understand? All they had was each other.

Delilah kissed the top of Kyra's head. "I can't imagine what you're going through, but you know I'm here for you, right?"

"I know. So, what are you going to do with your uncle's journal?"

"I wish I knew. I want to do the right thing, but I don't want to hurt the people I love. Do you know what it's like to make a decision like that? Do you know how it weighs on you?" Kyra laughed a cold, mirthless laugh. "More than you might ever realize."

CHAPTER 51:

Kyra was woken next morning by a gentle tap on her door.

She rubbed the sleep from her eyes. "Come in."

Delilah opened the door a crack. "Are you decent?"

"Like you'd care."

"Kyra Hughes, this is the south, we have manners down here."

"Only cos everyone's armed?"

"Got that right. Breakfast in ten, we'd love for you to join us."

"I'll be right down."

Kyra had slept deeply for the first time since coming to Yeuxville. She and Delilah had cried a bit more, made their excuses and gone to bed. The emotional release had exhausted Kyra and she'd crashed the minute her head hit the pillow.

The kitchen was filled with delicious smells.

"Mmm, pancakes."

Delilah was at the stove, with no make-up, wearing a t-shirt, jeans and a floral apron. "Hope you like blueberries."

"Love them."

Mimi patted the chair next to her. "Come and have a seat. Would you like some orange juice?"

Kyra stifled a yawn and surprised herself by asking. "Do you have any coffee?"

"Got a pot on the stove, be done in a minute."

Delilah put a plate of pancakes in front of Kyra and poured her some coffee. Funny how quickly she'd gotten used to drinking it.

"Didn't know you cooked."

Mimi laughed. "How's she gonna get himself a man if she can't?"

Delilah put a hand under her chin. "With these looks you even have to ask?"

The pancakes fed Kyra's soul as much as her stomach. They were moist and fluffy with a crisp brown crust. The blueberries exploded in her mouth, sweet and sour, every mouthful swam in maple syrup and salted butter. Kyra didn't look up till they were gone.

"I think I'll put on ten pounds if I stay any longer."

Mimi raised an eyebrow. "Like that would be a bad thing. So, I heard lots of tears last night, should I be concerned?"

Delilah took the pan off the stove and put her hand on her hip. "Aunt Mimi, were you eavesdropping?"

"Why no, you girls were making *so* much noise they could hear you in the next parish. I just want to know if everything's all right?"

Delilah rinsed her hands and came to sit at the table. "Now, don't be mad, but last week Sonya stopped me in the Piggly Wiggly."

"What did that woman want?"

"She wanted to give me something."

"I hope you told her where to go."

Delilah held out her palms and took a deep breath. "No, I went round to her house."

"You did *what*?!" Mimi shot to her feet, sending her chair reeling back with such force it broke one of the back spindles as it bounced off the floor.

Delilah got to her feet and held out her hands for calm. "I know how you feel about that family, but..."

"You have no business taking anything off that woman. It was her kin that killed your uncle."

"No, Aunt Mimi, I don't think it was."

"What lies has she been telling you?"

"She hasn't been telling me anything, Uncle Dan has."

Mimi stood and glowered at Delilah, breathing heavily through her nose for an uncomfortably long time. "What do you mean?"

"Uncle Dan gave Aaron some old floppy disks right before he died."

"Before Aaron killed him?"

"Now I've read those disks, I don't think Aaron killed Uncle Dan."

"And how did you read these disks?"

"On Uncle Dan's old computer."

"So that's what you were doing in the attic."

Delilah sighed and placed her hands on the table. "I got Uncle Dan's computer down so I could read them. He gave them to Aaron because he was afraid for his life and I think he was right to be. I think you'll agree when you read what's on those disks."

Mimi crossed her arms and tapped her foot. After a long pause she finally spoke. "I think you should show me what's on those disks."

CHAPTER 52:

Delilah took them up to her room and booted up the old computer. She showed Mimi what she'd shown Kyra last night.

Mimi took much longer to read her late husband's journal and when she was done there were tears streaming down her cheeks. "Times like this, wish I'd never quit smoking."

Delilah took her aunt's hand. "So, I did a bit of research, and I found the name of the guy to speak to at Internal Affairs. He's from the State Police in Baton Rouge. I'll have to give an affidavit against Sheriff Hawkins, along with a print-out of Uncle Dan's journal and the other evidence."

Kyra felt a cool foreboding. "You're going to contact the State Police?"

"It's what my uncle would've wanted, and I have to honor that. He died compiling this dossier, and if he's going to get justice, I have to get it to the right people."

"Is that wise? Sheriff Hawkins isn't a man you want to cross. You told me that."

Mimi pursed her lips. "I'm inclined to agree."

"Aunt Mimi, I've made up my mind. You and Uncle Dan brought me up to do the right thing, and this is the right thing to do. I'm not foolish, I'm going to pick my moment. He's up for re-election next month."

"With nobody challenging him. So there's your leverage shot."

"He'll be distracted, by the time he's elected, the investigation will be underway."

"He don't have to campaign, he's a shoo in. All you'll do is bring the town down on you for blackening the sheriff's name. And what if they start digging into your secrets?"

"Don't you think I've thought about that? But he might have killed Uncle Dan, and I can't let him get by with that."

Mimi fixed Delilah with a stare so hard it could've stripped paint. Kyra was glad she wasn't on the receiving end. As intimidated as she was by her aunt, Delilah stared right back. Mimi and Delilah were impossibly conflicted. Each trying to do the right thing when the right thing was as apparent as a white sheet in a snow storm.

Kyra cleared her throat and tried to change the subject. "Is it true you elect every official down here, not just your politicians?"

Mimi's face was careworn, but in her eyes Kyra saw she was relieved to be talking about something else. "We'd elect our crossing guards if they stood."

Delilah was also relieved to change the topic. "We hold elections for most posts in Louisiana. We're one of only five states to hold state elections in off years. We like to separate our state politics from national politics."

Mimi shot Kyra a knowing look, as if to say – *doesn't she likes the sound of her own voice?* "Politics is our favorite sport. It's entertainment in Louisiana."

"So, why do you have so much corruption?"

Delilah's tone was tart and acidic. "You don't have corrupt politicians in Chicago? Must be your lack of elections."

Mimi raised her eyebrows. "My father used to say, a politician is like a girl you take home from a bar. The first hour is great, but when you wake up, your wallet's gone and there's no number to call."

"What makes Sheriff Hawkins so popular?" Kyra was wary of returning to Hawkins, but she was curious.

Delilah was more dispassionate than Kyra might have imagined. "It's a lot of things. He's good with people. He makes folk feel safe. His brother's the priest, but he married the Mambo, so he can unite our two religious factions, no one else can, not even the mayor."

Mimi elaborated. "People like his story. He's a bad boy made good. His older brother was the good son, he was the black sheep. He dropped out of high school while his brother went to college. His brother joined the seminary, he joined a biker gang and landed in trouble."

"What kind of trouble?"

"It was hushed up. His family pulled strings and he went to Iraq to fight for his country. When he got back, his family pulled more strings and he joined the Sheriff's Department. Took to that better than anyone guessed. Then he met Céleste. She told me she couldn't stand him, but we knew different. Sparks flew between 'em. He stood for Sheriff soon after they married. It was a stormy marriage. They fought all the time, and she nearly left him, but there was passion there. He was never the same after she died. Something hardened in him, went bitter. He's been that way ever since."

Silence descended on Delilah's bedroom. Mimi tapped her chin, eyes toward the ceiling, weighing something up. Presently she spoke. "If you have to go ahead with this, I want you to be careful. There's no telling how dangerous Hawkins is. I couldn't stand to lose you too. You're all I have left."

Delilah hugged her aunt. "You won't lose me, I'll be careful, I promise."

Mimi hugged Delilah back and there were more tears. Kyra scratched the back of her neck, an awkward interloper. She stood in the doorway as Mimi and Delilah hugged and wept.

"Listen, guys, I'm going to head out. I need to catch a bus home and call my parents."

Mimi and Delilah broke their clinch.

Mimi nodded, a touch of remonstrance in her voice. "That's a good idea. I should think they'll be worried sick."

Delilah waved her over. "I'll give you a lift to the Piggly Wiggly, but first, come on over here."

Kyra came sheepishly over and joined the hug. When they were done she said, "I've got to pick up my backpack from Béatrice before I go. If you're going to contact Internal Affairs, I think it only fair to warn her."

Delilah frowned. "Are you sure?"

"Yeah, no, she'll be fine, honestly she's really cool."

"But she's Hawkins' daughter, won't she say something?"

"No, no, she's not like that, we can trust her. She's been good to me. She helped me plenty. I wasn't exactly straight with the police about who I was. Béatrice came and got me, she could've told on me but she didn't. She doesn't get along with her daddy."

"Kyra Hughes, you lied about who you are to the police?"

"I know, I know, I'm not proud. I've been making bad choices. But that's not the point. The point is, we can rely on Béatrice. She'll keep your secret, she's proved that."

Mimi made a pained face. "I don't know. I have a bad feeling."

"It'll be fine, really."

"If you say so. Her and her daddy ain't been close since he put her in that institution. So, there's that."

"Exactly, we can trust her. Plus it's only fair. This is going to affect her life. If someone was about to expose my Dad for something I'd want to know, no matter how I felt. How am I supposed to look her in the face, knowing all this, without saying something? What sort of person would I be if I didn't? You're trying to do the right thing here and so am I."

Mimi stood and stretched her back. "Everybody's trying to do the right thing. And yet I got a feeling it's going to turn out wrong."

Delilah smiled indulgently. "Aunt Mimi, not another of your 'feelings'."

"Don't mock me, child. I had the same feeling the day your uncle was shot. I knew something bad was coming but he wouldn't listen."

Mimi looked Kyra straight in the eye. "And I know something else bad is coming. But *you* won't listen."

CHAPTER 53:

As soon as Kyra stepped out of Delilah's van it started to rain. Tiny drops hissed on the asphalt, becoming steam as Kyra crossed the parking lot.

The drops got larger as she ran to the industrial park. By the time she reached the first set of units the downpour was so heavy it felt like swimming upstream. The rain fell in a thick curtain, as if the Mississippi had burst its banks and taken to the air around her.

The water was almost as warm as the air. A fetid deluge that overwhelmed the gutters, defied the drains and threatened to wash the whole town away. When Kyra reached Béatrice's unit, the rain had become a steady downpour, dampening the mid-morning heat.

Her sweatshirt and jeans clung to her skin like a toddler to their mother's legs. She couldn't believe Yeuxville could muster such Biblical weather. For the first time, Kyra was glad to be leaving.

She raised her fist to knock on Béatrice's door and let it fall. If she stayed a minute longer Kyra was certain she'd perish, inhale enough water to drown. Even still, something stayed her hand, stopped her from coming in out of the rain. It felt like panic and regret. How could she tell Béatrice what she knew? What would Béatrice think?

Her legs shook. Her eyes blinked from the rain. Maybe she wouldn't tell Béatrice, maybe she'd just grab her backpack and wait till the rain got light enough to leave. She raised her hand again but left it hanging within inches of the door.

Without any warning the door swung open. Béatrice dropped the bag of trash she was carrying and put her hand to her chest in surprise.

"Kyra! What are you doing out there? Get in here, you're soaked."

She grabbed Kyra's shoulder, pulled her into the unit. A puddle began to form at Kyra's feet.

Béatrice shook her head in disbelief. "What were you doing out there?"

"I came for my backpack, I'm leaving today."

"You should have waited for the rain to stop."

"I know, but I have a bus to catch."

"C'mon in back, we'll get you a towel and some hot tea."

Kyra followed Béatrice to the back of the unit where she grabbed a hand towel from the bathroom. Béatrice draped the towel over Kyra's head and tousled her hair. Kyra's head rocked with Béatrice's hands, which slipped gently down her neck to her shoulders and then her upper arms. The sensation was very intimate. A yearning ache rose in Kyra's chest and she had to stop her thoughts from wandering where they shouldn't.

Béatrice was at least ten years older. Kyra was just some dumb kid to her, a stray kitten she had to keep saving. But her smile said different.

"Don't we look a sight?"

Kyra felt the blood flush her damp cheeks, afraid they'd give off steam.

Béatrice chuckled. "I'll go get that tea."

Béatrice boiled water while Kyra tried to dry herself with the damp towel. A couple minutes later Béatrice handed her a cup of steaming, rose colored liquid. It had a sweet and floral aroma. Kyra took a sip. It was scalding, but it tasted good.

Béatrice pointed to the corner where Kyra left her backpack. "Got your things right here. Didn't even peek at your diary."

"I don't keep a diary."

"I know, wrote one for you, even put a list of crushes in the back."

Kyra tried to smile. Why did Béatrice have to be so lovely? She was even being flirtatious, wasn't she? No, not really. Well, maybe a little.

That just made things worse. How do you tell someone *their* dad's a serial killer and *your* best friend's about to turn them in? You can't just drop that into the conversation.

Maybe she should just grab her things and go. Delilah was right, she shouldn't get in the middle of this.

No, that wouldn't be right. Béatrice had been good to her. Kyra owed her this.

Béatrice put a hand on Kyra's shoulder, concern wrinkled the corners of her eyes. "Is everything all right?"

"No."

"Want to talk about it?"

"I don't know where to start."

"Beginning's a pretty good place."

Kyra took a deep breath, surprised at how ragged it was. "You remember I told you my birth mother was Caitlin Robichaud, the woman who was murdered fifteen years ago?"

"Yeah."

"Well, I found out yesterday who my real father is."

"And you're not happy?"

"No, well, I don't know."

"Anyone I might know? It's small town."

"Oh, you know him, the whole state knows him. It's Billy-Ray Johnson."

"The serial killer?"

"Yeah, only he didn't kill those women, not even my... not even Caitlin."

Béatrice frowned. "Why'd you say that?"

"Because *I* killed Caitlin. I didn't mean to, it was an accident, I was only two years old, but I did. It was me."

Oh God, were there tears in her eyes? Kyra thought she was all cried out. She put a hand to her mouth and blinked rapidly.

Béatrice reached out and squeezed Kyra's arm. It was a comforting gesture, without the frisson Kyra felt earlier.

"I'm going to go out on a limb here, okay?"

Kyra nodded, not trusting herself to speak.

"I'm guessing you didn't find this out by asking someone or reading about it."

Kyra shook her head.

"You saw this, didn't you? Saw it happen in the past."

Kyra caught her breath.

"Saw it through someone else's eyes."

The skin tightened along Kyra's spine. The tiny hairs there stood up, as if touched by a cool breeze. "How could you possibly know that?"

Béatrice looked her right in the eyes. "It's happened to me too."

"It has?"

Béatrice nodded.

"I'm not the only one?"

"You're not. In fact, it's why my daddy and Doctor McFadden had me put away."

"Oh my days."

"You see why I tried to warn you?"

Kyra swallowed and tried to get her breathing under control. "Am I losing my mind?"

"No, you're not."

"So, you know what's causing this?"

Béatrice looked away. She let go of Kyra's arm, walked to her work bench and sighed. For a moment she just rested her hands on the bench and hung her head. Then she spoke in a quiet voice.

"I do."

"Can you tell me?"

Béatrice's voice was low, her head turned away. "I really hoped it wouldn't come to this, hoped you'd be spared. Why'd you have to pick it up, why?"

This got awkward quick. Did Béatrice really know what was going on or was it a lucky guess? Maybe she should grab her stuff and go.

Kyra walked to the corner where her backpack lay. Béatrice seemed lost in her own world. She took hold of the straps but before she put the bag over her shoulders Kyra realized there was something she still needed to say.

"Hey, listen, you know I said Billy-Ray didn't kill those people, well, I think I know who did. But I didn't see this in the past."

Béatrice glanced at Kyra, her shoulders stiffened. She gripped the edge of the bench and looked over her shoulder at Kyra. "Really?"

"My friend's uncle was the Deputy Sheriff, before he was killed, and he worked the case. My friend discovered a journal her uncle kept, with a bunch of evidence. She's going to hand it to the authorities, because her uncle thought he knew who the real killer was."

"And who did he think the killer was?"

"Béatrice, I'm sorry, it's your daddy. He probably killed my friend's uncle, too, to cover it up."

"So, the killer wasn't *your* daddy, it was *mine*."

"There's a lot of evidence. He covered stuff up, kept things from the jury. I just, I just thought you ought to know before it all came out."

"Well, that's very thoughtful of you." Béatrice turned away again and stared up at the ceiling. She seemed to be talking to herself. "I suppose I should have prepared better, I kept putting it off, hoping it wouldn't happen, I guess it's unavoidable now. I'm relieved more than anything." She turned back to Kyra. "It's time for some more tea, the special blend this time."

Béatrice took Kyra's cup and disappeared into the kitchenette. She came back a few minutes later with another steaming mug.

"Sorry, I had to use the same cup, I don't have many in the unit." The tea had a unique scent, spicy, like the odor of the cabinet she'd stumbled on in the drug store.

Béatrice sipped from hers. "Try it. It's my mother's recipe, been in the family for generations. You won't have tasted anything like it. Go on."

Béatrice put her hand under Kyra's cup and moved it to her lips. Kyra had no option but to drink. It had a complex flavor, lighting up different parts of her tongue as she drank. She tasted jasmine, then roses then a bitter after taste that coated the back of her throat.

"Kinda bitter at the end. Do you mind if I leave it?"

"Try another sip, it gets better." Kyra tried another sip and pulled a face, Béatrice signaled for her to try one more. "Honestly, it grows on you."

Kyra tried a bigger gulp, to please Béatrice. Things were getting weird. She wanted this to be over. The rain had eased and she wanted to be out of there and on her way to the bus. She still needed to call her parents.

The taste of the tea intensified and so did the aftertaste. It spread out across her tongue and along the back of her throat, choking her.

Kyra felt a tingling in her fingers and toes. She was losing sensation in her mouth and lips, like the Novocain you get at the dentist. The floor was made of rubber, like trying to stand on a trampoline. The lights dimmed until Kyra could only see a small spot in front of her, looking out of a tunnel.

The cup fell from her fingers and broke on the floor.

Béatrice looked at the pieces in the small, brown puddle of tea. "A shame, I liked that cup." Her eyes met Kyra's. Kyra tried to say something, but her lips and tongue were too swollen.

"I'll explain everything in good time."

Kyra was unconscious before she hit the floor.

CHAPTER 54:

Cold and dark. Down in the bayou.

Always the bayou. Under the water once again.

Here where no light ever reaches. Here where darkness dwells supreme.

What was she doing here, down in the waters? How had they claimed her once again?

Was it the taste of these lonely waters, so bitter on her lips?

She'd drunk something. That's why she was here. Drunk something that took away her consciousness. But she wasn't alone. Something was circling Kyra.

It wasn't predatory or threatening. There was comfort in its presence. It was the presence that had been with her since she came to Yeuxville. It wanted to protect her and she now knew why.

Kyra wanted to reach out to it. She knew it wanted to reach her but the still, heavy waters kept them apart. Pinned her in position and pushed it away.

Kyra could feel its longing. Feel the regret for all the things it had wanted to say, all the things it had wanted to be for her. All cruelly denied.

The waters weren't just black, but bitterly, bitterly cold. Chilling Kyra to her bones. Sucking her energy. Snatching her will to live. Stealing the presence from her, further and further from her.

Till all that was left was the aching remorse that muddied the waters in its absence.

Kyra felt a stab of regret when she could no longer feel the presence. But its withdrawal brought warmth and movement to the water. She was no longer pressed into the bed of the bayou.

The blood in her limbs began to circulate. Her body became lighter and buoyant. The mud and rocks at the bottom of the bayou released their hold. Kyra began to rise. Slowly at first. But the further she rose the faster she got.

Her lips broke the surface of the bayou first. She hung there with her head tilted and her body floating just beneath the water. Only her lips showed above the meniscus.

Another pair of lips brushed against them.

CHAPTER 55:

The lips were full and warm. They pressed against Kyra's with a tender insistence.

Kyra blinked open her eyes and saw Béatrice. She could smell Béatrice's face cream and the subtle pheromones in her sweat. The air around her was filled with a thick blanket of incense.

Blood and sensation rushed back into her arms. She tried to move but couldn't. Something tied her wrists, holding her splayed against a concrete floor. She tried to move her legs and found her ankles were also bound.

Béatrice sat up, her eyelids hooded. She looked magnificent. She was dressed like the African statues on Aunt Mimi's altar. She wore a gold headdress, a crimson top with many cowrie shells, and a long gold skirt with a split up the side. Around her neck was a necklace made from snake vertebrae, with a snake's skull in its center.

She was kneeling astride Kyra. "Thought that might wake you."

Kyra was groggy. "Béatrice, what's going on? What are you doing? Why am I tied up? I can't feel my legs?" Kyra glanced at her hands and saw the ropes that held her were tied to metal pegs in the floor. They seemed to be in a storeroom in back of the unit.

Béatrice stroked her cheek. "It was the tea. An old family recipe. In small doses it puts you to sleep, in larger doses it's a poison. I got it from my mother, along with this outfit. Do you like it? It's worn by the high queen of the old ways. I'm thrilled I could fit into it. My mother never lost her figure, but I've put on a few pounds. What you get from sitting and painting all day, I guess."

"Béatrice, please stop this, you don't have to…"

Béatrice placed a finger across her lips. "Shh, shh, it's all right, I promise. Now, this next bit is important."

Béatrice reached behind her and produced a long, thin knife with an ornate handle set with semi-precious stones. She placed the tip of the knife in Kyra's left palm.

Kyra started to hyperventilate. "Don't, please don't, Béatrice. Really don't."

Béatrice dug the tip of the knife into her left palm, drawing blood. Kyra sobbed with the sharp, searing pain. Béatrice took the knife to Kyra's right palm and cut another gash. The pain was more intense. Kyra shrieked.

Béatrice placed the edge of the blade against her own palms and cut deep. She dropped the knife, sticky with their mingled blood and took hold of Kyra's hands, interlinking their fingers, pressing her sliced palms against Kyra's till they throbbed

"Now, we are sisters by blood."

Béatrice let go of Kyra's hands. With the blood fresh on her palms and fingers, Béatrice held up another object for Kyra to see. "Remember him?"

It was the strange fetish Kyra had picked up when she first came to Béatrice's unit. "He's responsible for all this trouble."

She removed the soil-filled phial from the center of the fetish. Béatrice scraped their mingled blood from her palm and let a few drops fall into the soil.

"I have to do this really carefully. I don't want to get blood on my outfit, it's been in the family for centuries. Dates back to the days of Marie Laveau."

Béatrice returned the phial to the belly of the fetish and placed it on the floor above Kyra's head. She got to her feet and placed black candles at Kyra's head, hands and feet.

Then she retrieved a burlap sack, filled with flour and cut a hole in it with the blood-stained knife. The flour escaped in a fine trickle and Béatrice drew a series of intricate patterns around Kyra.

"Béatrice, what, what are you doing?" She sounded like a broken record. Her voice high and scratchy from the drug. How long had she been out? How had things escalated to this point?

"I'm drawing a series of vèvès. These are the old ways we keep in Yeuxville."

"If this is about your dad, you don't have to do this, you don't. I won't say anything, I'm on your side. I was trying to help. I won't say a thing. I'll stop Del... my friend from going to the police. Stop this now, please, please stop it, you're scaring me."

Béatrice put down the bag of flour. "I can't stop. It's too late for that. It's been too late for a very long time. I really wish it wasn't, but it is." Béatrice picked up the knife and knelt over Kyra again, resting on her stomach.

She stroked Kyra's cheek with the back of her hand, leaving cold sticky smears on her cheek. "I like you, Kyra. Really, I do."

"I like you, too. Please let me go Béatrice, don't do this."

"If you weren't so young, if you hadn't got involved like you did, then maybe, who knows? But you did get involved, and it was far too late even then, far, far too late."

"It's not too late, Béatrice, let me go, please."

"You're wrong about my daddy. He's a dangerous man. He's capable of a lot of things, including murder, but he didn't kill those women. You'll see in a moment. You'll see everything."

Béatrice lifted the knife above her head. Rising up onto her knees. Towering over Kyra, lying prone on the floor as she'd lain so many years before on that kitchen table in her old apartment when another woman had threatened her with a knife. Why did it always have to be a knife?

Kyra couldn't kick or struggle this time. Her wrists and ankles were bound. She was helpless. More helpless than she'd been as a tiny child. Unable to defend herself in any way.

Béatrice's eyes were glazed like Caitlin's. Both of them high on something. Strung out on drugs and grief and anger. Why couldn't they have been kind? She deserved better than this.

"Béatrice don't, oh God, please don't. Don't do this, don't do this, please!"

Béatrice took a deep breath and began to chant, her voice high and lilting like a song:

"Simbi lan barrière;

  z'aut' poco connin moin.

  Ala nous rivé

  nour pr'allé gâté coumandé.

  Yé! Simbi Yandézo,

  Ian Paka Pong'oué!"

  "Béatrice, no, don't, no!"

  "M'di: Yé! Kim'boi salay!

  Salam a salay!

  Simbi lan barrière;

  z'aut' poco connin moin."

"Béatrice stop, please, please stop!"

Kyra closed her eyes and turned her head. Her body was limp and numb. Her limbs had little life in them. Her flesh betrayed her. She needed it alive. Needed to kick back against this danger. She didn't want to see the knife fall. Didn't want to feel it slice her skin and puncture her organs. She wanted to be free from women who attacked her with knives.

Kyra held her breath. Waited for the blade to bite. *Please let it be quick. Don't make it hurt.* She pictured it hanging over her. Pictured it falling. The sharpened tip getting closer and closer, tearing into her.

But it never did.

There was no pain. There was no tearing.

Only the tender sound of sharpened metal scraping skin and connective tissue.

Kyra kept her eyes tight shut. She didn't want to see. Didn't want to know what she was hearing.

Warm liquid sprayed her face. It smelled of salt and copper.

Something moist and gelatinous was pressed into the wound in her palm. It was round, like an orb with a dense and fibrous tail.

She wasn't going to look. She didn't want to see what was happening.

More slicing. More spray. Another orb pressed into her other torn and wounded palm.

Béatrice's fingers found hers, closed her hands around the orbs. She didn't want this. Didn't want to hold these warm, wet objects. The skin of her palms stung from the gashes. Her fingers betrayed her and squeezed the orbs as they were told.

The weight of Béatrice's body left her chest and Kyra heard her fall to the ground beside her. She listened to Béatrice's ragged breath. Felt Béatrice's fingers, slick and wet with blood, touch her cheek and turn Kyra's head toward her.

Kyra opened her eyes and saw what Béatrice had done with the knife. Béatrice's sockets were empty, blood ran like streaked mascara down her cheeks and over the bridge of her nose. A frayed eyelid, hung over one empty socket, lashes twitching.

Yet, for some reason, Béatrice was smiling, a beatific smile.

"Béatrice, what have you done?"

"It's okay. It didn't hurt much. I drank some of the tea, more than you, enough to poison me, and take away the pain. It's a merciful way to die."

"How can you say that?"

Béatrice put a sticky finger to Kyra's lips. "Shh, shh, it's a blessing really. The tea is a benison. In her later years, Marie Laveau would visit with prisoners. Bring comfort and solace to those condemned to death. In their final moments, she would give them the tea to drink. It would take away their pain and they could enter the next world with no fear. Enter it with a smile on their lips."

Béatrice reached out with both her blood caked hands and cradled Kyra's face. "I'm very fond of you Kyra. I've known you a short while, but I am. I need you to do something, I'm sorry to ask, but you signed up for this the moment you touched that fetish. There's a reason you came into my unit, you're connected to all this. It's all about to become clear."

Béatrice's hands went limp. She breathed out but not in. Kyra watched her nose and mouth. Willing her to draw breath again.

But she didn't.

The muscles in her face relaxed, lost all expression, the rest of her body did the same. Her limbs slack and free of tension. All trace of Béatrice's personality slipped from her face and body. Dissipated, like mist in the sun's rays.

And she was gone forever.

"No, Béatrice. No!"

A sob broke at the back of Kyra's throat.

Why had Béatrice done this. Was it too much to bear that her dad was a murderer? This wasn't on her, this was on him. Why had she killed herself? Had she done it to save Kyra? Changed her mind at the last minute, turning the knife on herself.

But hadn't she said she'd already poisoned herself? Sent herself on to the next world with the same potion Marie Laveaux used to help condemned prisoners?

So why do this? Why mutilate herself?

Oh God.

Kyra was still holding them. She couldn't let them go. Her fingers wouldn't move, however much she wanted to open them.

Kyra shivered. She was cold. The temperature in the space was dropping. A breeze was blowing across the floor. Where the hell had that come from? How was there a breeze in here?

The candle flames flickered. Listed to one side as the breeze got stronger. Then, one by one, the flames left their wicks and went out.

There was a CRACK. And then a BANG!

Sparks shot from the fluorescent lighting. They flashed and went out. The whole unit plunged into darkness.

The quality of the air shifted. Like the change before a storm. Before the skies shatter and roar with lightning, the clouds boil and the rains pelt the earth. When you know that wild, elemental forces are about to be unleashed and there is nowhere to hide.

Kyra had the sense that the fundamental order of reality had been altered. Switched in some unnatural way, by strange words and strong will.

Something wasn't right.

And it was about to get worse.

CHAPTER 56:

The darkness was absolute.

Kyra could not see a thing. Her sense of sight gone. Her other senses disoriented.

Was she tied to a floor by her wrists and ankles? Or was she hanging from a ceiling? Kyra couldn't tell. Her spatial awareness fled.

Was that her breath she heard, lifting her chest and rasping in her ears? Or was there a wind in this space roaring through the air? Lifting Kyra like a leaf and sending her spinning.

First up, then down. First under, then over.

Is she being distracted while things change further?

Yes.

She's being distracted.

There's another presence in here with her.

It's not Billy-Ray.

Kyra knows who it is.

And in knowing, in recognizing, Kyra calls it to her.

She feels the hands first. They come from behind. Reaching into her.

Into her back. Between her shoulder blades.

Through her cold skin and knotted muscles. Through the stiff cage of her ribs and into her warm, pulsating organs.

Then deeper still.

Into the heart of Kyra. Not her physical heart. The very essence of Kyra, at the core of her being.

This is wrong.

It's violation. Intense violation of the most intimate part of her existence.

It needs to stop.

But it doesn't stop.

The hands close around the most essential part of Kyra. And they begin to pull.

They pull her out of her flesh and bones.

They pull her through the floor to which she's bound.

They break every tie that binds her to the material world.

And they keep on pulling.

Down and down.

Kyra wants to reach out with hands she doesn't have and cling to her body.

Wants to anchor herself in the physical world.

Wants to stay in the known reality.

But the hands are too strong. The pull is too insistent.

Kyra has no idea where she is going.

And all she can do is surrender.

CHAPTER 57:

Surrender to the flow.

There's a flow. And Kyra's in it.

A constant liquid movement, one thing flowing into another. A continual change of form and being.

Kyra is in a fluid state. But not the deep, still fluid of the bayou waters. These waters are like the Mississippi when it floods. Untamed and uninhibited by levees. Full of alluvial deposits, rushing to the gulf to become sea.

She finds currents and counter currents. Fierce turbulence and extreme hazards. One wrong turn here, one tiny movement in the wrong direction and Kyra will be lost.

She doesn't know how to respond. Doesn't know how to protect or guide herself through this torrent. But she finds she doesn't have to.

Something is guiding Kyra. Moving her through the hazardous currents, keeping her safe as if they were swimming right behind her. She can almost feel their hands on her shoulders. They're the same hands that pulled Kyra out of her body and through the floor of the unit.

Kyra knows those hands. She has so many things she wants to say to their owner. So many questions she wants to ask. But Kyra has no way of communicating.

She pictures herself in her old body. Carried like a piece of flotsam by the tide. Guided by a set of hands she can't see. But that's just how her mind is interpreting what's happening. Kyra has no physical form. No mouth to speak.

She's more like a thought bobbing on a stream of consciousness. And if she *is* a thought, then that's how she'll communicate, with her mind. Because the mind behind those hands is closer to Kyra than anything else.

Béatrice, is that you?

Yes.

What's happening? Where am I? What have you done to me?

Relax, it'll all become clear in a moment.

What will? What's going on?

You're going to have to trust me.

Trust you? You tied me up, drugged me and threatened me with a knife. How can I trust you?

Okay, you need to keep calm and center yourself or I won't be able to hang onto you.

I don't think I can.

You must, it's essential to your survival.

Yeah, that's going to stop me panicking.

I'm sorry, I know this is a lot to take in. I'm having trouble myself. This is my first time here too. But you can leave, if you keep it together. I can't. That's why I've only got a short time to show you all this.

If I can leave, I want to go now.

There's something I need to show you first. Please, just give me a bit of time. If there was any other way to do this, I would have done it. Please believe me. I need you, Kyra. Need you like I've never needed anyone before.

Béatrice's mind is so close to Kyra's here. Not just pressed up against it, but overlapping it, like a Venn diagram. Béatrice can't lie to Kyra. Can't hide her feelings. Kyra knows she's telling the truth.

The current they're in changes direction and Béatrice banks to the left, then rises to catch a new one. That's how Kyra's mind perceives what's happening.

Where am I? Are we underwater?

Sort of, we're in a river.

Like the Mississippi?

Kinda, it has a lot of names and all rivers eventually lead here.

Thanks, that's so much clearer.

Okay, how to put this. You've heard the spiritual, Michael Row the Boat Ashore?

Yeah.

Well this is the River Jordan, or the River Styx as the ancient Greeks called it. But when I brought us here I thought of it as the River of the Guédé, the Loa of the dead.

This is getting clearer by the minute.

Why are you being so snarky?

I don't know, maybe getting torn out of my body and thrown in a dead man's river might have something to do with it!

I'm trying, Kyra. Please just bear with me a little longer.

So, am I dead?

No, your body is alive, unlike mine. You don't need to be dead to ride this river, and there are many ways to travel it. You can go from one place to another or one time to another. We're riding it in time, so I can show what happened fifteen years ago. It's like seeing the past through Billy-Ray's eyes.

Only Billy-Ray couldn't talk.

And I can. You're not sharing the past as I saw it, you're going to remember it with me. What happened with Billy-Ray, all those things you saw. I caused that. I didn't mean to, but I guess it was fated. You have to understand what drove me to this.

Okay. I missed my momma. I was so young when she died. I was so miserable and angry.

I can relate.

She was the Queen of Yeuxville. The town Mambo, respected by everyone, trained by my gramma who was trained by her momma before her. I was supposed to be next, but that was all snatched away when she was killed. I lost my birthright. It wasn't fair and I couldn't let it go.

The currents around them become less turbulent and Béatrice is able to guide them upward, toward what Kyra assumes is the surface of the River of the Guédé. As they rise, the dark accedes to light and Kyra's sense of sight kicks in.

Shapes swirl before her, like clouds of river silt churned by the current. As the clouds clear light breaks through. Béatrice guides them up toward the thin rays that seem to be playing on the surface of the river.

The closer they get, the more images Kyra can see. As if approaching a lighted window on a starless night.

Through the window she can see a tableaux. It grows larger, a cinema screen projected on the river's surface. Kyra and Béatrice dart toward the image. Break through the meniscus of the surface and find themselves inside the tableaux they saw.

They've moved back in time, along the river and they've entered one of Béatrice's memories. It's no longer a two-dimensional image. It has color and three dimensions and it is all around them. They float in the air, two non-corporeal entities in a very corporeal scene.

They're in an attic. Hovering in the rafters. Dust-choked cobwebs hang in forgotten corners and boxes of discarded junk lie scattered across the floor. Kyra can see everything clearly, but there are no sounds, no smell and she can't touch anything.

A teenage girl is on her knees in front of an old trunk. A penlight is lodged in her teeth and she's fumbling with the trunk's lock. Kyra recognizes the teen.

Is that you?

I'd just turned fifteen. This is my Gramma's attic, my daddy's momma.

What are you doing?

Using a skeleton key on the trunk and not having much success.

Why's the trunk so important?

It's my momma's. All her things are in there. My daddy hid them when she died, couldn't bear to look at them. Probably blamed them for her death. Couldn't throw them out, cos they were too valuable. Lots of folk came round asking about them but he shooed them away and put them in my gramma's attic.

Beads of sweat stand out on Béatrice's forehead. The skeleton key rattles in the trunk's lock, the penlight falls from Béatrice's mouth, but the lock on the trunk pops open.

Béatrice lifts the lid and stares with excitement at the contents. She shines the penlight into the trunk and starts examining every item, lifting up jars filled with colored powders, dried lizards and snake skins, and even a mummified black cat's paw.

Beneath the jars she finds costumes. Headdresses with semi-precious stones, crowns and coronets carved from ivory, long golden skirts and a necklace made of snake vertebrae.

Beneath the costumes, wrapped in crepe paper, are statues of saints and African carvings, candles of many colors, old fashioned toys like kaleidoscopes and magnetic lodestones.

At the very bottom of the trunk there's a library of books. Kyra watches Béatrice lift out leather bound volumes with titles like: *6th and 7th Book of Moses*, *The Egyptian Secrets of Albertus Magnus*, *Secrets of Voodoo* and *The Life and Works of Marie Laveau*.

The final thing Béatrice comes to is a large book with a magnetic clasp. She opens this book and scans the handwritten pages filled with drawings and diagrams.

Kyra wants to get closer to read over the young teen's shoulder, but Béatrice holds her back.

What's that?

My Momma's Grimoire. She wrote down everything she'd been taught by her Momma, every charm, hex, curse and spell. As if she knew she wasn't going to be there to teach me.

But you could learn it from this book?

I wanted to be a queen like my momma, revered by the community. Police and politicians visited my momma for help, and my gramma and their mothers before them. They had a lot of power.

What did you do?

I snuck the trunk out of that attic, and I hid it in a barn on our property. I read all the books. I memorized my momma's grimoire. I contacted the spirits, spoke with the Loas, learned hexes and spells.

So it did work.

I had my momma's gifts and I learned how to use them, but it wasn't enough. I knew she'd be proud of me, but I wanted her to see. I had to do all this in secret. My daddy didn't want me messing with that stuff, that's why he hid the trunk. I had no one to share my discoveries with. Reading that grimoire was like spending time with my momma. But in time, it just made me miss her more. Can you understand?

More than you know.

I wanted her back. I wanted the childhood memories I should've had. I wanted to go back in time and save her, stop her from being killed. That's why things turned out the way they did. Please keep that in mind. Will you do that for me?

Okay.

Thank you. It's time for me to show you something else.

They swim up through the roof of the attic, it looks solid. Kyra braces herself for the collision but, as they reach it, a ripple passes across her vision. The roof is two dimensional, nothing more than a reflection on the surface of a somnolent river.

A river into which they are diving.

As they enter the current, Kyra realizes she is no longer being pulled upward, but down into the River of the Guédé.

She is traveling from one of Béatrice's memories to another, along a river of the dead. Kyra isn't dead but Béatrice is.

Béatrice needs to share these memories. She wants to show Kyra something. But these truths involve Hawkins' crimes. And that means Kyra is about to learn something terrible.

CHAPTER 58:

Béatrice lets the current carry them down river. Kyra's vision is murky. She can't rely on her sight.

Kyra has so many questions about what she's experiencing.

Béatrice, are you a ghost now?

Let's say I identify as a spirit. One of the things I learned from my mother is that the human spirit, or the soul, has two parts – the Gros-Bon Ange *and the* Ti-Bon Ange. *That means big angel and little one. The* Ti-Bon Ange *is what makes you uniquely yourself. It leaves the body when you dream and when you take part in a ritual.*

Is that what I am? Is this my Ti-Bon Ange?

Yes, that's how I was able to take you out of your body. The rest of you is safe back in Yeuxville.

But your Gros-Bon Ange *is guiding us, right?*

Yes, the Gros-Bon Ange *travels this river as it returns to the* Gran Met, *the ocean of life from which every soul comes and to which they all return.*

But why all these memories?

You know how people say your life flashes before you as you're about to die?

Yes

That's what's happening, I'm taking you back to key points in my life.

But why are you doing this, Béatrice? What do you need from me?

I promise we'll get to that, in time.

We're not in time though, are we? We're traveling outside of it.

You're right, it's a turn of phrase. You just have to trust me, Kyra, please. Our next stop is up ahead.

The current moves back on itself, Béatrice and Kyra descend further into its depths. They are spiraling, caught in an eddy. Buffeted back and forth. But the turbulence feels less like motion and more like emotion.

The whirlpool that's forming seems to be caused more by personal conflict than the movement of water. Kyra realizes the river is mirroring Béatrice, moved by her regret and anxiety.

Light breaks beneath them. Kyra glances down and finds she can see something at the bottom of the whirlpool. There are blue skies down there, they're advancing toward them.

They move in ever decreasing circles, faster and faster until they're spun out of the river and into a wild expanse of cloudless sky.

For a moment, Kyra continues to spin through the air as she falls from a seeming height. Below them are fields and a canal.

It's the canal that Delilah took her to on the murder tour. With the grassy mounds Delilah insisted aren't levees.

The circles she and Béatrice move in get smaller and smaller, but instead of speeding up they slow down until they're floating above a scene on the top of the high mound. Once again she can see everything clearly, but there is no sound or other sensations.

There are two people beneath them. Béatrice and another girl. Béatrice has aged. Her body has filled out and there are traces of acne on her cheeks. Kyra can see a retainer when she smiles.

In spite of everything Béatrice has done, Kyra feels a stab of affection. Seeing her so vulnerable, an awkward teen, Kyra feels a deep, protective sympathy.

Béatrice is sitting next to another girl, with their legs over the other side of the mound, looking down at the water and the marsh grass that surrounds it. The other girl is very pretty, with flawless skin and long auburn hair.

As they move closer, Kyra realizes she's seen the other girl before.

That's Mary Jo Bernard. You knew Mary Jo Bernard?

We were in high school. She was popular. I wasn't. In 10th grade we went to the same art camp. We didn't know anyone there and we bonded over losing our mommas.

Mary Jo lost her mother in that bayou thing right?

Yes. We became friends but she wouldn't talk to me in school.

She ghosted you because you weren't popular?

It looked like that, at first, but we met up outside of school. She told me there was a reason. And this is when I found out what it was.

Mary Jo sidles closer to Béatrice. Their thighs are touching. Mary Jo tucks a strand of auburn hair behind her ear and smiles at Béatrice. Béatrice looks down at her lap, her shoulders hunched in embarrassment.

What are you saying?

She's curious about her sexuality, but she can't admit this to her friendship group. Or her dad.

Why not?

Her dad took her to a Purity ball, they were real big around this time. A lot of her friends went. They all made virginity pledges but few kept them. Only Mary Jo and one other. She knows I'm gay, but hardly anyone else does.

Why not?

It was the time. It was Yeuxville. It's a small town and I don't want people all up in my business. You know.

Yeah, no, of course.

Mary Jo wants to keep her pledge, but it's difficult. She thinks it will be different with a girl. She won't be breaking her word to God and her dad. He wouldn't understand but she's sure God will.

Mary Jo reaches out and runs her fingers lightly over Béatrice's cheek. Béatrice's smile is bashful as she drops her chin. Mary Jo slips her fingers under it and raises Béatrice's face.

She leans closer and presses her lips to Béatrice's. Their mouths open to one another in a tentative kiss. Mary Jo snakes her hand around Béatrice's waist and draws her closer.

Whoa, this is some memory.

I'm sorry, are you okay seeing this? It's important.

Yeah, yeah sure. Kinda vivid though.

I can remember every nanosecond of that kiss. It's never left me. The taste of peppermint gum on her tongue. The smell of moisturizer on her cheeks and the deodorant she used. The soft fabric of her blouse and the smooth denim of her jeans beneath my fingers.

They lie back on the grassy mound, lips pressed together, arms around one another, legs entwined. Mary Jo pulls up Béatrice's t-shirt, reaches around and unclips her bra. Her hand moves back and cups Béatrice's breast. She moves Béatrice's hands onto her own chest.

Mary Jo breaks the kiss, props herself up on one elbow and slips her other hand down the front of Béatrice's jeans. Then she bows her head and takes Béatrice's nipple in her mouth.

From above, Kyra sees Béatrice stiffen, a look of panic crosses her face.

Are you okay?

No, I'm scared. This is my first time too. She was moving so fast. I didn't know how to react. Didn't know how to touch her or what to do next. I just froze.

Béatrice's fly comes undone and Mary Jo's hand slides around to her crotch. Béatrice grabs Mary Jo's wrist and tries to pull her hand back. Mary Jo pays her no mind, her hand deep in Béatrice's jeans.

Béatrice tugs Mary Jo's hand out of her jeans and sits up. Mary Jo pouts and then smiles, her eyelids hooded. She reaches a hand around Béatrice's neck and tries to pull her into another kiss. Béatrice gets to her feet and fastens her fly.

Mary Jo frowns, her lower jaw pushed forward, her lips pressed together. She turns away from Béatrice and folds her arms tight across her chest. Béatrice sees this and a look of penitence crosses her face.

She kneels and places her hand on Mary Jo's shoulder. Mary Jo shrugs her off. Béatrice tries again, moves closer, puts her arms around Mary Jo's shoulders. Mary Jo pushes Béatrice away.

Béatrice falls back. Tears well up in her eyes. She puts her hands together as if in prayer, imploring Mary Jo.

Mary Jo narrows her eyes and turns to face Béatrice. Without warning, her right hand lashes out and slaps Béatrice hard across the cheek.

Béatrice puts her hand to her face and gets unsteadily to her feet. Mary Jo jumps to hers. Stabs at Béatrice's chest with her forefinger. The tendons of her neck distended, her face twisted with fury, spittle flying from her lips as she shouts at Béatrice.

Tears spill down over Béatrice's cheeks. She wrings her hands, pleading with Mary Jo, but this only inflames her. Increases the intensity of her verbal attack.

She's calling me a dyke. A disgusting, godless deviant. She's going to tell everyone what I'm like. My life is over. No one will talk to me when she's through.

What are you saying?

I'm telling her I'm sorry, over and over, but it just makes her angrier. I want things back the way they were. That kiss meant so much, but I was so inexperienced. I couldn't believe how wrong things had gone, and how quickly.

What a bitch.

It's not her fault. She felt rejected. I see that now. I didn't explain myself. I couldn't find the words.

Béatrice backs up to the edge of the mound. A steep drop behind her. Mary Jo takes a menacing step toward her. Béatrice cowers. A mean look steals across Mary Jo's face.

Her muscles tense and then she swings for Béatrice. Béatrice can see the blow coming and has time to step to one side.

Mary Jo's fist passes harmlessly through empty air. She leans too far forward and the momentum of the swing pulls her out over the edge.

Her arms flail. Her toes slip over the edge. Béatrice tries to grab her and misses. Mary Jo topples over and plummets off the edge of the mound.

One minute she's there. The next she's gone. It happens so fast it hardly seems real.

Béatrice peers down at the canal and Kyra moves closer, looking over her shoulder. The drop looks steep from this height.

Mary Jo's body is lying in the mud by the side of the canal.

She's completely still. Her arms and legs are splayed. Her head lies at a strange angle. Blood soaks the sharp rock next to it. A crimson pool is spilling from the back of Mary Jo's head, soaking her long auburn hair.

Her eyes stare into nothing. Her body is completely motionless.

Béatrice scrambles down the mound to the side of the canal. She kneels by Mary Jo and strokes her chin. Her eyes are wild and disbelieving.

She tries to talk to Mary Jo and when she gets no answer she shakes her. When that doesn't work, Béatrice touches her neck, feeling for a pulse.

Béatrice's face falls. She opens her mouth and starts to cry. Not just tears, huge roaring sobs that shake her chest.

Béatrice gets to her feet. She backs away from the body. She's not paying attention and she almost steps backward into the canal, righting herself at the last minute.

Béatrice backs up to the slope of the mound. The tears have stopped and she's breathing heavily. She can't take her eyes off her friend's corpse, they grow wide with terror. A wild hysteria takes hold, and Béatrice begins to scramble up the slope.

When she reaches the top, Béatrice turns once to look down at Mary Jo, then runs down the other side, back across the field and away from the canal.

Wait, you just left her?

It was wrong, I know that.

You didn't call 911, try to get an ambulance, tell her parents what had happened?

Kyra, you know I didn't.

I do, but I'm having trouble accepting what you did. How could you leave her there?

You've just seen what I went through. I was traumatized. I'd never seen a dead body before. Something just snapped in my mind. That's the moment I lost it. I've never been the same.

It wasn't your fault. It was an accident. Why didn't you tell your dad?

You don't know what it's like to grow up as the Sheriff's daughter. Everything I did or said was a reflection on him. I was terrified. Terrified of what he'd think if he knew what I was really like. Terrified he'd find where I hid my mother's trunk. I couldn't talk to him about anything. Least of all this.

I still can't believe what happened.

I made a bad choice, Kyra. A real bad choice. But I made worse. As you're about to see.

Kyra hovers over the mound, long after young Béatrice has left. The sun hangs in the wide, blue expanse, then it starts to move faster toward the horizon, like a time lapse video. A few scattered clouds appear and race each other across the sky.

Time is speeding up, as though it's reacting to Béatrice's impatience. Her need to make Kyra understand.

The sun sets. The stars wink then reel across the sky in a drunken whirl. The sun appears once more in the east.

It moves quickly to its midday height but slows as it drops into its afternoon spot. Time breathes a sigh and slows to its normal speed.

Béatrice appears on the other side of the field and makes the long walk to the mound. She's wearing different clothes. A satchel hangs from her shoulder. Her manner is furtive, but there's a grim determination on her face

So you're back. Feeling guilty?

Like you wouldn't believe. I'm going out of my mind. I only had one place left to turn.

Where was that?

My momma's books. Where I always looked when the walls were closing in. When I couldn't eat, breathe or think straight.

Did they help?

They always helped. But helping me feel better and helping me make the right choice aren't always the same thing.

No.

The books had a way of falling open at the right page whenever I asked a question. Especially my momma's grimoire. It was a form of divination, like consulting the tarot.

Or throwing the bones?

Yes, that too.

What page did it open at?

Well, that's the darnedest thing. The grimoire fell open and one page, toward the back, stood up straight. I looked closer and saw that two pages had gotten stuck together. I took a moment to separate them. I didn't want to damage the grimoire. It meant so much to me. But here were two pages I'd never read.

What did they say?

They contained a hex. A very hazardous spell that seemed to be the answer to all my problems. As though momma had been saving it for just the right moment.

Béatrice makes her way up the mound and scrambles down the other side. She stops at the side of the canal. Mary Jo's body hasn't moved. Nothing has changed since yesterday.

Except the blood has congealed and Mary Jo is deathly pale. Béatrice takes a jelly jar and a kitchen knife from her satchel.

First I had to take something from Mary Jo's body.

Béatrice kneels beside Mary Jo's body. She unscrews the lid of the jar and puts it on the ground next to Mary Jo's head. Chasing away the flies that swarm round her exposed brain.

Béatrice puts her thumb and forefinger on Mary Jo's eyelids, peeling them right back. Her eyeballs are milky with white constellations. The sun glints off the edge of the blade as Béatrice brings it closer.

That's enough. Take us out of here.

Out of where?

This memory. I don't want to see any more. I know what you did. You don't have to rub my face in it.

But we're not finished.

Yes we are. Take us out.

It doesn't work like that.

Yes it does. These are your memories. This is your life. You took us in, you can take us out.

Even though Beatrice is only a voice inside Kyra's mind, Kyra swears she hears her sigh.

Okay, you get the picture. We can go. But I warn you, what I'm about to show you is even darker and more troubling.

CHAPTER 59:

Béatrice takes hold of Kyra and guides her down to the canal. Her *Gros-Bon Ange* moving Kyra's *Ti-Bon Ange*, into the waters below.

As soon as they're submerged, Kyra realizes they're not swimming through the canal. They're back in the River of the Guédé. The transition is sudden and shocking.

It's like plunging into ice cold regret. Kyra senses an undertow. A longing is rising up from the dark bed of this river. A longing to go back and fix past mistakes. Every mistake that affects every person they've ever loved.

They sink lower and Kyra seems to lose more than her sense of sight. Dark, emotional sediment rises from the river's lowest ebb. Clouds the waters like the consequence of a bad decision.

Kyra senses a river bank. Béatrice is moving them toward it. She darts out of the river into what appears to be a burrow. Like an alligator's den. Kyra wonders what deadly predator would hide in a river of the dead.

They travel deeper and deeper into the burrow. Until it changes direction and begins to rise upward at a steep angle.

As they climb the dank tunnel, a light appears above them. At first it's no brighter than a flashlight glimpsed, at a distance, on a dark night. As they approach it gets larger and brighter. Kyra begins to see shapes and colors. It's the portal to another memory.

They come out in a hayloft. Teenage Béatrice is kneeling before the trunk from her gramma's attic. It's open and several jars have been taken out. The grimoire sits open in front of Béatrice.

She's winding wire and hair around a small hunk of dark wood, squinting in concentration.

What are you doing?

This is the hex I told you about.

Looks more like arts and crafts.

Same difference, magic is imagination and creativity. I'm creating an object of power.

Kyra notices a saucer between the jars. Two severed eyeballs, shrunken and deflated, are sitting on it.

Eew, are those Mary Jo's?

Yes.

I get why you didn't tell anyone. But why take her eyes. That's nasty.

It was for the hex.

The one you found in your mother's grimoire?

Yes.

Why did you need eyes?

The hex allows you to see the past through the eyes of someone who's already dead. The power behind it comes from the Petro Loa. You need blood to appease them. In this case you need to kill someone and take their eyes to perform the hex.

That sounds messed up.

It was, but when I saw what happened to Mary Jo, I realized I could perform this hex without hurting anyone.

You thought this *wasn't hurting anyone?*

I wasn't thinking right, Kyra. We've already established that. I wanted my momma back so badly and this hex offered me a way to make that happen.

By seeing the past?

Not only seeing the past. You can alter it. If you concentrate hard enough you can take charge of the person whose eyes you're using to see the past. Mary Jo's momma was there when my momma was killed. I thought I could use her to save my momma.

So, what are you doing with that wood and wire?

I'm making a fetish to concentrate and direct the energies of the hex. To embody them in a symbol of Met Kalfou, the Loa who stands at the crossroads of the past and the present. He is the one who lets you see into the past.

All at once, Kyra recognizes the object Béatrice is making. She's seen it before. She's held it in her own hands.

That's the fetish I picked up a couple days ago, it was on your altar.

Yes it was.

It was like I was drawn to it.

Its will overrode yours.

It has a will of its own?

Oh yes, and I think it chose you for a reason. You're a part of all this Kyra. You have no idea how involved you are. But you're about to find out.

CHAPTER 60:

Béatrice tugs at Kyra suddenly. Catches her off balance and pulls her down through the floor of the hayloft.

As she hits the floor it melts like liquid and she's out of the memory. The formless waters of the Guédé catch them and pull them down.

The transition is too sudden. Kyra's still trying to process what she's learned. She's drowning in emotions. Drowning in revelation after revelation. Drowning in the river where all drowned people go.

When she lifted the fetish in Béatrice's unit, she felt like it had called her from Chicago. Called her all the way to Yeuxville. Had that been Kalfou, the Loa Béatrice named? Were unseen forces manipulating all of this? Was that what Béatrice was about to reveal?

Kyra doesn't want to learn more about the murders. She's done with revelations. But Béatrice isn't about to let up.

She pulls Kyra up, fighting the weight of the river. Kyra can see skies the color of dusk beyond the surface of the river. The current lets them go, dwindles to nothing. They slip from its waters into the close heat of evening. Below them are the slow, brackish waters of a swamp.

They dart like kingfishers between the moss-covered cypress trees. Moving toward dryer land.

Where are we?

A few miles outside of Yeuxville. This area is mostly underwater now. It was used for picnics and community events when I was a child. In my momma's day it was used for gatherings.

They move to marshy grassland and leave the waters behind. A figure comes into view. She seems tired and beaten. She's moving in a strange and unnatural manner.

As they get closer, Kyra sees it's teenage Béatrice. Her face shows disdain and displeasure. But she seems to be mimicking those reactions rather than experiencing them.

She moves in a halting and uneven fashion. As if she's a marionette and someone else is controlling her body.

They move in much closer. Kyra can see Béatrice's eyes have rolled up into their sockets, showing only bloodshot whites.

What's up with you?

I'm seeing the world through Loretta Bernard's eyes, not my own.

The hex, it's working?

Yes.

Who's Loretta Bernard?

She was Mary Jo's mother. It's the anniversary of my momma's death, I took Mary Jo's eyeballs. I made the fetish of Kalfou. I worked the hex, and I made my way out to the bayou. I knew I had to be in the same place Loretta had been, all those years ago, at exactly the same time.

Otherwise it wouldn't take?

Exactly. I wandered around for more than an hour, trying to take the path she'd taken, but nothing happened. I was wet, and mad, and lost when it finally happened.

Did it start with your eyes?

Yes, I thought it was sunlight flashing off the water, but I wasn't near water, and it was late. The strange light filled my eyes.

Did you get patterns, like a kaleidoscope?

Lots, they filled my vision till I couldn't see anything, then I blinked, and I was seeing out of Loretta's eyes.

Béatrice lurches to her left and moves off in a different direction.

Is that what I look like when I'm seeing through Billy-Ray's eyes?

Yes, I imagine it is.

No wonder everyone thought I was on drugs.

You're not going to like this next part, but I need you to see what I saw. I'm going to take you inside my field of vision.

Young Béatrice seems to grow in stature, or maybe they're shrinking. Her face gets bigger and bigger. Her cheeks are wide plateaus. Her pores are craters and her eyes are deep lagoons.

They move toward her left eye and it becomes a lake and then a small ocean. The retinal veins become wide, red trenches, branching off into a network of tributaries.

They descend into the vein. Passing through the wall to become platelets. Riding the tide of plasma that gushes through the vein. Carried along on this crimson rapid until they come to the gaping abyss of the pupil.

As they spill over the edge into the gaping blackness, Kyra's vision whites out. Disappears completely.

When it returns she is no longer inside the retinal vein. She is seeing the world through the eyes of Loretta Bernard. Just as seventeen year old Béatrice did a decade ago.

They are in the grass land by the bayou. Loretta is tall and sees over the head of everyone around her.

She's walking behind an overweight man, with no hair, in a white suit. He's a good foot shorter than Loretta. He glances uncertainly about him. His glasses, misted with sweat, have slipped to the end of his nose. His cheeks and brow run with perspiration.

He looks down at the state department map he's carrying. Then he looks up in bewilderment at his current location. Unable to make the two match up.

Is that Reverend Lee?

Charming, isn't he?

Loretta turns from the Reverend to look at the rest of the party, trudging through the humid night. She glances to her left and sees a woman in her early forties. Dressed conservatively, a pale blue blouse and long black slacks. Her nose wrinkled, her lips drawn back in disdain.

That's Ethel Donovan. She's the mother of Frances Donovan.

The second victim's mother?

Yeah.

Walking next to Ethel is a woman in her mid-twenties. She's almost as tall as Loretta, with wide shoulders and a lumbering gait. She's wearing a white shirt, a short black skirt, knee-length socks and sandals. An outfit a twelve-year-old would wear. It gives her the appearance of an overgrown schoolgirl. Her jaw is set and determined.

Whitney Boudreaux, cousin of Elizabeth Boudreaux, the fourth girl who died.

There's hesitancy in Béatrice's thoughts. She isn't proud of this.

Is there something wrong with her?

She rode the short bus to school.

Thought as much. What's she doing here?

She fell for the Reverend's line. She's vulnerable, but he doesn't care. Whitney's the reason Loretta's here.

Why's that?

She's not religious, but Whitney's her niece. When her sister-in-law died, she made Loretta promise she'd look out for Whitney. Loretta tried to talk Whitney out of coming, but Whitney's a stubborn one. When Loretta couldn't talk her out of going, she decided to accompany her, to keep her out of harm's way.

How do you know this?

I spent a couple days, before this, seeing the world through Loretta's eyes.

Little episodes you mean, when you found yourself where Loretta would have been all those years ago?

Pretty much, it was a shock the first time, but after a while I went looking for it.

Been there.

The last woman, at the back of the party, has iron gray hair in a bun, and pious, wrinkled features too big for her face. Impractically, given the heat, she's wearing a red woolen cardigan, tartan skirt and tights.

That's Nicole Patterson.

Connected to Alison Comeaux?

She's her grandmother.

They're out here for the Reverend's community intervention, right?

Not much of a community. Three months campaigning and he convinced four townsfolk to come with him. They've been wandering around for two hours now, trying to find my momma's ceremony. The Reverend doesn't know these backwaters and the other women have never been to my momma's meetings. That's rare in Yeuxville.

So I've heard.

A grove of cypress trees comes into view. Reverend Lee turns away. Loretta sees a young Creole woman step from the trees, dressed in a white frock with a red sash around her waist and a white scarf on her head. She smiles at Loretta and beckons her to follow.

Loretta points to the Creole woman, who smiles and indicates the way through the trees. The Reverend turns round and marches up to the Creole woman shaking his head. He tries to shoo her away.

The Creole woman smiles politely and tries to explain something to him. The Reverend goes red in the face and wags his finger. Loretta puts a hand on the Reverend's shoulder. The Reverend shakes his head and sets his chin, so Loretta turns to the three other women, who don't look so certain.

Finally, Whitney seems to listen and makes to follow Loretta. She lets Whitney go on ahead and Nicole and Ethel continue into the grove. They follow the Creole woman for about ten minutes, and they come into a clearing, there's a white tent, similar to those in revivalist meetings.

Loretta glances behind her and sees a commotion among the trees. Reverend Lee charges into view, looking more enraged than ever. He pushes to the front of the party as the young woman invites them to follow.

The tent is filled with at least two hundred people. The crowd is diverse, white, black, Creole and even a few Asian and Native Americans. The men are dressed in white shirts and jeans. The women are dressed like the young Creole woman. Loretta follows Reverend Lee as he moves through the crowd, pushing everyone aside.

The central tent pole is covered in a spiral of green and red ribbon, surrounded by candles and statues of saints. Three drummers sit around the pole, pounding rhythmically on drums of different sizes. Four men, with no shirts, and four women, dressed like the young Creole woman, are dancing in a circle in front of the pole, throwing their bodies around in abandon.

In the center of the dancers is a beautiful Creole woman. She's dressed as a priestess in flowing golden robes. She doesn't have a headdress, but a large, golden bowl, filled with flaming oil, sits on her head. She is dancing a slow and sensuous dance, filled with intricate and graceful movements, the flames burn brightly but the bowl doesn't once move.

That's my momma, isn't she something?

She's stunning.

The Reverend stalks over to the drummers and knocks the instruments out of their hands. The drummers leap to their feet, berating him. The dancers stop and turn to see what's happening. A female dancer falls to the floor, throwing some kind of fit. The other dancers gather round her protectively.

Is that woman all right?

She's become a horse.

Transformed into an animal?

No, sorry, sometimes I think you know more than you do. She's being ridden by the Loa Erzulie Dantor.

Wait, what?

Okay, the Loa, are the spirits, or gods and goddesses if you will, that the followers of the old ways serve. We're called Servants of the Loa. The Loa act as intercessors between God and man, a bit like angels, and some angels are also Loa, like St. Michael, are you following me?

Not really.

Ceremonies, like this one, allow us to speak with the Loa when they possess one of the people present. When this happens, the Loa is riding the follower, and the follower being ridden is called a horse.

Right, so Erzulie...?

Dantor.

Erzulie Dantor is riding this woman?

See, you are following this.

The dancer breaks from the crowd and crawls to the Reverend on her hands and knees. The Reverend shouts at the dancers and the rest of the crowd, waving his Bible. The dancer vomits blood over the Reverend's shoes, her eyes red and bloodshot.

The Reverend steps away, a look of horror on his face. He takes the crucifix from around his neck and waves it in her face. The dancer gets to her feet and laughs. The Reverend raises his Bible and makes to strike her across the face. One of the drummers catches his arm and the Reverend struggles against him.

Béatrice's momma takes the flaming bowl from her head and places it on a stand before the pole. She steps between the dancer and the Reverend. She motions for the drummer to let go of him. The female dancer steps away and the other dancers crowd protectively around her.

Béatrice's momma speaks calmly to the Reverend, trying to appeal to his better nature. The Reverend points an accusing finger and starts waving his Bible at her.

Béatrice's momma points to the statues of the saints. The Reverend shakes his head. She draws the Reverend's attention to a portrait of Jesus over the entrance, but this only enrages him more. Finally she reaches into her robes and pulls out a crucifix. She turns to the assembled crowd and addresses them. At least half the people in the tent hold up the crucifixes they are wearing to the Reverend.

What's going on?

My momma's showing the Reverend that everyone here has accepted Jesus into their lives. They're not worshipping the devil.

Really?

Yep. The Reverend would have known that if he'd done his homework. It's why no-one in town has joined him.

The dancer possessed by Erzulie Dantor steps away from the dancers and shouts at the Reverend, waving her fist. The Reverend shouts back and the drummers step in to keep them apart.

The dancer smiles and taunts the Reverend, everyone in the tent laughs. The Reverend lunges for her and the drummers restrain him, veins bulging at his temples.

The dancer's manner changes, her look accusatory. She speaks with a cold, clear anger. Everyone in the tent looks shocked. The Reverend sags in the arms of the drummers and stares hard at the floor, his fists clenched, his teeth grinding.

What did the dancer just say?

Not the dancer, Erzulie Dantor.

Okay, what did Erzulie Dantor say?

She revealed the Reverend's weakness for underage boys.

Gross.

Tell me about it.

The drummers look repulsed, relax their grip on the Reverend, not wanting to touch him. The Reverend pushes them away, raising his arms and looking upward, imploring God for strength to smite the unrighteous. He grabs the bowl of flaming oil and holds it above his head. His eyes have a maniacal gleam and he doesn't notice the oil spilling over the sides or the blisters forming on his palms.

I didn't realize what he was going to do until it was too late. I had to act, I had to take control of Loretta, but I'd never done it before.

Loretta starts to shake, takes a single step forward and then freezes up. Several of the dancers move towards the Reverend, but Béatrice's momma stops them.

She was fighting me every step of the way. She must've thought I was a demon, trying to take control of her.

Loretta takes another faltering step, stalls, and brings her hands together in prayer. She remains rigid for a moment, then her hands are forced apart, they fall to her side and she walks toward the Reverend as everyone else backs away.

Loretta puts out her hands to the Reverend, imploring him to stop. She speeds up as she approaches. Something has snapped inside the Reverend. He doesn't recognize Loretta. He raises his foot and puts his heel in her solar plexus, knocking her to the ground.

This sends him sprawling backward and the flaming oil splashes the back wall of the tent. In seconds, the fire spreads along the wall and up into the roof.

Loretta lies on the floor, as panic grips those inside the tent. Béatrice's momma calls out and starts to direct them, making sure everyone leaves by the main exit in a calm, orderly manner.

As her congregation files quickly from the tent, Béatrice's momma turns to the Reverend and his party inviting them to leave. Loretta tries to get up, but falls back, winded from the blow to her solar plexus. As the flames engulf the roof, the Reverend places himself between the women and Béatrice's momma, holding out his palm to renounce her.

As the last of her congregation leave the tent, Béatrice's momma tries to hurry the Reverend and the women out. Ethel, Whitney, and Nicole try to leave by the main exit, but the Reverend holds them back and points to a side exit that's starting to blacken and smoke. He hustles the women toward this exit. Béatrice's momma calls out to them in warning.

This was my last shot at saving her, at changing the past, but it was so hard to control Loretta's body. It was bigger than mine, she was winded, and she fought me every step of the way.

Loretta gets up off the floor and stumbles to Béatrice's momma. She grabs her arm and tries to pull her toward the exit. Béatrice's momma resists, concerned for the others. The light flares, and Loretta turns her head to see fire racing down the ribbons of the tent pole.

The side exit becomes an inferno before the Reverend and the women reach it. The Reverend pushes Nicole to the floor as he flees toward the main exit. Ethel and Whitney try to help Nicole up. The tent pole starts to crack and list dangerously to the side.

Loretta manages to move Béatrice's momma toward the exit, but the Reverend collides with her as he flees. She sprawls into Loretta, knocking them to the ground. The tent pole falls, dragging the inferno down around them.

Béatrice's momma tries to get up, but she can't breathe from the lack of oxygen. She coughs violently. Loretta reaches out her arms to Béatrice's momma.

I was terrified. A little girl reaching out to her momma for comfort. It was my last chance to be held by my momma.

Béatrice's momma looks horrified, pushes Loretta's hands off and tries to scuttle away.

She flat out rejected me.

Loretta looks at her hands and sees that flames are racing up her arms.

And then I saw why.

Loretta is burning to death, but Béatrice's momma is untouched by the fire.

Kyra has reached her limit.

Okay, I've seen enough, take us out of here.

The burning canvas falls closer to Béatrice's momma. There's no way out. Flames finally find her golden robe, and the garment goes up.

I said stop it, Béatrice, I don't want to watch this.

Her hair catches light. Béatrice's momma panics, fear and pain twist the features of her face. She slaps at her scalp to kill the flames.

Enough, Béatrice, enough!

Her fingers blister and the flesh cracks open. Her cheeks and forehead blacken, the skin begins to peel away.

Stop, Béatrice! Stop this! Stop this! Stop This!

I can't!

You can, you did it before.

That was different. This memory's too strong. I can't fight it. I can't!

Loretta's head is consumed by flames. Her eyes boil in their sockets. Everything goes black. Kyra and Béatrice are spared any further visions.

With a wrenching lurch, they're pushed out of Béatrice's seventeen-year-old head and out of the vision she's having.

They rise a few feet above Béatrice, curled on the ground, in the exact place and position where they found Loretta's remains.

The ground is wet and fertile, marsh grass grows in profusion, covering every trace of the fire, as if to rebuke the memory of everything that happened there.

Young Béatrice shakes with grief, her limbs spasm, her chest rises and falls as she struggles to catch her breath and tears are drenching her cheeks. She is reaching out her hands to the spot where her mother died a decade ago.

You have to understand what this did to me. I lost my mother all over again. I thought I could save her and it went horribly wrong. She burned to death in front of me and I couldn't do a thing for her. Everything I did, from this point on. Everything I'm going to show you. It all happened because of this.

CHAPTER 61:

Once again, Kyra finds her *Ti-Bon Ange* and Béatrice's *Gros-Bon Ange* shrinking.

As they shrink, Kyra and Béatrice begin to descend. The blades of marsh grass become long slender spires. Young Béatrice's face becomes a wide expanse of skin.

Kyra knows this is an out-of-body experience, a kind of vision quest she is undergoing. But she can't help but feel vertigo as she approaches the teenager sobbing on the ground.

Shrinking is a lot like plummeting from an unimaginable height. Even though she has no body, can come to no harm, she feels a giddy fear in their descent.

The tear tracks on Béatrice's cheek are the size of crystal streams. As they get closer, the tear drop becomes an Olympic pool.

As they dive into it, Kyra feels her consciousness dissolve. Becoming one with the tear's moisture. It rolls over the edge of Beatrice's cliff-sized cheek and hurtles to the soil below. The ground rushes up to meet the tear and, as it crashes into the dirt, Kyra's vision is shattered into a million tiny drops.

Each drop of sight flies apart, dispersing Kyra's consciousness. As the drops reach the zenith of their explosion, some ineluctable gravity draws them back toward one another. As they meet they reform themselves into new sights, new visions.

Kyra is no longer in the bayou. She is inside another memory. Hovering over the living room of a small single-story house.

She sees Young Béatrice below her, on a couch with a girl of a similar age. The girl has brown, shoulder-length hair and skinny legs. She's wearing a floral print dress and costume jewelry. There are math textbooks open on the sofa and an empty pizza box on a coffee table. The two girls are drinking tea out of mugs.

Kyra is sure she knows the girl in the floral print dress.

Is that Frances Donovan?

I offered to coach her on Trigonometry. She was a senior, but so behind she accepted.

Frances drops her cup. Her body sways and slumps to one side. Her eyelids droop and close. Her chest moves slower and slower and then stops moving altogether. Béatrice checks her pulse.

Pain and dismay cross her face. She's appalled at what she's done.

You poisoned her?

It's the tea. It's very effective and you'd never know you were drinking it, as you know.

Thanks for the reminder. I guess this explains the mystery surrounding her death. How the killer got into a locked house with no forced entry. No-one guessed she let you in to help with her trig.

I guess they didn't.

Béatrice reaches into a large satchel at her feet. She brings out plastic sheeting which she places under Frances's head and body. Then she takes the same knife she used on Mary Jo Bernard from her bag.

Please tell me we're not stuck in this memory. I know I'm reliving your trauma, but I don't think I can take any more.

I don't want to see this either. We don't need to stick around.

Béatrice's shame descends on this memory like an anvil dropped from a height. The memory shatters and Kyra's vision disperses once again. Splits into a million little drops like mist over a meadow. It is disconcerting and disorienting.

Why is this happening again? I can't see properly.

We're traveling through my tears. God knows I shed a lot at this time. It'll clear in a moment.

There's one other thing that's bugging me.

What's that?

Hasn't the anniversary of your momma's death passed?

Yes.

So why did you take Frances's eyeballs?

So I could go back and save my momma. To put right what happened the last time. I thought you understood.

I understand your motives, but not your methods. Don't you have to be in the same place, at the same time, on the same day for the spell to work? That's how it worked the first time, it's how it worked with me and Billy-Ray.

That's how it works when the death is accidental. You can see through the eyes of someone connected to the victim, on the anniversary of the events you want to see. But there's a stronger, darker conjuration than that.

You're talking about murder, right?

Yes, if you purposefully sacrifice someone, you can choose the person close to them, whose eyes you want to see out of, and you can choose the exact time in their lives that you want to go back to.

That doesn't justify what you did. She invited you into her home and you killed her in cold blood.

She wouldn't have been dead if it had worked. If I'd saved my momma, then everything would've been different. Her mother would've been alive and none of this would ever have happened. I thought it was just temporary, I thought I could go back and fix everything.

You didn't fix it, though.

No, I went back and saw that night through Ethel's eyes. I tried to keep Reverend Lee away from the tent. When he refused to follow the Creole woman, I hung back and tried to stop him going after them. He pushed me over and charged away. I got lost, and by the time I found the tent, the fire had started. I raced inside and tried to drag my momma out, but she didn't know me, she wouldn't come, and she died in front of me, all over again.

You saw it all over again?

It was worse the second time. But not as bad as the third.

The droplets of Kyra's vision coalesce. Her sight clears, as though she's blinking away tears. They're in the hallway outside a one-bedroom condo. A girl scout knocks at a door, holding a basket with cookies and a flask. She's very tall for her age and her uniform doesn't fit. When a woman, in her early thirties, comes to the door, Kyra realizes what's so familiar.

You're the girl scout, the one neighbors saw.

I didn't think it would work. I hadn't worn that uniform since seventh grade.

Alison looks drunk. Béatrice shows her the cookies and the flask. Alison shakes her head, but Béatrice puts her hands together, as if in prayer, and pleads. Alison relents and invites her inside.

Your special tea's in the flask, isn't it?

Do I need to answer?

So long as we don't have to go inside. I know what happens to Alison. I don't want to see what you did to the body. I've seen the photographs.

The mutilation, that wasn't me.

I just saw you go in, Béatrice, I know what you're going to do.

I took her life, but I didn't cut her up.

Then who did?

There's more to see, but not here.

A cloud of mist descends on the scene, obscuring everything.

Nicole was Alison's aunt, wasn't she?

Yes.

How did she work out?

No better than Loretta and Ethel. Nicole was sixty-nine. She wasn't strong or fast. I tried to put out the flaming oil before the Reverend picked it up. I made her take off her cardigan and drape it over the flames, but the oil spilled and the cardigan caught alight and so did Nicole. She ran into the back wall of the tent, and it went up again. At least I was dead before my momma went that time.

You haven't told me who mutilated Alison.

I'm getting to that.

And all at once Kyra is aware that she might know, but she doesn't want to.

CHAPTER 62:

The hallway becomes two dimensional. A flat image with no depth or substance.

Long rivulets, like spilled tears, run down the image, smearing it. The image begins to run, washed by the tears like ink on wet paper. Colors run together and the image washes away, replaced by a mist of tears.

The tears evaporate. Kyra is in another three dimensional memory, replacing the last one. She is floating, near the ceiling of a large bedroom. The walls are covered with posters, punk bands and Haitian artwork. Béatrice is standing at the window in pajamas, peering through the curtains. She's just woken.

Firelight plays on Béatrice's face. It's coming from the back yard below. Worried, Béatrice turns from the window. She leaves her bedroom, and Kyra follows her down the uncarpeted stairs of the old, wooden farmhouse.

She reaches the kitchen, at the back of the house. The dishes are stacked by the sink. There's something in the tub. Béatrice walks over to see what it is. From over her shoulder, Kyra sees the tub is filled with water. Thick trails of fluid stain the water, dark crimson in the moonlight. A large hunting knife sits at the bottom of the tub. Its blade caked with blood.

Béatrice leaves by the back door. Out into the backyard. Her daddy is shirtless in the night air. Flames leap upward from a trashcan. He takes off his jeans, stained and splattered with blood. He puts them into the fire, along with his socks and shoes.

Béatrice is nervous. She tries to talk to him. He dismisses her, points to the house.

What're you saying?

I ask what he's doing. He says: 'Cleaning up'. I say: 'Cleaning up what?' He says: 'Your mess, now go on back to bed'.

So, your daddy was the one who...

He's trying to protect me, I'm all he has left.

How did he know it was you?

He's a cop, and my daddy. A daddy always knows, he'd say. But my daddy always goes too far.

The memory loses its depth and color. A torrent of tears wash the image away. Some unseen agent blinks those tears away to reveal the outside of the barn where Béatrice hides her momma's things.

Hawkins is leaving the barn. A canvas bag hangs from his shoulder. He's dragging the trunk Béatrice found in her Gramma's attic out into the yard. Béatrice rushes to stop him, tugging at his arm. She grabs the trunk, tries to pull it back into the barn. Hawkins is too strong. Her efforts come to nothing.

Out in the yard, is a can of kerosene. Hawkins empties it into the trunk, then throws a match after it. Béatrice rushes towards the trunk to rescue what she can. Hawkins holds her back, protecting her from the flames.

It's all I have left of my momma. I didn't think he would be so cruel. I thought, 'At least he hasn't got the grimoire. At least I hid that separately'.

Hawkins reaches into the canvas bag and pulls out the grimoire. He holds it over the flames. Béatrice tries to snatch the grimoire from his hand. He holds her at arm's length. She claws at his arm and grasps for the grimoire, just out of reach.

Hawkins hurls the grimoire into the burning trunk. Béatrice screams and launches herself at the pyre, trying to save her precious items. Hawkins grabs her round the waist and swings her away. She pounds his chest with her fists screaming at him, tears flow down her cheeks.

I told him I hated him. I said I never wanted to see him again. I asked him how he could do this? He said: 'Because I love you. Because I can't keep on protecting you. Because I don't want you to die by lethal injection!'

Béatrice struggles in his grip and breaks free. She runs from the yard to the front of the house. There's a truck parked in the front yard. She climbs into it and turns the key. Hawkins races up to the truck but he is too late. Béatrice drives off, away from the farm.

As Béatrice heads toward the road the memory freezes, becomes two dimensional and is washed away in a flood of tears.

I drive the truck into town. I'm aiming to ram-raid the Sheriff's office. But I'm crying too much. I can't see straight, and I hit a streetlight instead. The Sheriff's men take me into custody and call Doc McFadden.

Does he help?

No. I'm hysterical, and I try to tell McFadden what's really going on, what I'd done. He doesn't believe me, of course. He has me committed to an institution, with my daddy's full approval.

Why does your daddy do that?

To protect me. To keep me out of harm's way. Where I can't make any more hexes. To make certain no-one believes my confession.

How'd your daddy find the trunk?

He probably checked my Gramma's attic and then scoured the barns. He's a smart man, Kyra, and like he said, a daddy always knows.

The shower of tears trickles to a stop and a new memory comes into focus. Kyra recognizes the Godin house, from seeing it with Delilah.

It's night time. Kyra can see lots of teens through the lighted windows. There's a party going on. Béatrice is standing on the stoop. There's a crate at her feet. She rings the doorbell.

The door opens and a teenage boy stands in the doorway. His mouth opens in surprise.

Is that Steve Godin?

The very same.

Doesn't seem pleased to see you.

He thinks I was sent to the nuthouse.

Weren't you?

I broke out the night before. I told everyone at the party it was a rumor. I'd been sent to live with my aunt.

Steve is joined by other teens. They're reluctant to let Béatrice in. She opens the crate and pulls out vodka bottles. They invite Béatrice in.

Bought the vodka with my daddy's credit card. Laced it with a strong dose of the tea. I'd started keeping my own grimoire, you see. Had all my momma's recipes in it.

And everyone drank the vodka?

It was better than the keg they had. I made cocktails, but most people drank it neat.

So, that's how you drugged everyone.

It's not that difficult when you think about it. A house full of horny teens who want to get drunk and laid. Just bring alcohol.

Did you mutilate Elizabeth Boudreaux?

I gave her a bigger dose of the tea. Once she was out, I took her eyes, that's all. As soon as I had them, I lit out for the bayou to start the ceremony. My daddy called at the house an hour later. He knew I was out. He was searching for me. It was just luck he got to the house first. He sent his men after me to buy time.

To cut poor Elizabeth up?

He was doing it to protect me, to throw suspicion off me. He was trying to keep me from being locked up, or worse.

A mist of tears descends. The memory fades as a curtain of bitterness and regret is pulled across it.

They return to the bayou. Kyra sees Béatrice led away by two deputies. She's crying inconsolably, hardly able to stand.

But he did lock you up in that institution.

I wasn't well. Beside myself with grief. One last chance to save my momma and I blew it.

It didn't go well?

It was horrendous.

Whitney was hard to control?

No, it wasn't that. There wasn't much going on upstairs, you get me?

Yeah.

And by that point I'd had practice taking control. It didn't help. As soon as my momma put the bowl of oil down, I had Whitney run and grab her. Threw her over my shoulder and ran for the exit. I was hoping to get clear of the place, but my momma fought and kicked. Her followers blocked the exit. I tried to fight, Whitney was strong, but there were too many. Then things played out the way they always did.

I'm sorry.

I brought it on myself.

Kyra and Béatrice move away from the memory. They fly out until they find the somnolent waters of the bayou and plunge deep into them.

So many mysteries surrounding the murders now make sense. But Béatrice hasn't revealed why she's showing Kyra.

There's a deeper purpose at play here, and Kyra fears it is darker than she knows.

CHAPTER 63:

They are no longer traveling through Béatrice's tears. That part of their journey is over.

They are back in the River of the Guédé. But Kyra senses the journey is coming to an end.

Béatrice is flagging. The force of the current weighs heavily on her *Gros-Bon Ange* and Kyra is afraid Béatrice's grip on her own *Ti-Bon Ange* might falter. She could be lost to the river. Unable to make her way back.

The temperature of the river has changed. It's tepid, like deep fatigue. Bone-weary exhaustion. Like Béatrice wants to lie down and let it all go.

Are you okay?

Yeah, no, I'm fine. I've enough energy for this last part, don't worry.

So, we are getting to the end.

Nearly there.

Is that why you're tiring?

It's not that, I've been living with these memories so long. They take a toll. I've tried to make up for what I've done but they're a burden I can't carry anymore.

So, you're trying to pass them onto me?

No, no of course not.

Then, what, Béatrice?

What do you mean?

This whole trip down the river of the dead. Horror show after horror show. There's a reason for it. There's something you want me to do. What is it?

You're right, I'm getting to that. Please trust me. There's just one more thing I need to show you.

Béatrice guides them upriver. Kyra knows they're still moving through time as they ride the currents, but she has the sense they're getting closer to the present day. There's a familiarity about the timestream they're entering, as if she's lived through it.

They move closer to the river bank. Up ahead there's an opening. Not a rough one, like the alligator's den. This one is lined with concrete. It's a culvert overflowing into the river. As Béatrice bucks the current and moves them into the culvert, Kyra tries not to think about the kind of underground tributaries that would flow into the river of the dead.

The culvert is tight at first but the round, concrete walls seem to expand, growing larger and further away. Until Kyra realizes the culvert isn't expanding, they are shrinking. She feels the same disorientation she felt the last time. It's a sensation she will never get used to.

They take a sharp turn upward through a smaller pipe that gives out onto a maze of plumbing. Kyra loses count of the twists, turns and new pipes that they take. As the pipes get smaller, so do they.

Finally they make their way up a drainpipe. They follow the U-shaped bends of a P-trap and rise through a drain hole into a sink. Water is slowly emptying into the drain. There are thin traces of scarlet in it.

Not more blood.

No, just paint.

Kyra sees huge logs in the water that are topped with bristles. As they rise up through the water, she and Béatrice regain their normal stature, even as they remain bodiless and invisible. Kyra's perspective returns and she sees the logs are thinly tipped paintbrushes. They are hovering in the storeroom at the back of Béatrice's work unit.

This is the present, right?

Nearly, it's about a week before you turned up at my workshop.

Béatrice is sitting cross-legged on the floor in front of an old, battered suitcase. It's full of junk that Béatrice is sorting through.

She pulls out a stack of old notebooks, tied with gold ribbon. The top notebook is covered with a pattern of hand drawn symbols, like the ones Béatrice drew in flour.

That pattern, it's a what-do-you-call-it?

A Vèvè, yes.

Those are the notes you made from your momma's grimoire.

That's right. My daddy was throwing a bunch of junk out of the farmhouse. I was surprised when he asked if there was anything I wanted. I took this suitcase.

Beatrice traces the *Vèvè* with her finger. Her face wistful. She puts the notebooks to one side. She lifts some gold scarves from the suitcase and stops dead. Something has caught her eye. Horror shows in her face.

She reaches into the suitcase. Stops, and pulls her hand back out. She bites a knuckle, staring at something Kyra can't see. She goes in again and pulls out a small object. It's the fetish of *Kalfou* Kyra saw on her first visit.

Béatrice takes the fetish into her work area. She holds it over the trash, but she can't seem to throw it away. She's wrestling with herself.

She goes instead to her altar and places it in front of the objects there. She turns to walk away, pauses, and turns back shaking her head.

Béatrice lifts the fetish off and goes to the trash. She stops half way and goes back to the altar. She hides the fetish at the back. Then changes her mind and puts it back at the front.

I thought it went missing years ago. The minute I saw it, I knew everything was going to change. Then you walked into my life. It was calling you, that's why it turned up again. It was calling you into my life.

All the way up in Chicago?

The time was right. That's why it brought you to me.

I had my own reasons for coming.

Doesn't mean it wasn't calling you.

That's why I couldn't help myself. Why I had to pick it up.

That's what I've been trying to show you. This started way before you left Chicago.

But why me?

You're connected in some deep, personal way.

Through my birth mother, Caitlin, when I killed her?

You killed your birth mother?

I didn't mean to. It was an accident. She was abusive. Came at me with a knife. I was two years old, kicking and flailing, trying to get away. My foot hit the knife. It went right into her eye, and she died almost instantly.

That explains a lot.

Does it?

The hex was never closed down. I wasn't in a fit state. They locked me away. By the time I was better, I was done with Voodoo. I didn't realize the hex was active till you touched the fetish.

But why did it pick me?

Caitlin's death was connected to the ones I caused. The hex has certain rules and, without knowing it, you followed them.

But I was two.

I'm afraid that doesn't matter. You killed someone, it was an accident, like my first time, but you took out her eye. That's what the hex needs. It waited until you were ready and then it called you to come complete the hex. You remember when you touched it?

Knocked me on my ass.

Exactly, all the power that surged between us. That was the hex starting up again. Soon after you started seeing through someone else's eyes, am I right?

Yeah, it was Billy-Ray Johnson, my birthfather. I learned about Caitlin, how she abused me, and how I killed her. Billy-Ray was stalking her, to keep an eye on me, because he knew what she was doing.

And that's how you learned he was your daddy?

Is that why I could see out of his eyes?

Because he was your daddy? Yes, but it was also because he was intimately connected to your momma.

I wouldn't say they were intimate.

But they had a child together and that's enough for the hex.

The last time I saw him I was two years old. I'd completely forgotten about it until I saw it again through his eyes. They took him away after that.

That was my fault.

They killed him you know. Lethal injection. He told them he was innocent right to the end. No one believed him. But he was. I know that now.

I'm so sorry.

Why didn't you do anything? Why didn't you tell anyone?

I tried, but they locked me away. Everyone thought I was crazy. No one believed me. My daddy saw to that. No lawyer could have put me on the stand or taken a deposition. I was delusional, that's what my health records say.

But he paid for crimes that you committed.

If I could change places with him, I would. Truly I would. I've been in hell ever since. That's why I did all this. Took you here, showed you these things.

You still haven't told me what you want.

There's one last thing I need to tell you.

Why don't you just tell me what you want?

I will, but this is important. I need to warn you.

Warn me about what?

The person whose eyes you saw the past through, Billy-Ray.

What about him?

I've had issues with the people whose eyes I looked out of.

What kind of issues?

Well, let's say they didn't always want to leave the party.

I'm not following you.

They don't always go. You may have seen their pasts, but they can hang around in your present.

In what way?

It's hard to say. It's different every time and it may never happen. When I was in the institution, and for a few years afterwards, I could feel them around me like a presence, do you understand?

I know how that feels.

But it wasn't just me, sometimes other people felt them—

How do you mean?

Objects would move. Books would open at certain pages, especially Bibles, as if someone was giving me a message. People around me would feel a hand on them that wasn't there. Occasionally they'd be nudged or spill something. Nothing major, but it happened enough not to be coincidence.

Like a poltergeist you mean?

Something like that.

Now you need to tell me what you want from me.

It's a big ask. Probably the biggest thing anyone's asked of you.

Kyra knew in that moment Béatrice was right. And she had no idea if she could do what Béatrice was going to ask.

CHAPTER 64:

Kyra's not in her body. She's experiencing Béatrice's memories as a spirit. A *Ti-Bon Ange* Béatrice calls it.

Even still, she senses a change in the air. A crackling energy that's just out of her perceptive range. Something is about to happen.

The memory in front of her appears a little distant. As if she's taken a step back from it. Time begins to speed up, just as it did by the side of the canal. Béatrice moves in a blur, working, turning off the lights, leaving for the day, then returning seconds later for a new day's work.

She goes through this routine in a blur. Then Kyra appears. She touches the fetish, falls over, wakes up, leaves. Beatrice works. Kyra comes back, leaves, then comes again and leaves her backpack. She comes one more time, drinks the tea and collapses. She wakes and finds herself chained to the floor. Her whole time in Yeuxville reduced to a couple of minutes.

In a last, violent finale to this frenetic tableaux, Béatrice takes a knife to her eye sockets and presses her eyeballs into Kyra's bloody palms.

Time slows to its usual speed. She is almost back in the present.

Kyra has been viewing this memory from above, bobbing near the ceiling. As the flow of time slows, she floats gently to the floor. Settling beside her unconscious self and Béatrice's corpse.

Kyra's mouth is open. Her eyelids are hooded and only the whites of her eyes are visible. A trickle of black saliva runs from the corner of her mouth.

Until this moment, Kyra has not been visible in Béatrice's memories. She's been a bodiless and insubstantial presence. Now the outlines and contours of her *Ti-Bon Ange* start to glow. It's as if she's been sketched on the air in shining lines of light.

Kyra holds her hands up to see. They're transparent, outlined in bright pulsing lines. The rest of her is the same.

The air on the other side of the room sparkles and ripples, like light playing on the surface of a lake. The same glowing lines from which Kyra is made draw an image in the empty space of the unit. Kyra recognizes what it is right away. Béatrice is materializing.

This is what my Ti-Bon Ange *looks like?*

It's how I picture it. So, this is how we both appear.

Kyra looks down at herself.*It's pretty.*

We don't have much time left.

So, stop being evasive. I'm not going to ask again.

I know. What I want is to close this hex down, once and for all.

How do we do that?

It sounds simple, but it might just be the hardest thing you'll ever do.

No pressure then. What do you need from me?

To close this hex, I have to be released.

And how do I do that?

You have to forgive me.

Forgive you?

I did terrible things Kyra. I murdered three people. I took the eyes from four corpses. I sent an innocent man to his death and robbed you of a father. I'm deeply, deeply sorry for the things I did. I'm tired now. Tired of struggling with the memory of what I've done. Tired of trying to make up for it. Trying to redeem myself with good deeds.

All that volunteering. I thought you were too good to be true.

I thought if I lived a good life, if I did good things and helped people I could be redeemed. I was wrong. My sins found me out, like in Numbers 32:23. *I'll never be absolved, but I might just be understood. I might even be forgiven.By me?*

By you.

What makes you think I'll forgive you?

I have no right to ask. I certainly have no right to expect it. But Kalfou *called you to me. The Loa want an end to this disruption. To close this circle and banish the spirits. You're a part of this hex. You've been a part since you were a tiny child. It haunts you too.*

I know it does. But I've only just found out. It's a lot to process.

It's a big ask, but can you forgive me?

I don't know.

Béatrice's *Gros-Bon Ange* is clearer now. Her lines sharper and more defined. She's pulsing with the power of her plea. With the need to be forgiven.

Kyra looks in her eyes – those beautiful, pain filled eyes – and sees a little girl who never stopped missing her mother. Who couldn't live with the random injustice of the world and did something terrible as a consequence.

She glances down at Béatrice's body lying next to her own. The discarded, eyeless husk with its blood-streaked cheeks and vacant face.

Kyra can't help seeing Caitlin, on the kitchen floor of her old apartment, all those years ago. She did terrible things too, most of them to Kyra. But she never killed anyone.

Only Kyra and Béatrice have done that.

There is blood on Kyra's hands, and that's not all.

There are so many things Kyra regrets. So many things she has to make up for. There's the ten grand she took. It wasn't hers. She didn't have permission. She knew she shouldn't take it. But she was so mad.

There are her parents who must be worried sick. They haven't heard from her in days. They have no idea where she is. They don't even know if she's alive or dead.

There's the people she lied to. Delilah and just about everyone she met in Yeuxville, even Sheriff Hawkins and his deputies. And there's people she forced to lie, like Béatrice.

Given everything she's learned about Béatrice, that doesn't seem too bad. But Kyra is still in the wrong. She shouldn't have put Béatrice in that position. Her crimes don't excuse Kyra's misdemeanor.

Are Béatrice's crimes so much worse than hers? Only a few nights ago Kyra was ready to murder Caitlin all over again. To use Billy-Ray to take revenge for all the abuse she suffered at Caitlin's hands.

Caitlin had failed her so badly as a mother. She should have protected Kyra. Should have nurtured Kyra's sense of wonder and interest in the world. Not terrorized and beat her into submission.

When Kyra thinks about the tiny child she was, simply trying to survive in that environment, trying to navigate Caitlin's explosive moods and selfish behavior, she gets so mad.

No child should be treated that way. Made to feel so frightened and powerless. How could a grown adult do to Kyra's delicate body what Caitlin had?

This is where her anger originated. The molten core of lava that burns unceasingly deep inside Kyra. That turns this anger inward, to continue the abuse Caitlin started.

Because Kyra also blames herself. As stupid as it sounds, she does. Blames herself for letting Caitlin treat her that way. Even though she was too small to do anything about it.

And Kyra blames herself for Caitlin's death. Even though it was in self-defense. Even though she'd forgotten all about the murder until she saw it through Billy-Ray's eyes.

A tiny part of her consciousness has not forgotten. Has held onto the memory of her crime and tortured Kyra ever since.

All this sits like a toxic dump at the core of Kyra's being. Poisoning every part of her life. Every decision she makes. Every relationship she has. Especially with her parents.

She blames her parents for all the things they can't fix because they're the people she loves the most. The people who love her the most. And if this is all Kyra's fault, and they still love her, then they must be to blame too.

As crazy and twisted as all this sounds, she knows it's true. Where is all this coming from? She's made more breakthrough in the last hour than most people make in years of therapy. How can that be?

Is it something to do with being outside of her body looking in? Doesn't *Ti-Bon Ange* mean 'good little angel'? Is this part of her higher self? Is she wiser and smarter when she's like this, or simply less distracted, more able to make the insights that change her life?

Whatever the case, Kyra sees clearly for the first time in an age. She's not to blame and neither are the people she loves the most.

Kyra has to accept that Caitlin will never apologize for the things she did and never explain them. Billy-Ray won't tell her why he left her at Caitlin's mercy, why he didn't fight harder for shared custody. Kyra will never get closure for these things unless she grants it herself.

These things are her problems now and only *she* can fix them. She has no power over any other person, or anything that's already happened. But there is one thing she does have power over and that's how she reacts to it all. How she lets it affect her.

Having this one thought is the single most inspiring thing that Kyra's ever done. Because she knows this is something she *can* do. She *knows* it to be true.

She needs to forgive Caitlin, Billy-Ray and her parents and, more importantly, she needs to forgive herself.

But how does she do that?

How does Kyra forgive herself when no one is more aware of her sins?

Maybe it's because Kyra is still in her *Ti-Bon Ange*, but suddenly she knows.

To forgive herself she must first forgive everyone who has ever hurt her in any way.

And that includes Béatrice.

Kyra comes back to herself. She realizes she's been lost in reverie for ages.

Or was it just a moment? Time is so elastic in this state, she could easily experience a lifetime of revelations in a single beat of her heart. Just as in a dream.

She's back in the unit. She sees her unconscious body on the floor and Béatrice's body sprawled next to it. She looks from the bodies to Béatrice's *Gros-Bon Ange*.

She reaches out her hands to Béatrice, who reaches back. They can't touch or feel one another, but as their hands overlap, the glowing light that outlines them grows brighter and pulses with a greater intensity.

Of course I forgive you. I see you and I know the path you've walked to get to this moment. I've walked it with you.

Kyra senses a rush of emotions emanating from Béatrice. They flow from her and into Kyra from their overlapping hands. Much as her memories had flowed into Constance, just a few days ago. That had been an unpleasant experience. This is pleasant, though no less intense.

What flows from Béatrice is relief, and gratitude. Deep, deep remorse for what she's done and love, pure unbridled love toward Kyra, for forgiving her, in spite of all she knows.

Thank you, Kyra. Truly, thank you.

Kyra has the sense that the universe is changing gears. That some hidden machinery behind the curtain of reality is grinding into life and changing the scene. It's unnerving and disorienting because it challenges everything Kyra knows about the way things are.

The two far walls of the unit are suddenly gone. As if Kyra has just realized she's standing on a film set. But instead of cameras and crew on the other side of the set, there is an endless void of unknowable existence.

A single shining road stretches out from what was once the corner of the room. Somewhere, in the distant void beyond, another equally shining road crosses it. Two figures stand next to this intersection.

Kyra can't make out their features. Something tells her she needs to imagine what they might look like and the more she does, the clearer they become until she has a crystal-clear picture of them both.

The first figure is a beautiful, young Creole man. His hair falls in long dreadlocks and an enigmatic fire burns in his piercing eyes. He is dressed in black and red the color of the sky at twilight.

Opposite him, on the other side of the crossroads, is an older African man, with a broad-brimmed straw hat on his head and a corn cob pipe in his mouth.

He is dressed in simple work clothes, a white shirt and dark pants, his hands rest on a cane.

Is that Kalfou at the crossroads?

Béatrice turned to look.

Yes it is.

Who's that with him.

That's Elegua.

Like at the shrine, on the crossroads just out of town.

Yeah, that's the one.

Do they always hang out together?

Béatrice smiled.

Some people say they're brothers. Others that they're rivals. Either way, they're both involved in this.

The hex you mean?

Yeah.

You have to go now don't you, with them?

I do.

What happens after that?

I honestly have no idea. Guess I'm about to find out. Maybe one day I'll tell you all about it.

I'd like that.

Béatrice pulls her hands back, turns and walks toward the shining road. She stops, just before she reaches the corner, turns back and waves.

Kyra waves back. Béatrice looks reluctantly out along the path at the two waiting Loas.

She puts her shoulders back, lifts her chin and steps out onto the road.

There's a blinding flash of light as she does.

Like a distant sun going supernova it grows and grows in size. Kyra can no longer see Béatrice, or the road or the two Loas awaiting her.

The light fills her vision. If she weren't in a spirit form she would likely be blinded. As the light reaches its brightest point, Kyra is sure she sees five fleeting shadows appear from nowhere and race toward the center of the light, as if they were chasing Béatrice.

The first four move in unison and the last seems to be trailing behind the others, as though hesitant and uncertain if it will be accepted.

The shadows are gone so quickly Kyra is not even sure she's seen them. But she is almost certain that one resembles Loretta and another Whitney. And she could swear the last shadow was cast by the woman who gave birth to her.

The walls rush back in. The unit is as it was. But emptier, hollow, even a little forlorn. The light begins to dim, a leaden gloom descends on the room and Kyra is gripped with the sudden certainty that something terrible is about to happen.

CHAPTER 65:

The gloom gets thicker, almost viscous, as if someone has melted the shadows and let them trickle across the room.

Only the center is visible. The center where Kyra's body and Béatrice's corpse lie.

Béatrice's face is blank. An empty slate. As lacking in personality as her sockets lack eyes. Even her limbs are sacks of meat hugging bones.

Kyra will never speak with Béatrice again. Never hear her voice, brush her lips or hold her hand. Never look forward to seeing her, with that anxious desire she hardly dare admit.

Her soul has been released. Her *Gros-Bon Ange*, her *Ti-Bon Ange*, every kind of *Ange.* Everything that animated Béatrice's physical form and made her uniquely herself is gone. All that's left is flesh. Abandoned. Irredeemably dead.

Kyra's own body is almost as immobile. Only the set of her eyebrows, a slight twitch at the corner of her mouth and a restless tension in her muscles suggests she's not dead.

Kyra doesn't want to go back. Doesn't want to inhabit that physical form again. The idea appalls her. Stepping back into her body would be like stepping out of the shower with freshly washed hair and lightly scented skin. And seeing a pile of clothes on the floor.

Clothes that are caked in mud and stink of sweat. That would scrape her skin and make her smell. Making her feel small and dirty and inhibited.

As a *Ti-Bon Ange* she can traverse time. Ride the River of the Guédé and relive the past of another. She can witness Loas and the roads they walk beyond the known states of man. Why would she give up that freedom for the crippling limits of flesh?

But the liquid gloom at the outskirts of the room grows darker and claims more space. Moving in on Kyra and Béatrice's inert bodies. It's goading her. Hemming her in and pushing her back to her body.

Kyra knows she can't step into the darkness. Can't let it touch her. She can't exist there and it's giving her no choice. Soon there will be nowhere to go but her body.

But something terrible is going to happen as soon as she slips back into that body. Kyra knows this for a fact. She doesn't want to face this. She wants to escape.

She wants to part the darkness. Beat a path to the wall and pass through it like the ghost she is. She wants to flee Yeuxville. Hurry home to Chicago and be with her parents. But she can't leave her body to the fate that awaits it.

If only she could pick it up. Move it out of the unit and away from danger. But the only way to do that is by returning to it. Sinking into that frail and limited flesh for what's left of her limited life.

Kyra takes a couple steps closer and wonders if there's a way of getting her body to move without inhabiting it, of guiding it to safety.

She reaches out a hand toward it. That changes everything, she realizes too late.

The thin, glowing line that runs like an outline around her transparent form comes away from the end of her left index finger. Like thread unraveling it spools toward her forehead, right between her eyebrows.

Kyra's hand is disappearing. As more and more of the glowing line that once traced it is pulled into Kyra's body. She takes a step back in panic. Her heels brushing the darkness. Tries to pull what's left of her hand free. But that only speeds up the unraveling.

As her hand vanishes entirely, Kyra grabs her wrist with her right hand, tries to hold it together. This is not a good idea.

As Kyra's wrist and forearm unravel, so does her right hand. Two threads of glowing light are tugged from around the outline and pulled toward the center of her chest and the middle of her stomach.

Pretty soon Kyra's arms have lost their form, the glowing lines that defined them drawn back into her body. The darkness edges in, swallowing Béatrice's body, till the only thing Kyra can see is her own body and the glowing lines that once traced her *Ti-Bon Ange* are being gathered back into her flesh and blood.

Her body pulls her spirit closer. The tips of its toes touch the edge of her right arm and they too unravel. The lines that run from them are pulled into the base of her spine and that tiny spot between her bottom and her crotch.

As the legs of her spirit-self unwind and are lost, Kyra shrinks in size. She feels a tug at her crown and one last glowing line escapes her *Ti-Bon Ange* and moves toward the top of her body's head.

This last line stops before it reaches her head and winds itself into a glowing ball that floats above it like a spool. All the threads that once made up her outline are being wound back into her physical body. Each spot at which they enter her body is like a spool, spinning Kyra back into her flesh.

Her body is greedy to reclaim what has left it. Demands her *Ti-Bon Ange* return to its rightful place. The trickling darkness of the gloom leaves Kyra no place to exist outside.

But she doesn't want to go.

Please, please don't make me.

I don't want this. I don't want to do this.

This is against my will.

Let me go.

But she can't go. Can't leave and still live. Kyra knows that.

But she also knows her body is in peril

That it might not live much longer.

And there's nothing she can do.

CHAPTER 66:

There's nothing she can do.

Her body is quicksand pulling her under.

It's a blackhole from which her light cannot escape.

It's the suit of a prisoner condemned to life. She can no longer shed it.

She's back in her cell. Her cage of ribs, bones, skin and muscle.

Kyra's lost everything that she was.

She was her good little angel. Combing through the memories of a lost soul who'd lost her mother. Who'd committed one atrocity to cancel another and when that didn't work committed more crimes to make good.

She'd been closer to Béatrice than almost anyone in her life by the time Kyra forgave her. Forgave her and closed down a hex that was conjured when Kyra was barely a child.

She'd discovered things about herself that would affect her for the rest of her life. Let her heal wounds she'd hardly known were there.

But the rest of her life might not be that long. And she might not have the time to let those wounds heal.

Kyra was back in her body. She felt panic as a physical response. She was in danger. Mortal danger. Life threatening danger.

It was there. Waiting for her.

The moment she opened her eyes.

CHAPTER 67:

The moment she opened her eyes, Kyra knew something was wrong. She just couldn't tell what it was. Her body was waking up. One pain and discomfort at a time.

The concrete floor was cold and damp. Her wrists were sore and chafed, her ankles too.

Her muscles were stiff and cramped from lying spread-eagled. Her head throbbed. Her throat was dry and there was a sharp pain in her right side. It was causing her to rock.

Her body was moving from side to side. The ceiling of the industrial unit was a blur as Kyra's head was jerked along with her body. The fluorescent lights a streak of bright that burned an image in her retina.

Someone had their boot in Kyra's side. Moving their foot up and down to shake her awake. She wanted them to stop. She felt sick.

The gorge rose in her throat. Kyra turned her head to the left and tried to aim at the floor. Her stomach had been empty for too long. All that came up was milky, gray bile. It burned her throat and tasted of the bitter herbs in Béatrice's tea.

It spilled from the corner of her mouth and stained the side of her t-shirt. Kyra turned back to the boot, still rocking her. She tried for the words to stop it, but her lips and tongue were too groggy.

Kyra saw the tanned leather of a cowboy boot. Her eyes moved to khaki chinos. A light tan shirt. The bright gold star pinned prominently on the chest.

And above that, the grim countenance of Sheriff Hawkins.

CHAPTER 68:

"Nice of you to join us, Sleeping Beauty. Mind telling me what you've done to my daughter?"

Kyra's heart began to race. Her breaths came quick and shallow. Her mouth found the ability to form words again.

"I haven't done anything to Béatrice."

Hawkins nodded to her hands. "Then why are you holding her eyeballs?"

Kyra's palms stung. She remembered the cuts, tender and scabbed. And the cool orbs that sat on them. Sticking to the scabs. Her fingers still curled about them.

She forced them back. Opened her hands and shook them. The eyeballs peeled away from her wounds and slithered to the ground with a wet plop.

Hawkins narrowed his eyes. "This some kinda sex game gone wrong? She push you too far with the knife? Till you took it off her?"

"I didn't do anything. How could I? She drugged me and tied me to the floor."

Hawkins looked over to Béatrice's corpse. He pursed his lips and nodded. "She's given to that kinda behavior. Guess I spared the belt too much. She didn't have no momma growing up. Wasn't set a good example. Nor were you, I imagine. Certainly don't do as you're told."

"Can you untie me please? I'm very sore."

Hawkins pushed the brim of his hat back. "Don't quite know what to do with you yet."

"Just untie me. Let me clean up and go catch that bus. I can come back later and make a statement with my parents, I promise."

Hawkins folded his arms. Let out a breath and shook his head. "That bus left over two days ago. You're gonna wish that you were on it."

"It can't be over two days. I only missed the first one. I was on my way to catch the next. I came here to collect my bag and Béatrice did this to me."

Hawkins said nothing.

"How long was I out?"

"I was you, I'd be more worried about how long you're going to get."

"Get for what?"

"Murder of my daughter."

"But I didn't murder her. She drugged me. Tied me up and poisoned herself. Then cut out her own eyes."

"Good luck convincing a jury. D.A. might even ask for the death penalty. He won't try you as a minor."

"So you're going to frame me?"

"I'm simply going to present the evidence."

"Like you presented the evidence on Billy-Ray?"

Hawkins opened his mouth then shut it abruptly. A succession of micro-expressions crossed his face. Maybe Kyra was hyper-aware because of the danger she was in. Or maybe it was the after effects of the drug. But she could read every one.

Surprise. Calculation. Curiosity.

"What would *you* know about that?"

This was Kyra's only edge. Her one chance to get out unscathed. But Hawkins was dangerous and unpredictable. Kyra's fate hung on the next words she spoke. For some reason, she thought of her dad, the lawyer, and knew she had to channel him.

"I was you. I'd be worried about who I talked to, not what I know. The D.A. might consider not trying me at all if I can give him a bigger fish. What's a minor compared to a corrupt public servant."

"Corrupt public servant, that's a mighty strong accusation."

"It's a mighty long rap sheet. Suppressing evidence, tampering with a crime scene, even a couple murders."

"My daughter put these ideas in your head?"

"She might have done."

"Well, that's some death-bed confession. A shame the D.A. will want more than hearsay on a crime committed while you were in diapers."

"You're not the only one with evidence."

Hawkins stood very still. Hands on hips. Eyes hooded to slits. "You got a smoking gun, little miss?"

"I got better. I got a dossier from one of your dead deputies."

Hawkins blinked once, drew a deep breath and turned his back on Kyra. He took off his hat, held it to his chest and let his head fall back, gazing up at the ceiling.

"Dan's faggot nephew. Didn't give Delbert enough credit."

After what was probably a minute, but felt like eternity, Hawkins bowed his head, put his hat back on it and turned to address Kyra.

"Back when I was your age, a person kept their word. If they promised they'd do something, by God they did it. Not today. Your generation is more worried about pronouns than keeping their word. I guess you didn't get role models."

Kyra didn't like where this was going. Didn't like the implicit threat in Hawkins' voice. Had she overplayed her hand?

"See, I keep my promises, always have done. You broke yours when you weren't on that bus. But you put me in a difficult situation. I told you to leave my town. I made you a promise. I told you if you didn't, I'd make you disappear into the system. You weren't on that bus, but now I can't make you disappear into the system."

"Why not."

"Cos I have to make you disappear altogether."

CHAPTER 69:

Sheriff Hawkins reached into his left shirt pocket and produced a set of mirror shades. Like something out of an 80s movie.

He put on the shades and his expression was unreadable. His face blank and implacable. Kyra felt the urgent need to go to the bathroom.

Moving slowly, and with precision, he reached around to the back of his belt and produced a hunting knife.

"What are you doing?"

There was more desperation in Kyra's voice than she liked. It was the sight of the knife. Every time she saw one, she got nervous.

Hawkins stood astride Kyra's body and bent forward, pointing the knife directly at her. Kyra closed her eyes and turned her head. She strained against her bonds and clenched her teeth to stop a scream escaping. It came out as a high pitched whine. She shook her head and thrashed her limbs. All to no avail.

Kyra felt her left hand jerk as if someone was tugging the rope around her wrist. The rope went slack and fell away, releasing her hand. Hawkins had cut through her binding.

Kyra opened her eyes and watched as he cut the rope that held her other wrist and the ropes around her ankles. Hawkins stood and slipped his knife back into its sheath.

Kyra curled into a ball to protect herself, too afraid to do anything else. Her arms and knees pulled up to her chest. Her hands covering her face.

She felt his large, rough hands grab her under the arms and haul her to her feet. She opened her eyes as he lifted her arms, bent his knees and slung her over his shoulder.

He let out a sharp *huff* as he straightened up. His shoulder pressing into her gut. He grunted as he found his feet and staggered toward the door. Kyra flushed at his discomfort.

Had she put on that much weight since she got here? She hated herself for worrying about this. But she was powerless and he was going to decide her fate.

No. He'd already decided it. She just didn't want to admit it.

He carried her through the exit into the parking lot. Kyra turned her head to look at the sky. It was dark and full of clouds. Only a few stars could be seen, the others afraid to come watch what was happening.

Hawkins hoisted Kyra off his shoulder and set her on her feet next to his cruiser. He was so confident she was in his power that he didn't bother to cuff her. Just sauntered to his vehicle.

Kyra's brain was screaming at her to run. To take off into the night and find a dark, quiet corner to crawl into. But her legs wouldn't listen. Wouldn't take a single step. All they could do was shake with fear. It was like a nightmare in which danger was creeping up and she couldn't avoid it.

Hawkins opened the cruiser door and pointed to the back seat. Kyra knew, with a sickening certainty, that if she got in that car and sat on that seat, if she let that door close on her, no human being would see her alive again.

Then a light came on in a unit just across the way. And someone stepped out into the lot.

CHAPTER 70:

He was a tall, wiry guy in his late 50s, wearing light blue overalls and a baseball cap. Kyra couldn't run from Hawkins, but she could shout. She could shout at the top of her lungs.

"Please, mister, please, you've got to help me. I'm being abducted. He's going to kill me."

The guy put his head and shoulders back, took off his cap and scratched his short, thinning hair in bemusement.

"I know he's the Sheriff. And I know what you're thinking. But it's not like that. He's done things. Terrible things. Killed people. And he needs to keep me quiet. Please, you can't let him take me. You've got to help me get away!"

The guy smiled, shook his head and addressed Hawkins. "Got a wild one there, Sheriff."

"Drugs are a terrible thing."

"Got that right. Kids these days." He shook his head.

"Say hi to Eileen for me."

"Will do, Sheriff."

"Jed." Hawkins tipped the brim of his hat.

Jed went back inside his unit.

Hawkins put his hand in the small of Kyra's back and marched her to the car. Kyra's knees gave as she was forced into the backseat. He brought his face so close to hers she could see the pores on his skin and smell the sour whiskey on his breath.

"And what did that accomplish?"

"Nothing."

"That's right. Nothing."

He took the cuffs from his belt and snapped them around her right wrist. The cold, carbon steel bit into her skin and Kyra winced. Hawkins clipped the other cuff to the partition in front of her. She was trapped. There was no running now. Unless she gnawed off her hand like a coyote in a trap.

Kyra looked at her slender white wrist, pinched by the shiny cuff, and wondered if she could do it. Chew through the skin and flesh. The tendons and bone joints. All to be free. Anything to take her mind off what was coming.

Then the driver's door closed and put an end to her thoughts. A chill panic settled in her gut and began to creep through the rest of her body.

The light in the unit across the way went out.

Along with any hope of Kyra surviving this.

CHAPTER 71:

A bush leapt into the cruiser's headlights then cowered back. Hawkins leaned into the bend. No stars, no moon looked down. They hid their faces in the clouds.

Where were these backroads leading? Out to the bayou or further into the dark wastes beyond? Kyra was lost, alone and in terrible danger.

Her wrist screamed every time they took a bend or hit a pothole. Cuffs grinding bone. Made it hard to think or plan, to plot her escape.

Dislocate her thumb and slip her hand out the cuffs. It was pale and swollen from lack of blood. She'd hardly feel the pain.

Then what?

Open the door, get free. Could she do that? The car was moving at speed. Would she survive the fall? Tuck her head and roll? Maybe. She'd never jumped from a moving vehicle.

Then what?

Run and hide. But where – a ditch, a clump of bushes, an old barn? What if she broke an arm or a leg jumping out? Could she crawl and hide nearby? Wait until morning, get to the nearest town?

Hawkins wouldn't just let her go. He'd come find her. He knew these roads and she didn't. He'd drag her back to the car and things would go worse. Could they go any worse? She was trapped in a cop car with no return journey. This fare was strictly one way.

She'd reach through the partition. Grab his gun and shoot Hawkins in the back of the head.

Then what?

What if the car hit a tree? Would she survive? What if the gas tank exploded? Kyra was handcuffed to the partition. She'd die in the flames.

Go for his gun when they got out the car. Play possum, catch him off-guard, grab it from his holster and put one in his gut.

Kyra thought about pulling the trigger. Watching Hawkins double over and collapse. Could she do that to another human being? Even one who wanted to kill her?

She'd killed before, but that was as a child. A tiny defenseless babe who didn't know any better. A two year old in fear of her life. She had no sense of what she'd really done. There was no intention in the lucky kick that ended Caitlin's life. It was pure accident.

Kyra was no cop killer. She couldn't spend the rest of her life on the run with a new identity. Never able to see her mom and dad. Killing just wasn't in her.

It *was* in Hawkins. She knew that better than any living person. She'd seen the things he'd done. The bodies he'd mutilated. The cops he'd killed.

He knew she'd seen these things. That's why she was trapped in his car. In the dead of night. Driving some place remote. So Hawkins could cover up his daughter's crimes one last time. And cover his own ass while he was at it.

He was going to commit one more atrocity, in a long stream of atrocities. Only this time he was going to do it to Kyra.

Was this how it ended? Were these the last few moments of her life? She was so young. She hadn't graduated high school. It couldn't be all over. Not here, not yet.

Her senses were so alive. Her taste, her touch, her sight. Things were so clear and vibrant to her. How could that be about to end?

No one else thought like Kyra did. No one saw the world the way she saw it. She'd seen through two other peoples' eyes, so she knew this was true. This meant something. It was important.

She'd experienced miraculous things. Touched magic so deep it had healed the wounds on her soul. This was precious. It should be celebrated and protected. Not snuffed out like a candle. Not by someone like Hawkins.

But what if she had no hope left? What if all her miracles were used up and the darkness won?

Who would look after her?

Kyra needed her parents. Longed for them. Wanted to be a child again, curled up in their arms. Craved their help. Her mom's advice and her dad's unwavering support. If she could only see them one last time, tell them how much they meant to her, how sorry she was about everything that had happened.

If they could only save her from this man and the fate that awaited her.

If only anyone could.

CHAPTER 72:

Hawkins reduced his speed. This trip was coming to an end, but Kyra didn't want to think about that. He glanced back at her through the partition.

"I don't take any pleasure in this. It ain't personal, but you've left me no choice. Should've left when I told you. Your missing person's report put me in a bind. Could've reported you, but that would've brought attention I didn't want.

"So I tried to send you home. You were young so I was gentle, but I guess some people are just too dumb to help. Moment I saw you I knew you were trouble. I got a nose for these things, an intuition you might call it. I always know, I used to tell Béatrice when she was little. A daddy always knows. Her momma might've had the old ways, but I always knew."

The road got narrower and the bushes thinned out. Hawkins put the lights on full and Kyra caught the dark waters of a canal.

"That's why I called on her tonight. Knew something bad had happened, another mess to clear up, just like always. Gonna be a long night for me. Tomorrow I'll visit Delbert. That's who's got this dossier ain't it?"

He meant Delilah. A cold bath of adrenaline washed over Kyra and her heart rate spiked. She'd put Delilah in harm's way.

"It was Béatrice, she's the only one who knows. She compiled the dossier and gave it to me for safe keeping. In case something happened to her."

Hawkins didn't reply. Didn't turn his head or even move his hands on the wheel. Somehow that was more intimidating than anything he'd done. Kyra couldn't bear the silence.

"Really, Delilah had nothing to do with this."

Hawkins growled, low and disapproving.

"I'm telling the truth."

"I been Sheriff a long time. Heard just about every lie at one time or another. So, I got a nose for BS. I know when a person's pretending to be something they ain't, like a man wearing a dress. And I know when a person's pretending something happened. Like getting a dossier from a woman they claim killed themselves 'in case *something happened to her.*' What was my daughter afraid was gonna happen, someone *else* was gonna kill her? *I* was gonna kill her? After everything I did to protect her. She'd gather evidence against me when that evidence would land her and me both in prison? Does that sound like someone who's telling the truth?"

Kyra tried to swallow. There was no spit in her mouth.

"What are you going to do?"

Hawkins' tone softened. "His uncle was the finest man ever served under me. Would've had my job when I retired if he'd kept his nose out. I won't make his nephew suffer. Dress him in one of his frocks and leave a note saying he couldn't 'take the shame' anymore."

Delilah was going to die. Just like her uncle. She was going to die and there was nothing Kyra could do. Because she'd be dead herself.

Unless she could find the right words. Strike a bargain with Hawkins that would save them all. She was still breathing. There was still a chance.

The deal with the dossier hadn't worked. She needed to change her approach, find a way to get Hawkins to let them go. Kyra didn't know how she was going to do that, she just knew she had to do it soon.

She had maybe minutes left. She needed to come up with something now. She took a breath, swallowed but when she opened her mouth...

her mind went blank.

No words came. No great ideas or clever stratagems. No plan for saving her life and Delilah's. Her jaw moved for a moment, chewing on invisible sentences that never passed her lips.

Then the partition in front of Kyra blurred as her eyes welled up and a wracking sob burst from her mouth. She couldn't find the words, couldn't find anything but sobs and tears.

Hawkins was unmoved, but his voice was soft. "None of that now. Show a bit of dignity. It's almost over, it'll be clean and quick, I promise. The pain won't last. It'll be over before you know. I'm not a monster. And when I'm done, I'll put you where they'll never find you."

Never find her. Kyra's parents would never know what happened to her. Kyra slumped back against the seat, her wrist dangling from the cuff.

She stopped sobbing, too stunned, too numb, too devasted to resort to tears. *A daddy always knows,* that's what Hawkins had said. Would her dad know what happened to her? Her mind began to drift away from her body, and the backseat that held her prisoner, like a balloon slipped from the fingers of a fairground child.

Kyra was with her dad. His arms about her, tight. She could smell his aftershave, subtle but expensive. Feel the soft wool of his sweater pressed against her cheek. She was five again and he was the bravest, strongest, kindest man in the world and he wouldn't let anything bad happen to her, ever.

Hawkins couldn't let her have that moment though. Couldn't let her escape even into her memories. He had to pull her back. Had to shatter her one haven as if he could see her fragile thoughts and bring a hammer to them.

"Guess you're worried what your parents are gonna think. Didn't think of that when you took off, did you? As a man who's just lost his only daughter, I can tell you this. First thing he's gonna feel is relief. Sounds cold, right? You'd think it would be anger, grief or dismay. No. He's gonna be relieved. Lighter, like a burden's been lifted from his shoulders."

Until that moment, Kyra's feelings for Hawkins had been ambivalent. He was someone to avoid, someone she suspected. Now they blossomed into hate. That he could feel this way about Béatrice, could suggest her dad would feel that same. It filled Kyra with loathing.

He picked up these thoughts too.

"When I saw her on that floor next to you. Cold, with no eyes, I was relieved. I wouldn't have to clean up after her no more. Well, maybe one last time, but that's a blessing in disguise. You see, grief's gonna get me eventually. It's gonna hit like a freight train, but until then, I gotta stay busy, keep it at arm's length."

Hawkins stopped talking as the temperature suddenly dropped. One minute it was a typical humid evening, the next it was like they'd just hit Alaska. Hawkins tried to adjust the AC on his dashboard.

His voice soured. The tone changed, became distant, as though the acoustics in the car had changed.

"I did nothing but clean up for that girl and she threw it all back in my face. I loved her, I was her daddy, but I knew she was gonna come to a bad end. Some people just have that vibe. My daughter was one. You're another. It hangs around you like a bad presence."

There it was.

The magic term that manifested all this.

Presence.

The word had been stalking her since the bus station in New Orleans. It always brought him to her and now was no different. She no longer feared him. He was a comfort and she welcomed him.

Hawkins did not.

His first inkling that something was wrong was the cruiser's speed. It climbed at an alarming rate. The engine's revs became a roar as the throttle was released.

Kyra was thrown backward and the cuffs bit into her wrist. She heard Hawkins stamping on something. She guessed it was the brake, but it did no good.

"The hell? Work, damn you."

Through the partition, she could see his knuckles, white on the wheel. His shoulders hunched and his elbows out. He was fighting the wheel.

Kyra caught Hawkins' face in the rearview.

His skin was white. He was terrified for his life.

CHAPTER 73:

Hawkins had lost control of the vehicle.

Kyra was forced into the backseat, her wrist about to dislocate. The scenery a savage blur in the cruiser's headlights.

They hit an intersection and the cruiser took a sharp right. Hit a two lane blacktop and crossed a bridge over the canal. Kyra was thrown left and the pain tore down her right arm, leaving her fingers numb, her palm throbbing.

This was not the quiet little spot he had picked out. He fought the wheel, grunting as it refused his will. Then slapping it in frustration. They must have been doing 140 with no sign of letting up.

Hawkins hadn't realized, but an old friend was back with them. Béatrice had warned her of this. It was the final remnant of her hex. The people whose eyes you saw through don't always leave. They can manifest in strange ways.

Hawkins was smacking the dashboard and the wheel. Lashing out with his boot at the pedals.

"Goddamn!"

The tires squealed beneath them, losing traction with the asphalt. They began to swerve, listing dangerously across the road.

Kyra grabbed at the cuffs with her free hand. Minimizing the damage to her right wrist as her ass slid back and forth across the upholstery.

Burning rubber and grinding metal screeched in unison. The cruiser went into a skid, swung a full 360 and was thrown up onto its two right wheels.

"No!"

Hawkins barked, as if he were commanding one of his men. As if he could right the vehicle with nothing more than the authority invested in him by state.

Kyra thrust her fingers into the partition mesh and clung on. Through the windshield she watched as the road ahead of them turned 180º. Her body swung and her feet hit the roof as it bounced off the asphalt and the car continued to roll.

Time stopped moving at its normal speed. Kyra had heard of this, but never experienced it till now. Each second got longer than the last and Kyra's metabolism slowed with it. In the center of the sudden maelstrom she found a strange calm.

But no less danger.

A single crack snaked its way across the windshield from corner to corner, bifurcating again and again like a bolt of lightning. More cracks ground through the glass, intersecting and forming a giant web. The side windows too.

The car righted itself. Bounced once off its spinning wheels and went back into a roll. This was too much for the glass and it let go of its shape. The car filled with lacerating shards as it became a blizzard of sharp edges and spinning prisms.

The roof was a sheet of paper in frustrated hands, crumpling in on itself. The front passenger door detached itself with a shriek of torn metal and went whistling off into the night.

Kyra pulled her knees up to her chin, still gripping the partition. Grinding her teeth and fighting gravity, which kept changing its mind about where it wanted to pull her. She wanted to be as small as possible. A sleeping babe, curled in its cot. Away from harm.

She had seconds to live. She didn't want to be here. Like a child's fingers opening around a balloon string, Kyra's body let go of her mind. Let it float into the cloudy sky above the wreckage and away into her memories.

She was back in her dad's arms. But they weren't her dad's arms.

But they were.

They were the arms of the daddy she hardly knew. The one who'd left before she could properly remember him.

She'd seen this through his eyes. Only yesterday. Now she was seeing it through her own. With a clarity she could hardly believe. The smells were vivid. As they were when she was two years old.

There's crisp, salty marsh grass and her daddy. He's a complex aroma of cigarette smoke, male musk and soft leather jacket. Her head is on his chest, her arms around his neck. His arms cradle her as he runs.

They run for miles. Away from the terrible, violent woman she feared and hated, but loved more than anything in the world. The woman she'd never see alive again.

She listens to his heart beat faster as he runs. Hears the words he says over and over again as a low reverberation in his chest. They're his mantra.

It's all right. Daddy's here. Daddy's got you.

It's all gonna be okay. Won't let nothing bad happen.

You're safe now.

Daddy's here.

And daddy was here. In this memory with Kyra. Experiencing it with her. His *Gros-Bon Ange* looking out for her *Ti-Bon Ange*. His good-big angel carrying her little angel like a babe in his arms.

He can't share his thoughts like Béatrice, and Kyra can't see him. But she can feel his presence all around her. Better than she ever has before. She can sense his true intentions. His love, his pride, his affection for the child she was and the person she's become.

And though he can't tell her, Kyra knows he has to leave again. Just as he left her that night in the trailer park. Neither of them knowing they'd meet once more in the memory of their final parting. Fifteen years and one day later.

The memory of that night fades and Kyra catches a brief glimpse of the crossroads where she left Béatrice. The roads that lead off it have their own inescapable force. One grabs her daddy and sends him on to his ultimate destination. Another grabs Kyra and sends her back where she came.

There's time for one last pang of longing and regret. For everything Kyra never knew about her daddy and never will. For never thanking him for what he's done, before they're torn forever from one another.

Billy-Ray has saved her for the very last time.

And she knows she's yet to face the worst.

CHAPTER 74:

Seven Days Ago – T-Minus Four Hours till Departure:

Kyra was alone.

Alone in her room. Alone in the house. Alone with her thoughts.

This was the worst.

Everything was unravelling. She was suspended from school with only a semester and a half left of her senior year. She wasn't speaking to her mom or dad. She'd wanted to find her birth parents for the longest time and, after years of stonewalling from faceless bureaucracy, she'd finally discovered her birthmother was a victim of her favorite serial killer.

For some reason her parents and teachers thought it best to exclude her from friends and studies. Like that was going to do anything for her mental health or grade averages. Because the best thing for her depression and anxiety was obviously to keep her locked up with only her intrusive thoughts for company.

Thoughts that goaded her rage. Pushed her further down the spiral of hatred and dismay. Hatred for herself and dismay at where her life was going.

She couldn't go on like this much longer. Something had to break and it couldn't be her. Something had to give and it wasn't going to be her parents. Something had to change and Kyra had to make it.

If she had to stay in Chicago one more night things were going to get dark. Darker than the singed flesh on the inside of her thighs. For the longest time Kyra's heart had been elsewhere. In a small town in Louisiana that almost no one knew of. And now she knew why. It was the town of her birth.

Kyra had been planning to visit since she first read *Eyes for the Killer*. But something always prevented her. Her parents thought it was too far for Kyra to travel by herself. Maybe, once she'd been to college she'd be old enough. They'd take her themselves, but her dad had used up his vacation.

It was always just out of her reach. A reminder she wasn't old enough to live her own life or make her own decisions. Yeuxville had become a threshold. Once Kyra crossed it her life could begin.

It was the only place that could save her from the train-wreck her life had become. She needed it more than ever. Her past was a series of puzzles and the more she learned the harder it was to solve any of them. If she was ever going to get answers, it wouldn't be at home.

She had to leave and she had to do it now.

Kyra couldn't let anything stop her. Her parents would be mad but screw them. They'd done nothing to help her recently. She'd take the punishment when she got back. She was leaving for college next year anyway. What's the worst that could happen? Whatever it was, it would be worth it if she could get to the bottom of her problems.

Her mom was out until late this evening. She had back-to-back viewings on two different properties. Her dad was in court with a pro-bono case, this meant he would work late to keep up with his paying clients.

Kyra wouldn't have this much time to herself for another eight days. And that would be too late. She had to act now. In five days' time it would be the anniversary of Caitlin's death. Some urge, some deep intuition told her she had to be in Yeuxville on that day.

It was a clarion call, as clear as a summons. Some power, outside of her control, needed Kyra to be in Yeuxville, and she couldn't deny it. She had to go.

Her parents had left at 7:30 that morning. They insisted Kyra was out of bed and dressed before they left. Even if she had no school. She'd had the rest of the day to plan this.

Kyra had been packing her backpack for days. She started before she'd even admitted what she was doing. Stuffing more and more items into the pack as they occurred to her. Until she could hardly zip it shut.

She'd checked and re-checked the bus times. She couldn't risk buying a ticket online. She'd have to use one of her parent's cards for that and they'd be tipped off straight away. They'd find out where she'd gone and come get her.

Kyra needed time in Yeuxville. She needed distance from Chicago. She didn't want anyone denying her. She'd buy her ticket and pay for everything in cash. And she knew just where to get it.

Her dad's home office was in the basement, and so was the safe. Kyra hadn't been down there in months. She'd been avoiding her dad for a while. The wooden steps creaked their accusations as Kyra entered.

The safe was on the far wall. Behind her dad's desk, hidden by a framed poster. In shades of red, Eddie Vedder jammed beneath the heading PEARL JAM LIVE, SOLDIER FIELD, CHICAGO 1995.

Kyra lifted the poster from the wall. She'd never opened the safe or even seen her dad open it. But she knew what the combination was. It was the same numbers he used on every passcode. The date her mom and dad officially adopted Kyra.

She punched in the numbers and pushed the handle down. There was a click and the thick, metal door swung open. There were three shelves inside. The top two contained bonds and official documents in folders and satchels. The bottom shelf was full of neat stacks of cash.

As well as pro-bono clients, her dad represented people who, for various reasons, could only pay in cash. This was where he kept their payments.

The cash was stacked in bundles of $10s, $20s or $50s. Kyra had no idea how much cash was in the safe, or how much she'd need for her trip. She wasn't even sure how long she'd be away. She lifted a bundle of twenties. The currency band was crisp and clean, but many of the notes were worn and crumpled.

Kyra took two more bundles and felt an icy sweat break out on her skin. Her heart was beating abnormally fast. The room pitched, like she was on the deck of a ship, and she had to sit in her dad's leather work chair. Was this a panic attack or her conscience?

Whatever it was, Kyra was facing another threshold. If she stepped over, there was no turning back. She would never be the same person. This was theft. Kyra had never done this. Her parents had always given her whatever she wanted.

No, it wasn't theft. She'd pay every cent of this back. She was just borrowing it. Taking an advance on her inheritance. If her parents knew how much she needed to do this, if they really understood, they'd give her this money. When she got back she'd make them understand why she had to go. Kyra counted out $10,000 which seemed to be about half of what was in the safe. That would be enough, wouldn't it?

She closed the door, replaced the framed poster and took the money up to her room. Her backpack was already bulging. There was no place for the cash. Kyra unzipped it and took out a few non-essentials. Then she remembered a few things she hadn't packed and began checking her drawers.

On top of a stack of notebooks, on the second drawer in her nightstand, Kyra saw the handkerchief she'd bought her dad. It would be his birthday in a week. She was still mad at him but, seeing the embroidery, other feelings rose up– love, frustration, respect and annoyance.

Maybe she could still convince them she needed to do this, get her dad to listen.

No. There wasn't time and she couldn't risk the delay. Kyra looked at the Little Prince, standing next to the long eared Fox, his scarf blowing in the air. She traced the letters of the quote with her finger:

"One sees clearly only with the heart.

"What is essential is invisible to the eye."

This was too important not to pass on.

Kyra carried the handkerchief into her parent's room. A pile of books lay on her dad's nightstand. Unlike Kyra, who spent her last waking minutes scrolling through her phone, Kyra's dad liked to read before sleep. He kept his current book, plus a selection of others, by his bedside.

At the bottom of the pile she found his dog-eared copy of *The Little Prince*. She slipped the handkerchief between the pages and returned the book to the pile. When her dad read it, he'd understand what Kyra had done. She was seeing this trip with her heart. Seeing clearly for the first time. That's why she had to go.

She couldn't turn back now even if she wanted. Her course was set. Her life was a speeding car with its own trajectory and someone else at the wheel. She had no other options. Her life in Chicago was a car crash. She needed a new pasture.

After all, how much worse could things get in Yeuxville?

CHAPTER 75:

Someone was shaking Kyra. Was it time to go to school?

A power tool revved up outside. Yard work? Someone trimming the shrubs? Sounded like someone cutting into her walls. Why were they doing that? Who was shaking her? Her wrist hurt like someone was standing on it.

Her palms stung, her bladder ached and she needed to pee. She didn't want to wake up yet. There was something in her bed digging into her back. She reached for the covers to roll over but there were no covers and she couldn't move her right arm.

Something was very wrong.

The whine of the power tool increased. Kyra opened her eyes. Light streamed in above her and to one side. She was in a glass and metal box.

No. She was in a car. She was lying against a passenger door. It was Hawkins' cruiser. It wasn't the right way up. The car was on its side and Kyra was cuffed to its partition. Her wrist, swollen and bruised, throbbed as soon as she saw it.

The noise was coming from a pneumatic saw. Sparks flew from the door directly overhead. Someone was cutting into it. The door shook then it was lifted clear and Kyra could see sky overhead.

A young man in a paramedic's uniform filled the space where the door had been. He looked surprised.

"You're conscious."

He looked over his shoulder and shouted: "We've got a live one."

Kyra heard commotion outside, and the paramedic turned back to her. "Miss, can you hear me okay?"

Kyra nodded. "Yes, fine."

"Good, now, without moving too much, I want you to tell me if there's any part of your body you can't feel and if you're in any pain."

"I can feel everything. The only thing that hurts is my wrist." Kyra rattled the cuffs. "They're too tight."

"Okay miss, we'll get to them in a minute, is there anything you're having difficulty moving?"

"No, nothing. Just a bit cut and bruised, is all. Can you guys get me out of here?"

"I've got you, give me a minute."

The paramedic disappeared and reappeared thirty seconds later with a set of bolt cutters. He leaned in through the open door and cut through the cuffs, freeing Kyra.

Another voice called out to him.

"How's it looking?"

"Stable enough to climb in with the spinal board."

"You sure?"

"Supports are holding."

The paramedic climbed in and another paramedic passed him a plastic board with black, fabric straps. Moving gently and methodically the paramedic guided Kyra onto the board and strapped her in place. Another paramedic reached in and took hold of the bottom of the board and between them they lifted Kyra out.

As they carried her away, Kyra saw the destroyed police car was surrounded by a makeshift wooden structure to stop it from falling any further into the ditch. It was early morning. Kyra had been unconscious for hours.

The road was cordoned off, and there were police cars, a fire truck, and an ambulance parked along it. In the middle of the road, lying on the asphalt, was another stretcher with a long, tall body on it, covered by a blanket. The body wasn't moving. A boot was poking out from under the blanket. Kyra recognized it as Hawkins.

Was this retribution for Billy-Ray?

Kyra was taken to the ambulance where yet another paramedic, called Cindy, checked her out and treated the worst of her cuts and bruises. Cindy, a feisty strawberry blond with a nose ring and tattoos, shone a light in her eyes and checked for concussion and signs of brain injury.

When she'd cleared Kyra for that, she dressed the cuts on Kyra's palms, gave her some painkillers and asked about other injuries. Kyra told her about getting hit by a car a few days ago, and Cindy checked her ankle.

"You're sure it was this ankle?"

"Definitely, I could hardly walk a few days ago."

Cindy pointed at the ankle. "Can't see any bruising or swelling, doesn't look like it's been damaged at all."

Cindy was right, Kyra felt her forehead and found the bump there had gone as well.

"I have to ask this," Cindy said. "But you're sure it happened a few days ago, and not a few months? There are no visible signs of head trauma, but is there a chance you're getting your timelines confused?"

"I've only been here a few days. You can check with Doctor McFadden, who saw to me."

"Well, if the accident was as bad as you say, I don't see how it could have healed so fast."

Kyra wondered if she should say anything but went ahead anyway. "My friend's aunt also treated me. I guess you could say she was a healer."

"This aunt from Yeuxville?"

"Yeah."

"She follow the old ways?"

"Uh, yes, actually."

Cindy nodded. "I come across this sort of thing from time to time. Find it best not to question it. Guess you're good to go, but I'd like you to see a medical professional in the next forty-eight hours, in case there's any problems we've missed."

"Okay." Kyra got up and left the ambulance. Outside she found Deputy Guillory and Deputy Patterson waiting for her.

Guillory shook his head and narrowed his eyes. "Why am I not surprised to see you?"

"Are you done with her?" Patterson asked Cindy.

"For the time being,"

"She injured badly?"

"Not that I can tell."

"So, you're not going to take her in for more treatment?"

"No, she's in remarkably good shape for someone who just walked away from a car crash. If they hadn't just pulled her out of the wreckage I wouldn't have believed it. Must've had an angel looking out for her."Patterson turned to Kyra. "You got an angel looking out for you?"

Kyra thought of Billy-Ray and those last moments before she lost consciousness. She shrugged in reply and stared at the ground.

Patterson took off her cap and ran a hand over her cornrows. "Cos I'm having trouble believing you walked away from a car crash myself."

Guillory squared his shoulders. "So am I."

Patterson put her cap back on. "I think you should come with us."

Kyra stuck her hands in her pockets, winced at the pain in her wrist and took them out again. "I was kinda hoping for a lift to the Piggly Wiggly. I need to catch the bus home."

"Chicago, that right?"

"Yes."

Guillory put his thumbs in the front of his belt. "You ain't going nowhere."

Patterson took a step toward Kyra. "I'm afraid my colleague's right, we can't allow you to leave town at present."

"But I have to see my parents."

"You're the principal witness in two homicides. We need you to help us with our enquiries."

"Two homicides?"

"The unlawful deaths of Sheriff Hawkins and his daughter Béatrice."

Guillory stepped up behind Kyra. "Way I see it, you're more suspect than witness."

"But I need to get back home. I need to call my parents."

"Are you refusing to cooperate with a police investigation?"

"No."

"I'ma have to insist you come with us, miss."

Guillory grabbed Kyra's shoulders and spun her round so Patterson could slap a fresh set of cuffs on her.

Cindy climbed out of the ambulance and headed toward the deputies. "Hey, hey, is that really necessary? She's already got a damaged wrist."

Patterson stepped in front of Cindy, blocking her route to Kyra. "Ma'am, I'ma have to ask you to go about your business and let us see to ours."

"Is that girl under arrest?"

"Ma'am, please get back in your vehicle."

"She's a minor, you can't treat her like this."

Before Cindy could say anything else, Guillory hustled Kyra toward their police cruiser, pushing her between her shoulder blades. Kyra stumbled on the second push and nearly lost her balance. Guillory grabbed the back of her t-shirt and hauled her to her feet.

"Told you I'd put you away, didn't I?"

Kyra felt a cold, hollow sickness in the pit of her gut as it occurred to her that Guillory might just get his way.

CHAPTER 76:

Patterson and Guillory drove Kyra to the station house, marched her down the same corridor, and dumped her in the same tiny interrogation room. They gave her nothing to eat or drink. They didn't remove the cuffs. They just left her to stew.

The painkillers were starting to wear off and Kyra felt woozy and tired. Her shoulders ached, her wrist throbbed and she had a pounding headache.

Finally, the door opened. Guillory switched on the camera in the corner of the room, and Patterson removed Kyra's cuffs.

"This is Deputy Patterson and Deputy Guillory, interviewing Kyra Robichaud concerning the murders of Sheriff Jacob Hawkins and Béatrice Hawkins." Patterson also stated the time and date.

They still didn't have her proper name.

"Kyra, do you want to tell us, in your own words, what happened at the Park Vale Industrial unit rented by Béatrice Hawkins?"

"Um, okay, I called in to see her yesterday morning. I think it was yesterday, I've been unconscious, so time's kind of scrambled for me."

"I understand, and what was your reason for calling on Ms. Hawkins?"

"I was on my way to catch a bus and I stopped at her unit to pick up my backpack."

"She was looking after it for you?"

"That's right."

"Is this because you were staying at her house?"

Kyra balled her hands into fists and buried them in her lap, her fingernails biting into her palm. She couldn't carry on lying to the police. She was linked to two murder scenes. She had to be as open and transparent as possible.

She spoke in a quiet voice, head down, avoiding eye contact. "No, I wasn't."

"You weren't what?"

"Staying with Béatrice."

"But you told officers of this precinct that you were staying with her, am I right?"

"Yes."

"You are aware that giving false information to an officer of the law is first degree misdemeanor."

"I panicked and I lied. It was dumb."

"Is that the only lie you told us?"

"Yes." Except for her name, but she couldn't tell them that now.

"Where have you been staying?"

"At the local motel and I'm now staying with a friend."

"And what's this friend's name?"

"Delilah Landry."

"Who?"

Guillory grunted. "She means Dan Landry's nephew."

"She identifies as a woman."

Patterson frowned. "I don't care if he identifies as a fence post or an elephant. In the eyes of the law he's a human male." She turned to Guillory. "What's his name again?"

"Delbert."

"Delbert, that's right. So, how long were you at the Landry household?"

"Just a night."

"Then you left next morning to catch a bus?"

"Yes."

"And you stopped at Ms. Hawkins' industrial unit to pick up your luggage."

"That's correct."

"Then what happened?"

"She made me some tea, only it was special tea, but I didn't know that when I drank it."

Patterson raised her eyebrow and exchanged a look with Guillory. "Special tea?"

"It knocks you out. It's like a Voodoo thing. I'd guess you'd call it 'the old ways' here in Yeuxville. Her mother taught her how to make it, her mother was a priestess, I'm sure you know."

Patterson smiled a tight, humorless smile. It was the sort of smile her mom gave her dad when he was mansplaining. The sort of look someone who grew up in Yeuxville might give an outsider when they mentioned 'the old ways.'

"This would be the same mother who died when Béatrice was a girl?"

"Yes, only she didn't teach it to Béatrice when she was a girl."

"No?"

"No, Béatrice learned it from her mother's grimoire, that's a book where you write down spells and stuff."

"And what happened to this grimoire?"

"Her daddy, Sheriff Hawkins, burned it when she was a teenager, but she kept a copy of the spells, in a journal, including this tea recipe."

Deputy Patterson rubbed her forehead. "Let's get back to the morning in question. What happened when you drank this tea?"

"It knocked me out."

"Rendered you unconscious?"

"Yes, and when I came round, I was tied to the ground, in the back room, and Béatrice had put out stuff for a ceremony."

"That would be the paraphernalia we found."

"Yes, the candles and stuff."

"Did you assist her with this?"

"No, I was unconscious."

"I see, go on."

Neither Patterson nor Guillory were buying this. She knew how it must sound, but it was the truth. If she stuck to the truth, they'd have to let her go.

"So, she, um, she told me she was going to conduct this ceremony and she had, uh, she'd drunk some of the tea herself, a lethal dose."

"Was this before or after you drank the tea?"

"After, I suppose."

"Go on."

"So then she cut my palms with a knife and then she took the knife, she took the knife and she…"

Kyra screwed her eyes shut and dropped her head in her hands. The chair tilted or was it the floor, rocking like the deck of a ship. Visions of blood and blades filled her mind. Caitlin and Béatrice with empty sockets.

She'd seen too much. Hadn't stopped to process it. Hadn't realized its enormity until she tried to put it into words. Put it on the record for two police deputies. She was frightened and angry and wounded and she couldn't deal with it.

A sob broke in the back of her throat and she collapsed in tears, just as she had in the back of Hawkins' cruiser. Patterson's response sounded remarkably sympathetic.

"It's okay, take a moment, gather yourself." She turned to Guillory. "Go get her a soda."

Guillory left the room reluctantly and Patterson handed her a tissue. Kyra did her best to dry her eyes and compose herself. Guillory returned with a can of Dr Pepper. Her throat was raw, the soda stung, but the sugar and liquid helped.

Patterson smiled, genuinely this time. "Better?"

Kyra nodded.

"So, just to recap. Ms. Hawkins gave you those cuts on your palms, with the knife *she* was holding. Then what happened?"

"She turned the knife on herself. Put it in her sockets and cut out her eyes. She put the eyeballs in my hands and then she died, from the tea. She said she'd taken an overdose."

"An overdose of what?"

"The tea."

"When did she say this, before or after she hurt herself?"

"After, she said the tea killed the pain."

"Doesn't sound like any tea I've heard of."

Guillory folded his arms and hunched his shoulders. "Nor me."

"What did you do then?"

"I passed out again."

"And what happened when you came to?"

"Sheriff Hawkins was there, he woke me up."

"What did the Sheriff say?"

This was going to be difficult. Hawkins was their boss. How could Kyra put this so they'd believe her? They already doubted her account.

"He asked me what I'd done to his daughter, then when he saw I was tied up and couldn't have done anything, he said he didn't know what trouble she'd gotten herself into, but he was going to make sure I paid for it."

"So the Sheriff had cause to suspect you of murder?"

"No, I was tied up and unconscious when he found me."

"But he said you were going to pay for his daughter's murder, that's what an officer usually says when he arrests you. The Sheriff had a lot of experience with crime scenes, if he was going to arrest you, there must have been a reason. Wouldn't you agree?"

"Under normal circumstances, but this was different."

"How was it different?"

"Because the Sheriff was going to frame me."

"And why would you assume a seasoned officer like Sheriff Hawkins, with an exemplary record, would want to frame you?"

"Because he's done it before."

Did it just get really chilly in the room? The mood certainly cooled. Patterson and Guillory fought to control their reactions, trained not to give anything away in interrogations. But Kyra could see their backs stiffen and their eyes narrow.

Patterson spoke in measured tones.

"And who do you think Sheriff Hawkins framed?"

"Billy-Ray Johnson."

"Billy-Ray Johnson, the serial killer?"

"Yes."

Kyra was testing Patterson's control. The hint of derision in her voice was palpable.

"A man caught and convicted by an inter-departmental taskforce, based on forensic evidence of the highest caliber. I studied that case in the academy. I know some of the people who worked it. You're telling me Sheriff Hawkins framed Billy-Ray Johnson and let the real killer go free?"

Kyra rubbed at the bruises on her wrist, unable to look Patterson or Guillory in the eye. "Yes."

"You have any proof of this?"

"A friend of mine does."

Patterson and Guillory exchanged another look. It was quick and covert, but their manner changed again. The skepticism giving way to a more guarded approach.

"And can they produce this evidence?"

A cool spasm of fear gripped Kyra's guts. Had she said too much? Was she making the same mistake she made with Hawkins? She was just trying to make them aware of the truth.

"You'd have to take that up with Internal Affairs."

Patterson nodded, her eyelids hooded. "So, your friend's handed this proof to IA already?"

"I'm not sure."

Patterson furrowed her brow. Her voice became harsher.

"You're not sure. But you're claiming that Delbert, I'm assuming it's Delbert, thinks he has some evidence of misconduct on Sheriff Hawkins' part. Evidence that he may, or may not have handed over to IA. And on that basis, you expect us to believe our boss was trying to frame you?"

"He said he was."

"He used those words, those exact words: 'I framed Billy-Ray Johnson and now I'm going to frame you'?"

"No, he didn't use those words. Like I told you, he said I was going to pay for the trouble his daughter had gotten into."

"And you took that to mean he was going to frame you?"

"Yes, you don't know what he's like."

Deputy Patterson raised an eyebrow. "I've been working with the man, every day, for the last three years, you've met him what, twice?"

"Three times."

"Oh, three times, I'm sorry, of course you'd know him much better than me. Let me suggest another take. He finds you, next to his daughter's body, covered in her blood and he intends to arrest you for her murder. Doesn't that sound more plausible?"

"No, because he didn't arrest me. He put me in the back of his car, and he drove me to the bayous to kill me."

"Wait, a second ago you said he was going to frame you. Now you're changing your story? Because that's a serious accusation."

"I'm not changing my story, I'm telling you what happened."

"You said Sheriff Hawkins was going to frame you. When I asked you for proof you started making wild accusations and then you said he was going to kill you."

"No!"

Kyra's voice rose and she balled her fists. Guillory pursed his lips, sat up in his seat and his eyes widened with anger. Kyra took a moment, breathed and relaxed her hands. She couldn't afford to lose her temper, no matter how much they tried to twist her words and confuse her.

"He was going to frame me until I told him what I knew. Then he decided he needed to silence me."

Patterson was no less furious than her partner, but her tone remained level.

"Sheriff Hawkins was going to kill you. He said that: 'I'm going to kill you'?"

"No, he didn't say anything."

"So, an officer of the law places you in protective custody, after finding you at a murder scene and you assume he's going to kill you. What did he say that made you think that?"

"He said, 'the pain won't last for long', that he wasn't a 'monster'."

"That doesn't sound like a threat to me. Sounds like he was trying to reassure you, wouldn't you say?"

"No, you didn't hear the way he said it. And if he was taking me to jail, how come he didn't drive me here? How come he crashed way out of town?"

Patterson sat back and folded her arms. The anger left her eyes and she returned to her cold professionalism.

"Good point, let's talk about the crash. Do you know what caused it?"

"Um, no."

Deputy Patterson leaned forward. Looked Kyra right in the eye. "You hesitated, are you sure you don't know? Maybe it slipped your memory. If you take a moment, it might come back. Trauma can do that to you. I'ma ask you again, do you know what caused the crash?"

"He lost control. The car went into a roll and when I woke up, the paramedics cut me out."

Deputy Patterson sat back in her chair. "See, this is where I have a problem. Our preliminary investigation says the vehicle had no technical faults. There was nothing on the road that could have caused an accident, and Sheriff Hawkins was an experienced driver, I've ridden with him many times. But you're saying he suddenly lost control of the car and it went into a roll."

"Yes."

"Was there something in the road that made him swerve?"

"I don't know, it was real dark."

"You didn't see anything?"

"No."

"He just," Deputy Patterson made quotation marks with her fingers, "lost control."

"Yes."

Patterson shook her head. Then she pushed her chair back. This was a signal. She was ceding the floor to Guillory. A vein throbbed in his head. He pushed his jaw out, got to his feet and leaned so close to Kyra she could smell his breath, even with her head bowed.

"Enough with the bullshit! We know what happened. You and Ms. Hawkins were into some kinky dyke stuff. It went too far, you grabbed a knife and Béatrice called her Daddy to come help. By the time he gets there Béatrice was already dead. Sheriff Hawkins arrests you, but you freak out and grab the wheel, hoping to escape. Instead, you crash the car and make Sheriff Hawkins your second victim."

"That's crazy!"

"Is it?"

"Yes."

"Crazier than voodoo, magic tea, and Sheriff Hawkins framing a serial killer?"

Kyra had nothing. Guillory was right. Her story was crazy, even if it was the truth. Truth was supposed to set you free, not make you look guilty.

Guillory leaned in closer. Kyra shrank into herself. She could feel his breath on the top of her head.

"How could I?"

"What?"

Kyra took a deep, uneven breath. "How could I kill Beatrice when I was tied to the ground? How could I have grabbed the wheel of the police car from the back seat? There was a partition between us, and I was handcuffed. How could I cause the crash?"

"I'ma find out, and when I do, you're in big trouble."

Guillory collapsed back in his seat and Patterson moved forward. "Now, if you don't mind, I'd like to go over your story again."

And they did. Over and over for the next two hours. Picking holes in it, trying to catch Kyra in a lie. When they were done, they left her in the room, by herself. Her wrist throbbed and her head ached so badly she couldn't see.

Half an hour later Patterson and Guillory returned. Patterson was cold and perfunctory.

"Kyra Hughes, I'm arresting you for the murders of Béatrice Hawkins and Sheriff John Hawkins. You have the right to remain silent. Anything you say can and will be used against you in a court of law. You have the right to have an attorney. If you cannot afford one, one will be appointed to you by the court. Do you understand these rights?"

"But I'm a minor."

"This is murder, and under Louisiana State Law you can be charged as an adult. Now, I'll ask you again, do you understand these rights?"

"Yes."

Guillory pulled Kyra out of her seat and led her into the corridor. "I'ma see you get the death penalty."

Why had she told them what happened? She should have just kept quiet. That's what her dad would have told her. Now they were going to put her in jail and there was nothing she could do to stop them.

CHAPTER 77:

Guillory took Kyra to the holding cells in the basement. Three tiny, barred rooms. Each contained a metal bunk with a plastic mattress, a metal toilet with no seat, and a sink.

Two cells were occupied. Guillory put her in the empty one. On the other side of the corridor was a tall, broad African American guy. He didn't acknowledge anyone. Just stared at the floor and smacked his fist into his palm every few seconds.

There were two women in the other cell. They were dressed in tiny crop-tops, even tinier shorts and huge stiletto heels. One had red hair, the other was a blonde. They perked up as soon as they saw Kyra.

"Ooh, fresh meat."

When Guillory left, Red called out to her. "Hey honey, what you in for?"

Kyra didn't say anything. She sat with her back to the bars, staring at the peeling white paint.

"Hey, hey, I'm talking to you, what they bust you for? Hey, talk to me."

The blonde spoke with a sing-song voice. "She don' wanna talk to us, Dolores. Maybe she killed someone."

"Naw, she ain't no killer, Jaime. Are you honey?"

"Yeah, she is, look at her eyes. Bet she wasted a pig."

Dolores and Jaime cackled.

"Is that what you did, honey, did you murder a pig?"

Kyra turned to look at the women. She spoke without any expression. "Yeah, the Sheriff and his daughter. That's what I'm in for."

The women fell silent. Dolores frowned and shot Jaime an enquiring look. Jaime shrugged. Neither of them spoke after that. Kyra turned back to the peeling paint.

A few hours later, a deputy arrived pushing a trolley. He unlocked an opening in the cell doors and handed the occupants a tray. Then he turned to Kyra's cell, unlocked the opening and a pushed a tray through.

"What's this?"

"Dinner, baloney sammich, creamed corn, and a carton of juice."

"Um, what's the vegetarian option?"

"The what now?"

"The vegetarian option. I don't eat meat. I can't have this."

"There isn't any option, this is what you get."

"But I can't eat it."

"Pick out the meat, eat the bread."

"Are you sure there's nothing else?"

The guard wasn't much older than Kyra. He had a shaved head, muscular arms and a gut that spilled over his belt. His eyes were brown and beady, his forehead prominent, but he had a kindly expression.

"You really can't eat this?"

Kyra shook her head. "Sorry."

"Bet you're hungry too."

"Oh hell yes."

"Well, there ain't nothin' in the station, but I got a break coming up. There's a drive-in couple miles up the highway. They do a bean burger. Would you like one of those?"

"Really," Kyra's stomach growled, she hadn't eaten since breakfast the previous day. "You'd do that for me?"

"Well, I ain't supposed to, but my momma raised me to help my friends out. You do wanna be friends, don'tcha?"

"Sure."

"You want some fries and a milkshake, too?"

"That would be amazing."

"I can get it to you in the next thirty minutes, that be okay?"

"That'd be great."

Kyra couldn't keep a tremor out of her voice. Her eyes were misty. The cops in Yeuxville had not been kind. They'd harassed, threatened and even tried to kill her. Now they'd arrested her for crimes she didn't commit.

Kyra had come to distrust, fear, and even to her shame, despise the Yeuxville PD. Just when she was ready to tar them all with the same brush, this one deputy had disproven her. This single act of kindness had restored her faith in law enforcement.

The deputy put the tray down on the ground.

"'Course, there is something you can help me with in the meantime, seeing as we're friends and all. You do wanna help me, don'tcha?"

"What do you mean?"

Kyra was staring up at the deputy's face. The look in his eyes made her drop her gaze to his chest. She heard a fly open and saw his ample belly push up against the bars.

Though she was afraid to, Kyra let her gaze travel down to his crotch. Jutting through the bars was his erect penis. The end was the color of raw liver. An angry, purple vein ran down its thick shaft and a tiny bead of pre-come glistened in its hole.

It wasn't the first penis Kyra had seen. But her reaction confirmed something she'd suspected for a long time. There was no way she'd want to be intimate with that part of a man's body. No matter how much she liked the man, she did not want to touch or feel a male member.

The deputy breathed out, heavily.

"I think you know what to do with that."

Kyra folded her arms, turned her back on the deputy and glowered at the wall. Refusing to look at him or dignify anything he said with an answer.

Dolores and Jaime whooped and laughed, calling out from the cell opposite.

"Open wide and blow his mind, honey!"

"Time for the veggie to taste some meat."

"Only the best pork served in this joint"

The deputy told them to, "Shaddap!" When he addressed Kyra there was a whiny undertone to his words.

"Hey, I thought we had a deal, I'll hold up my end, but you gotta hold up yours."

Kyra hunched her shoulders and dropped her head, trying to wish the deputy and his genitals away.

"Hey, c'mon, play nice."

Why wouldn't he just go? Why wouldn't he leave her alone? How could he be so brazen about this? He wasn't allowed to act this way. Eventually, the deputy huffed his disapproval.

"Screw you, then,"

This was followed by a succession of clatters and wet thuds as the deputy emptied the tray onto the floor of her cell.

Kyra listened as he pushed the trolley back up the corridor. Jaime called out after him.

"Hey, Dolores here will blow you if you get me a hamburger."

"Blow him yourself, I'll have your fries."

When she was sure the deputy had gone, Kyra went to the bars and called out to the women opposite.

"You saw that right? He's not allowed to do that."

Dolores scowled. "Honey, I didn't see nothing, and neither did you."

"He should lose his job for that, we should report him."

Jaime curled her top lip. "You ain't from round here are you?"

"I was born right here in Yeuxville."

"But you didn't grow up here, can tell that from your accent. Don't know what it's like up north, but down here you don't make trouble for the cops, not when they got you in custody."

"But he can't do that."

"He can do what he likes and I'll just look away. So will you if you know what's good for you."

Kyra slunk back to her cot. Soon after, the women and the African American guy settled down to sleep. Kyra closed her eyes and listened to their snoring and the buzzing of the fluorescent lights. She was too hungry to sleep.

Slipping from her bunk, she checked to make sure the others couldn't see her. Then she picked the sandwich off the floor, pulled out the baloney and set it aside. She scooped as much of the creamed corn off the floor as she could and washed it all down with the juice.

It was cold and bland and processed. But her body screamed with joy at the sustenance. She wasn't proud of herself, but Kyra imagined there would be far worse to come.

CHAPTER 78:

Kyra gave up on sleep long before morning. She dozed fitfully for a few hours but kept waking in an anxious sweat, her chest tight and her skin clammy. The mattress was too thin. The bunk was too hard and Kyra was too bruised to get comfortable.

In the cells opposite Jaime and Dolores stirred, but slept on, and the African American guy rolled onto his back and snored some more.

Eventually, Kyra heard footsteps in the corridor outside. She propped herself up on her elbow. Guillory approached her cell.

"On your feet."

Kyra slipped from her bunk. Guillory unlocked her door hatch and beckoned.

"Step forward, put your hands through here."

Kyra complied. Guillory snapped cuffs on, tight enough to make her wince. He unlocked the door and led Kyra up to the interrogation room where Patterson was waiting.

"Sit down, please."

Patterson handed her a document containing several sheets of paper.

Kyra didn't want to touch it. "What's this?"

"It's your confession, I'd like you to read and sign it."

Kyra flicked through the pages. They outlined the deputies' accusations.

"I can't sign this."

Guillory's neck reddened, his hand balled in a fist. "You will, if you know what's good for you."

Kyra shook her head, groggy from lack of sleep and food. "But it's not true. I didn't say those things. I can't sign it if it's a lie."

Patterson spoke in a more reasonable tone. "If you confess now, you won't get the death penalty. We'll convince the judge to go easy on you. You'll be out in fifteen to twenty years. You're still young, you could start over. But we can't help you if you don't help yourself."

"How am I helping myself if I sign a false confession?"

Guillory slammed the table with both of his fists. He got out of his seat and thrust his face at Kyra. It was such a sudden, violent movement that Kyra shrank back in her seat, bringing her left arm over her face, hugging herself for protection.

"I wrote that confession, based on all the evidence. Are you calling me a liar?? Are you gonna start accusing me of framing people now?!"

"No."

Patterson stood and placed a hand on Guillory's shoulder. She guided him back down into his seat.

"It's okay, I got this."

She produced her phone, tapped the screen a couple times and showed it to Kyra. There was a photo of a good looking African American man. His hair was cropped close and his thick mustache sat atop a broad smile.

"This is my fiancé."

She flicked through a few more photos till she came to one that showed the same man unconscious on a hospital gurney.

"He was also a deputy of this department, until he took a bullet in the spine in the line of duty."

Patterson changed the photo again. This one showed her fiancé, in athletic gear, sitting in a basketball chair. "This is my fiancé last month, trying out for the Paralympics, know how he got there?"

"No."

"Because Sheriff Hawkins, my boss and mentor, raised the money for his physio and that wheelchair. Bake sales, community events, sponsored activities, you name it, he did it. He worked tirelessly for two years to make sure a man who worked under him wasn't forgotten or left behind. So he could rebuild his life. Do you have any idea of the debt my fiancé and I owe Sheriff Hawkins? We were never going to repay that, and now we never will, because this man was taken from our community."

Kyra looked at Patterson's phone. She thought about the back seat of Hawkins' cruiser and being driven to her death by the man Patterson was talking about. She thought about Delilah's uncle, and Billy-Ray, and the things he'd done to them. The man who'd done those things, hurt those people so badly, just didn't square with the person Patterson was describing.

Did Kyra have Hawkins all wrong? Could a man who did the things Delilah was suggesting be capable of such altruism? Capable of commanding the respect, gratitude and love that Patterson and Guillory showed. Despite what she'd been through, Kyra couldn't help but admire him when she heard Patterson speak.

Patterson moved closer to Kyra. Her body was relaxed and open. Her deep, brown eyes were full of sympathy and understanding.

"You don't have to let this sit on your conscience for the rest of your life. You don't have to look in the mirror and hate the person you see. This is day one. You can make a clean break. We're not here to hurt you Kyra. We can help. If you get this off your chest, I promise, you won't believe how good it'll feel. How much lighter you'll be. Work with us here. Let us help you rebuild your life and become the person you want to be."

She passed Kyra the pen and Kyra took it.

There was a loud bang.

Kyra looked up. Patterson and Guillory swung round. The door flew open. A five-foot, bottle blond tornado tore into the interrogation room.

"This interview is over."

CHAPTER 79:

A middle-aged woman in a cheap suit pointed a finger at Kyra.

"Don't say another word. Not one."

Guillory curled his lip. "We got her confession."

"She sign anything?"

"She's about to."

"You've questioned her twice without me present. You can't use any confession. First thing I'll do is get the judge to throw it out, you know that. Now, I'ma need you to leave so I can have some time with my client."

"This is bullshit."

"This is due legal process, now git. And remove those cuffs before you go."

Patterson scowled. "They're for your protection."

"I'll take my chances."

Patterson took the key from Guillory, and unlocked Kyra's cuffs. She spoke softly to Kyra. "Think about what I said."

"You'll do no such thing." The woman held the door for Guillory and Patterson who traipsed out reluctantly. Suddenly there was room to breathe in the tiny space.

The woman sat down and pulled a slim folder from her battered briefcase. "I'm Elaine Sienkewicz, your court-appointed attorney. You wanna soda? I got diet cola, I always bring a can for my clients, cos I know the pricks here."

Kyra nodded gratefully and Elaine took a can from her briefcase. The soda was warm, but Kyra had only had a tiny carton of juice to drink since yesterday.

She drank half the can in one gulp, the bubbles stung her throat. She coughed and burped.

"You okay there?"

Kyra nearly dropped the can and covered her mouth with her hand.

"I was thirstier than I realized."

Elaine put on a pair of spectacles, and peered at Kyra, taking in her bruises. "They knock you about, hon? Cos I know what these pricks are like when one of their own's dead."

"This is from an accident, had a few recently."

"Careless, huh?"

"I guess."

Elaine flicked through the pages in the folder. "Well, you're sure in a heap of trouble."

"But you're going to help me, right? You can get the charges dismissed."

Elaine snorted. "I can't get them dismissed, hon, this is a serious matter. Best I can do is get the first charge, murdering your girlfriend, down to manslaughter. Blame it on some sex game gone wrong. I can't do anything about the Sheriff's murder, that's an automatic murder one charge in this state, and they want the death penalty on this."

"I didn't do anything, it was a car accident. It wasn't my fault."

"I'm afraid that doesn't matter."

"It matters to me."

"Maybe so, but it all comes down to what you can prove. Can you prove it was an accident?"

"Can they prove it wasn't?"

"They'll give it a good try, and they have a big legal team. Listen, if you're willing to plead out, we can get the death penalty off the table. You could get twenty-five to life and, with good behavior, be out in fifteen. You'll be young enough to start over."

"That's what the deputy said. Pleading out means saying I'm guilty, right?"

"Trust me, it'll probably save your life."

"But I'm innocent."

"Only until they prove you guilty, and this isn't going to play well in front of a jury, not in this state."

Elaine glanced at her watch, gathered her things and stood up. "I'm really sorry, hon, but I'm afraid I have to go now, these pricks gave me the run around, so we'd get as little time as possible."

"That's it, that's all you're going to give me?"

"No, that's not all I'm going to give you, but that's all we have time for at the moment. I'll be back as soon as I can."

"So, you're just going to leave me here to rot, what kind of a lawyer are you?"

Elaine sat down and massaged the bridge of her nose. The care lines around her mouth seemed to deepen as she spoke. "I will do my damnedest for you, but right now I have two clients in Youngsville and another in New Iberia. I'll need to break the speed limit to see them all. I work sixty hours a week as a public defender, because my ex-husband won't pay child support. Some months I barely make minimum wage. I'll bust a gut to make sure you get the representation you deserve, so don't question my integrity."

"I'm sorry. I'm not supposed to be here, I'm not even eighteen. They haven't given me my phone call and my parents don't know where I am."

Elaine's expression softened. "Give me your parent's details. I'll get in touch. I'll chase the bastards about that phone call, but I can't promise anything. You'll definitely get a call when you get to the state penitentiary, I'll see about getting you moved to a juvenile facility as soon as I can."

"Wait, state penitentiary?"

"Aw hell, didn't they tell you? Sorry, hon, they're moving you out first thing tomorrow."

CHAPTER 80:

There was a ten ton weight on Kyra's chest.

She couldn't see it, but it was there. Crushing her ribs. Stifling her breath. Making her heart pound.

Sweat trickled from her forehead. Pooled in her armpits and the backs of her knees.

She was so, so tired. But sleep, like a swollen sea, kept washing her back to the shore. Denying her its still and soothing depths.

In restless dreams she turned over and over in a runaway police cruiser. Its roof buckled. Its windshield shattered. Shards bit into her flesh. Adrenaline burst through her system. Jolting her awake.

Where the ten ton weight would find her. Squeezing the last of the hope from her bones.

The ceiling fell. Stopping at what felt like inches from her face. The floor rose up under her bunk. The walls pushed in until Kyra was sealed in a coffin of brick and bars and concrete.

She screwed her eyes shut. The walls and ceiling disappeared. There was nothing around her but an empty, howling void. Her bunk spun endlessly through this baleful vacuum.

Until she opened her eyes and the fluorescent lights showed her cell unchanged.

The weight on her chest was the certainty that Kyra did not want to go to jail.

Not even for one night.

She'd barely survived high school, how would she manage the state pen? Images of every series or film she'd ever seen about women's prison spooled through her mind. And Kyra knew the reality was going to be worse.

Why had she ever come to Yeuxville? What did she think she was going to achieve? Connect with her past? Learn who her parents were? She'd done all that and look where it had gotten her.

Back in Chicago her bed would be clean and made. The sheets fragrant with the softener her parents used. Her books would be on their shelves, her clothes all over the floor and her mom would tut every time she passed Kyra's door.

God she missed them. Like a phantom limb. Like a deep, internal ache. Like air to a man who's breathed his last. They must be looking for her now. Fretting and worrying. Fearing the worst. Hoping for a call. Never in a million years would they expect her to wind up in jail. Even her dad, with his exhaustive searches, wouldn't think to look for her there.

Dad, where are you? Please come. Please, please come.

Dolores snored in the cell opposite. A grim dawn chorus to end the worst night of her life. She had no doubt there was worse to come.

Keys rattled in a lock. A door creaked open. Footsteps echoed round the long corridor between the cells.

Kyra propped herself up on her elbow. Patterson, Guillory and the deputy who'd propositioned her strode into view.

Guillory banged the bars with his baton. "Rise and shine, everybody on their feet."

Dolores's snores choked off. "What's going on?"

Jaime groaned. "Where's my breakfast? Whose dick do I gotta suck for an Egg McMuffin?"

Patterson raised her eyebrows. "Very funny. C'mon it's time to go."

Jaime pointed to Kyra and the deputy. "I ain't joking. I want the deal he offered her. I'm hungry."

Guillory brought his baton down hard on the bars. "Enough! Anymore and you'll get this upside your head. Now haul ass."

Kyra rolled off her bunk, joints aching, legs dead. The weight still on her chest, stealing her breath. The ground spun. She gripped the bars. Everything closed in on her.

A scream built in her throat and she clenched her teeth to hold it in. She could still hear it in her mind, protesting this injustice. *Stop it! This shouldn't be happening to me! I didn't do anything! I didn't do anything!*

Patterson approached Kyra's cell with the keys. "Step away from the bars."

Kyra tried to comply, but her fingers wouldn't leave the bars. Her legs wouldn't move.

Patterson banged the bars with her baton. "I said step away."

Kyra ground her teeth, tugged her hands away and stepped back. The cell spun. Her breath was quick and shallow. Sweat broke on her back, nausea grew in her gut.

Dolores, Jaime and the African American guy were already out of their cells, standing in a line while Guillory put cuffs on their wrists and ankles.

Jaime giggled. "Kinky."

Guillory growled and she rolled her eyes.

Patterson unlocked the cell and gestured for Kyra to leave. "Join the line."

Kyra stepped in behind the African American guy, dwarfed by his height and bulk. Guillory cuffed her ankles. The cold metal bit into her shins. She winced and Guillory smirked. He looped a chain around her waist tight enough to impede her breath, hooked the cuffs onto it and slapped them on her wrists.

Patterson watched. "You double lock them?"

"Nope."

He shot her a malicious smile that spoke of cuffs tightening and further discomfort.

Guillory banged the wall with his baton. "All right, move out."

Kyra shuffled along behind the others. The leg cuffs made it hard going, especially on the stairs.

At the top of the stairs the prisoners stopped and Kyra walked into the back of the guy in front. He shrugged as if a fly had buzzed him. Kyra couldn't understand the hold up until she peered around the guy in front.

The corridor that led to the rear lot was lined with deputies. A tall man with a thick mustache caught Kyra's eye. There was murder in his gaze.

The three prisoners ahead of her were hurried along, chafing against their leg irons. Kyra was held back. She was going to have to run the gauntlet. The deputies closed in around her, making her squeeze past.

They stared her down with dead eyes and folded arms. Shaking their heads, spitting at her feet, withering her with their loathing. They'd lost one of their own. A Sheriff they loved and admired. They wanted to see Kyra get what was coming to her.

Kyra shrank into herself. Bowed her head, brought her knees and elbows in. Still they bumped and jostled her. And the door to the lot never got any closer.

Finally, Kyra was pushed past the last two deputies and out into the glare of the early morning sun. The prison transporter sat waiting in the lot, dirty white with slatted windows. Kyra stumbled up to the door.

Jaime and Dolores were on the front seat.

"They gonna love a sweet little thing like you in the pen."

Dolores made a 'V' with her fingers and slipped her tongue between. They both laughed.

A voice called out. "Wait, sir, stop, you can't go back there. Sir, I need for you to stop or I'm going to shoot!"

Footsteps raced up behind.

"Release that prisoner," a voice shouted.

Kyra recognized it instantly.

CHAPTER 81:

The voice, the wonderful voice with its northern accent rang out. "I have a court order demanding you release that prisoner into my custody,"

Kyra hardly dared turn her head. She took a breath and he was there. His hands in the air, an official document clutched in his right for all to see, his briefcase lying at his feet.

Two deputies advanced on him, weapons drawn. One of them barked orders.

"Down on the ground, hands behind your head!"

More deputies spilled out of the back door, unclipping their holsters, circling him.

He didn't flinch, he didn't move. He used his voice, his deep clear voice.

"I have a court order with a clear mandate. You need to release that prisoner into my custody."

More weapons were pointing at him. Patterson stepped forward, her hands out to calm the situation. "It's okay, it's okay, stand down, he's not armed. I've got this."

"You need to release that prisoner."

Patterson shook her head. "No can do. Paperwork's already signed. She's as good as on that bus, and that bus isn't stopping till the State Pen."

The other deputies stood around, weapons lowered. Guillory barged forward. "You ain't her lawyer, how come you've got a court order?"

"What does that matter?"

"It matters to me. Who the hell are you?"

"Who am I?"

"That's what I said."

"I'm her father."

No, she wasn't going to cry. She wasn't. Her legs were shaking, her chest was heaving but she wasn't going to let the tears out.

Her dad had dropped his left arm but was still holding the court order up in his right hand. "My daughter is not getting in that vehicle."

"Like I said, it's as good as gone."

"Except it's not. I know that's what you planned, giving me the runaround yesterday, refusing to confirm you had my daughter in custody, shipping her out first thing in the morning, before I'd get here. But that's not going to happen."

Guillory narrowed one eye and pushed out his chest. "And why's that?"

"Failure to comply with a court order is a disciplinary offense. So is failure to report the location of a missing person, misleading legal counsel and questioning an underage suspect without a parent. I've already got enough to take your badges. If my daughter gets on that transporter, your careers are over."

"Where do you get off?" Guillory stepped up to her dad.

Patterson stepped between them. Guillory was taller and broader than her dad, but he didn't flinch. "Go ahead, add assault to the charges. Lose that badge and do some time."

"Good luck making that stick, I got witnesses who'll saw you tripped and fell."

Her Dad pointed to the prison transporter. "And I've got three witnesses who'll testify to the contrary, especially if I arrange a plea bargain."

Jaime called out. "Hey, I'll say whatever you want, if you get me a court order."

Dolores waved. "You're kinda handsome for an old guy."

Patterson sighed. "I think we need to talk. Come on inside."

"Not without my daughter."

"Your daughter will come, too." Patterson spoke to the guy behind the wheel of the transport. "Sorry, Joe, it's just gonna be three this morning."

"But I already filled out the paperwork. It's my ass if I turn up without her."

"Right now, I don't give a damn."

Kyra followed her dad and the two deputies back into the station. She would have to run the gauntlet of the deputies once again. But now she had her dad at her side.

Let them try and jostle her.

CHAPTER 82:

The station was in an uproar. An angry hubbub followed Kyra and her dad as they were led back to the interrogation room. They had to find another chair for Kyra's dad. They didn't record the meeting.

Patterson was emphatic. "Given the severity of the charges against your daughter, we can't release her into your custody."

Her dad was just as immovable. "No, you *have* to do that. I have a court order *demanding* it. Failure to comply will result in charges of contempt and insubordination for both of you. The charges aren't just severe, they're ridiculous and you're going to drop them all."

"Say what now?!" Guillory made to stand.

Patterson grabbed his arm and moved him gently back into his seat. "Mr. Hughes, we have your daughter's DNA at two murder scenes. We're not going to drop any charges."

"I beg to differ. I know that in Louisiana, Kyra can be tried as an adult if the charge is murder, but you're not allowed to take her DNA without my consent, and you never contacted me. So, any DNA is inadmissible, meaning you have no evidence tying her to the alleged murder scene."

Kyra's Dad reached into the briefcase he'd brought and pulled out a handful of folders. "What's more, you can't prove either death was a murder."

Now Patterson looked like she was going to spring out of her chair. "Béatrice Hawkins' eyes were taken out with a knife, Mr. Hughes. Your daughter was the only person present when that happened. It won't be hard to prove murder."

"I disagree, my daughter was tied to the floor and incapacitated."

"So she states, we only have *her* word."

"There are photos of the crime scene showing the restraints. We'll have her clothing checked for rope fibers, and you can bet we'll find them. There is no way she could have overpowered Ms. Hawkins. You've made no claims about Kyra's prints being on the knife, so I can assume you haven't found any. Secondly, the initial autopsy shows the victim didn't die of ocular trauma, she died of poison that she most likely administered herself."

Patterson was looking more uncomfortable. She glanced at Guillory. "Your daughter could have administered the poison."

"While she was tied to the floor? Good luck proving that. Plus my daughter told you, in an interview that's inadmissible by the way, she was unconscious at the time. Soon as we leave here, we'll get an independent tox-screen, as well as having her clothes forensically combed, bet you we'll find evidence of sedatives in her blood stream."

Guillory couldn't contain himself. "You're not her counsel. Where are you getting all this?"

"As her parent, and a lawyer, I can add myself to her legal team. I read her case file and contacted the coroner who e-mailed me the initial report, perfectly legally."

Guillory sat back and crossed his arms, a sneer stealing across his face. "Some lawyer, you deal in building contracts. Yeah, I checked you out. You're not the only one who does their homework."

"I did five years of criminal law, before moving into property, and the fact that you checked me out only adds to the misconduct charges I could file. It proves you knew who I was, and yet you withheld evidence, failed to tell me you'd located my daughter, even though she was an official missing person. I can have your internet history subpoenaed to prove this."

Guillory ground his teeth, fists in his lap. A vein throbbed on his temple. This wasn't going the way he and Patterson expected. Patterson made one last attempt to get things back on track.

"We still have your daughter on a murder one charge."

Kyra's dad let out a short, dismissive laugh. "No, you don't. Without your other charge to corroborate, the whole case falls apart. Kyra was handcuffed to a partition in the back of Sheriff Hawkins' car. The partition is specifically designed to ensure felons are safely contained in the backseat, with no access to the front."

Guillory breathed out through his nose. "How do we know she was in the backseat?"

"That's where she was found in the wreckage."

"She mighta been thrown back there when the car went off the road."

"If that's really the story you want to go with, I have to warn you, I'll introduce photographs of the bruises on her wrists. I'll put the paramedics, who cut her from the vehicle, on the stand and ask where they cut her out and whether she was cuffed at the time. I'll get experts to testify how effective the partition is in protecting officers in the front seat from felons in the back, not to mention how impossible it would be to be thrown from the front seat into the back. And we all know how that'll end—with a full acquittal."

"Well, maybe we'll let a jury decide that."

"So you're banking on the jury siding with the prosecution because a cop's been killed? Is that all you've got? Because it makes a pretty flimsy case. And I have to warn you, if you proceed with this line of enquiry, I'll be forced to enter evidence that speaks to the character of the 'so-called' victim."

"What are you talking about?" Kyra's dad pulled out a huge manila file from his briefcase. "I have in my possession a dossier, compiled by a late deputy of this department, showing Sheriff Hawkins' complicity in crimes surrounding the Billy-Ray Johnson case. At the least, it's proof of tampering with evidence, corrupting crime scenes and perjury. At its worst, it cites Sheriff Hawkins as the culprit responsible for the murders."

"The hell?!" Guillory sprang to his feet, knocking his chair over.

Kyra flinched, her dad gave no reaction, just handed the file to a shell-shocked Patterson. "Go ahead, check it out, it's all here in black and white. This copy's for you."

Patterson hesitated, then took the proffered dossier. "Are you threatening us with this, Mr. Hughes?"

"No, as a professional courtesy, I'm giving you a heads up on my defense strategy. If you proceed with these charges, I'll be forced to hit you both with a misconduct suit that will effectively end your careers. Then there's the press attention that'll come when this dossier gets into open court. Do you really want to be the guys who brought that kind of heat onto the Sheriff's Department?"

"What are you saying. Mr. Hughes?" Patterson's voice was dry and tired, struggling to hide her defeat.

"I'm asking you to take a moment and consider your career paths. Are you sure you want to go to court with two cases you can't prove, because your evidence has already collapsed? Sheriff Hawkins lost control of his vehicle on a road twenty miles from here. A road that doesn't lead to this station or any other detention center in the state. He didn't call in the arrest, and no officer knew he'd detained her. She knew about this dossier, and I have witnesses who can attest to that. My guess is Sheriff Hawkins was taking her somewhere to silence her, like the dossier suggests he did with those other five women."

"Can you prove any of this?"

"Read the dossier. It's all going to come out if you go ahead with a trial. Serial killer cop, the press will have a field day with that. There'll be reporters camped out here, twenty-four-seven. That's what you're facing if you press charges."

He sat back in his chair, crossed his legs and folded his hands across his stomach, totally chill. It was a power move, even Kyra could see that.

Guillory righted his chair and sat down. Neither deputy spoke. There was a calm in the room, like the still air before a weather front blows in. Their eyes were narrowed, their jaws set, their muscles coiled with a seething impotent rage.

Guillory indicated the door with his chin. Patterson nodded. Without saying anything, they got up and left the room.

Had Kyra's dad just kicked their butts?

CHAPTER 83:

They were alone.

Outside, the station buzzed with chatter and expectation. Inside, Kyra was with the one person she needed more than anyone.

She met his eyes. A smile stole across his face. A hesitant crack in the façade and Kyra saw how hard he was trying to keep it together. All the confidence and bravado masked the pain he felt at seeing her like this.

Shame, relief, regret, gratitude welled up inside her. So many unfinished sentences formed and died on her lips and all she could manage was. "Dad, what the hell?"

He put a finger to his lips. "They're probably still listening. We need to choose our words carefully while we're here. We shouldn't have to wait too long."

"You think they'll let me out?"

"I haven't left them any choice. It won't take long to talk it through. There'll be one call to the Parish DA, and they'll be right back."

"But the dossier?" Kyra held up her hands.

"Your friend Delilah. Nice kid, printed it out and everything. She cares about you."

"How do you know Delilah?"

"I've been combing Yeuxville the last two days. Always a few hours behind you, at the motel, at Aunt Mimi's house."

"You met Aunt Mimi?"

"I met a lot of people, including Dr. McFadden, but not you. I kept missing you. Then I learned about your friend, Beatrice's industrial unit, by the time I got there it was a crime scene. I checked with the Sheriff's Office to see if you were involved. Fearing the worst at that point. They knew nothing about your missing person's case, even though I'd filed the paperwork."

"That was the Sheriff's doing, I'll tell you about it later."

"At first, one of the deputies admitted your arrest, but then the whole station clammed up, refused to confirm they had you in custody. I smelled something fishy, so I got in touch with the courts and found your counsel. Got the whole case file from Elaine. She's a character."

"Don't get me started."

"When I told Delilah what had happened, she gave me the dossier, said it would probably save you. It's dynamite. I knew they couldn't hold you on anything, and so did they, that's why they'd been giving me the runaround, trying to hide you from me, did the same thing to Elaine."

"She was pissed."

"They didn't want you conferring with anyone. Because you were young, they thought they could frighten you into confessing"

"They gave me a confession to sign, but I wouldn't do it. It was all lies."

Kyra saw her dad's eyes narrow, and his jaw clench. More cracks in the façade. Anger trickled through. He looked away, shook his head.

"Assholes."

"Did you just cuss?"

"Don't tell your mother."

"Is she listening too?"

The anger passed, he almost smiled.

"They gave me the same runaround. When I saw the prison transporter I knew they were trying to move you, the deputies at the desk refused to look at the court order. I had to jump over a gate in the back of the building."

"I thought they were going to shoot you."

"So did I. Figured it would be worth it if I could get you out."

The door opened. Patterson and Guillory were back. They walked with a slow, heavy step. They were trying for poker faces and settling for thinly veiled scowls. They dropped back into their chairs, shoulders slumped, peering up with bowed heads.

No one spoke. Kyra found it unbearable. She shifted in her seat, rattling her cuffs. Her dad placed his hand lightly on her shoulder, encouraging her to hold out. He wasn't going to blink first.

Eventually Patterson spoke. "Okay, we just got off the phone with the DA."

Kyra's Dad shot her a conspiratorial smile. *Told you.*

"We're willing to release your daughter, but *only* if you hand over all copies of this dossier, electronic and hard copy. We also reserve the right to continue this investigation, so you can't leave the Parish."

Kyra's dad shook his head. "Not acceptable. You *have* to release Kyra into my custody. I have a court order demanding it. If you're going to continue building a case I'm going to keep this dossier. In fact, I'll be forced to enter it into the public record so we can use it in court, and that'll be even more of an embarrassment to the Sheriff's Department."

Like a cornered beast Guillory began breathing hard. "How you going to do that?"

"Continue with the charges, you'll find out."

Patterson dropped her head, sighed and then shook it. Total resignation and surrender. She turned to Guillory, a rueful half-smile on her lips. "Told you it wouldn't work."

Guillory pursed his lips, folded his arms and turned his head away, morose and betrayed.

Patterson addressed Kyra's dad. "So why show us the dossier? What's your play?"

"I'll hand over all copies of this dossier when I get a signed agreement from the governor's office that all charges against my daughter have been dropped and the state will not pursue them again."

"The DA's not gonna like this."

"She'll find a way to live with it. Now, take these shackles off of my daughter, we're leaving."

Patterson looked at Guillory. He ignored her. She cleared her throat. He reached into his pocket and handed her the keys with sullen disregard. Patterson's raised eyebrows and tilted head said – *so, it's going to be like that.*

She knelt in front of Kyra and unlocked the leg cuffs. Pain shot through Kyra's shins. Pins and needles bit into her foot. Her wrist screamed as the cuffs came off. Air flooded back into her lungs as the chain around her waist lost its hold on her diaphragm.

Kyra glanced at her dad, teeth clamped on his bottom lip, his eyes full of pain. Summoning his last reserve. Holding back the tide of anger and concern that threatened his composure. He reached out and brushed a single lock of hair behind her ear, like he used to when she was a little girl. Their first meaningful contact since she'd seen him this morning.

Kyra's Dad put his hand on her shoulder and led her out of the interrogation room. The staff who'd turned out to see her off were milling round the office. Shock and anger on their faces as they watched Kyra collect her things, and sign for the backpack they'd recovered from Béatrice's unit.

Kyra wasn't facing them in chains, like some animal dragged to a truck. She wasn't a murder suspect. She was free. She was with her dad, and she'd never felt prouder, or more grateful, to be in his company.

CHAPTER 84:

This wasn't happening.

When Kyra had woken this morning, she was going to prison. She wasn't ever going to see her parents again.

Now she was free, leaving the station with her dad. Crossing the road to where he'd parked.

Kyra knew the street, recognized the buildings, felt the heat of the morning sun, but it didn't seem real. Was she dreaming this from a seat in the transporter? Or had she woken from the bad dream of her holding cell?

Her dad stopped by a white Toyota Corolla. This wasn't his car. He didn't drive a hatchback. But he produced a key fob and the locks bleep-bleeped open. It was a rental. He popped the trunk and dropped in her backpack.

Kyra stood gazing at the strange car. What should she do now? Her dad opened the door, climbed inside and opened the passenger door. He signaled for her to get in. Of course, that's what she should do.

She scooted onto the front seat and for a moment she and her dad just looked at each other. Then she did what she'd wanted to since she first saw him in the parking lot, since they'd sat for an interminable period in the interrogation room and since she finally left the station. She threw her arms around his neck, buried her face in his shoulder and let out every tear she'd been holding back.

Her dad hugged her right back. His chest heaved against hers and she felt his tears on her neck. Was it minutes that they sat like that, sobbing in the front seat, or hours? Kyra didn't care and she didn't care who saw them.

The car was baking by the time they stopped hugging. The sun was rising and they weren't in the shade. Her dad wiped his eyes with the heel of his palm.

"Kyra, I am *so* sorry."

"What? Dad, you were awesome in there. You saved my life. You nearly took a bullet for me."

"Okay, I know, but this is important. I've spent the last two days tracking you down. Trying to work out what you were thinking and feeling, what your motives were so I could find you. I did a lot of thinking, and I realized I let you down. I didn't see how important it was for you to come to Yeuxville and how it was affecting your mental health."

"No, Dad."

Her Dad took her hand in his. "I wasn't there for you, not like I should have been. You were angry all the time and I didn't know how to fix that. I thought if I found your birth parents you'd stop being so mad. Stop getting in trouble at school. But your problems were more complex."

"I think maybe I should get therapy."

A pained look crossed her dad's face. "Yeah, I think maybe we all should. Look, my generation, we're not great when it comes to mental health. Things were different when we were teens. You didn't talk about those things, there was a stigma attached. I guess I didn't want to admit you had a problem, because then it would be my fault and I'd be a bad parent."

"How was it your fault?"

"I'm your dad, everything's my fault. It'll be my fault till you've gone through a score of therapists."

"Don't be silly."

"I'm serious. I didn't want to face up to what you really needed. I kept trying to fix things practically. I poured all my time and energy into finding your birth parents and I neglected your feelings. No, I need to be honest, I was avoiding the way you were feeling."

"For real?"

Her dad looked sheepish. "Your anger made me angry and we kept clashing. I couldn't get through to you. You've seen what Granny and Grandpa are like."

"Oh yeah."

"I wanted so much to be different. To not raise you like they raised me. But suddenly I was acting just like them. I was ignorant and out of touch and I hated it. I just couldn't connect, I couldn't talk to you, and we'd always talked."

"I know."

"Right? I know it sounds lame, I know I'm your dad, but you're one of my best friends and more than anything I missed you."

"I missed you too, I couldn't work out why you were acting like you were, why you'd changed. But I didn't think about how I was treating you."

"I blamed myself. I'm your dad, I'm supposed to fix all your problems, but I couldn't fix this. It was too big. Being your dad is the most important job I have, and I felt like a failure at the one thing I wanted to do best."

"You're the best dad I ever had."

"I'm kinda the only dad you've ever had."

"That's not strictly true."

Kyra's dad looked down and massaged his forehead with his fingertips. "No, you're right. And, if we're being real honest, I guess I was jealous."

"Of what?"

"Of your birth parents. I know it sounds stupid, but I thought you wanted to find them because I wasn't good enough. If I'd been a better father, you wouldn't need to find them. I couldn't understand why your mom and me weren't enough."

"Dad, you're so much better than my birth parents. My birth dad only saw me when he was stalking me."

"Honestly?"

"Oh yeah, and Caitlin was awful. She took drugs and slept with other people's men and, she abused me, badly."

"Oh Kyra, I had no idea."

"Neither did I till I came here. And you know what the most messed up thing is, I still miss her, I still love her, and I did the worst thing to her."

Everything disappeared in a mist of tears. Kyra felt her dad's fingers on her cheek, gently brushing them away. She took a breath and blinked her eyes clear. There was so much love on her dad's face, so much concern.

"Is this a recovered memory or did you ask around?"

"I saw it, not through my own eyes, but I saw it."

Her dad tilted his head and looked at Kyra quizzically. "I'm not sure I follow you. How did you see it?"

Kyra took a deep breath, pushed her hair back from her face and put both hands in her lap. "Can we go get a coffee? There's a place I know, and there's a lot I have to tell you, plus it's too hot to stay in this car."

Her dad started up the engine. "Would this be The Naked Bean?"

"You know about The Naked Bean?"

"I combed the town looking for you, showed your picture to everyone. You were in there with Delilah a few days ago, that's how I tracked her down."

"Let's go then, I'm starving."

"I'll treat you to breakfast."

"Thanks. Listen, I have a lot to tell you, and I need you to keep an open mind. Okay? A real open mind."

"It's not drugs is it, or something worse?"

"No, Dad, it's not drugs."

"Okay."

It *was* something worse. And Kyra had no idea how she was going to tell him.

CHAPTER 85:

The first thing Kyra told her dad about was the cash she'd taken from his wall safe. But she waited until they'd ordered and eaten.

Kyra had the vegan breakfast special, and half of her dad's beignets. They were just as good as she remembered. She'd chosen a corner table, by a window. The waitress didn't get to them as often, but no-one would eavesdrop.

It wasn't the strangest, and it wasn't the worst thing she had to tell him. But it was the hardest.

When she was done she put down her fork. He was quiet, staring out the window at the town's historic square. Kyra knew her dad well, she could see the cogs in his mind grinding as he weighed up his response. Should he be a traditional parent, like his folks, and scold Kyra? Or should he listen and help?

He chose the latter. Meeting her eyes and taking a breath.

"Have you spent it all?"

"I have about seven and a half left, probably more, it's in my fanny pack."

"The one we've just collected from the police station? That's likely to have been searched."

"I'm sorry, I had nowhere else to put it. I've not been making great decisions, but I never expected any of this to happen. I was on my way to catch the bus home."

Again, her dad glanced out of the window. Weighing his response – scold or try to understand.

"It's okay, it's probably there. I know you had a rough time with the Sheriff's department, but I've had a lot to do with cops, and they have a moral compass."

Kyra made a dismissive noise with her mouth. "Except the crooked ones."

"No, even the crooked ones. They might be on the take, but they have lines they won't cross, people they won't take from. We're all human, we all make bad decisions, cops as much as anyone."

Kyra frowned. "Okay, I get it, *I've* been making a lot of bad decisions. I just said that."

"I think our whole family has been making bad decisions. And this is where we're at. But that's not what matters. What matters is how we move on."

"I'll pay you back every penny."

"I know you will in time. Meanwhile, we'll call it an interest free loan."

"Does mom have to know?"

Her dad rolled his eyes. "She's my wife, she'd have my balls if she found out I didn't tell her."

Kyra blinked in surprise, put her hand to her mouth and giggled. "Dad, that's my mom you're talking about."

"Exactly, so, you know why I can't keep this from her."

"I guess so."

Her dad drained his cup. "Can I ask you a question?"

"Sure."

"You spoke about your birth parents as if you'd found them. Do you know who they are?"

"Yes, but you won't believe how I found them."

"But you know who your..." He was having trouble saying the word, finding a term he could live with.

"My birthfather is, yes."

"Who is it?"

"It's Billy-Ray Johnson."

"Get out of here."

"Seriously."

"How could you possibly know that?"

"It's true, dad. I'll explain everything, but you're going to have to trust me."

Her dad was still processing this. "Your birthfather, was a serial killer, was the man who murdered your birthmother?"

"He didn't murder Caitlin."

"Yes he did, I watched the YouTube videos."

"What videos?"

"The ones you sent me."

"You watched those?"

"Of course I did. You sent them to me. It was important I watched them."

"Why didn't you say something?"

"I wanted to, I was dying to discuss them with you, but we were hardly talking."

"That's true. But the videos were wrong, so were the books and newspaper articles. It's a colossal miscarriage of justice."

"You're serious."

"I am."

"Then who killed your birthmother?"

"I did."

Her dad's mouth literally fell open. "What?"

"I killed her."

"Kyra, you were two years old. Caitlin Robichaud's body was stabbed and mutilated, the killer painted on the walls in her blood." He stopped when he realized he was talking about the woman who gave birth to Kyra, "Sorry to get graphic, but how could you possibly have done all that when you were barely a toddler? You were only just walking when you came to us, you were barely potty trained."

"It was an accident. She was a real bad mom. She came at me with a knife. I was on my back, on the kitchen table, kicking and screaming. I caught the knife with my foot, knocked her hand back and she stabbed herself in the eye. Sheriff Hawkins mutilated her body and wrote on the walls. He did that so he could frame Billy-Ray for all the murders."

"That's a pretty wild story, Kyra."

"It gets wilder."

"How did you learn all this?"

"It's in that dossier about Sheriff Hawkins, I thought you knew most of this."

Her dad's face flushed. He smiled sheepishly and rubbed the back of his neck. "I haven't actually read the dossier. Didn't have time. I just got the basic facts from Delilah."

"Dad, you threatened the police with it."

"I wouldn't say 'threatened.' I used it as leverage to get you out of custody."

"You're lucky it's all true."

"Delilah's uncle *was* a cop. I figured it would have *some* substance. So, everything you've been telling me, you learned from the dossier?"

"Not all of it. The dossier doesn't tell the whole story. I'm going to need another latte to tell you that."A slight scowl crossed her dad's face. "As your dad, I'm a bit concerned about all the caffeine you're drinking. Can we get you a juice, or a soda?"

Kyra full-on scowled. "Dad, there's likely to be as much caffeine in a soda. I know it comes from a place of love, but if you want to be my best friend, you have to stop treating me like a child."

"Duly noted."

He signaled to the waitress for two more lattes.

The waitress brought their drinks. Kyra took a deep breath and began her tale. She didn't hold anything back, not the presence, nor what happened when she met Delilah. Though she still cringed at the way she acted. She opened up about flirting with Béatrice and when the episodes started. She tried to make her dad see it all, through her eyes just as she'd seen through Billy-Ray's.

He wiped milk-froth from his lips. "So that's how you got hit by a car?"

"How'd you know about that?"

"I spoke to Dr. McFadden. I was thorough, I told you."

Kyra went on. She told how the episodes continued, how the past opened up for her and how she came to Sheriff Hawkins' attention. She spoke of her rage, of the revelations, of Caitlin's cruelty. She spoke of the 'K' she'd carved into the past and the oak that still bore this out.

She relived the impossible decision. Between letting Caitlin die, when it was in Kyra's power to save her, and never seeing her dad or mom again.

Kyra's dad gripped her hand. "That's what the voicemail to your mom was all about."

"You heard that?"

"Your mom didn't pick it up."

"She never does."

"Her phone wasn't even charged. When I finally heard it, I realized where you'd gone."

"How did you work that out from the message I left?"

"I told you, I'm thorough."

Kyra wrinkled her nose.

Her dad shrugged. "Call it father's intuition."

Despite the skepticism in her dad's eyes, Kyra continued. Conjuring an account of what she saw on the anniversary of Caitlin's death, what Delilah had revealed and how Kyra went to warn Béatrice. Her capture, the ceremony, and how the visions Béatrice had bought with her death flowed between them, as Kyra had flowed down the river of death.

Finally, she took her dad for a ride in the back of Sheriff Hawkins' cruiser. They listened to his threats, were rescued by Billy-Ray's ghostly presence and managed to survive a car crash that was fatal to Hawkins. Then, to cap it all off, they were arrested and charged for murder.

Her dad's eyed narrowed to slits. His knuckles were white from gripping his water glass. A thin crack appeared.

"Dad, stop, you're going to cut yourself."

Her dad blinked, looked down at the cracked glass and let go of it. He put his hands to his temples, grimaced and dropped them in his lap.

"I'm sorry, I've been running round the past couple days, fearing the absolute worst. Or I thought it was the worst, but I was so wrong. Kyra, what you faced, I don't even know where to begin. I pushed you away and you ran here and, I would have died, seriously, I don't think I could have gone on living if Hawkins had..."

Kyra took her dad's hands in hers. "Dad, it's okay, I survived, I'm still here. You were who I thought about in the back of that police car, how I consoled myself. When I was struggling with saving Caitlin, you were the one I looked to. I did what I thought you'd do. You mentioned moral compasses, well my needle points to you. You're my due north."

He reached across the table and stroked her cheek, with tenderness and love. He blinked rapidly, he was trying to hold back his tears and failing miserably. "Thank you, that's one of the nicest things anyone's ever said to me."

"I mean it."

"I know, and I know you believe everything you've told me. I'll be honest, I'm struggling with it. Voodoo, ghosts, changing the past, that's not part of my worldview. I'm not saying I don't believe you, I'm keeping an open mind, I am, but I need a bit more proof. So, stick with me."

"I'll stick with you. We'll find proof. For now, I need you to believe *what* I'm telling you, even if you don't believe *how* I found out. Deal?"

"Deal."

Kyra knew where she had to take him next. She prayed her dad would realize how important it was. To Kyra, and the injustice she was going to fight.

CHAPTER 86:

"That's the K?"

Her dad ran his fingers over the soft edges of the carving, where it was still visible in the wrinkled bark. They'd pushed through the dense bushes to get to the old oak. A light breeze shook the Spanish moss that hung from its gnarled branches.

Kyra pressed in next to her dad. "Just where I said it would be. That's your first bit of proof."

"It would be better if you had a photo of the tree before you altered the past and then after."

"It doesn't work that way. I changed the past when I made Billy-Ray carve that K, and I altered the present and every moment in between. Even if I'd taken a photo on my phone, the minute I altered the past, the K would have appeared on my phone too. Cos I changed the past fifteen years ago and only took the photo two days before. But if you'd been here with me, when I first came to this trailer park, you'd have seen there was no K, and now there is."

Kyra's dad looked at her with admiration that became a sudden realization. "So, what you're saying is: 'the essential is invisible to the eye.' You're asking me to see clearly with my heart."

Kyra clapped her hands in child-like excitement. "*The Little Prince*, yes, that's exactly what I'm asking."

She led him out of the bushes and back to the main walkway. His eyes darted left and right, uneasy, checking for trouble. He tried to be surreptitious, but

Kyra could always read him. For all his restless spirit and open mind, her dad had never been in a trailer park in the deep south.

"Well, bon soir dere, stranger."

Kyra recognized that voice. She'd been so busy trying to steer her dad out of the bushes and away from trouble, she hadn't noticed they'd walked right past Gail's trailer. Gail was out in the yard, waving to them.

"Regarde ça, ya came back to see me."

"Hey Gail, how's things?"

"Comme ci, comme ça, but what ya gonna do? Who's dis feller?"

Kyra opened her arms to indicate her dad, like some magician's assistant. "Hey, Gail, this is my dad." It felt hokey, she quit doing it.

Her dad gave his best winning smile and offered Gail his hand. "Dennis."

Gail batted her eyelashes. "Well, ain't you de handsome one."

Her Dad's smile broadened. "You're not so bad yourself."

Kyra rolled her eyes. "Gail used to look after me back when I lived in Yeuxville. We met up a few days ago."

"She's hardly changed in all dat time."

"Bet you haven't either."

"Da-ad, enough already."

Her dad shot Kyra a contrite smile and winked at Gail. "Sorry, sweetheart."

"So, how ya been since I last saw ya?"

How should she answer that? Probably best to be honest. "Not great. I was in a car accident and I got arrested for something I didn't do, but my dad got me off."

"Dat how ya got dem bruises, from de accident, I mean?"

"Yeah."

"Oh, hon, I'm sorry to hear dat. Sounds rough."

"It was for a while, but things are on the up. Gail, can I ask you a question?"

"Sure."

"Did you know Billy-Ray Johnson?"

"De Killer?"

"Uh, yeah."

Gail turned from Kyra and walked straight back to the door of her trailer. Kyra was surprised. Why was she acting like this?

Gail turned in the doorway. "Best to come on in, I ain't gonna discuss dis in de open."

Kyra looked to her dad. He shrugged and they both followed Gail inside the trailer. It hadn't changed a bit since her last visit.

Gail invited them to sit at the small table and went to the stove. "Who wants coffee?"

Kyra glanced at her dad. "Do you have any soda?"

"Sorry, hon, just coffee and water."

Kyra's dad sighed. "Coffee's fine, for both of us. I have a feeling we're going to need it."

"Cream and sugar?"

"However it comes."

Gail made coffee and joined them at the table. "Truth is, I ain't never told nobody 'bout dis, but I dated Billy-Ray for a few months, 'fore your momma took up wid him."

"Wow, I had no idea."

"Hardly anyone did. Kept it to myself, n'a rien dit. He wasn't like dey said wid me. He was always a gentleman. Quiet and kinda sweet, y'know. But when I heard what he did to yer momma and all dose odder women, I was shocked. I woulda never believed it of him."

"Did he start seeing Caitlin straight after he was seeing you?"

A bitter tone crept into Gail's face and voice and Kyra regretted the question. "Wouldn't be de first time, nor de last."

So, she knew all along. Kyra took her hand. "I'm sorry about that."

"Dat was yer momma, ya had to take de good wid de bad. She could light up a room when she wanted to, make ya feel like de most important person in de world. But she was always drawn to odder women's men. Her own daddy left when she was a babe see, and her momma treated her real bad, 'specially when she got older. Couldn't take the competition from her own daughter. So,

Caitlin was always looking for male attention, cos she never got none when she was young. And she always saw odder women as her rivals."

"I never knew that. It explains a lot. About Caitlin and how she treated me."

"She weren't a good momma, c'est vrai. I did my best to look after ya when I could.

Never had no children o' my own, havin' ya round so much, well it too de edge of dat, made knowin' yer momma all dat much better, bon vieux temps."

Kyra squeezed Gail's hand. "You know, I came to Yeuxville to find out who my parents were. The authorities wouldn't tell me after I was adopted."

"Expect dey wouldn't, given what happened."

"Caitlin gave birth to me, sure. But you raised me, Gail. You were more of a mother to me than she ever was."

Gail put her other hand up to her face. "Stop, yer gonna make me tear up in front o' yer handsome daddy."

Her dad blew on his coffee. "You're both going to make me tear up."

They finished their drinks and said their goodbyes, promising Gail they'd come and visit whenever they were back in town.

As they pulled away from the trailer park her dad looked thoughtful. "Okay, the jury's still out about the tree carving, but it seems Billy-Ray could've been your birth father, and he probably didn't commit those murders."

"Probably?"

"Hey, I'm trying here, give me that."

She did give him that. He was keeping an open mind. She just had to make sure he didn't let it slam shut. And she knew the perfect person to help.

CHAPTER 87:

The door swung open and there stood Mimi, beaming at them.

She threw her arms round Kyra. "We were so worried. Come in, come in."

She ushered them into the house, and they followed her to the kitchen. Mimi put her arm round Kyra's shoulder. "I made offerings to Saint Expedite and Marie Laveaux for your safe return, they never let me down."

Kyra was puzzled. "Marie Laveaux, really?"

"Oh yes, she's a powerful spirit. In the last days of her life she dedicated herself to helping the condemned, she sat up all night with some prisoners on the eve of their execution. There's no better spirit to call on when you want to help someone who's been unjustly incarcerated."

"Unjustly incarcerated, that definitely sounds like me."

Her dad put his hand on her shoulder. "But you're out now, thanks in no small part to Mimi and Delilah."

Mimi smiled. "My niece is at work, but she'll be back later. She'll be so relieved to hear you're okay. I was the one who persuaded her to give Dennis the dossier. As soon as your dad told us you'd been arrested, I knew it'd help. Oh, look at your face, did the deputies do that?"

"No, Mimi, it happened in the accident. The Sheriff's car went off the road, he was killed, and they tried to blame me."

Mimi shook her head. "I wish I was surprised, but I've known the deputies too long."

"I'm sure they're not all bad."

"I was married to one. I *know* they're not all bad, but they ain't all smart neither, Dennis."

Her dad flushed. "Of course, sorry."

Mimi guided them to the kitchen table. "Sit, sit, I'll get my things, you stay right there."

Mimi returned with a jar of unguent, a roll of bandages, some herbs and a small statue. She lit a candle in front of the statue and said a silent prayer. She put the unguent on Kyra's wounds and bandaged her wrist with the herbs.

"You'll feel an improvement tomorrow morning, by the next evening they should be all healed."

Kyra's dad was unconvinced. "It'll take longer than that."

Maybe this was the proof he needed. "It won't, the bruises I got from the car healed two days after Mimi saw to them. Seriously, check these bruises in a couple days' time."

He screwed up his face, he was trying, she could see that, but he had a way to go. He pointed to the statue on the kitchen table. It was about eight inches tall. An African man with straw hair that covered his head and fell to his feet. His face was covered with a headdress made of cowrie shells and he was carrying a rattle in his left hand.

"Who's this?"

Sensing his skepticism, Mimi spoke slowly, as if explaining something to a clever child. "He has many names, San Lazaro, Ọbalúayé, Shopona, he's the spirit of healing and infectious diseases. He's very powerful, be warned, you should treat him with veneration and respect."

"He looks a bit like Cousin It, you know, from the Addams Family."

"Way to go on the veneration and respect, Dad."

"Sorry."

"You'll have to excuse him, he's new to all this. I mean, so am I, but he's really new."

Mimi collected the herbs and unguents together, leaving the candle to burn. "I'd expect nothing less. But I'd bet on the strength of my faith over the power of your skepticism any day."

Her dad looked genuinely contrite. "Is this what Kyra meant when she told me about the old ways?"

"I would imagine so."

"Do you mind if I ask how old these ways are? Do they trace their roots back to Africa?"

"Everyone traces their roots back to Africa, it's where humanity was born."

"Good point."

"The old ways can be traced back to Benin, at least a thousand years ago, although it's likely some of the rituals and beliefs were ancient then. Some of our ways are newer than folk like to believe. The old ways came with us on the slave ships from West Africa, but they were met by the faiths of our captors. These people wanted to rob us of our faith and supplant it with their own. But some beliefs are stronger than others. Our truths could accommodate their truths without losing any of their strength or power. My niece, Delilah, would call this 'syncretistic', but all the best religions are syncretistic. Christianity is syncretistic and so is science. Our ways accommodate them both and still remain every bit as powerful."

"So, you believe in Christian saints and ancient spirits, biology as well as bewitching?"

"We believe in what works, Dennis."

"And it does work, dad, trust me."

"Okay, I'll try."

Kyra took his hand and squeezed it. She also had questions. "Can you clear up some stuff for us?"

"I'll try."

"There's a ritual Béatrice got from her momma, it lets you see the past out of other people's eyes, she also used it, or something similar, to travel along the River of the Guédé to show me the past."

Mimi held up her hands. "Child, you need to slow down, you're not making a lot of sense. Is it any wonder your poor Daddy's having problems following this. Come over here and help me peel these vegetables, you tell me all about it while you prep, start at the beginning and don't leave anything out."

So that's what Kyra did. She started with how she met Béatrice and picked up the fetish, explained about the episodes she had and how Béatrice had shown her the past. She went into greater detail than she had with her dad, and at times he looked alarmed. As she talked, Mimi passed her vegetables, and prepared rice for jambalaya.

By the time she was finished Kyra's throat was sore, and incredible smells were coming from the pot on the stove. Mimi set four places at the kitchen table, one for Delilah when she got back. The vegetable jambalaya was sweet, spicy and full of flavor, Kyra's dad had three portion.

When they were done, Mimi took them into the back yard so she could smoke and made them swear not to tell Delilah. "Béatrice's mother, Céleste, had a lot of secrets. The Papillons passed some dark knowledge from mother to daughter."

Kyra's dad coughed. "The Papillons?"

Kyra did her best to explain. "It's like a dynasty of priestesses who practiced the old ways. They conducted services out in the bayou for generations, apparently the whole town used to come."

Mimi blew a plume of smoke. "Up until recently."

"They were revered by the community, and it was always passed from mother to daughter."

Kyra's dad batted an insect away. "That's why Béatrice was so upset about losing her mother, why she went looking for her spell book."

Mimi stubbed her cigarette out. "It's called a grimoire. And it would have been a fearsome one. Powerful knowledge, some of it frightening. As you found out, Kyra."

Kyra's dad, ever the gentleman, held the back door so they could all go in. "Has Kyra got anything to worry about?"

"I shouldn't think so, not anymore. The hex has more or less played itself out, Kyra and Béatrice closed it down."

Kyra bit her thumb, thoughtfully. "Béatrice said sometimes the dead don't leave, you can call them into your own time. Like when Sheriff Hawkins crashed the car, I'm pretty sure that was Billy-Ray. Should I be concerned about him coming back again?"

"The dead are a curious lot. They like to know what's been going on since they left, but they get bored of being ignored. The living don't pay them much heed, 'specially not these days. Eventually they get lonely and move on. If you're worried, go visit Billy-Ray's grave, and say your goodbyes, that'll allow you both to move on."

Kyra and her dad cleared the table and made a start on the dishes.

"I've been texting your mom, by the way."

"What did you say?"

"I told her you were fine, that everything was taken care of and she shouldn't worry. I said for her to sit tight, and we'd be home in a couple days."

"What did Mom say?"

"It's your mom, what do you think she said?"

"That she's on the next flight here?"

"She's booked us a hotel in Lafayette. She thinks we should spend some quality time together."

"I think she's right."

"She's going to be mad, to begin with."

"I know, but I don't care. I miss her."

The next evening, they were waiting for Kyra's mom to land at Lafayette Regional Airport. While her dad waited on the concourse, Kyra went to the bathroom and removed the bandages. When she'd inspected Mimi's handiwork she came out and showed her dad.

He was incredulous. "That's not possible. I saw what happened after that crash. No one heals that fast."

"You gotta have a little faith, dad. You should have trusted me about this."

Her dad put his arm round Kyra and pulled her to him. "I should have trusted you about a lot of things. And from now on, I promise I will."

CHAPTER 88:

TWO WEEKS LATER...

When Kyra looked back on the events of that long, strange fall, she came to realize everything began to go right as they passed Tunica, heading north on Highway 66.

Fall was giving ground to winter. Temperatures in Louisiana were falling to bearable levels. In Chicago the leaves had fled their branches to lie in brittle piles on lawns and strew the sidewalks. Here they'd only just begun to swap their green for ocher, rust and flaming red.

The sedan her dad had rented was making good time, but the air conditioning was taking forever to kick in, even with the lower temperatures outside. Her dad was at the wheel and Delilah was draped across the backseat looking stunning in a black, layered midi shirt dress with tulle skirt layers to add volume and black buckled boots that were to die for. Kyra felt frumpy in jeans and t-shirt.

Delilah fluttered a black hand fan. "Tell me we'll get to visit St. Francisville."

Kyra snorted. "Why would you want to? It's trapped in a re-run of *Gone with the Wind*!"

"Kyra Hughes, you have no poetry in your soul. It's idyllic, I want to tour at least one antebellum mansion."

"Seriously?"

"I love local history, and I'm proud to be southern. I want to stand on a porch and imagine myself, two hundred years ago, sipping iced tea, looking out over the estate."

"Watching the slaves pick cotton?"

"Kyra, I'll forgive you that remark, because you're southern by birth. It's not your fault you were raised among infidels."

Kyra's dad turned his head to address Delilah. "I think you'd make the perfect southern belle. I can just see you in a silk evening gown, turning every head at the ball."

Delilah put a coquettish hand to her mouth. "Why, thank you, Dennis. It's nice to know some northerners still have manners, not to mention chiseled good looks."

Kyra rolled her eyes at Delilah. "Oh, my days! Are you flirting with my dad?"

"I think you'll find he's flirting with me."

Kyra's dad grinned. "Just don't tell your mother."

Delilah brought the back of her hand to her forehead in a dramatic flourish. "My life is full of married men."

Kyra and her dad laughed, an easy silence settled on the car. Kyra had missed Delilah. They'd messaged regularly and facetimed over the last couple weeks, but it wasn't the same as hanging out.

Back in Chicago, Kyra had been required, by her school, to write letters of apology to all her teachers. She also had to enroll in a catch-up program and attend summer school, even though her grades hadn't actually slipped and, as it turned out, she wasn't behind in any of her lessons. She would also be marked as a chronic truant on her school record. All this sucked but, as her dad pointed out, the school could have suspended or even expelled her. So she got off lightly, all things considered.

The Yeuxville Sheriff's Department had agreed to drop all charges against Kyra and would not pursue the investigation any further. In return, Delilah and her dad were required to hand over all copies of the dossier to the Sheriff's Department. Kyra, Delilah and her dad also had to sign some pretty comprehensive NDAs. Again, all of this sucked, but it meant Kyra was free from prosecution.

Her dad arranged a session with a family therapist soon after they got back. He thought it would do them good. Kyra and her mom appreciated the chance to talk to each other without being interrupted but decided family therapy wasn't for them. Her dad was disappointed but respected their wishes.

He was showing Kyra a lot more respect and that was doing wonders for their relationship. If anything, that was the single best thing to come out of this long, strange fall. He no longer embarrassed Kyra in front of her friends, his genuine interest in other people, and his affable charm won people over.

Kyra had seen another side to her dad in Yeuxville, a strength and courage she wasn't aware he possessed. He'd faced down the entire Sheriff's department, with guns drawn, and demanded they take Kyra off a prison bus. He'd forced them to drop all charges when they thought they had an ironclad case.

His real strength wasn't in his ability to face down or outargue people. It was in the depth of his moral convictions. His sense of what was right. In her blackest moment, lost and alone in a darkened field in Yeuxville, with her whole world crumbling, Kyra had found her own moral core, her sense of the right thing to do. It had all come from her dad and the example he had set. He didn't know this, but it was the best thing he'd ever done for her.

Inevitably, Yeuxville had pulled Kyra back. She needed to lay old ghosts to rest. One ghost in particular.

Kyra kept coming back to what Béatrice had told her about calling the dead into our own time. She didn't feel Billy-Ray's presence as strongly as she had those first days in Yeuxville, but she knew he was still there and that it wasn't good for him. She'd dwelled a lot on what Mimi had told her about saying her goodbyes.

When she told her parents she needed to go back to Louisiana, and explained her reasons, her dad booked a flight and hired a car without any questions. Even her mom accepted without a fight, or her usual million conditions.

The Angola Prison Rodeo and Arts passed by on their right, Kyra checked the directions on her phone. "We need to hang a right onto Main Street at this next crossroads."

They turned onto Main Street and drove through the tiny town of Angola. On their left, in the distance they could see the vast complex of the Louisiana State Penitentiary, on their right rose the steep Tunica Hills, studded with tall, proud hardwood trees. The two sights a stark contrast to one another. The natural sprawl of a deciduous forest springing from the hillside opposite the brutal architecture of a prison, designed on an industrial scale to capture and crush human life, kept apart by a single blacktop.

Kyra stared out of the windshield at the airstrip and the scattered buildings beyond. Strangely, they didn't appear as imposing or terrifying as she'd imagined. "So that's the largest maximum-security prison in the country?"

"Apparently." Her dad's eyes were on the road.

Delilah sat forward and rested her arm on the back of Kyra's seat. "It's larger than Manhattan. Can you believe that?"

"Seriously?"

"Twenty-eight square miles they say."

"I could have been a part of that, if it wasn't for you guys."

Her dad put a hand on Kyra's shoulder. "I would *never* let that happen."

"I'm serious. You guys came through for me."

Delilah added her hand to Kyra's dad's. "We love you. That's why."

"Really?"

"Even with your unforgivable dress sense."

"Ouch! I won't forget what you did, though. I'm sorry about your uncle's files."

"That's okay. I'd do it again, in a shot. I'm sure my Uncle Dan would've approved and so does my aunt."

"Really?"

"Totally, we wanted Hawkins to pay for his crimes, but once he died it didn't seem so important, not when you were in trouble. Besides, I didn't destroy every copy."

Kyra's dad put his hand back on the wheel, looking concerned. "That was a comprehensive legal document you signed, you could get in a lot of trouble if they find you've got those files, they're entitled to check your property."

"Don't worry, Mr. hot-shot lawyer, I read that entire document, several times, and it didn't say anything about password protected cloud files."

"Even still, if someone got access."

"They won't, because it's encrypted, and I'll never tell anyone the codes. Besides, it's helped me dig up other stuff about Hawkins and I didn't sign anything saying I couldn't disclose something I subsequently discovered. I don't know what I'll do with it, but if they come after me, I've still got leverage. Besides, you let Kyra publish her blog."

"And I monitor that closely for any infringements of the agreement we signed."

Kyra sighed. "Not to mention spelling, grammar and anything else you can bug me about."

Delilah rested her chin on her palm. "How's it going?"

"Traffic's pretty good, lots of feedback, most of it haters who think I'm a 'libtard slut who's going to hell'."

"Can't fault their accuracy."

"Ouch. All I want is to help an innocent man clear his name, but without that dossier..." Kyra groaned, exasperated. "Why is that Sheriff's Department so corrupt?"

"Hey, my uncle was part of that department. He wasn't corrupt. He put his life on the line to compile that dossier."

"And look where that got him."

"Thanks for the reminder."

Kyra hung her head. "Sorry, but maybe you wouldn't be so pro cop, if you'd suffered what I have."

Her dad reached out and took her hand. "Kyra, honey, neither of us can imagine what you went through, and, as your father, I don't want to, but Delilah has a point. Those deputies thought you were a cop killer. You didn't see them at their best. You can't judge every cop on the basis of this experience. You're too young to lose faith in an entire system, and I love you too much not to challenge you on that. I have to believe most cops really do want to protect and serve."

Delilah clapped her hands. "Oh my God, a liberal with a conscience!"

"Says the redneck in black lace. Don't we make a pair."

"He's got bite! I like him."

Kyra smiled. "Okay, guys, I'm sorry, maybe the whole department isn't corrupt, but I didn't see the best of it, I'm still raw."

Delilah leaned forward and hugged her. "I'm sorry too, hon, I know I give you a hard time, but that's because I love you. You're my dearest friend. I was worried sick when I heard you were arrested."

Kyra hugged back. "I love you, too, you're my best friend, that's why we fight so much."

"Amen to that."

Kyra's dad pulled off the road and parked by some hardwood trees. "I think we're here guys."

CHAPTER 89:

They got out the car and walked along the white rail fence to the entrance.

It was flanked by two square, white columns. A wire arch ran between them with the word 'CEMETERY' on it. Inside the fence the overgrown lawn was filled with rows of white stone crosses, many without names.

Kyra looked around. "I don't think this is the place."

Her dad held up his cell. "This is Point Look Out Cemetery. It's right here on the map."

"But Billy-Ray's buried in Point Look Out 2. I'm pretty sure it's the place we passed on our left. It's on the other side, just a few minutes from here."

"Okay, this is your show, lead the way."

Kyra led them across the road and along the grassy verge. They passed a large field with a barn, and came to a cemetery annex, surrounded by the same white rail fence. Set back from the road, on the far side of the cemetery, were rows of white stone crosses, interspersed with a few traditional tombstones.

Kyra's dad surveyed it from the entrance. "So, is this like an overspill for the other cemetery?"

Delilah joined him. "It was opened in the mid-nineties. If you die in Angola and no-one wants you, this is where you end up."

"Why are there names on most of these graves, but hardly any in the main cemetery?"

"Because they have no idea who half of the people are."

"Really?"

"Yeah, it was built in 1927, the previous one was destroyed by a flood. It washed all the caskets out of the ground and left the corpses to rot on the levy. A common thing in these parts. We lose a lot of cemeteries that way."

"Is that so?"

"Sure is, the prison buried over three hundred bodies in an unmarked grave and put up those markers to memorialize them."

"You really are the fount of all knowledge, aren't you?"Delilah inclined her head and fanned herself. "I do my best."

Kyra walked along the rows of gravestones and the others followed. "It's kind of sad. They were locked away their whole lives and the world forgot about them even in death."

Delilah pointed to a grave. "Wait, Kyra, I think I've found it."

Kyra and her dad joined Delilah. The porous white stone of the grave marker was flecked with lichen. It bore the name BILLY-RAY JOHNSON, and the dates of his birth and death.

Kyra's Dad put his arm around her shoulder, and she leaned into him. "Do you need a minute by yourself, hon?"

"I think I'd like you both here." Kyra reached into her jeans pocket and pulled out two folded sheets of paper. "I, um, I wrote some stuff, to say, I feel a bit weird now I've got to read it, so you'll have to hang in there."

Delilah smiled. "We're not going to judge, take your time."

Kyra cleared her throat. "Billy-Ray, there are so many things I want to tell you, I'm not even sure where to begin. Mrs. Johnesee, my English teacher, who is actually kinda cool, said the beginning is the second hardest thing to write, endings are the worst. I guess everyone's story ends the same way, eventually. Yours ended too soon, and it ended unjustly. I can't change the way it ended, but I can fight to clear your name, because your name is my name. You were my first Daddy, and I love you."

Kyra had to stop as the words on the page misted up and she blinked away the tears. Delilah and her dad placed their hands on her back in support. She waited until she got her composure back and continued.

"I've no idea how many times I met you, I only know of one occasion we were together, because I saw it through your eyes. You had to love me from a distance, spying on me from behind a wall or a fence, or the barrier that separates the living from the dead. You missed all my birthdays, you weren't there when I lost my first tooth, had my first kiss, or got my first A on an English paper. But you *were* there when it mattered most, you saved my life, and I think it's fair to say I wouldn't be here without you, and, as long as I'm alive, I'll always remember that.

"I wish I'd gotten to know you better, found out more about you. Simple things like the teams you supported, the music you listened to, and what beer you drank. I did get to spend some time with you, though it was probably the weirdest father-daughter time anyone's ever had, but at least I got to see the world through your eyes, literally. I know the world sees you as a monster, but I don't. I know the truth about you, and your life, and I'm going to make sure that one day, *everyone* will know the truth. I'm going to make everyone see you through my eyes, a loving father, who looked out for his daughter and never let her down, no matter what it cost him."

Kyra felt the tears on her cheeks, but she didn't bother to hold them back, she paused to let them flow, then carried on. "I read the inmates sing a song when they bury one of their own, it goes: 'I'm free, praise the Lord, I'm free. No longer bound, no more chains holding me. My soul is resting. It's just a blessing. Praise the Lord, Hallelujah, I'm free.' I think you and I were trapped by our mistakes, and by our secrets, and there's no worse kind of prison. I think that's why I came to Yeuxville, I think you were one of the forces that called me back, to show me the truth and set me free. Well, now it's your turn, I'll never forget you, I owe my life to you, but now it's time for you to finally go free."

Kyra folded up the sheets again and placed them on the ground in front of the gravestone.

Delilah wiped a tear from her eye. "Kyra, that was beautiful."

Her dad agreed. "Yes, it really was."

The air around them was completely still, sluggish as the animals in the fields and the townsfolk drowsing on their porches. There was no breeze, but something stirred the pages on the ground. They fluttered, turned and unfolded themselves. Then they were lifted straight up into the air, as if a strong gust had caught and picked them up. The pages continued to rise high above the grave. Kyra craned her neck and watched them recede into the vast blue expanse, until they were tiny white dots that eventually disappeared.

Delilah was also craning her neck to watch them go. "Well, that was weird. It's like they up and left."

The pages weren't the only things that had left.

"He's gone." A chill ran through Kyra, like the wind through a derelict corridor. It was all so sudden and acute. Billy-Ray had been a constant presence in Kyra's life since she'd arrived in New Orleans. She hadn't seen or heard him, she didn't even know who he was until she saw out of his eyes, but he'd become a permanent fixture. Always close, menacing at first, then protective and finally even comforting.

Now, he'd been wrenched from her, carried up into the wide blue expanse like the pages that held her words. Her protector, her father, her constant companion had deserted her. The shock was akin to snatching a heavy cloak from her shoulders on a cold night.

"He's really gone."

She was empty and ached deep inside, as if a vital organ had simply vanished of its own accord. She knew it was time for Billy-Ray to go but she never imagined it would hurt so much. She would never sense his presence again and only now did she understand what she'd lost.

Kyra closed her eyes. She was two years old again, standing in a trailer park in Yeuxville, crying and reaching out for her Daddy. Terrified and confused. Sure of only one thing, that as he melted back into the shadows of that night, she would never see her father alive again.

"He's gone."

It was all too much. Kyra had worried about tying Billy-Ray to the world. Worried his presence would never leave. Now she couldn't imagine being without it. Yet he was gone, irrevocably.

He'd abandoned her again and with him went her ability to speak or even stand.

The ground loomed up and her dad caught her before she fell. She put her arms around him as she fought to stay upright and looked into his eyes. Her mouth moved but her words had fled with the pages the sky had taken.

He nodded. "I know, sweetheart, I know. You set him free. And, speaking on behalf of both your dads, we could not be prouder of you."

Oh God. Why did he always have to say the right thing at just the right time? And now she wouldn't be able to control herself.

As she let go of her absent father, Kyra clung to her present one. Buried her face in his shirt. Breathed in his scents. Fabric softener and the musk of fresh male sweat. The corded muscles of his arms enfolded her, kept her upright when her legs couldn't. Their strength gave her permission to fall apart. To surrender to her grief.

Delilah sniffed and let out a ragged breath. Her dad took an arm from Kyra's shoulders and beckoned to Delilah. "Come join us."

"Honestly I can't, I'll just bawl."

"Then come bawl."

Delilah slipped her arms around Kyra and her dad. He pulled them all closer. Delilah broke down too, her tears a tributary of the wide river of grief that flowed through them all. They wept for everyone that had been taken from them. Absent fathers, lost uncles, departed friends and enemies. Mourned them among the headstones of the unnamed dead.

Finally, Delilah let go and disengaged. "I think you need time to yourselves. I know I do."

"Okay, we'll see you back at the car."

Kyra could only nod her head. Delilah left the cemetery and Kyra clung to her dad.

She needed to find the bottom of her sorrow. Needed to let it flow out into a deeper ocean of remorse before she could sink down to its floor and then, and only then, could she rise up and break its surface.

Her sobs slowed to sighs, her tears trickled into mist, and she felt the ground at her feet once more. She lifted her head from her dad's chest and looked at the damp patch she'd left on his shirt.

Kyra rubbed at it. "Sorry."

Her dad reached into his jeans pocket and pulled out a handkerchief. "Good thing I brought this."

"You're such a boy scout."

"Be-prepared is my middle name."

"I thought it was Brian."

"It is, 'Be-prepared-Brian', that's me."

Her eyes were nearly dry but Kyra still dabbed at them. The handkerchief felt familiar and she caught sight of the patterned edges. She unfolded it and saw two carefully embroidered figures – a Fox and the Little Prince.

"You found it."

"You reach for some strange lifelines when you're panicking. When I couldn't find you anywhere, when I realized you were gone, I grabbed our favorite book from my nightstand. Only there was something in the pages. You were going to give it to me on my birthday, right?"

Once again Kyra felt riven with guilt at everything she'd put her parents through. "Dad, I…"

He held up his hand. "It's okay. I cried when I saw it, you know. I'm not afraid to tell you that. Especially when I read this."

He pointed to the quote embroidered on it.

'One sees clearly only with the heart.
'The essential is invisible to the eye'.

"That's what I kept telling myself as I searched for you. I had to look with my heart, not my eyes. It was like you'd given me the key to finding you."

"I think it's the key to a lot of things."

"Yes it is. It's brought us close again and I couldn't be happier."

"Me too."

"Are you done here, or do you need more time?"

"I'm good, we can't keep Delilah waiting. She has to get back and make sure the cotton's picked."

They left the cemetery. The sun was sinking in the sky, the day lapping at the shores of evening. As they made their way down the side of the road Kyra reached for her dad's hand. She wasn't certain why. She hadn't held his hand since her third day at kindergarten, when she decided she'd outgrown it. Maybe she just needed to stay close to him. It surprised him as much as her.

Please don't make a thing out of this.

He didn't. But she saw a tiny smile play around the corners of his mouth.

Billy-Ray may have left her again. May have hardly been around her whole life. But her dad was still there. In all her early memories. Picking her up when she cried, mending her toys when they broke, making hot chocolate before bed and sneaking in marshmallows when her mom wasn't looking.

Then a rift opened between them and Kyra hadn't recognized him. Couldn't equate the person he'd become with the man she'd known all her life. When she looked back on all the people she'd met that long, strange fall, all the masks that had fallen from their faces, it occurred to Kyra there was only one person who'd remained who she truly thought. And that was her dad.

The man who loved her unquestioningly, as if it was programmed into his DNA. Who loved her without any conditions. Who didn't expect her to look a certain way or do a certain thing. Who always wanted to know every tiny detail of her day. Who accepted her just as she was and adored her the more for it. His love an endlessly renewable resource, that existed simply because *she* did. There would be few people who would give her this kind of love, and none so unfailingly as her dad.

She remembered his mad dash to the prison bus and the guns the deputies had trained on him. How one wrong move, one wrong word, could have ended his life, his love for her, forever. A fierce, protective passion rose inside her, and she knew there was nothing she wouldn't do to keep him in her life.

He snored so loudly you could hear him in the next room. His running shoes stank out the front porch and you couldn't ask him anything without getting a lecture. But there was no other man on the face of the planet that Kyra would have wanted to raise her.

She stole another glance at him. His gentle hand clasped about hers. His broad shoulders thrown back in contentment. His hair swept back from his face as if the soul of a biker or a beach-bum sat secretly in his breast. He met her eyes and grinned, full of paternal pride, and she loved it.

She'd viewed the world through Billy-Ray's eyes and what she'd seen most of all was the man her dad *truly* was. She saw him now, more clearly than ever, with her heart.

And she knew this essential truth would remain, for as long as her heart kept beating.

HOPE YOU READ THIS WITH YOUR HEART, GENTLE READER, AND ITS ESSENTIAL TRUTHS WEREN'T INVISIBLE TO YOU.
IF YOU DID, THEN I'M GUESSING YOUR EYES WON'T BE DRY BY NOW.
BECOMING A FATHER WAS PROBABLY THE SINGLE BEST THING I EVER DID WITH MY LIFE. MIGHT I SUGGEST, IF YOU HAVE A DAUGHTER, OR IF YOUR OWN FATHER IS STILL IN YOUR LIFE, THAT YOU GO GIVE THEM A CALL AND LET THEM KNOW WHAT THEY MEAN TO YOU.
IF YOU DON'T HAVE A FATHER OR A DAUGHTER IN YOUR LIFE, SEND LOVE TO SOMEONE YOU CHERISH. TRUST YOUR UNCLE JASP ON THIS, YOU KNOW IT MAKES SENSE!

ACKNOWLEDGEMENTS

Acknowledgements are strange things aren't they? Like the mints that come with your check at the end of the meal. If the mints were made of cardboard and mostly tasteless.

I read them, at the end of most novels, when I have a hangover from the story. When the author's voice is still in my mind and I don't want to let go. When I want to wring every last drop from the prose I've just read. But as soon as I get to the list of names I don't recognize, I my eyes glaze over and I skip huge chunks of text.

Another way to look at the Acknowledgements, would be to think of them as the reverse check. Imagine if the chef sent you a little note, at the end of your meal, thanking everyone who'd helped them prepare your meal and inspired them in their career. Would you read it?

I'd like to think I'd give it a cursory glance. In the same way I've always sat through the credits at the end of movies, even before the MCU started dropping those little teasers in at the very end. Much to the annoyance of my wife and daughters, who sit there smiling with embarrassment at the cleaning staff who are waiting to sweep up the popcorn in the few minutes they have between screenings. But, I tell myself, *someone* has to at least attempt to read all the names of the Prop Department, so their valiant efforts don't go unappreciated. Especially as my son-in-law-to-be is now one of those names.

There are a huge list of names I have to thank for their help in writing this novel. And I guess I'm writing this preamble as a way of holding your attention, so they won't be the only ones reading through this to spot their namecheck.

I'm never sure if anyone reads these sections, but for those of you who do, I want to give you a little incentive, a thank you for reading this far. At some point in the following list of names, I'm going to hide a codeword in amongst them. If you drop me a line on my website at https://www.jasperbark.com/contact and tell me what this codeword is, I will send you a free eBook from the Bark Bites Horror line as a way to say: 'thanks, but you really need to get a life'.

The first person I'm going to thank is Lisa Jenkins. Not for her help with this book, but because she was instrumental in helping me improve the prose of what finally became the *Draw You In* trilogy and I forgot to thank her in the Acknowledgements at the back of that! I know, right?! How could I be that much of an ass? So, hanging my head in shame, I'd like to thank her, belatedly, for that and hope this will go some way to making up for my oversight!

The next person I'd like thank is Ann Giardina Magee for reading a very early draft of this novel in order to make sure I portrayed Cajun Country, and her state, authentically. She picked me up on quite a lot of things. Anything in this novel that seems authentic is down to her careful eye. Any howling mistakes are entirely mine.

Monique Snyman edited a very early draft of this novel, back before it was part of the Bark Bites Horror series. It has improved immeasurably since and that's in no small part thanks to her excellent editorial eye. Look how few ellipses there are now, Monique, and did you spot the single semi-colon hidden in the early chapters?

The codeword is BayouBotherer, by the way. I told you I'd sneak it in. Thanks for reading this far. Now you've made it all this way, you may as well soldier on to the (not so) bitter end.

Many, many drafts and much sweating and soul-searching later, my editor Poppy McDonald worked her magic on the MS I handed in to Crystal Lake, whole-heartedly agreeing with Monique that the novel needed to be purged of all the ellipses that had fastened themselves onto the prose like ticks on the hide of a feral cat. She had my back and I'm very grateful for all the improvements she patiently suggested.

I'm also grateful for the careful eye, and meticulous red pen of Jodi Shatz, who sifted through the final proofs to winnow out all those irritating and embarrassing typos that dog my work. Making me look so much better than I deserve. Jodi, you are a great first reader and I value your opinions as much as your proofreading skills.

The crew at Crystal Lake Publishing are all superstars. Jaco Nieuwoudt, Charlene du Toit, Naching T. Kassa, Anita Stewart, Lisa Lee and Lisa Vasquez are always so patient, helpful and supportive, it's an honor to work with them! Thank you all so much.

Penultimately, thanks to the head honcho, CEO and Camp Counsellor of Crystal Lake, Mr. Joe Mynhardt himself. I've been working with Joe for over a decade, since appearing in Crystal Lake's first ever, official publication. From day one, his mission has been to create a publishing house that gives authors the chance to create their very best work and be rewarded properly for it. A publisher that nurtures the next generation of horror writers and leaves a lasting legacy to the genre. He's not only the best publisher I've worked with, he's also a close, personal friend. He'd have to be, to put up with me as much as he does!

Finally, thanks to you, whether this is your first time with one of my books or you've read every one of them so far. I really appreciate your time and attention and I hope you'll drop in again soon. I have so many stories I want to tell you and I promise you won't have read anything quite like them.

ABOUT THE AUTHOR

Multiple award-winning author, **Jasper Bark** is infectious – and there's no known cure. If you're reading this you're already contaminated. The symptoms will manifest any time soon. There's nothing you can do about it. There's no itching or unfortunate rashes, but you'll become obsessed with his mind-bending books. From the acclaimed Draw You In trilogy and the ground breaking Bark Bites Horror series, to graphic novels like Bloodfellas and Beyond Lovecraft.

Then you'll want to tell everyone else about his visionary horror fiction. About its originality, its wild imagination and how it takes you to the edge of your sanity. We're afraid there's no way to avoid this. These words contain a power you're hopeless to resist. You're already in their thrall, you know you are. You're itching to read all of Jasper's bloodstained books. Don't fight this urge, embrace it. You've been bitten by the Bark bug and you love it!

Would you like to read four more of Jasper's books absolutely free?

Of course you would. I mean, who doesn't like free books?

Jasper's infamous novella, *Stuck On You* is now free to own as soon as you join Jasper's cult and sign up to his mailing list with this link:

Don't worry, you won't have to shave your head or unalive any celebrities (for the first couple of years). But you will get all of Jasper's latest, videos, podcasts, blogs, breaking news on upcoming books and other crucial information to help you cyberstalk him.

What's more, you'll get two more short novels, a graphic novel and a spoof picture book, just to sweeten the deal! That's five free books just for signing up. These books are exclusive to this offer. You won't get them anywhere else.

Are we crazy? Of course we're crazy! We're asking you to join Jasper's cult!

Don't be the only weird kid on your block to miss out. Don't delay. Sign up today.

THE END?

Not if you want to dive into more of Crystal Lake Publishing's Tales from the Darkest Depths!

Check out our amazing website and online store or download our latest catalog here.

We always have great new projects and content on the website to dive into, as well as a newsletter, behind the scenes options, social media platforms, our own dark fiction shared-world series and our very own webstore. Our webstore even has categories specifically for KU books, non-fiction, anthologies, and of course more novels and novellas.

Readers...

Thank you for reading *Harmed and Dangerous*. We hope you enjoyed this novel.

If you have a moment, please review *Harmed and Dangerous* at the store where you bought it.

Help other readers by telling them why you enjoyed this book. No need to write an in-depth discussion. Even a single sentence will be greatly appreciated. Reviews go a long way to helping a book sell, and is great for an author's career. It'll also help us to continue publishing quality books.

Thank you again for taking the time to journey with Crystal Lake Publishing.

You will find links to all our social media platforms on our Linktree page. https://linktr.ee/CrystalLakePublishing

Follow us on Amazon:

MISSION STATEMENT

Since its founding in August 2012, Crystal Lake has quickly become one of the world's leading publishers of Dark Fiction and Horror books. In 2023, Crystal Lake officially transitioned into an entertainment company, joining several other divisions, genres, and imprints, including Torrid Waters, Sinister Smile Press, Crystal Lake Comics, Crystal Lake Games, Crystal Cove Press, Crystal Lake Kids, Memento Mori Ink, and The House of Shadows & Ink on YouTube.

While we strive to present only the highest quality fiction and entertainment, we also endeavor to support authors along their writing journey. We offer our time and experience in non-fiction projects, as well as author mentoring and services, at competitive prices.

With several Bram Stoker Award wins and many other wins and nominations (including the HWA's Specialty Press Award), Crystal Lake puts integrity, honor, and respect at the forefront of our publishing operations.

We strive for each book and outreach program we spearhead to not only entertain and touch or comment on issues that affect our readers, but also to strengthen and support the Dark Fiction field and its authors.

Not only do we find and publish authors we believe are destined for greatness, but we strive to work with men and women who endeavor to be decent human beings who care more for others than themselves, while still being hard-working, driven, and passionate artists and storytellers.

Crystal Lake is and will always be a beacon of what passion and dedication, combined with overwhelming teamwork and respect, can accomplish. We endeavor to know each and every one of our readers, while building personal relationships with our authors, reviewers, bloggers, podcasters, bookstores, and libraries.

We will be as trustworthy, forthright, and transparent as any business can be, while also keeping most of the headaches away from our authors, since it's our job to solve the problems so they can stay in a creative mind. Which of course also means paying our authors.

We do not just publish books, we present to you worlds within your world, doors within your mind, from talented authors who sacrifice so much for a moment of your time.

There are some amazing small presses out there, and through collaboration and open forums we will continue to support other presses in the goal of helping authors and showing the world what quality small presses are capable of accomplishing. No one wins when a small press goes down, so we will always be there to support hardworking, legitimate presses and their authors. We don't see Crystal Lake as the best press out there, but we will always strive to be the best, strive to be the most interactive and grateful, and even blessed press around. No matter what happens over time, we will also take our mission very seriously while appreciating where we are and enjoying the journey.

What do we offer our authors that they can't do for themselves through self-publishing?

We are big supporters of self-publishing (especially hybrid publishing), if done with care, patience, and planning. However, not every author has the time or inclination to do market research, advertise, and set up book launch strategies. Although a lot of authors are successful in doing it all, strong small presses will always be there for the authors who just want to do what they do best: write.

What we offer is experience, industry knowledge, contacts and trust built up over years. And due to our strong brand and trusting fanbase, every Crystal Lake book comes with weight of respect. In time our fans begin to trust our judgment and will try a new author purely based on our support of said author.

To date we've published around 300 books, and with each launch we strive to fine-tune our approach, learn from our mistakes, and increase our reach. We continue to assure our authors that we're here for them and that we'll carry the weight of the launch and deal with third parties while they focus on their strengths—be it writing, interviews, blogs, signings, etc.

We also offer several mentoring packages to authors that include knowledge and skills they can use in both traditional and self-publishing endeavors. This includes Shadows & Ink Creators on our The House of Shadows & Ink YouTube channel and our Crystal Lake Academy.

We look forward to launching many new careers.

This is what we believe in. What we stand for. This will be our legacy.

Welcome to Crystal Lake Publishing—Where Stories Come Alive!

www.ingramcontent.com/pod-product-compliance
Lightning Source LLC
Chambersburg PA
CBHW022020300726
48970CB00003B/977